Fair Winds
and
Following Seas

Part Two

By

Melissa Good

©2021 by Melissa Good
Second publication 2021
Flashpoint Publications

FLASHPOINT
PUBLICATIONS

ISBN 978-1-61929-478-3

Cover Design by AcornGraphics

Editors Verda Foster and Mary Hettel

Books by Melissa Good

Dar and Kerry Series

Tropical Storm
Hurricane Watch
Eye of the Storm
Red Sky At Morning
Thicker Than Water
Terrors of the High Seas
Tropical Convergence
Storm Surge (Books 1 & 2)
Stormy Waters
Moving Target
Winds of Change (Book 1 & 2)
Southern Stars
Fair Winds and Following Seas
(Part 1 & 2)

Jess and Dev Series

Partners (Book 1 & 2)
Of Sea and Stars

Chapter Eleven

Kerry trotted down the steps of the condo with Mocha at her heels and started out along the road at a brisk pace leaving the golf cart behind her as she stretched out her abused muscles from the previous day.

Ahead of her, and to her left she saw the makeshift guard station at the next condo section entrance, and she made no bones about looking curiously at it as she approached. "Now, what do you think that's all about, Mochie?" She asked the brown dog. "You think it's spooks, like Grandma said?"

Mocha sneezed.

Some VIP, no doubt. Kerry knew political goons when she saw them, and after studying the men as she neared them, she decided they weren't national level goons, but instead, a more local variety.

The governor? Perhaps. The state capital where the governor usually hung out was in Tallahassee, which was, as Dar often said, a lot closer to Georgia than Miami, a matter of some hundred and fifty miles versus four hundred eighty.

It would make sense for the governor to, if he had to stay locally while examining the damage, get a place where he could at least have power and air-conditioning. She didn't begrudge him that, having enjoyed very much chilling out in her kitchen that morning. Comfortably cool while her muffin toasted.

The guards watched her, and after a moment of internal debate, she angled her way toward them right up the driveway. She removed her sunglasses as she reached the barrier and the two guards straightened up and watched her with benign interest.

"Hi." She came to a halt, and signaled Mocha to do the same. The Labrador took a seat next to her, his tongue lolling.

"Hello, ma'am," the nearer one responded with civil respect. "Can I help you with something?"

"What's all this?" Kerry asked, straightforwardly, gesturing at the blockade.

The man looked at her awkwardly. "Well, ma'am... we have a dignitary visiting and this is controlled access," he said. "Do you live here?"

"I do," Kerry said. "Right over there." She pointed behind and to the side of where they were standing. "Who is it?" She asked, in a tone that clearly expected to be answered. "Is that their helicopter sitting on the green?"

"Um... we can't really say," the second man spoke up.

"C'mon guys, I'm not the Miami Herald," Kerry said. "I'll just use my binoculars from our patio. We all have the same outside view. Or bump into whoever it is over breakfast in the Mansion." She grinned easily at them.

Both guards relaxed a little, glancing around behind them.

"She's right," the first man said. "It's John Beringar. He works for the governor. He and his team are staying here so they can evaluate all the damage."

Kerry nodded. "Makes sense," she said. "I spent all day over in the city yesterday. No one wants to stay there."

"No, ma'am." The second guard came closer, nodding at her. "Got to say I was happier than a clam to get sent out here. First night since the storm I got any sleep."

"True that," the first one said. "So, what's your name, ma'am?"

"Kerry." Kerry extended a hand. "We're in unit 4A," she said. "Not many owners are residents in that area, but we're full time. If you need anything, just ring the bell," she said. "We own an IT company, and my father-in-law's a retired Navy seal. Sometimes we're useful."

She winked at them, and then put her sunglasses back on before she turned and started back down toward the road, giving a cluck of her tongue for Mocha to follow.

"Huh," the first guard looked at the second guard. "Wasn't how I expected that to go."

"Seems like a nice lady," the second said. "Not like some of the folks around here." He glanced around. "Remember what number she said. Never know when these guys need something last minute, you know? Specially IT stuff. Everyone's always forgetting something."

"Cables and stuff. Yeah, absolutely."

****

Dar got the ladder positioned against the wall that separated their buildings' entrance from the street and climbed up to the top of it.

She set down the converter and roll of cable on the top of the wall, then removed a screwdriver from her pocket and started to remove the cover off the light mounted on one of the elevated posts.

It was a long metal tap screw, and once she'd seated her driver tip inside and her hands began twisting it, she looked over the wall to find something to occupy her attention while the task was in progress.

Across the road, she saw a team of men running a pump to drain the last of the storm caused lake over the golf course.

The helicopter was gone, but on either side of the pump team Dar saw maintenance trucks with crews at work. Dar watched a golf cart pull up to one of them, and then she had to turn her attention back to the cover that was coming loose.

She pulled it aside and peered into the casement, where a camera was now exposed, it's dome relatively unscathed. Inside it a three-hundred-and-sixty-degree camera was positioned under a light overhead, hidden in the fixture.

Dar studied it, trying to remember if she had always known there was a camera looking at their front door, and the entrance, and decided she probably had.

Were they elsewhere though? Thoughtfully, she straightened up and searched the area, thinking about where it was lit up at night.

"Hey! Hey, Ms. Roberts!"

Dar looked down to find Lou, in his golf cart, at the entrance. "Hey." She leaned her elbows on the wall. "What's up?"

"Listen, I wanted to let you know, they got the ramp working," Lou said. "I know your dad asked about it. So, if you need to, we got the ferries operating. They're kinda slow, because there's a lot of stuff in the channel, but they're going."

"Nice." Dar nodded "Yeah, that's great news, Lou. Thanks for letting me know. How's it going beside that? I see they cleared the course."

Lou swung sideways in his cart and leaned his elbow on the steering wheel. He was dressed in a cotton polo shirt already discolored with sweat stains and khaki golf shorts. "Not so bad. You really helped us out fixing that system, I gotta tell ya," he said. "Sorry I wasn't really appreciative the other day on it, there was just so much stuff going on."

"No problem." Dar half smiled. "Glad it worked out, and this thing too." She indicated the adapter. "Win win, you got these things installed."

Lou grinned. "You betcha." He nodded vigorously. "That new camera system is a lot better, and the cams are great, hi def and all that. Is that what you're doing? Putting that thing in there and connecting up to the club?"

Dar nodded. "Closest one to the house, right?" She asked.

Lou paused thoughtfully and eyed her.

"Y'know, I can hack in and find out for myself." Dar smiled in a completely different way. "And given the bullshit I have to take from the other residents, might turn out messy for everyone," she warned. "Except me."

"No no!" Lou waved his hands at her. "I was just trying to think about where they are. Honest, they weren't that stupid, you know? Like most of the residents have lawyers on retainer they got nothing to do but file suit about stuff like that."

Dar chuckled. "I wouldn't bother with a lawyer."

"No, listen." Lou got up and came over to the wall. "You're not somebody I want to mess with, straight out. Even Jim didn't want to mix it up with you, and he said we were smart to get you to help with the cams, you know?"

"Yeah, I know," Dar said, her eyes twinkling a little. "He doesn't like me, but he knows I'm good at what I do."

He put his closed fist, knuckles first against the wall. "They got them out on the beach, to watch the frontage, and once the wall meets up with the common area, they're all over there." He said, in a serious tone. "Nothing in the back, nothing facing the windows or nothing like that. Only this one here, at the door." He inclined his head toward the half disassembled light fixture. "Okay?"

Was it true? Dar decided she would take the time, later on, to check one of the lights in the back and for now she just accepted the pitch.

"Okay." She nodded. "I'm going to run this along the walk and up to the stairs, then in the window there. That's my office." She pointed. "Can I get the landscaping team not to cut it please?"

Lou pulled a small notepad out of his pocket, and now he scribbled on it. "I'll let em know," he promised. "Hey, one more thing. We're only running the ferries in daylight, you understand? It's too dangerous at night."

"Got it." Dar lifted her hand and waved a goodbye, as he went back to his cart and returned the wave, then rumbled off back toward the maintenance trucks. "Probably less dangerous if we stay home," she remarked dryly, then went back to connecting up the converter to the post.

****

"Hey, it's Kerry!"

Kerry closed the door to the cottage behind her, already pleased to leave behind the muggy heat and enter the crisp, clean smelling villa. "Hey, guys."

Angela came in from the kitchen with a plate of croissants. "You got sunburned," she said. "You get breakfast? They just brought some stuff in here for us."

The staff all looked freshly scrubbed and were dressed in their island merchandise. They seemed relaxed and happy. The two programmers sat on the floor with their laptops on their laps, pecking away.

"Boy do we have voice mails." Angela sat down at the dining table, where her laptop and a pad of paper were sitting. "Me and Cel here are trying to sort them out for you." One of the VoIP phones was on the table next to her, a cable running from it over to the server rack.

"I can only imagine." Kerry then realized she'd forgotten something. "Hold that thought." She unclipped the radio from her pocket and brought it up to her lips. "Dardar, you there?"

There was silence for a long moment. Then a crackle. "Go ahead, Ker."

"You almost ready to join us? If you are, could you bring my laptop with yours?" Kerry asked. "I forgot to grab my backpack."

"No problem," Dar responded. "See ya in a little."

Kerry unkeyed the radio and clipped it back on. "Is there another one of those phones?"

"Two of them," Angela said. "We had the phones forwarded but it got crazy. Have them going back to voice mail for now."

Elvis scrambled to his feet and fished in the case. "Hang on." He pulled out another phone and cable. "Where do you want to park, chief?"

"Table's fine here in the corner." Kerry took possession of the end chair, and watched as Elvis unrolled the cable and brought the phone over. "I want to call Baptist and see how Tomas is doing."

Celeste was seated next to Angela, busy with pages of notes. She glanced up as though feeling Kerry's eyes on her and grinned briefly.

Kerry winked at her. "Okay, where do we start?" She asked. "Give me the pissed off ones first, might as well get that started and out of the way." She leaned on her elbows. "How are you all doing? Everyone sleep okay?"

"Are you kidding?" Arthur had his head down. "That freaking bed's awesome."

Elvis nodded in agreement.

"It was nice," Celeste said, after clearing her throat a little. "And the shower's really nice too."

"We lucked out," Arthur said. He finished typing something and then studied the results. "Okay I just checked that back in. Dar's gotta look at it."

He looked over his shoulder at Kerry. "The Feds want to get their mittens on her. That guy, Scott? He even sent us emails all frantic."

"Well, he'll have to wait another half hour," Kerry said. "I can hardly wait to see all the exclamation points in my inbox."

Elvis resumed his seat. "The guys upstate sent us some pictures of their rig up there. Pretty nice," he said. "We all going to go up to Melbourne? I have a couple of cousins near there."

"Maybe," Kerry said. "Colleen was looking for space."

"How far is that from Disney World?" Arthur asked. "Someone said like an hour?" He looked around at Kerry. "That might be cool."

"Hmm. I like Disney World," Kerry admitted. "How would your dad react to you moving?"

Arthur laughed. "He's wanted me to move out forever. But he and Mom would move to Cocoa. They're like from the nineteen fifties space world anyway."

Kerry got up. "Okay let me get some coffee before I start calling." She went into the kitchen and found a large coffee dispenser, like one you'd find in a convention, and a huge basket full of snacks. With a slight smile, she fished amongst them and found a granola bar, sliding it into her pocket before she retrieved a heavy porcelain coffee mug.

She took the coffee back to the table and picked up the receiver, checking her relatively useless cell phone for the number to the hospital.

****

Dar closed the door to the condo and went down the stairs with Chino in close attendance. It was even hazier out now, and the air had so much moisture in it she almost felt like she was in a steam bath. But at least there was a breeze coming off the water, and as she started walking, it cooled down a bit.

She'd swapped her werewolf shirt out for a navy sleeveless tee with their company logo on the back in steel gray and traded a pocketful of hand tools for the backpack on her back that had both her laptop in it and Kerry's.

At the edge of the driveway she paused, then looked up at the sky. Then she retreated back down the slope into their parking area and put the backpack in the back of her truck, holding the door so Chino could jump in after it. "G'wan, girl."

She got behind the wheel and started the engine, letting it idle for a moment as it hesitated a bit. A few feeds of gas later it steadied, and she put it into reverse and backed out.

The maintenance trucks were gone, and the pumping rig had been pulled out and set alongside the road, its motor turned off. There were three SUVs camped in front of the next residential entry though, and as she put the truck into gear to move forward, five or six khaki clothed men moved toward them along with a short, dark haired man in a bush hat and jeans.

He was young and lithely built and had a slightly aggressive walk.

One of the men walking with him opened the door to one of the SUV's in a respectful gesture. He paused before getting into the car, gesturing with a sharp, impatient motion toward the gate.

A young woman hastened from the opening and crossed to the car. She carried a briefcase and a raincoat over her arm. She had curly red hair and glasses, and she circled the SUV to get in on the other side.

"What do you think, Chi? That Mister Helicopter?" Dar commented, as she accelerated past them. "Seems like a jackass that might land a helicopter on a putting green."

"Growf." Chino sat behind her and looked out the window.

"Yeah, I think so too." Dar maneuvered the truck around the SUV's, and headed off toward the club, while the group of them went off in the other direction, toward the ferry ramp. "Well, good riddance for now anyway." She got back on the road proper and continued around the bend.

Landscaping crews were hard at work on either side, dragging debris off to flatbed carts. Dar lifted a hand off the wheel and waved at them, then she slowed and rolled down the window as she came even with the supervisor. "Hola, Jorge."

"Buenos Dias, Senora Dar." The man came over, greeting her with a relaxed smile. "*¿Todo está bien con tu casa?*"

"*Si.*" She nodded. "*Hay un cable que atraviesa el patio delantero. ¿Intenta no cortarlo?*" Lou or no Lou, it never hurt to do something yourself, and no telling when the security chief would remember to take the pad out of his pocket and recall her ask.

"*¡No hay problema!*" He reassured her. "*¿Ves a tu nuevo vecino? Del*

Gobierno." He cast a skeptical eye past her, down the road, then he touched both fingertips under his eyes, and then pointed them back toward the entrance to the condos."

"Yeah, got it." Dar winked. "Glad you all made it through all right. Let me know if you need anything."

Jorge smiled at her. "Have a nice day, Ms. Dar. We will watch for your cable." He backed away and went back to the crew, who had paused to lean on their long-handled tools. Dar rolled up the window and drove on.

She spotted the outline of their golf cart near the front entrance of the mansion and she detoured over to park next to it. She saw her parents on the steps talking to a couple of other residents. "Hang out here, Chi." She rolled the back window open and got out. "Keep an eye on the truck, okay?"

Andy and Ceci spotted her and they were half turned, waiting for her to climb up the steps to where they were standing. Dar recognized the two men standing next to them as two of her less annoying neighbors. "Good morning." She greeted them all, as she reached the top step.

"More rain coming," Andy said. "Ahm gonna go put the tarps up and start the pumps on them boats."

"Thanks," Dar said. "Hey, Bob, Rene. "

"Morning." The two other residents nodded amiably. "How's it going?" Rene asked.

"Ramps up," Dar said, briefly. "Daylight runs only."

"Hot damn," Ceci remarked. "I wanted to go run some dead traffic lights and watch Miami Beach try to handle four way stops."

"Hey that's great news." Rene looked surprised. "They told us it wouldn't be until dinnertime, didn't they, Bob?"

Bob looked annoyed. "Bastards," he grunted and shook his head. "I knew that asshat was lying. Probably getting paid on the side to reserve space on the ferry." He glanced behind them at the door to the mansion. "Everyone wants off."

"Yeah, not all of us have a boat docked," Rene said. "Like you all do."

Bob eased from between them and headed for the steps. "I'm going to grab my car. See what the office looks like."

"Wait up." Rene followed him. "Thanks, Dar!" Bob called over his shoulder. "Man, I was wondering what I was going to do the rest of the day. I'm bored crazy watching the news."

"No problem." Dar watched them go, then turned to her parents. "Anything new here? I'm heading over to the cottage."

Andy had his arms folded. "That is some good news there, Dardar," he said. "Want to swap buggies? Ah'll drop on over to the shop," he said. "For that word gets out and we got a big old line waiting."

"I'm game," Ceci said. "Let's get out of here before the story spreads around that you hacked the ramp to get it working." She eyed her daughter. "You didn't, did you?" She asked, after a brief pause.

"No." Dar fished the keys to the truck out of her pocket and offered them, taking the fob for the cart in return. "I bumped into Lou. He told me," she said. "Let me get my backpack and the dog from the truck. Anything going on in there?"

"Usual griping." Ceci led the way down the steps. "Though what the hell people have to gripe about on this island I can't fathom. No one out here should be bitching about anything. Did you see West Miami, the news?"

"I saw."

"Everyone's whining they can't get cable television here, and no phones," Ceci said. "Oh, and they're all pissed off at whatshisface your satellite guy because it's slow."

Dar rolled her eyes, as they reached the truck and she opened the back door. "C'mon, Chi." She grabbed the backpack and hoisted it over one shoulder as Chino jumped down, tail waving. "Glad I went through all that effort."

"Well, he charged them like five hundred bucks apiece for it, kid," Ceci informed her. "And I saw someone trying to use it. They got a point."

"He oversold the bandwidth he claimed he had," Dar said. "Moron. But what are they trying to use it for? It worked fine for mail."

"Streaming video, I think. Some program on HBO," Ceci said. "And one of them wanted to live stream their kids' quinces to some relatives in Jersey."

Dar paused in mid motion and tilted her sunglasses down, exposing her blue eyes and sharply raised eyebrows.

"No, huh?" Her mother smiled. "Yeah, I recognize that look." She lifted a hand and went around the other side of the truck to get into the passenger seat. "Have fun, and good luck. We'll stop by the beach club and bring the gang some supplies."

"Lord." Andy sighed and shook his head. "You heard yet from that lawyer?"

"Not yet." Dar pushed her sunglasses back into place. "Let me go see if that's in my inbox. Let us know if they need anything out there, Dad."

"Ah will do that."

Chino was already in the back of the golf cart waiting for her, and Dar got in the front, turned the cart around and headed along the road toward the path that would take her between the mansion and the club, and the cottages they used as high priced hotel rooms.

She passed by the oceanfront side of the mansion and turned down cobblestone lined accessway beside it, carefully avoiding a peacock and then went between the buildings.

"Growf!" Chino barked at the peacock, who turned and spread his tail, shaking it at her.

"Sh." Dar said to the dog. "Don't make it start screaming. That's all I need." She sent the cart into the grass around the animal as it shook its feathers again, clicking its beak in a triumphant sort of way.

"Growwwffr," Chino rumbled softly.

"Stop," Dar muttered. She pulled around the back of the cottage and saw the satellite rig, its dish extended and pointed toward the horizon. From behind the partially opened double doors to the van she heard loud voices.

She strode toward the door as Chino scrambled to follow her, hiking boots crunching on the gravel outside

****

Kerry put the phone receiver down and scribbled a note on her pad. "That's the most urgent of the non-locals," she said. "Where's my, where's my, where's my."

"At least the support desk is up," Angela said. "Nobody's got nothing to say about that."

"No, that was a good call to move them upstate." Kerry checked the list she had in one hand and looked back and forth from the pad. "Damn I'm glad we didn't take on any twenty-four seven yet."

The other phone rang, and Angela picked it up. "Roberts Automation, good morning. How can I help you?" She listened, then started to write on her pad. "That's right. Okay."

Kerry picked up her phone and dialed a number. After a minute, it was picked up. "Hey, Col."

"Oh my God!"

Kerry blinked and stared at the phone. "Colleen?"

"You are all back up? It's back?" Colleen asked. "You're on the inside line! And holy Mary the mail's back up!"

Kerry glanced around the cottage. "Well, no," she demurred. "It's kinda complicated. So, how's it going up there? We're still bunked out over here on the island, but we've got some comms up on satellite."

"Well, we're surviving," Colleen said. "I was able to talk to the landlords here in this co-op, and they've got some space they can offer us, but if you're that close to getting things back up there…"

"No, no, no," Kerry said. "So, right now me, Angela, Arthur and Elvis, and Celeste are here in one of the   billion-dollar rental cottages near the Vanderbilt Mansion with a rack of servers and cables everywhere."

Colleen digested this. "Do I know Celeste?"

"Sort of. You do since she was ILS security." Kerry soldiered on. "Jerry from the day door is back at the office."

"Ah heh. So should I add them to the books then?" Colleen took it all in stride. "How's Maria? I heard all about you running about there and all that. You do know you ended up on CNN, right?"

"Yeah, I'll get their information and you can… what?" Kerry halted. "Wait, what?" She repeated. "Okay hold on first things first, yes, Maria and Mayte are fine, and Tomas is in Baptist. He's got a broken leg and broken ribs, but he's stable."

Colleen chuckled.

"That's not really funny, Col."

"No, it's not, and I'm glad they're fine, but it was a great surprise to us all to look up on the television and see you without your shirt on, I'll tell you that." Colleen said. "I guess you didn't see the cameraman there at the army headquarters."

"Totally didn't," Kerry admitted. "I was focused on getting help for Tomas." She sighed. "No idea there was a camera crew around."

"Oh, for sure," Colleen said. "And to give em credit, it took a couple hours before I got the call after they figured out who you were," she said. "One of the army guys there was interviewed and spilled your name. Probably a fine thing you were out of pocket, but we got some great press out of it."

"Jesus." Kerry rubbed her temples with one hand. "We don't have cable out here," she said. "Only local feed, and it's just weather." She looked up and across at Angela, who was still taking notes on the phone. "Angela is picking up the office admin line but I don't think anyone's found it yet who isn't a customer."

"Good thing," Colleen said. "We can keep it like that. I don't mind lying my behind off all the day long here. I can't answer any of those broken PC calls," she said. "But would be a nice thing to have some of the technobobs up here for interested parties to talk to."

"Good idea," Kerry said. "Let me get hold of Mark and send him and his wife up there. I owe it to him after yesterday. If he can grab some of the business analysts that showed up at the office, they can be a lot more useful there than here."

"Perfection, my dear. We'll hold the fort until then and watch out for more of your adventures on international news," Colleen teased. "And don't forget to send me the info for our new staff. I'm glad I can now get hold of you all when needed."

"Thanks, Col. Talk to you soon." Kerry put the phone down. "Ho boy. Got a feeling there's not going to be enough coffee for this day."

****

Dar came around the van to find her two hapless coconspirators standing with their backs to the doors, and three men facing them all with angry faces and accusatory finger shaking in progress.

Why were people so jackass? Dar wondered. She removed her sunglasses and came up next to the two satellite vendors. She slid the glasses into the front of her shorts pocket. "Hey."

The voices cut off at her presence. Chino sat next to Dar's leg and sniffed suspiciously.

"Oh, hey." John seemed, if anything, glad to see her. Or glad for an interruption, at any rate. "How are ya?" He glanced at the three fuming men. "Maybe she can help us with this problem."

Dar sighed. "If I had a buck for every time someone said that to me, I'd own this damn island." She paused, then waited for someone to enlighten her. After a long silent moment, she looked at John. "So, what's the problem? Aside from the fact you've got a lot of people using a little bandwidth."

"So, you know about this?" One of the men asked.

"Yes," Dar responded. "Look. I'm not getting into the physics of this with you all. What is it exactly that you're having a problem doing and I can tell you if there's anything we can do to fix it, or if you're just going to have to wait for some other connection."

Alex had disappeared into the back of the van and now came out with an armful of folding stools, that he flipped open and set down on the gravel. "Here, siddown." He perched himself on the edge of the van floor. "Take a load off."

The three men and Dar took a seat, the nearest man wiped his forearm across his sweat covered head. "Okay." He had a vaguely midwestern accent, and he looked like he'd spent some time in the boxing ring, from the crooked profile of his nose and his bull neck.

The two other men were underlings. They sat there and just watched their boss.

"What do you mean, some other connection?" The boss asked, diverted. "Like what?"

Dar cleared her throat. "Reason why there's no TV and no Internet on this island is that the other end of the long cable coming out here is connected to something that's got no power," she said. "You want a definitive end to the dealing with satellite issue? Fix that. Go waste your energy and money or influence or whatever you got in getting AT and T to get their asses back up."

The man looked thoughtfully at her.

"Everyone is using the only route they got to get anything out anywhere, a satellite," Dar said. "We're using this, but everyone on the damn mainland needs all the space up there and that includes the military and the government. Guess who gets priority? They do," she said. "And before you ask, no it can't get any faster. Every single bit's being sent up to space and back."

John just nodded along like the dog in the back of a car, on a long highway ride.

"It's a freaking miracle this thing's working at all," Dar concluded. "So, I'm gonna ask you again, what is your particular problem?"

"I'm a GC. Your governor's an old family friend," the man said, shortly. "I've got probably a million people over there who need repairs and emergency construction on their houses, their roofs, the sidewalks... and I can't do shit about it, because I got no way to get pictures or orders for material or anything else outta here."

"Hmm." Dar grunted thoughtfully.

"Can't send pictures. Been trying to send one all morning," the man continued. "I thought by paying this guy, I'd get what I needed."

"David Barrow," he added, finally, extending a hand out to her. "And you are?"

Dar reached over to meet his hand with her own. "Dar Roberts," she said. "Okay. How much stuff do you need to send up right now?" She released his hand. "You got it on a laptop? Or a drive? Bring it here," she instructed. "Someone's gotta do something. It's a crap show out there. I saw the news."

"How much stuff? No idea." He turned to his minions. "You know that? How much?" He asked. "These are my IT guys," he explained as an aside. "I don't do that. I don't touch those computers. I just yell and pay the bills."

"It's a lot," The shorter of the two said. "Not sure how much."

"It's not on a drive. It's in a big database," the second offered. "So, the guys in the field they get the reports together and we have to send them to our processor in Canada. They place orders." He watched Dar warily. "We got a server back at the house. We got it here this morning."

"I've got a server in that cottage," Dar responded amiably. "Lucky for me all I'm sending up is the equivalent of text files. Just code." She stood up. "Find out how much and get the IP of the server you're using and bring it here to me and I'll see what I can do."

"Can you do something?" David asked, his tone skeptical.

Dar looked briefly at him. "Bring it or don't. Your choice." She patted her leg. "C'mon, Chi." She turned and went around the van to the double doors that led to the living room of the cottage. She opened them to slip inside.

"Well?" David looked at them. "This worth my time?" He asked. "Or should I just fly one of you guys out to Atlanta like we talked about?"

The two IT techs looked at each other, then at him. "Yeah. It's worth your time," the taller one said. "Cause I know who that is." He glanced aside. "You do too, Eddy."

"I sure do." The shorter one nodded. "Let's go see if we can export that send file and get it on a drive." He stood up. "Or maybe…get the transfer site config and get back here. Maybe we can do an IP to IP transfer if she'll go for that."

David regarded them. "Do I know who this is?" He asked, aggrievedly.

"No. It's an IT thing." the shorter one said. "It's okay boss. It's legit." He pulled at the neck of his shirt, blinking some sweat out of his eyes. "You going to stay here? Can we take the cart back?" They both started moving toward the path, looking over their shoulder at him in question.

"Go on." David pointed at the cart. "Make it fast."

"We will."

The two techs disappeared, leaving David by the van with John and Alex. He looked at them. "So, what's the deal?" He asked. "You know whoever that was? What's her story?"

"We don't know," John said. "Just someone told us to talk to her after the storm. They said she could help us get the satellite up."

"She did," Alex confirmed. "She figured out how to take stuff from this van and make it go to all the houses and got some gear that made it all work." He half turned and looked toward the cottage. "They got a whole IT rig in there with some guys working on it."

"Yeah?" David looked at the door with interest. "Let me go see if I can find out what the deal is with them." He winked at them. "Might be useful for the governor, y'know?" He made his way around the van and went toward the door.

John stuck his hands in his pockets. "He's gonna regret doing that."

"Hell, at least he's not here yelling at us." Alex fanned himself with a brochure. "Tell you what. Let's go hide in that villa they gave us, and just put a sign here saying to go ask her for help."

John turned and stared at him. "I notice you didn't tell them you knew about her."

"Pofft." Alex shoved his sunglasses up onto his nose. "Let him go figure it out."

****

Kerry looked up as the door opened, her ears picking up the ticky tacky noise of dog toenails on the ceramic tiles outside. "Hey, hon," she greeted Dar, who entered behind Chino and closed the door. Mocha came rambling out of one of the bedrooms and greeted them.

"How's it going here?" Dar came over and took the chair next to her. "Mom and Dad took the truck over to the office."

Kerry indicated the pad she'd been writing on. "Those are the top five in order of urgency." She said. "You need to call the Pentagon, by the way."

"Do I?" Dar had swung the backpack off her back and fished inside it. She pulled out both laptops and put them on the table. "Aren't they swimming in Bob? What do they want me to do about that? Reroute him via Alaska?"

The sound of laughter made Dar looked up, with a faintly puzzled expression.

"Don't give them any ideas." Kerry pulled her machine over. "Got a couple more ethernet cables, El?"

"Scott from Colorado sent me like twelve emails." Elvis rooted inside the crate. "Something you sent him before the storm?"

Dar looked up from plugging in the power for both laptops. "Latest build of the DOD rig," she said. "Is that what the Pentagon wants to talk to me about?" she asked. "They ran it in sim that day before. They were talking about me coming up to demo it."

"Again?" Kerry was still scribbling notes. "Hon, you promised John Deland his checkpoint on Friday." She looked up at her partner. "He says he knows, he's seen the news, and he doesn't care. Either we make the deadline or he's canceling."

Dar clicked the network cable Elvis held out to her into place. "Fuck him."

"Totally not interested," Kerry responded calmly. "You're my one and only." She grinned briefly at the chuckles in the room. "Anyway, you should at least call him and give him some kind of status."

"Wait." Dar paused and straightened up. "Is tomorrow Friday?"

"Today is Thursday, so yes." Kerry got up. "Let me get you some coffee," she said. "Restart your brain." She got out of the way of Elvis running a final cable and went back into the kitchen to retrieve a second ceramic cup and fixed coffee to Dar's preference.

Behind her, she heard the laptops booting up and after the previous day's extreme efforts she found herself glad to contemplate nothing crazier than wading through days of email.

She was a little sore, the sunburn a little uncomfortable under her light cotton clothes, her shoulders stiff from all the shenanigans on the airboat. "Hey, Dar?" she called out. "I ended up on CNN again."

Kerry carried the cup back into the main room, now full of keyboard clicking as the two programmers got down to work. Dar studied her screen and now glanced up at Kerry over the top of it. "You hear me?"

"I heard." Dar turned her screen around so Kerry could see it. "You certainly did." She pointed at the picture displayed on it as large as the screen was. "Nice."

"Oh my God." Kerry set the cup down and stared at the screen. "Local business owner rescues staff. Jesus." She reached up to pinch the bridge of her nose. "What the hell."

Dar took a sip of her coffee. "Well, that's what happened, Ker," she said mildly. "Looks like the media found them and interviewed Mayte," Dar added. "Sit down and read it. Let me see where John's framework is." She pulled the pad and the phone Kerry had been using over.

The back door to the cottage opened, and they all looked up as David Barrow entered. He blinked in relief at the air-conditioning inside. He paused and looked around at them and there was a moment of silence.

Then Elvis finished something on his keyboard. "Hey, Dar, I finished the modules for the State Department. I think you need to look at them though they're in the repo."

Dar picked up the phone. "Pentagon first," she said. "Buddy, if you want to sightsee, go somewhere else." She directed that at David. "We got a lot going on here."

"Who is that?" Kerry whispered.

"Governor's contractor," Dar responded. "Wants me to push some data through for him so they can start supply." She dialed the phone.

Kerry got up and went over to the newcomer. "Hi." She extended a hand. "Kerry." She waited for him to somewhat hesitantly take her hand. "What can we do to help?"

"Who in the hell are you people?" Barrow asked her.

"Long story. Want some coffee?"

****

Mark sat on the picnic table outside, his arm outstretched on his knee, covered in a bandage. "We didn't know what the hell was going on," he told Andy. "After you guys left last night, we all crashed. Then at three a.m., all hell broke loose outside."

Carlos nodded. "Sounded like fireworks on fourth of July," he said. "I thought... hey maybe they're fixing the power and those are transformers, y'know?"

"Wishful thinking," Ceci said.

"Kinda." Carlo's big, rugged face creased into an unexpected grin. "We ran the fans off the generator but man, it's hot." He turned and pointed to one corner of the inner yard. "We set up a sun shower over there. Didn't trust the water inside."

"Yeah, anyway, I hauled ass downstairs to see what the deal was," Mark said. "Hank was at the door, and Pete had just come over from the back. We heard people running and yelling outside, and guns going off." He paused. "I mean, we know they were guns now, but then we had no idea."

"We had no idea." Carlos pointed at himself and Mark. "Those guys knew what it was." He indicated Pete. "They were trying to haul us back inside."

Pete glanced over with a look of mild amusement. "You kids are nuts," he said. "Bullets flying around all over and there you all were, eyeballin."

Ceci was seated on the table, just listening. Along with Scott's RV, Mark's big bike was parked somewhat haphazardly, and two other cars were a little way away next to Hank's rigged up Humvee, with its owner sprawled asleep in the front.

"That is a big old mess," Andy said in a mild tone.

"Big one!" Carlos agreed. "Whole road out the front was full of guys with sticks and I don't know what else. Guard was chasing them, or maybe it was the cops. Too dark to see what the deal was." He had a cut on his head, and a splotch of dark crimson on his jeans. "I went out to see better."

"Good lord, boy." Andy gave him a severe stare.

"I knew he was going to say that," Carlos said to Mark. "Next thing we knew the whole crowd of whoever it was came hauling up to us wanting to get inside the building. We were not going along with that."

Ceci covered her eyes with one hand.

"Yeah that's true," Mark said. "I guess they didn't know maybe who all was still in here. Hank and Pete put the trucks and my bike in the back," he said. "Maybe they thought it was empty and they could hide inside."

"Just a bunch of jerks," Carlos said. "Anyway, Hank started shooting off his revolver and then stuff got wild," he said. "He was just trying to scare them back, y'know? Keep them out of the hallway until we could get back inside and close the door."

"It got crazy," Pete admitted. "There were about two dozen perps and a dozen who knows what, chasin' em."

"Wow," Ceci muttered.

"So, then the Guard caught up to everything and came over and started putting people on the ground," Mark said. "And they grabbed us, and then we got lucky because the guy in charge of the Guard was one of the guys that was at the Doral place when I was in there messing with their servers."

"So, in all that he recognized you?" Ceci asked, her voice raised. "Seriously in the dark and all that?"

Mark shrugged a little. "He said he did! They had me up against the wall of the building then one of them said to hold on, he knew who I was."

Pete was grilling the bacon and had a pan of scrambled eggs and peppers heating up. He glanced over at the table. "It was nuts between the cops yelling in Spanish and the Guard cursing and the perps crying like babies," he said. "So, the Guard came in after they dragged all the perps off and turns out they know you, Big A."

Andy looked surprised. "Me?"

"They do," Mark said. "They're from Alabama, or somewhere around there. They were the guys we bumped into out west. Kerry made friends with them."

"Oh boy," Ceci muttered. "This is getting weirder by the minute."

Andy frowned, perplexed. "Ah don't know me any Guard from Alabama," he said. "And ah ain't been back there for more'n a minute for a damn long time."

All the chatter had woken Hank up and he peered over at them, opening one eye. "Knows the family, Andy," he said. "Some of them are from those parts." He closed his eye again and pulled his cap down over his face, wriggling a little to get a bit more comfortable.

"Wall." Andy's brows creased. "That could be."

"So, what were the guys who they were chasing doing?" Ceci asked. "I mean, just running around shooting off guns in the rain or what?"

"Building down the road, they broke into it," Carlos said. "They started up a fire to make some... I don't know to cook or something and it caught the building on fire. They tried to put it out, but it just got out of control and then someone saw it and called the cops."

"And the cops called the Guard, I guess," Mark concluded. "Anyway, it all got settled down and we went back to sleep. Figured we'd let you all know this morning after breakfast, but here you are."

"Here we are," Ceci agreed. "And we've got supplies in the back of the truck, but honestly, people, I think we need to get you all out of here. This isn't good."

Carlos shrugged a little. "My apartment's trashed," he said. "It's way more put together here."

"So's our house," Mark said. "It was actually not that bad sleeping on the couch in my office last night." He went over and accepted a paper plate with some eggs and bacon on it. "Thanks, Pete."

"He's got a point," Pete said. "Nothing around here's worth shit. At least here it's close enough to the water to get a breeze and there's entertainment around." He winked at them. "Haven't had this much fun since I mustered out."

Ceci glanced aside at Andy, who was listening thoughtfully, head slightly tilted to one side. The rest of the occupants of the office were emerging, drawn by the smell of the bacon and the sunshine. She recognized now five or six new faces, staff, who waved at her in greeting.

She waved back. "Well," she said. "It's a sturdy building."

"It is," Carlos agreed. "That's what the Guard was saying when they were around, you know? Like a fort."

"Lord." Andy stood up. "Let me go get on the radio." He headed for the inner door.

"That load in the truck all for us?" Carlos asked. "We'll go hump it in."

"It is," Ceci said. "Most of it's camping gear. There's a... well, it seemed like a whole squad of Coast Guard out by us, and Andy stopped by there and loaded up before we came over."

"Sweet." Carlos looked up as his two lifter buddies came over, with three more Ceci didn't recognize. "Hey, guys."

"Morning," the cute, curly haired one said. "So, Joe, from the gym said we could go in there, but it's skanky," he said. "Could we move the plates and stuff over here? Set up in the corner there?" He pointed at one corner of the open space, where a concrete pad lined up along the short side of the building. "Better to sweat in the sun than smell that carpet."

Carlos eyed Ceci. "Think the bosses would go for that?"

"Sure," Ceci said, without hesitation. "The more big friendly guys like you around, the better." She got up and dusted her hands off. "In fact, if you unload the truck, I'll drive it over and you can use it to move stuff."

"Hot damn," the cute, curly haired man said. "Gonna be a great day!"

****

Kerry sat down at the small, linen covered kitchen table with David, intent on giving Dar the time to deal with her current slate of questions before loading her up with more.

Dar was brilliant. But she was also single-tracked and having multiple things pull her in different directions didn't end with good results. So Kerry tried to draw off the distractions to let her focus. "So," she said, as David sipped appreciatively at the excellent coffee in its ceramic cup. "What can I tell you about us?"

He relaxed a little. "Glad to be out of that heat," he said. "Jesus, it's hot here."

"It is. Took me a while to get used to it," Kerry said. "I'm from Michigan."

"You sound like it," he said. "My families all in Chicago. Anyway. So, my guys are going to bring over the stuff we need to get sent to the main office. You think that'll happen?"

Kerry took a sip of her coffee. "Did Dar say it would?"

He shrugged a little. "Said she'd try. What does that mean?"

"It means she'll try," Kerry said, dryly. "But generally, Dar does achieve whatever it is she's trying to do, so if she agreed to try it, it'll probably be fine." She smiled at him. "If it was just not going to happen, she'd have told you that."

David nodded thoughtfully. "So, who are you people?" He reverted to his original question.

"Who are we people. Well." Kerry settled back in her seat. "We are, as in, Dar and I are the owners of Roberts Automation. That's an IT services company." She paused. "Which you I am sure have never heard of."

"Truth." He agreed readily.

"We do custom services for companies. Strictly B2B. So, if you're a company who wants to do something like roll out new technology, you call us, and we evaluate what your choices are, recommend one, and help you roll it out. Or..." She cleared her throat a little. "Or if you have a need for custom software, to do something that you can't get off the shelf, and you need it fast and need it to work..."

"Not like the tax website."

Kerry chuckled. "If you need it to work, we do that as well."

"But for small stuff. Because you just got what... six people here?" David watched her with a shrewd expression.

"We actually have around a hundred and fifty employees." Kerry smiled at his surprised look. "I sent our support groups upstate so they could keep answering phones for us and our accounting director is there too. But Dar and I live here." She indicated vaguely the island around them. "So, we brought our main server stack and some of our programmers over to keep working since we have power here."

"That rig in there."

"That rig in there," Kerry confirmed. "We loaded it onto the deck of our boat and brought it over a few days ago."

David looked at her, his head dropped forward a little bit, one eyebrow lifted.

Kerry smiled at him, lifting her coffee cup in a mock toast. "We sell being a non-traditional option. Everyone can do IT, you know? We try to assume whatever we're asked is out of the box," she said. "And yes, we do a lot of work with smaller companies, but we also have government contracts, both local and federal."

"Interesting," he mused. "My company's kinda like that too. I don't build buildings or houses or stuff like that. We come in when they need stuff fast, and no screwing around. You know?" He eyed Kerry. "Get around the ... sometimes the government's way of doing things takes too much time."

Kerry did understand. "My parents worked in the federal government."

"So, you get it." David now smiled more confidently at her. "So anyway, I got a call to come down here and get things moving to help the guard and everyone put on temporary roofs and fix things. You know."

"Got it."

"I didn't figure on not being able to talk to nobody or send emails," David said. "Like I said outside, I don't get into all the IT stuff. I just give orders to people. I don't like the IT stuff. I don't understand it. I thought we'd at least be able to use the... what do you call them? The cell phone things."

"MiFi's," Kerry supplied. "Yeah, we didn't expect it all either. Don't feel bad. We had satellite phones..." She held up hers. "But you know, they don't really work well."

"No, ma'am, they don't. The governor's guy I'm here with tossed his in the water this morning."

"We have a marine radio relay set up to talk to our office, but Dar was really glad when those guys with the satellite came to her because at least it meant we could do some small, basic things," Kerry said. "But with everyone using it, it's kinda pitiful."

He leaned on the table and regarded her. "So, what's she going to do for us?"

"Mm..." Kerry pondered the question. "Probably prioritize the traffic. Dedicate some bandwidth to you to get the data through."

He looked blankly at her.

"Grease the skids for you," Kerry translated, with a small grin. "VIP pass."

Immediately, his expression cleared. "Now that I understand." He leaned back and took a long swallow of the coffee. "Now you're talking my language." He put the cup down. "She can do that?"

"Oh yes," Kerry said. She got up and refilled her cup and raised her eyebrows toward his. He nodded, and she put her cup down and took his, setting it down next to the dispenser as she picked up the plate of breakfast pastries and offered him one. "So, where are you guys starting in all that?"

He took a pastry. "Mayor's neighborhood." He took a bite. "Got someplace you're interested in?"

Kerry sat back down. "I might have." She put the plate down on the table. "Let me find out what it's going to take to get a real connection back up here, and maybe we can do a little business together."

He smiled at her, an expression of calculating predation and startling transparency on his face. "Governor's gonna really appreciate that."

Governor's going to probably have to get in line. Kerry thought, with an internal, wry sigh. "Here we go again."

****

Dar shifted her position on the chair and glanced outside the window at the breeze lashing the storm battered plants outside. "Scott." She took a breath to continue the argument. "Listen—"

"No, no, no, no. I know what you're going to say." Scott cut her off. "We'll send a jet for you. Ever take a ride in a fighter?"

"Yes."

"It's great, you'll love... wait. What?"

"Long story," Dar said. "What's the rush, Scott? What can't wait until after the weekend? By then things should be a little better here." She looked around the cottage, briefly distracted by yet more mail coming into her inbox. "We've been working on this for six months."

"I can't talk to you about why it's a rush," Scott said. "I mean, like, I can't. You know? But honest to crapazoid, it is. You gotta come up here, and show the big guy what it does, and let us go beta on it."

"Haven't they all evacuated? All up in the hills somewhere? Scott, no one's even in DC this week."

"You need to come here," he said. "Here to Cheyanne." He paused. "So, we're going to send a jet for you. What time is it, ten? Can you get to the airport by noon?"

Something on the screen caught Dar's attention and she swiveled in the chair she was sitting in, reaching over to open a page. "Hold on." She focused on the screen, reading rapidly for a long minute, aware of Scott's breathing on the other end of the phone. "Okay, " she murmured. "What the..."

"Okay? Great. See you here by two, our time. Thanks, Dar. You won't regret it. I swear to you. This is gonna be big." Scott hung up the phone as Dar was drawing in her breath to answer him, leaving her with nothing but a slightly digital sounding dial tone in her ear.

"Wait," she said, then stopped, her shoulders relaxing as she put the phone back into its cradle. "Shit. I didn't mean to say okay to you ya little..."

"Problems, boss?" Angela asked, from across the table. "You don't look so hot."

"Just got some unexpected news," Dar muttered. "Very unexpected."

She hesitated, torn between the email on her screen and the terminal screen open behind it, cursor blinking, waiting on her input.

Kerry came back in the front door, closing it behind her. "Hey." She came over and sat down next to Dar. "What's up, hon? I think I got rid of our new friend for a while." She eyed her. "You okay? You have a funny look on your face."

For an answer, Dar turned her laptop screen around, so it faced Kerry, and gestured at it. "Here. While I was reading that, I committed to flying to Colorado in two hours."

Kerry's' eyes slowly lifted up past the top of the laptop screen, deferring her attention from the email for a moment. "What?" She asked, in a startled tone. "Fly to Colorado? Like… as in right now?"

"Read it." Dar pointed at the screen. "It'll give me a few minutes to figure out what the hell I'm going to tell John Deland about his deadline for tomorrow."

She folded her hands and watched Kerry read, as her pale brows slowly drew together and she moved, almost unconsciously, closer to the laptop screen until she paused and looked up at Dar, her green eyes round and wide.

"Dar is this … does this say what I think it does?" Kerry's voice rose in consternation. "Did he, the landlord, sign the title to the building over to us?" She reread the email. "Is that what this says? Is he serious? Is he for real?"

"Apparently." Dar felt obscurely comforted by a reaction almost a mirror image of her own. "Doesn't have the money to fix it. He carried only the minimum insurance." She regarded her hands, long fingers calmly clasped. "I guess he was just over it."

"Son of an ice cream sundae." Kerry went back and read it again. "Dar, this is insane!"

"Mm." Dar nodded. "Who does that? Nobody does that," she said. "Except people who know us, I guess." She reached up and pinched the bridge of her nose. "Didn't need to read that in the middle of a half dozen customers yelling at my ass."

"He's moving to Costa Rica with his boyfriend." Kerry sat back. "Holy shit."

"Now I hope that deal didn't go through. We don't have the cash to do both these places." Dar rolled her head to one side and regarded Kerry. "Though we could sell that office, I guess. With the land it's on it's worth something."

"Instead of fixing it," Kerry murmured. "But where are we going to go, Dar? We have jobs we have to do. We can't just move everyone… can we?"

Dar shrugged faintly. "We moved them there."

"That was before a hurricane blew apart most of the class A office space in three counties." Kerry reminded her. "Shit, I better call Coleen and see how much space they've really got up there." She gave her head a little shake. "Son of a biscuit."

"Graham cracker."

It made Kerry smile, despite the shock that was still lifting her nape hairs. "Well, okay. That was unexpected." She turned the laptop around again to face Dar. "So, you said you have to fly to Colorado? To Cheyanne Mountain?"

Dar nodded.

Kerry's brow creased again. "All at once? That's a sudden hair on fire?" She asked. "Why? What's so urgent? They know what's going on down here. We've been working that project for months."

"They won't tell me."

In the act of opening her own laptop, Kerry paused and stared at Dar. "Excuse me?"

"They won't tell me why they want me to fly there, but they're sending a plane for me. In two hours," Dar said. "So now I've got to get a ride over to the airport and hope to hell they're open and they let me in."

Kerry stared at her. "What the hell is going on, Dar?"

"So, I guess I'll take my laptop with me and work on John's framework on the way." Dar soldiered on doggedly. "Unless they really are sending a fighter jet for me." She shook her head and pulled her laptop closer. "Can't open one of these in that back seat."

"A f…" Kerry paused.

"Yeah. Told him been there done that." Dar pecked at her keyboard. "Arthur, are the modules all linked for Dect Pharma?"

"Yeah," Arthur answered from his position on the couch. "I put the new libraries up there. They said they all compiled." He shifted the laptop on his lap. "But that stuff is a little weirdo."

"A little," Dar muttered. "Where is that… there it is." She focused on the screen, fingers moving rapidly over the keys. "C'mere you..."

Kerry shut the laptop. "Okay..." She stood up. "I'll go back to the house and pack a bag for you and pick up my car so I can drive you to the airport," she said. "You stay here and get as much done for him as you can before I get back."

Dar glanced up at her, "Thanks, Ker. Sorry for the chaos."

"No problem, maestro." She walked behind Dar and squeezed her shoulders. "Angela, call Colleen for me would you please?"

"Sure." Angela put pen to pad and waited. "Whatcha want her to do?"

"Tell her to see what she can work out to house the whole company up there," Kerry said. "Tell her to think of it as picking up the whole building and moving it up there. And add in what it's going to cost to house everyone in the area until we get settled."

"You got it."

"I'll be back." The bizarre events of the last few minutes just made her shake her head, as she went around the table and to the door. "Lock the door when I leave. You guys don't need distractions right now."

"Gotcha." Angela followed her. "Gonna be one of those days."

"Another one of those days."

****

Ceci perched on the picnic table and watched the activity in the center of the complex. It was hot, and sticky, and uncomfortable. The gym kids had all taken off their shirts as they went back and forth setting up things to their satisfaction on the far end of the space.

They were covered in sweat, but seemed happy with the results. Two of them were using wood debris they'd dragged in from the parking lot to build a rack for the bars they'd brought to sit on.

"I don't know, Andy. Is this really a good idea? What happened last night is scary," she said. "I don't think it's safe for these kids to be here. I know their houses are all messed up, but we should find a different place for them."

Andy regarded the weightlifters, and the Humvee parked in the center of the square. "Wasn't too good," he admitted. "Easy to get all wrong, in that dark, with guns round." He folded his arms over his chest. "Ev'erbody getting all het up."

"Do you think those guys were trying to hurt people?" Ceci asked. "The ones who set that building on fire?"

"Ah don't," Andy said. "Think they just didn't have no place to go to, and that there building let them in." He studied the lifters. "Ah went over there and looked round some. Bottom level there had a shop in it."

"The sandwich shop, yes," Ceci agreed. "That had a grill."

"Done had."

"So, they were just looking to… were they cooking in there?"

"Seems like," Andy said. "Probly didn't mean nothing." He shrugged. "Found me a fella holed up nearby there saw it all. Just folks lived in one of those camps down the road there."

"Homeless guys?"

"Yeap. Got them out of the rain, fella said. Thinks those cops came down too hard for it."

Ceci could imagine it. It had been a gas grill, and had gotten out of hand, maybe with people using it who, like her, had no idea how to cook over an open flame. "I can see it," she said. "After all, we have this grill back here." She indicated the now quiet area.

There was a propane tank connected to it, and two more standing by. "But we put it outside, on the concrete." She noted, the grill seated in the open, a big plastic tarp folded nearby to cover it when they were done for the day.

"Ain't nobody here without good sense," Andy said. "But ah don't know you're right, Cec. Coulda gone bad here, even with Pete and them round." He studied the open space. "Figure something out."

Mark's bike was gone, he'd headed off toward home and now some of the staff who'd showed up were busy inside the building, its windows all thrown wide open to the languid air. A half dozen more had appeared after breakfast.

"Ahm goin to go try and raise up them kids," Andy said. He walked back into the building and along the hallway down to the room on the end, a small utility space that had a large window that faced east.

It was open, and he smelled the salt water as the breeze shifted a little, rustling the dead leaves outside. He heard the sound of flapping tarps and hammers, and an echo of incoherent shouts somewhere in the distance. He had to concede that the area, even with guards, wasn't that safe.

Inside the room was a battered table with a radio set on it, and a long coaxial cable that went out the open window and up to an antenna fastened to the wall and extending up to the top of the second floor.

A battery was attached to the radio, and he checked the charge before he turned it on. He sat down on the wooden stool in front of it and reached out to tune the dials.

An earlier attempt to contact the island was unsuccessful, though it was hard to say at the time if it had been technical issues or just Dar and Kerry being busy.

After an adjustment to the frequencies, he picked up the mic. "Lo! Lo there you all." He paused. "Lo! You all listening?" He released the transmitter and waited.

After a moment of silence, a bit of crackling emerged. "Go ahead, Dad," Kerry's voice responded, and behind it he heard the distant sound of a helicopter. "What's up? I'm just heading back to the house."

"They all had a dust up here last night," Andy reported. "Evry'body's all right, but Cec don't like the idea of keeping folks ovah here. Thinks maybe we should get them all outta here, and let that boy handle the fixin."

There was a pause. "Well," Kerry's tone sounded like a mix between resignation and amusement. "Actually... there's a complication."

Uh oh. Andy had known his daughter-in-law long enough by now to read her verbal cues, always more subtle and nuanced than Dar's. "What's the story, kumquat?" He asked. "Ah thought that landlord be back today to get hisself sorted out. Ain't showed up yet though."

"He signed over the property to us," Kerry said. "We now own the place."

Andy stared at the radio. "Say what?" He managed, after a pause. "You all mean that boy done ran off?" He knew a moment of honest shock and surprise. "For real?"

"Yeah. For real. He had title to it, I guess. Didn't have the money to fix anything, so he cut his losses and left us on the hook for it while he escaped to Costa Rica," Kerry said. "And oh, by the way, we're going to be on our way to the airport in a few minutes. Dar's got to fly to Colorado."

"Scuse me?"

Kerry's voice now held resigned humor. "Anyway, I have to get her bag packed. I'll stop on the way back and fill you guys all in. But we kinda should try to keep the place in one piece."

Andy looked around the inside of the room, at a loss for words. Finally, he picked up the mic. "Roger that," he said into it, in an almost mechanical way. "Talk at ya later."

He put the mic down and stood up, then reached over and turned off the radio to save the battery before he walked out into the hallway and looked down it. Overhead he heard the sound of people walking around upstairs, and the scrape of chairs against the now bare floors.

He could smell mold, and debris from the outside, and the dusty scent of canvas and plastic from the materials they sealed the roof vents with.

He heard the laughter upstairs of the workers, and it sounded so relaxed and carefree. "Some bitch," he said. "Some damn bitch."

Pete came out of the first level washroom, wiping his hands on a paper towel. "Sup?" He paused. "You look like an eel bit ya."

Andy put his hands on his hips. "Fella what owns this place done ran out on us."

"That punk haired little scoot?" Pete came over. "Wasn't worth much anyhow. You all had to board up this place your own self, you said."

"Ah know that. Figured they'd come in here and fix it up after we done that, but the little bastard just handed over the keys and took off."

Pete stared at him. Eyes widened. "No shit," he finally spluttered. "Left this all up to you all?" He made a vague gesture around the lower floor. "All this fixin? All that mess? For real?"

"Seems like." Andy shook his head and exhaled in disgust. "Swear to the Lord, ain't a situation we don't get all up into."

Pete folded the paper towel neatly into a square and shoved it into his back pocket. "Well, buddy, we better go round up some more of our old friends then, cause more stuff like last night's gonna take more than me and old Hank."

"Lord."

"Specially if you own this thing now. Sure don't want it to be set on fire."

"Hell and damnation."

Chapter Twelve

"So that's that." Kerry dropped a leather overnight bag on the dresser. "As if things weren't complicated enough, now we have Crazytown happening at what suddenly is our property. Jesus."

She was talking specifically to herself, the condo otherwise quiet. Only the sound of the air-conditioning plant cycling in the background.

"This is nuts," she continued, as she sorted through the drawers and selected underwear and socks, she then neatly tucked into the bag. "Totally nuts."

She went into the closet and grabbed two of Dar's favored short sleeve silk shirts and two pairs of jeans, folded them and added them as well.

For dealing with the government, especially the military, Dar always preferred to dress down. Kerry wasn't sure that really made sense, but she didn't argue with it. And considering it was coming into fall where she was going, she added a light sweater as well.

She ducked into the bathroom and opened one of the cabinets. She pulled out a small bag and sorted out travel bottles of body wash and shampoo and a fresh scrubbie, then tossed in a little bottle of Advil that was Dar's concession to medical necessities.

She pulled out her phone and opened it, checking the calendar in the mostly useless device, glad to see that neither of them was close to cycling. "One small blessing," she muttered and shoved the phone into her back pocket again.

She brought the small bag out into the bedroom and put it in the overnight bag, pausing a moment thoughtfully, before she went back out into the main part of the condo and into the kitchen. She opened up the refrigerator and pulled open one of the small partitions.

Inside were a supply of Hershey's kisses. She removed a handful of them, their tightly foil wrapped surface cold against her skin as she returned and added them into the bathroom kit before she zipped up the whole thing and dusted her hands off.

"Okay." She brought the bag into the living room and dropped it onto the coffee table and paused to stand thoughtfully for a moment in silence as she considered if there was something else, she needed to do before going back to the cottage.

She checked her watch and decided she had time for a cup of tea, and went into the kitchen to put up some water for it, pausing to glance out the kitchen window at the partly cloudy weather outside.

It was breezy, and past the battered outside wall of the garden she spotted two men working to remove debris from the edge of the water where rollers were still coming up and surging past the gates.

They would need to rebuild the beach; she'd heard one of the other residents say. Have a barge come out and pump sand in from offshore to rebuild the edge of the island. Kerry recalled them sounding impatient about it, as though that was the most important thing in the world to get done.

Here they were, she shook her head a little, sitting out here with all the comforts in the world. They had power and air-conditioning, people to get them pretty much whatever they wanted, without worrying about dark nights and people looting their homes.

She remembered talking to Maria and Mayte earlier. Tomas was resting comfortably. The hospital had operated on his broken leg, and given him antibiotics.

Maria told her all about how grateful they were to be in the little residential hotel next to the hospital, and how there was even a little Cuban cafeteria open in the lobby where they'd had Cafecito and pastalitos. They felt so lucky when they saw what was going on elsewhere.

Mayte had told her about how the Miami Herald had found them and interviewed them and hoped Kerry didn't mind too much about it.

The water pot hooted gently, and she poured the water over her loose tea ball, the scent of the green leaves with their faintly seaweed tainted steam rising to her nose.

She hadn't minded. Kerry watched the tea steep. Even if she had, she wouldn't have told them that of course, but she really didn't, since it wasn't as if they hadn't told the truth. And frankly if she was going to have her picture on CNN, she'd much rather it be for doing something laudable.

She wondered if someone had chased down what her mother's view of it was. A faint smile twitched on Kerry's face, as she removed the tea ball and added a drizzle of local orange blossom honey to the tea. She imagined her reaction to the picture of her daughter, in a pair of drenched cargo shorts and a sports bra, streaked with mud, yelling at the National Guard.

She lifted the cup and took a sip, swallowing it around a grin. Once they had decent access, she was looking forward to watching the clip. She wondered if one of the mails in her box she hadn't had any time to look at was from Angie, who surely would have seen it.

She wondered what her father would have said. Kerry stared out over the water. "He'd have taken the good press." She decided, with a wry grimace. "Probably wouldn't have mentioned Maria's family are immigrants though."

Or maybe he would have. Kerry felt she could grant that posthumous reasonable doubt.

She took the cup into the living room and sat on the couch, extending her legs out and crossing her ankles, stretching out muscles sore from the previous day, taking the moment of quiet to consider what direction her plans were going to take next.

****

Dar studied the screen in front of her. "Pain in the ass not having those damn double screens here." She scribbled a note on one of the pads Angela had passed over to her. "I'm never going to be able to read these stupid notes."

"Yeah, sucks," Arthur agreed. "Could we go get them?" He looked up and over at her. "That ride on the boat was fun."

"Fun," Elvis agreed. "All right, Dar, I finished that recompile and checked it back in."

"All right." Dar paused. "Hey maybe we can ask my parents to bring them back," she said. "Hang on." She unclipped the radio from her belt. "Ker? Ker, you there?" She paused to listen, clicking the transmit button impatiently. "Ker?"

"Go ahead. All done packing here. I was just having some tea," Kerry's voice answered a moment later. "Had to grab the radio off the counter."

"Did you get ahold of Dad?" Dar scrolled down the page and reviewed the code on her screen. "If he's coming back can he throw the screens in the programmer's cubes into the truck? We need the eyeball space here."

"Sure, I can ask," Kerry said. "I just got done telling him about the landlord. He might have stopped cursing by now. They had some kind of kerfuffle there last night with the police. Everyone's fine," she hastened to say. "But it sounded like it shook them up."

"Huh." Dar diverted her attention. "That doesn't sound good. "Maybe we should head over there."

"I told them I'd stop by on the way back from taking you to the airport to get all the details," Kerry said. "Anyway, let me see if I can raise them again about the screens, then I'll be over to pick you up."

"Okay." Dar went back to checking the code. "This isn't going to be done in time, Ker," she added, in an almost mutter.

"Keep working at it. We can talk about it when I get there, to see what to tell John," Kerry told her. "See you in a bit."

Dar put the radio down and concentrated on the programming in front of her. "All right let's see how that works out."

A knock came at the front door, and Celeste hopped up to answer it. "Hello?"

"Um." There were two young men in polo shirts standing outside. "We have some data here that can maybe get sent?"

"Let 'em in," Dar called out, her sensitive ears catching the voices. She half turned as the door opened and the two techs entered. "You got it on a drive? Bring it over here." She held out one hand to them. "C'mon, don't just stand there. I've got a dozen things to do."

The nearer tech came over and unzipped a case, removing a hard drive in a housing and offering it up to her. "Here it is. It's pretty big."

Dar inspected the connection to the drive. "USB." She stood up and went over to the rack. "We got anything here I can plug this into that's not secure?" She examined the stack of servers. "No."

"Spare lappie?" Elvis suggested. "Got one in the bottom of that case."

"Good idea." Dar went to the case, fished a laptop out and brought it over to where the router sat on its small table, whirring away, its fan causing the linen cover on the table to flutter.

"So, what are you guys doing here?" The tech who'd handed her the drive asked, hesitantly.

"Coding stuff," Arthur muttered. "What the hell does it look like we're doing here, dude?"

"Hey, I was just asking."

Dar got the drive connected and quickly examined the contents. "Hmph." She grunted. "That's gonna take a while." She plugged the laptop directly into the router and attached the hanging configuration cable to it, resting the laptop itself on top of the bulky device.

It was taking time out from her work, and now she regretted even getting involved in the situation. Regretted deciding to step in and do this guy a favor. With an irritated sound, she opened up a configuration window and examined what was going on inside the router.

"Is that what's running everything?" The tech asked.

"Dude, sit down." Elvis pointed at a chair. "Don't bother her."

It made Dar smile, safe enough as her back was to the room. There was a period, naturally, of skeptical wariness when she'd first hired on her new programmers, not the least of which had been her own internal doubt on whether she was really suited for the work anymore.

She'd never really left it, always dabbling a little bit in the craft with her gopher and the monitoring programs that were, probably, still in use at ILS somewhere. But she hadn't focused on it like she was now. And projects hadn't depended on her coding skills like they did now.

So as a way to start, she'd thrown the code of the business systems they were running Roberts Automation on up into their newly born repository and invited them all to have at it in terms of fixing problems and suggesting improvements.

Because, she knew these folks she'd hired knew who she was. She knew she'd been known in the industry for long enough and had been public enough but never in this arena. That wasn't what she'd been in the business mags for. Wasn't even what she'd mostly ever done for ILS.

That had ended well. She'd gotten a budding respect from them out of it, had used the app framework to develop a programming design guide for the group. And with the participation of her new team, shined up the old pile of code and added features and functions that surprised and delighted the rest of the company in the bargain.

Now the programmers were stuck to her like ticks, and felt an almost hilarious sense of possession. And it did, in fact, make her smile as she stood there, her fingers moving over the keyboard.

She set up some configuration and put it in place, then went back to the laptop's interface and checked the drive's contents. "This text file the end point?"

"Yes." Both techs had sat down on the couch and they answered almost together. "We're just curious, y'know. We do this too." The second one told Elvis. "I mean, IT."

Dar studied the text file. "You FTP this file?" She half turned and looked at them, her eyebrows hiked.

"The thing it's going to is a dBase 4 datastore," the nearer tech told her. "We're lucky it has an ethernet bus."

Dar blinked at them, both her eyes widening. "dBase FOUR?"

He nodded. "It was written by the bosses uncle or something to do building site management back in the day. They never updated it. He says it still works, leave it alone." He shrugged a little. "Which, I kinda get. My grandpop worked for the phone company, back in the day."

"Ooookay." Dar turned back around and opened a terminal program, cutting and pasting the config into place and watching the session connect. "You do this all manually?"

"Filezilla."

"That what's on the other end of it?"

"Yeah, it puts the file in a directory, then the box picks it up and sucks it in. It's just a CSV with embedded links to the pictures." The tech got up and came over, curiously peering over her shoulder at the laptop. "Oh. Yeah there it is, that's the right screen there."

In another window, Dar opened the file she was getting ready to send. "Thought you all just got here?" She closed the file and started the transfer, watching the small text pinwheel whirl. "That's a lot of data."

The tech remained silent, and after a moment, Dar looked at him. He was a good-looking kid, with tightly curled brown hair and a dark skin. "How'd you get it in so little time?"

"We don't ask that stuff," he finally said. "Boss got it where he got it, you know? From the governor."

"Okay," Dar responded mildly. "It's on its way." She waited as he peeked at the screen, then backed off and went back over to the couch to sit down. "Probably take about an hour."

"Awesome."

She turned back to the screen and re-opened the file in another session, running her eyes over the data that seemed to mostly be names and addresses. Curiously, she selected one of the embedded pictures and opened it, finding a hi-res picture of a nice looking home inside.

Thoughtfully she closed the windows, and then went back to her seat, pulling it up to the table and putting her attention back on her programming. "We should have my dad throw the gamer chairs in the truck while he's at it," she muttered. "Take this stupid furniture out of here."

"That would rock," Elvis said. "Like, who sits on stuff like this?"

"Nobody, for very long. It's for looks," Dar said absently.

"Lame," Arthur said.

"Lame," Elvis agreed. "We should swap em out for beanbags."

****

"You're going to what?" Ceci looked up from pouring lukewarm iced tea into a cup. "Wait... what?"

Andy came in and sat down at the conference table, propping his head up on one fist. "We got us a big old mess here," he said. "Ain't gonna be nobody to come fix this place if it gets wrecked."

Ceci put the jug down and sat in the seat next to him. "No, I get that," she said. "That landlord turned out to be the exact turd I thought he was. Got it." She held up a hand. "But do we need to turn this place into a fortress?"

"Ah do think so," Andy replied in a mild tone. "Ah sent Hank and Pete out to round up a few more fellers for it," he said. "Specially if these here folks are goin to stick round here."

Well, that made sense. Ceci paused. No, really none of it made any sense at all, but in the world that revolved around her daughter and her daughter-in-law that was relatively normal.

She looked around the conference room. "Well," she said. "I've wanted to redo this place. It's too damn dark. Even if we have to sell cupcakes to finance it."

Andy pursed his lips thoughtfully. "Ah'd like me a cupcake," he said, in a serious tone.

"Of course you would." Ceci got up. "Okay, well, I'm going to grab a pad and start taking down ideas on what we need to get done to get this place back in order. And stick my head out on the street and see if anyone's out there selling cupcakes."

Andy grinned as she purposefully walked out. He picked up the cup of warm tea she'd left behind and took a sip from it.

The conference room was right next to the front door, and that was also wide open, to get as much of a cross breeze through as possible, the generator being saved for the evening to run the fans that made the building habitable.

It wasn't horribly uncomfortable. He'd been in much worse places, in worse situations and here he could go around in a tank top and not have thirty pounds of gear strapped on him.

Even the stress of the landlord abandoning them was relative. It meant they now could do what they wanted with the place, and though there was a ton of money involved, there was nothing around here unfixable.

A flicker of shadow caught his attention and he looked up and through the doorway as a slight figure entered and looked around with wide eyes. "Lo there," he called out. "That you all, Zoe?"

Zoe reacted to his voice with a relieved sound, and a smile. "Oh, Mr. Andy!" She said. "I am so glad to find someone here."

"Plenty of folks round," Andy told her. "You all doing okay?"

Zoe sat on the chair Ceci had so recently vacated. "Our house is gone," she said. "It fell into pieces. We just went from the shelter to there to see it. My mama says, at least all of us is alive."

Andy consciously gentled his voice. "That's a true thing, Zoe. Ain't nothing nowhere as important as your family," he said. "Building's just a thing. Ya'll can always fix a thing. Can't always fix people."

Zoe nodded. "Yes. But they told us, it will be a long time before anything can be done. So, my papa said, I should come here to see if there was something I can do, because the shelter is so... " She made a face. "There are people there who are not so good." She hesitated. "They are angry and mean."

"Mean to you all?" Andy asked, quietly. Zoe had a cleft lip, like Hank, and the surgery to fix it had left her face a little twisted and disfigured, and given her a faint lisp to her speech.

She had wavy light brown hair and pretty almost purple eyes and she wore shorts and a company logo T-shirt. She had on a backpack that had a little stuffed kitty keychain hanging from it.

Zoe nodded. "My brother got in a fight last night. He got hurt," she said. "So many people there."

"Kind of a big old mess here," Andy said, a touch apologetically. "Got no power, and the roof got some wet."

"Kerry told me yesterday," Zoe said. "But there are good people here. You are here, and Mr. Carlos is here. My papa said, it would be okay."

Well. Andy regarded her. Maybe Kerry would want to take her over to the island later on, with the two programmers. "Yeap," he said. "Let's go see what we all can get into. Ah think mah wife's out there counting carpets."

Zoe followed, calling out happily as she spotted Carlos down the hall, with now more familiar faces newly arrived, a buzz of conversation filled the space.

Lord. Andy sighed internally. What ain't gonna happen next.

****

Kerry pulled up to the curb in the arrivals level at Miami International Airport, pausing to regard the building as she put her car in park. "Jesus, Dar. Are you sure this is open?"

The front of the airport was completely covered in metal shutters, and halfway down the concourse the overhang that sheltered the outside entrance had collapsed, twisted metal structure draped all down the street and blocked all but the leftmost lane.

Past that was nothing but wreckage. The far end of the terminal invisible. Part of the parking complex, which filled the inside of the departure and arrival loop, had collapsed, and between some of the debris cars left parked in the lot could be seen.

There were four police cars, and three military SUV's parked in front of the one visible entrance, and that was it. The rest of the landscape was barren and empty, save bits of debris being blown about by the wind.

Dar seemed a bit nonplussed. She had the overnight bag at her feet and she took off her sunglasses to study the wreckage. "It's not open for commercial flights, no," she conceded. "That's what the radio said, anyway." She indicated the AM station playing in the car. "So, I guess it makes sense...."

"Can they even land an airplane here?"

"Governor's buddy showed up."

"Maybe they drove."

Dar regarded her with a hint of skepticism.

"Yeah, okay, that's a long drive. Let's get you inside." Kerry shook her head a bit, then she opened her door and slid out of the SUV and glanced around to see if there was anyone to talk to about leaving it parked there.

Literally no one. She'd been to this airport dozens of times and never seen it this empty, not even when dropping Dar off for a 5 a.m. flight. "Holy bananas, Dar."

"Holy bananas, Ker." Dar checked her watch, then got out of the passenger side and shut the door, slinging the bag's strap over her shoulder. "C'mon. Let's see if anyone's inside."

They walked together along the debris covered sidewalk, the wind howling a little through the struts of the collapsed overhang. "What a mess." Dar studied the luggage check in station, busted into a thousand pieces scattered over the sidewalk.

She picked up a bit of the check in station. "Plywood." She dropped it to the ground. "At least it's not pressboard."

"Pressboard? Dar that wouldn't last fifteen minutes in this climate."

"Never stopped them before."

They went to the closed sliding door and it stayed closed as they reached it. Dar shaded her eyes with her hand and pressed against the surface, peering inside. "Lights are off."

Kerry sidestepped a foot or so and knocked on the other door. "You sure he said this airport, Dar?"

Dar studied the dark interior and searched for any motion. "No, I'm not sure, matter of fact. He said the airport," she muttered. "Then he hung up. But if they were sending any reasonable sized plane it would have to be to here."

"Or Lauderdale."

"It's a bigger mess than this is. This is inland at least," Dar said. "Wait, there's someone in there."

Kerry knocked again and wrapped her keys around her hand to add a staccato tang to the sound. "Hope he knows who you are. I'm not really in the mood to be hopping the airfield fence today."

"Not sure I expect him to know who I am, but if he can't find me someone who knows about military planes I'm turning around and going home." Dar stepped back as the figure inside came to the door and peered at her suspiciously. "Not really in the mood to be arguing with a rentacop today." It was a tall man in a security guard uniform. He looked from one to the other of them for a long moment.

"What do you think he's thinking, Dar?" Kerry stepped back as well and slid her hands into her front pockets. "We're some dumb chicks who are lost?"

She saw the man reach for his belt and for a brief moment she felt a tingle of alarm, but it was just to retrieve a ring of keys and she relaxed as he took his time hunting through them.

"We'll find out in a minute." Dar slid her sunglasses back on and glanced around, lifting her head a little, sniffing reflectively. "That's jet fuel," she said, after a moment.

"What is?"

"That smell." Dar rocked up and down on her heels.

"Well, it's an airport. Is that unusual?"

"In a closed airport?"

Kerry paused and gave her a sideways look and saw a brief grin and a wink appear on Dar's face. Then watched the guard, who was now fitting a key into the inside of the door. After a moment it clicked but didn't move.

The guard got his fingers into the crack between the doors and hauled at them, causing them to open with a scream of objecting metal tracks.

A gust of air puffed out at them, full of mildewed carpet and musky, sweating security guard. Highly unpleasant. "Hello?" Kerry said, in a mild tone. "Sorry to cause you so much trouble."

The man got between the doors, wedging his body sideways and shoving against them with both hands. They opened all the way up and he turned to look at them. "Well? Whatcha want?" He asked, impatiently. "Airport's closed!"

"Yes, we realize that." Dar stepped forward, and almost instinctively, the man stepped back. "I was asked to come over here and meet a military plane," she said. "Is there anyone from the Department of Defense I could talk to inside?"

It totally wasn't what he was expecting, Kerry evaluated, and so, he had no idea what to say to Dar to that question. Dar was a half a head taller than the guard and was staring at him with that peculiar intensity that she well remembered from that very first moment she'd faced her in the doorway of her small office.

"Well..." He glanced around. "I don't know nothing about that."

"Did a plane from Colorado just land here, by any chance?" Dar asked. "Probably either Air Force, or Naval aviation?"

The guard got out of the way and gestured inside. "C'mon in and look around, ladies. I got no idea what you're talking about but sure. C'mon. Least you smell good." He gave in with surprising grace. "There's some guys in the back, in the office. Maybe they can tell you."

"You can head back," Dar suggested to Kerry, as they edged through the door. "I'll…"

"You can't call me. Let's find out if you're going anywhere and save us both the trouble." Kerry put a hand on her hip and nudged her forward. "Otherwise I won't be able to think straight."

Dar grinned, a little, but shifted the strap on her bag and started after the guard, who was trudging through the gloom inside. He headed down the concourse toward a bit of illumination coming from somewhere inside.

Somewhere something was leaking. Dar could hear water hitting the polished concrete floor and the inside of the building smelled about what you would expect a huge public space to smell like without air-conditioning for days when it required that to keep mold spores at bay through pure humidity control.

South Florida was a swamp. Both because it was, most of it being at or only slightly above sea level, but also because it had a true tropical, humid climate that had more in common with the Bahamas and the other islands of the Caribbean basin than the rest of the continental US.

Everything was air-conditioned. It was the only thing that allowed people who worked and lived in the area to wear anything but bathing suits. As they slogged through the musty, humid air Dar already missed the at least slight air movement of the outdoors.

"Mess in here," the guard muttered. "Stupid assholes turned off all the air to save them a buck."

"Much damage?" Dar asked as they went between the dark check in counters and along the concourse.

"Yeah. Everything from G down's screwed," he said, cheering up a little at the opportunity to share bad news. "Like, really screwed, y'know? Shutters got ripped off and the windows blew in. Whole thing's a wreck."

"Wow."

"Least in D, here, the entrance is in the curve. Backside of it got wiped out though," the guard said. "And forget the sky bridges. Stupid idiot managers were supposed to drive them against the terminal wall, but they didn't. What a god damned mess that is. Wrecked half of airside."

"You can drive an air bridge?" Kerry asked, distracted. "Really?"

"Sure," he said. "Just the front part, right? Where the plane goes. You can drive it back so it's flat to the wall mostly."

"Huh," Kerry said. "Seems like a crazy thing to forget."

"In a rush. Everyone wanted outta here. Now they all want to get back in." The guard shook his head, muttering under his breath as he stumped along ahead of them. "Can't blame em I guess. Glad I was in the ride out crew, got me a cot and everything."

They walked past the security stations, all packed up and covered in plastic. Beyond that Dar could now see light was coming from the American Airline VIP club in what, in operation, would be the secured area. The stores on either side were shut tight with rolling doors and on either side the boarding gates still had shutters in place, giving the entire facility a dark, dank atmosphere.

However, as they walked closer to the club the air around them stirred and moderated, and by the time they got to the entrance, you could feel the air-conditioning. The guard pulled at his shirt as they walked inside. "That's better," he muttered. "Lemme find somebody for you to talk to."

Inside the Admiral's Club, the space had been taken over as a control center for the airport staff. There was power inside, and the coffee makers were going full force to service the dozens of men with papers and clipboards scattered across the small courtesy tables.

The smell of the coffee and pizza were prevalent, with a tinge of old cold doughnuts on its fringes. Where there would be a little buffet set out for the airlines' guests, boxes and bags of warehouse store bought sugar and creamer and paper plates were stacked.

The men closest to the door looked up as they entered, and they attracted attention immediately. A tall, silver haired man in a guayabera came over to them, glancing at the guard before focusing on Dar and Kerry with a look of perplexed concern.

"Hi." Kerry short circuited him. "We know you're busy here, so let's just ask our question and get on our way. Have you had a military plane land here recently? We're supposed to meet them."

Dar made one of her little grunting noises that were half amusement and half satisfaction. She wrapped her fingers around her overnight back strap, content to let Kerry do the talking, while she glanced around the room and tried to reconcile her own memories of it as a passenger with the somewhat organized chaos she saw now.

"Hel...lo," the man said. "I'm not really sure..."

"No, I get it." Kerry smiled at him. "We're just interrupting you. Sorry about that but you know what it's like working with the government. They just tell you to go somewhere and here we are. Should we talk to flight operations maybe?"

"The... airport's closed," the man finally said. "So, I'm not sure..."

"Would they stop a Department of Defense flight from landing?" Dar spoke up for the first time. "Assuming the field is cleared for them to do so safely?"

The silver haired man half turned and focused on her. "Department of Defense?" He repeated. "Okay well, that's a different story. Come with me, ladies." He turned his head. "Miguel, I'll be back. Let me take these folks over to control."

"Si," the man he'd been talking to nodded. "I'll keep going with this." He pointed at a clipboard full of dirty papers.

Their guard friend waved at them. "Good excuse for coffee. Good luck."

They exited the club and went along a corridor that got progressively warmer and mustier, until the silver haired man turned and swiped his card on a large metal door. He waited until it blinked green before he pushed the door open.

Inside it seemed metallic and the air dropped back down to a dank chill. The floor switched from carpet to linoleum tile, and the walls to painted concrete block, with a thick layer of off green that anyone having gone to public school would likely recognize.

Sounds echoed, and their steps were squeaky distinct, though the floor had a section in the middle where the wax had worn down and was scuffed.

Delivery carts were lined up against the walls, mostly empty. A few with supplies stacked on them, including tape and bags of bags, and some folded tarps.

"Thanks for taking the time to take us where we need to go," Kerry said after a moment. "I know it must be crazy."

"Well." The man led the way down a long hallway, with anonymous metal doors with cryptic identification blocks next to them on either side. "Yeah, it's a mess, but to be honest, administering this facility's a mess at the best of times. So, it's all relative." He glanced around at her. "My name's Steven Hillingdon, by the way. I'm in charge of the civil side of this place."

"Where to start, huh?" Kerry sympathized.

"Where to start." He paused at one door and swiped his card again. "Hope you don't mind the stairs...." Here he paused and looked at both of them in question, finely distinct eyebrows lifting just slightly.

"Sorry," Kerry said. "Kerry and Dar Roberts." She indicated herself, and then her partner. "We run an IT consulting company that does business with the government and they don't view a major hurricane as a travel impediment."

"Got it." Hillingdon stepped back and pulled the door open. "Hey if the government is sending a plane here, it must be important. They know what kind of a mess this place is in, but on the flipside, they've got hardware that can deal with the mess."

"Third floor." He indicated the steps. "Sorry about that, but they have the elevators turned off. Not sure if it's more power savings or the fact we don't have to have to have the firemen in here if someone gets stuck."

"No problem." Dar started up the steps. "Least there's no carpet in here to get wet."

"That is the truth. Certainly stinks on the public side."

"Certainly does."

****

"All right." Andy stood on the landing in the center of the open central space of the building. Hank's Humvee was back, and now Pete's Wrangler was parked next to it, it's shortwave whip antenna with its frowny face topper waving gently in the breeze. "Get this here mission all started up now."

Carlos emerged behind him and came up to the edge of the concrete slab. "Whole deal got changed, huh, pops?" he said. "Crazy crazy just got even mo crazy. Now we got skin in the game here for sure."

"Some bitch changed all the right," Andy said. "Ain't gonna have no more of that all mess from last night round here." He sniffed reflectively. "Nobody's going to get no ideas when we're done with it."

"Little punk."

Andy glanced at him. "That landlord?"

Carlos nodded. "He never did crap for us," he said bluntly. "So, you know, I'm glad it went down that way, even if it's a mess for the bosses to handle." He folded his brawny arms over his chest. "We'll figure it out, even if we gotta go barter for stuff."

Andy smiled, just a little. "Ain't no doubt," he said. Along with Hank and Pete, there were now eight more men in their mid-thirties and forties in the central area, all in worn jeans or camo pants and faded T-shirts and ballcaps, all a bit battered by life looking.

As Andy himself was.

They were enjoying relaxing near the Humvee, laughter and trash talking echoing a little over the tattered grass, one of them pointing over at the lifting area now with obvious approval.

"Buddies of yours, pops?" Carlos asked, in a casual tone. "You got a lot of em."

"Wall." Andy thought about that. "Most folks who done served ah at least'll chitchat with cause we got that in common," he said. "Got good and bad like ev'rywhere else. But these all boys are good nuff for me to let near my kids."

"Uh huh," Carlos mused. "Pops, you know they can kinda kick ass themselves, right? Our bosses, I mean."

"Still mah kids." Andy was unrepentant. "But, yes, ah do know that. Dar done took one of them boy scouts down by the Hunter place last night." He chuckled a little. "Tackled him so hard his damn ears near came off."

Carlos could imagine it. He knew his boss had a temper and wasn't shy about being physical. "Guess we know where that comes from." He grinned as Andy gave him a side eyed look. "Hey, total respect! Between you and her it's an honor to be allowed to be security around here."

Andy smiled briefly. "Dar done grew up where being able to scrap was normal," he said. "Ah never did tell her she got a pass for being a girl."

"Hey, did they get that place?" Carlos asked, after a brief pause. "Holy crap if they've got to mess around with that, too?"

"Ah do not know, but I spect it's likely cause they do get into every damn situation." Andy sighed. "Lord it don't never end."

"Hey."

Andy and Carlos both turned, to find one of Scott's ex friends standing there, hands in pockets. He wasn't the same man who'd showed up the other day. This was one of the hangers-on, who'd stood on the fringes of the group most of the time.

"Lo," Andy responded. "If y'all are lookin for that wheelchair man, he's not round."

"No, I know where Wheels is," the man said, with a slight shake of his head. He had curly black hair and a scar across the side of his face that twisted it just a little. "Joe was here. Said maybe you were looking for some help around here or whatever."

Andy turned all the way around and studied him for a long moment. Carlos remained silent, withholding judgement or deferring it. "What you all got a mind to do?" Andy finally asked.

"I can do construction," the man responded. "Y'all gonna need new walls up in there. I do that," he said. "And I might know where to get my hands on some stuff to do it with," he added. "If you got some way to move it."

Carlo's eyebrows lifted. "You do drywall?"

"That's lathe backed." The man jerked his head toward the building. "Gonna need to be taped and jointed. Yeah," he said. "I do that. "Before you ask me why I don't just make everyone out there no offer, it's because you done what you done for Wheels."

"Scott," Carlos corrected him. "We don't call him that here."

"C'mon inside," Andy said. "Let's have us a cup of joe and chitchat." He gestured toward the door. "See if we can make us a deal."

"Always use a cup of joe."

****

Kerry slid her sunglasses back over her eyes as she emerged from the dark tomb of the closed airport into the murky sunlight, gratified to find her car right where she left it tucked against the curb.

In normal times, there was no doubt she'd be running around chasing a tow truck for it, but today it just sat there, behind the government and military vehicles, unmolested and unremarked.

There was still no one anywhere around, but her ears detected the sound of jet engines warming up. She hoped Dar was sitting comfortably inside along with her two friendly young pilots.

It was an Embraer jet, but converted to military use, and it was blocky and a bit ugly. But Dar was assured it had been kitted out with regular seats and she wasn't going to be stuck sitting on strap webbing or on top of a cargo box.

Dar wouldn't have cared. Kerry got into her car and almost envied that escape from their current reality into what was a vaster normality once you got out of the South Florida area.

She started the SUV and then paused, regarding the wrecked upper level blocking her path. "Well, hell." She did a three-point turn and went down the wrong way, down the inbound road to the terminal and hoped she didn't encounter either police or a truck until she reached a place she could hop the curb to an egress lane.

She got to a point where she could see the field and pulled over near the edge of the road so she could watch the one small moving point making its careful way around the debris on the field toward the runway. It waited, as a larger plane, also military, but gigantic in size landed and reversed its engines, the deep rumble vibrating loud and itchy inside Kerry's ears.

The smaller plane scooted over to the end of the runway and paused, heat wash visible to Kerry's eyes from its jet engines.

Kerry's eyes shifted as it started to move, rapidly coming up to speed and then launching itself up into the air and arching around, its engines thundering in a somewhat scary to watch maneuver.

Kerry closed her window and smiled, guessing Dar was enjoying the ride. She put the car back into drive and cautiously edged her way out of the airport.

It was going to be a long time, she realized, until the airport was ready to handle commercial traffic. It was one thing to clear the runways enough for emergency transport, and something else entirely to have a facility that was capable of handling normal people.

She shook her head and got up the ramp to the highway, merging into the very sparse traffic at midday with the sense of having a unique experience that wasn't particularly wanted.

Once she was down on street level again, she paused at the corner where she normally would have turned left to go to the office, and pondered, freed from having to make an instant decision by the lack of traffic. She resisted temptation to drive down to Hunter's Point and headed left.

They had gotten most of the biggest debris dragged out of the main street, and she was able to move along despite the frequent puddles with relatively good speed, but she was able to look right and left at what had been a familiar landscape now turned horror show.

In front of where there had been a small sandwich shop there was now a handmade cart, with people gathered around it, and she recognized the woman behind it with her hibachi grill as the owner of the sandwich store.

Instinctively, Kerry pulled over and hopped out, reaching back to make sure she had her wallet in her pocket as she closed the door and headed over to the cart. "Sasha!" She called out, as she stepped over a pile of branches and between two debris covered cars.

The bronze skinned woman waved at her. "Hello, Kerry!" She stood behind the cart, a fan in one hand, waving the smoke from the hibachi. "How are you in all this crazy time?"

Four men were sitting on the hood of one of the wrecked cars nearby, munching on sandwiches purchased from Sasha's cart. A fifth was waiting for his order, strips of meat grilling for it on the grill.

It smelled really good. Sasha was Vietnamese. She and her brother were brought to the US when they were small children. They made their living with the small shop that sold pho and bahn mi sandwiches. It was a favorite place of the staff.

On the cart, aside from the hibachi on its sturdy metal platform were containers of pickled vegetables and beneath it on the lower shelf a plastic container of baguettes.

"How am I?" Kerry looked up and down the street, with its wreckage. "How's anyone?" She asked. "I see you got set up though."

"Just like in Saigon." Sasha smiled at her, eyes twinkling. "Right on the street. And anyway, all the freezer unfroze in the store. I must do something with it. Might as well sell sandwiches! Maybe tomorrow I can do a pot of pho. Kiki is seeing if he can do the noodle for it."

"I'll take one," Kerry said at once. "Matter of fact, give me three, since my parents-in-law are at the office and I'm headed over there."

"One with the vegetables then," Sasha said. "Carlos was here before, with some of his gorillas." She opened a container and removed a handful of meat strips, laying them expertly out on the grill. "He told me all the stuff that went on last night."

"The fire and the police and all that?" Kerry glanced down the road. "Crazy."

"Crazy." Sasha split open a baguette and loaded it down with meat and vegetables, adding a squeeze of sauce and some sliced cucumber to the top before she handed it over to the waiting man. "Here you go."

"Looks great," he said. "What kind of food is this?" He was dressed in a guayabera and cutoff denim shorts, with hiking boots and a straw hat. He took a bite of the sandwich. "Mmm."

"It's from Vietnam," Kerry said, as Sasha was busy flipping the meat on the grill. "It's great.

The man chewed thoughtfully. "Vietnam," he said, after he swallowed. "Interesting." He lifted the sandwich and wandered back down the street.

Both Kerry and Sasha watched him go. "He is not from here," Sasha commented. "Probably a reporter taking pictures of all the damage."

"Probably," Kerry agreed. "There's a lot to take pictures of. I was just over at the airport and wow." She watched Sasha assembling the sandwiches. "How'd your shop end up?"

"Not so bad," Sasha replied. "Water came in, but the roof held up okay, just a little leak in the back where the storage is. If we had power..." She glanced up. "We could open, you know?"

"Us too," Kerry commiserated. "If you end up with anything left, c'mon down. I've got about a dozen people living in the building there." She took possession of the three sandwiches and handed over a bill. "They didn't make out as well as you did with the store."

"Carlos said," Sasha responded. "Don't worry, I know where my customers are. I said I would be over there tomorrow morning." She winked at Kerry. "We get through this, all of us. Even with all the bad things. We know each other, we help each other."

Kerry grinned and retreated with her armful of baguettes. As she went back to the car, though, she had to wonder if that was really the truth. Places like Sasha's—she could see her using her cart and selling her sandwiches until power came back and business picked up, but the rest?

The rest of the places on Main? Kerry set the wrapped sandwiches down and started the SUV up. How many would just stay abandoned and destroyed? How many people would do what their landlord had done, and just walk away not wanting to bother with the hassle of rebuilding?

Kerry started forward, thoughtfully regarding the mess on either side. Maybe Dar's thought of just selling the property had merit. Maybe moving the company upstate made sense. They could service the rest of their clamoring customers who didn't want to hear about rebuilding or lack of power.

Angry, impatient customers who wanted what they wanted, and didn't want to hear excuses, and had no tolerance for natural disasters.

She parked in front of the office, and as she opened the door, she heard music and the noise of hammering coming from inside.

The pile of garbage, she noted, was gone from next to the building. She picked up the sandwiches and headed for the door, which was standing wide open as were all the windows to let the breeze, what there was of it, go through. And why the sound of music was so loud.

Kerry stepped inside and heard voices. Unfamiliar drawling male ones, and some more familiar to her along with Ceci's crisp commentary.

"Oh, Ms. Kerry!" Zoe trotted down the stairs. "Hello!"

"Hey, Zoe!" Kerry took off her sunglasses and slid the ear of them into the collar of her shirt. "Where is everyone?" She looked both ways, but the hallway was otherwise empty. "I didn't' know you were here."

"Yes, I am glad to be here," Zoe said. "We are doing a lot of things. Papa Andy is outside and there are a lot of people there too," she said. "They said you would be coming. It is true, they made this building our building?"

Kerry sighed. "It's true all right."

"This is good," Zoe said, surprisingly. "Maria was saying just the last week it would be a good thing if this was ours because we would take care of it properly."

That was true. Kerry smiled back at her assistant. That was true but was it really their business to do that? How distracting would it be to have to handle their own facilities? Where did that fit in the budget, a budget now blown to hell by the storm?

Zoe didn't seem to sense any reluctance. "Would you come see? Already they are making preparations to fix things." She pointed at the door to the central compound. "So many people!"

"Sure." Kerry shifted her grip on the sandwiches. "Let's go find out what's going on." She started for the interior door, catching the scent of newly cut wood drifting on the wind.

****

"You doing all right back there, ma'am?"

"Just fine," Dar responded, her legs sprawled out across the floor of the plane, her laptop on her lap. The power cable from it ran across the steel to a generator bolted to the surface behind the cockpit, and the sound of the engines inside the plane was reasonably tolerable.

It was an odd configuration. Behind the nose of the plane, where the pilots were, and a locked compartment behind them, was a row of plush, leather first class airplane seats, four in total. And behind that a large expanse of nothing but empty steel.

It suited Dar just fine. The seats were as comfortable as the ones in a private jet, and there was plenty of leg room. If she'd wanted to get up and do cartwheels there was space for that too.

She didn't. She was comfortable enough to be able to concentrate on her screen, working out the intricate frameworks for the new program to evaluate products for her small pharma client. It seemed like an obvious thing, a database of all the drugs and ingredients they used. But she'd folded in some of the proprietary AI potential from her networking program to allow them to analyze what things they had they could use for other uses.

Off brand, they called it. Something beyond Dar's experience and knowledge, but important to them, and something they were convinced would give them the edge in sales. And one they wanted urgently because times had recently been tough for them.

This was a gamble. Dar reviewed the structure of the database and scrolled back to look at the logic. A gamble that put pressure on John Deland, who had called her out of the blue. A friend of a friend of someone she'd known at ILS, who now had to prove to some new CEO why the expense.

She got it. She understood why he was pissed off. And if she'd been in his shoes, she'd have been just as cranky, saying just the same things about why she didn't care what anyone's local problems were, she had a delivery she'd been promised.

So here she was, in a military jet, on her way to talk to yet another demanding customer. She needed to work out a knotty bug in this last set of programming before they could hand it over.

Her life was weird. Dar changed a bit of the programming, and recompiled it, then ran the sequence again to watch it fail, in a completely different way. "Crap," she muttered under her breath, reverting the change. She drummed her fingertips along the edge of the keyboard.

What the hell was it? Why was this one sequence so screwed up?

"Hey, ma'am, want a Coke?"

"Sure." Dar took the bit of code and focused the screen on it.

The copilot had climbed out of his seat and ducked into a tiny compartment behind the cockpit and returned with a   familiar red can in each hand. He handed Dar one and then sat down in the chair across from her with the other. He opened his can and took a sip.

"Thanks." Dar paused to open the can and joined him. She decided a moment of distraction might get her brain cells realigned and turned her eyes from the screen to the pilot. "So. What'd you think of all the damage?"

He was young, probably in his mid-twenties. He had a stiff crew cut of dark hair that matched the dark brown eyes. There was a little bit of stubble on his square jaw and he seemed, Dar thought, like a great model for a GI Joe.

"Man, that was crazy," he said. "Only thing I ever seen like that is bombed out places in the Middle East, you know? In flight vids." He took another swallow of soda. "I didn't realize hurricanes were like that, you know?"

"They're like that," Dar said, mildly. "Like a tornado, only bigger, slower moving. And comes with a wall of water from the ocean."

"Crazy." The copilot got up. "Let me go let Josh stretch his legs," he said. "Hey, if you need the use the head, there's one right there in that corner, behind the door." He pointed. "It's kinda small, so watch your head.'"

"Thanks." Dar watched him go back to the cockpit and waited a moment to see if the other pilot was going to come out to distract her before she returned her eyes to the screen. She reviewed the code while she let her mind linger briefly on the words they'd just exchanged.

She'd seen the pictures of the damage, and the pilot had circled the city before they'd headed out over the Gulf of Mexico toward the west. And now something the man said niggled at her.

That it was like bomb damage. Dar looked at the screen without reading it. A result that happened from two very different sources, completely different applications of energy that had nonetheless ended up producing an end stage that was apparently the same.

Two different paths bisecting.

She blinked a few times, just breathing quietly, her hands still over the keyboard. Then, thoughtfully, she selected a section of the code, and deleted it. She then typed in a replacement statement and linked it, referring back to an earlier section of the program and adding a line.

Two different paths, two different instances, and where to determine where they bisect?

She recompiled, and reran the program, and this time the code finished without complaint. Dar saved the framework with a tag, and then picked up the soda and took a swallow. Not failing, of course, didn't mean it worked.

It just meant it didn't stop. She regarded the screen. But it was progress and that was more than she'd had ten minutes ago. Dar considered the segment, and pondered a way to test the logic with the small set of test data she had.

The pilot of the plane came out and used the head, as she retrieved and reviewed the data stacks, and then he came over and sat down in one of the seats. "So," he kept his voice low. "You're the one who wrote that new sim, aren't you?"

Distracted, Dar glanced at him. "Yeah," she said, after a blank moment. "You've seen it?"

The pilot, a cherubic looking youngster with curly blond hair, nodded. "I got to go in it. I was a tester for the mock, you know? It was freaking amazing. It was like I was there. I've been in simulators before, we all have, but this was like it was real. How did you do that?"

Dar hesitated. "Well..."

"Was it the helmet? The things... "The pilot touched his face, near his temples. "Hey, I realize you can't really talk about it. I was just so… it was cool. I was glad I had a chance to try it. So, congrats." He got up and went hurriedly back to the cockpit, where the sound of radio communications crackled.

Dar stared after him, wondering what in the hell she was flying into.

Wondering what in the hell they'd done.

****

Zoe stuck her head into Kerry's office. "Ms. Kerry, the police are here. Would you like to speak with them?"

Kerry sat in the window seat at the back of her office. It allowed the light outside to provide enough visibility for her to read a pad of notes she was working on. "Not really," she said. She shifted the pad against her upraised knee. "Any idea what they want?"

"No," Zoe said. "I will go ask them." She disappeared, and a moment later her footsteps echoed on the wooden, now carpet less steps.

The police were here. Kerry ran her eyes over the notes, the grid lined pad neatly capturing her regular well shaped script. Four projects, cancelled. She read them and shook her head slightly. Were the police going to bring her more problems?

Or did they want cookies?

She didn't need any more problems. Four cancelled projects, and a half dozen out of area customers who were fuming because progress on theirs had slowed down or stopped, even though it had only been for.... Kerry's brows creased.

Had it only been a week? Less than a week?

Jesus. The languid breeze stirred her hair, and Kerry glanced out the window, toward the water. She caught some motion by the sailing club, and as she watched, two men came around the corner of the storm wracked building, one of them carrying a clipboard.

Denim shirts and hiking boots, and one had gloves tucked into their belt in the small of his back. Contractors? Insurance adjusters?

She welcomed the distraction, from this grim accounting of their fortunes. She'd been light with it with Dar. They joked about her selling off brain cells, but the understanding that all these people around them were depending on them weighed on her.

Dar was much more likely to take it as it came. "We'll figure it out." Was her view on most things, focused on real time problem solving, giving up as pointless what ifs.

In most cases, that was astounding and priceless. Dar's ability to be wholly in the moment. Her instinctive understanding of details and potential really, truly was the baseline of their success. She could make it happen, whatever it was that 'it' was that Kerry needed her to.

She could go to Dar, and say she needed a flying pig. And Dar would start figuring out where on the pig the wings needed to be to properly support it in flight. Dar didn't care why Kerry needed a flying pig.

She, on the other hand, wanted a plan, and direction, and scope, and structure. That was why she did what she did to take that ability and focus it into something that had a business wrapped around it.

So, looking at the pad, it was a little bit of a lonely escarpment to be sitting on. Here in this musty and warm office because she couldn't share the burden with her staff. And even if Dar were there, Dar would just shrug and… "We'll figure it out."

Dar would bring her a chocolate chip cookie, and a kiss. The transition of their lives had brought out the aspects of her personality that had been stuffed down under that need to be the master of her environment and had allowed her sometimes surprisingly random nature to come to the surface.

Kerry loved that. But she also got that it meant her responsibilities had changed as well and therefore here she was,   writing down all their problems and thinking of ways to work around them, or in the worst case, replace business they'd now lost.

She shifted her eyes back outside, wanting the distraction.

One of the men, she noted, took pictures as they slowly made their way around to the dockside and its shambles.

What would they think of the makeshift plank dock, she wondered suddenly? Should she go over there and talk to them about it? Now that the ferry was running, she didn't think they'd need to use it anymore, but you never knew in situations like this.

She got up and closed her pad, walked over to her desk and put it away, along with her fountain pen. Then she turned and went into the hallway to head to the back stairs. She would go out and find the sailing club inspectors, and make sure they understood what the planks were for, how they got there and who'd done it. Kerry nodded to herself, mentally checking off that internal note.

Then she remembered Zoe and the police and realized she couldn't really leave her hanging with them.

"Ugh." She turned around and went to the front stairs, rambling down them and listening for her assistant's voice as she headed for their open front door.

She caught a flash of dark blue outside and went out into the sun, where she found two officers standing there casually talking to Zoe in Spanish. "Hi, there." She drew their attention. "What's up?"

"Hello, ma'am. Are you the manager here?" One of them asked.

"This is..." the second officer backed up and looked up at the sign, "a business, right?"

The two policemen were almost like twins. They both were middling height, with black, cropped hair and tanned skin, cleanshaven and wearing sunglasses. They were probably in their low or mid-thirties, and they had that distinctive Miami accent Kerry knew well.

"It's a business," she said. "Roberts Automation. I'm the co-owner." She stuck her hands in her front pockets. "What can we do for our friends at the City of Miami Police department?" She asked and tilted her head in friendly inquiry.

City police, not the county police, and not the state police she'd seen parked at the airport. Different politics. These were their actual local cops, as Coconut Grove was a part of the city.

"Ms. Kerry they were asking about the trouble we had last night," Zoe said. "I was going to get Papa Andy to tell them. Should I go get him?"

"Depends." Kerry regarded the police, retaining her friendly demeanor. "What is it you all want to know? Wasn't our trouble, actually. We were just in the way," She said. "Some of our security staff were here."

She paused and watched them watch her. "Want to come inside and sit down? It's not much cooler in there but we have a conference room inside the door here and you're welcome to come in."

They were sweating. The uniforms were short sleeved, but the fabric they were made of was thick and they wore a T-shirt underneath along with their heavy-duty belt holding cuffs and guns and other blocky things Kerry wasn't familiar with.

"That'd be great, ma'am," the first one said. "My lieutenant just asked us to come down and ask about what happened."

"C'mon inside." Kerry gestured to the door. "Zoe, can you go get Carlos? He saw everything." She stepped back to let Zoe dart inside, and the cops followed. "Want some cold water? We got a chest of ice." She led them into the conference room.

"That's very nice of you," the slightly taller of the two said. "Oh, hey... you guys are really prepared huh?"

The room had been tidied up and organized. It was where they had centralized their supply storage. On one side of the room were folding tables stocked with boxes of snacks, crackers and ramen noodle soup, bags of chips and pretzels.

Cases of paper plates and cups, two big cases of powdered cream and sugar for beverages. Stocked in one corner were three big bags of Cuban bread.

Along the short side of the room against the wall were cases of water, both gallon jugs and bottles and underneath the jalousie windows open to the front was a long ice chest that Kerry went over to and opened. She pulled out three bottles of water and handed one each to the cops, then sat down with one for herself.

Gratefully, they opened the water and sat down. "Thanks." the one closest to her took a swallow of the water. "We appreciate the hospitality."

Kerry smiled at them and took a sip of her own water. "Law enforcement is always welcome here," she said. "We had a bunch of folks from Miami-Dade here a day or so ago."

"Yeah? What were they here for?" The cop sitting a little farther away asked. "This isn't their territory."

Kerry sipped at her water thoughtfully. "Why were they here," she mused. "It was after the storm, and I guess... you know, I don't know really." She responded honestly. "I'm not sure they said why they were here."

The two cops exchanged glances.

"And we were kinda busy sorting ourselves out here, you know how it was," Kerry added, with an apologetic expression. "Checking damage and all that."

"Oh, sure." The nearer cop nodded. "No problem, we get it. Everything was crazy."

"It was," Kerry said. "I'm sure it was triple crazy for you guys."

Both cops relaxed just a little bit. "Oh yeah. I live in Sweetwater. What a mess," one said.

Carlos entered, with Zoe at his heels. "Hey, boss." He looked at Kerry, then at the cops. "What's up?"

"Sit," Kerry offered. "C'mon in, Zoe." She indicated the other seat on the far side of hers. "These officers were asking about what happened last night. Can you fill them in? I figured it was better for them to hear it from the source."

Carlos regarded the officers for a long moment, then he shrugged and pulled a chair out. He sat down and folded his muscular arms over his chest.

"Sure," he said. "Whatcha want to know?" he asked. "We were all sleeping when all hell broke loose," he added, when they hesitated. "Like the first thing we knew were bangs and stuff."

"Who's we?" The second cop asked. "You all just camping here? I saw the camper in the middle there through the door."

"Carlos is, and some of his security guard friends, and a few other of our staff whose homes were not really habitable," Kerry said. "We took some roof damage, water came in, but it's pretty whole in all."

One of the cops took out a small pad and a pen and   nodded. "You get a good look at the guys that busted up that store?" He looked up at Carlos, the pen poised to write. "They from around here? You know them?"

Carlos took his time about answering, his eyes shifting off to one side as he considered. "I didn't see any of em," he finally said. "It was dark, they were all running around... cops were all running around.... National Guard was all running around... all we wanted was to stay the hell out of it."

The cop nodded again, scribbling. "Did they seem like... was it... did it look organized to you?" He asked. "You know what I mean," he added, when Carlos hesitated again. "Were they talking to each other outside?"

"You mean like, was it a gang?" Kerry asked. "I thought you had all those guys. I mean, as in, they were arrested."

The cop looked over at her. "Jurisdiction got screwed up and they all got let go," he said, briefly. "So now we gotta start at square one. What about it?" He looked back at Carlos. "They local? I know you got some drifters and bums around here. I chased a bunch of them a couple weeks back."

Carlos shook his head. "Just a bunch of guys in dark clothes all wet," he said. "Just a big mess."

"Lo there." Andy's tall frame filled the doorway and he ambled in the room. "What do you all want?" He took a seat in the chair at the end of the table and rested one hand on the table. He looked steadily at the cops with an expression that reminded Kerry irresistibly of Dar.

A forthright, raw challenge, very much like Dar might do when she wanted to knock whoever she was dealing with off their balance. And that same claiming of space in the room.

It surprised her a little, because her father-in-law was usually on the friendly side with anyone in uniform, having that background. Kerry felt there was something going on she wasn't quite clued to.

"My father-in-law, Andrew Roberts," she introduced him. "They're interested in the brouhaha last night, Dad."

"Ain't that interesting," Andy responded. "Thought you all had it wrapped up." He glanced at Carlos. "Y'all did say they took all them folks off."

"They let em go apparently," Carlos told him. "Paperwork problem." He leaned back, visibly content to let Andy take the lead in dealing with the police.

"That so." Andy regarded the cops. "Do tell."

"Were you here, sir?" The cop asked.

"Ah was not," Andy said. "Howsomever ah did take a little bit of time today to go over and see what all went on ovah by that burned out place and ah will tell you ah do not think them fellers meant no harm."

The cop nearest looked steadily at him. "What makes you say that, sir?"

"They were just some homeless fellers," Andy said. "Vet'rans, some of em."

"We do have some around here," Kerry said, into the awkward pause that followed. "We hired one in fact. What makes you think it was a gang? I haven't seen that around here, at least before the storm."

The nearer cop tapped his pen on his pad. "We heard about maybe some gangs or maybe militia down here," he said. "You wouldn't know anything about that, would you folks?"

Oh. Kerry was a bit nonplussed, since viewed objectively, given armed men and armed military vehicles, she might in fact know something about that. She exchanged glances with Andy, who regarded her with a slightly raised eyebrow.

"We're a computer company," Kerry finally said, indicating herself, and Zoe. "Do we look like a militia to you?" She asked, with just a touch of amused disbelief in her tone. She watched the cops carefully. "I'll admit to being a registered gun owner, and my mother's a senator but...."

Ah. She saw the minute reaction, and the wariness. "If my father-in-law said those guys were just poor homeless folks, chances are that's what they were. Everyone's just trying to keep themselves above water here, you know?"

Andy cleared his throat. "Ain't nobody no half ass militia down here," he added, in a dismissive tone. "Folks got guns round here, they know what to do with em." He stopped speaking and waited.

"Are you one of those people, sir?"

"Ah am." Andy smiled without much humor. "Done made mah livin with em for a good long while."

The cop closed his pad up and put it in his pocket. "Let me give you folks a little advice. This isn't a war zone. We're not going to tolerate any of that."

Kerry put her bottle down. "Buddy." She leaned forward and folded her hands on the table. "You need to go have a conversation with the National Guard, and the cops who were here last night. If there's anyone out there who thinks they're in a warzone, it's them. Not us."

She stood up. "Now if you'll excuse me, I have to go tell our neighbors who put up a dock in their marina and call the governor." She took the bottle and dropped it into the trash can near the door, and then kept going, feeling confident Andy could handle the fallout. "I'll be back. C'mon, Zoe."

Zoe scrambled after her. "Oh, my goodness, Ms. Kerry!"

"What?" Kerry led the way around the corner and headed for the back door.

"The police, they didn't like that!"

Kerry chuckled. "Well, we are the troublemakers they think we are, Zoe. The point was to let them know we're better friends than enemies." She pushed the back door open and emerged onto the loading dock and headed for the concrete steps down to the ground. "They should go find someone else to mess with."

"Oh!" Zoe trotted after her. "Would they do that?"

"For everyone's sake I sure hope so."

****

Scott was waiting for her when they landed. Dar saw him behind the doors, a tall, thin, blond man with a crew cut, horn rimmed classic nerd glasses, and wide, astonished looking dark grey eyes.

Well. Here we go. Dar shouldered her overnight bag and adjusted the backpack on her back that held her laptop as she followed the pilots down the metal, green gray steps onto a sun-drenched tarmac brushed with a pleasantly dry breeze.

"This way, ma'am." The pilot indicated a painted walkway with a stick figure on it and they made their way between carts and other planes toward the single level bunker looking building that had government literally painted all over it.

It was faintly nostalgic to Dar, growing up where she had. She knew when the door opened it would smell like wax and old paper. As she followed the pilots inside it didn't disappoint as they stepped from concrete to dark green speckled linoleum that gleamed with a dull shine.

Still it was better than the airport she'd left and at least this one was fully powered and functional. They went past a row of doors that emitted a low buzz of conversation and somewhere, faintly, the sound of someone transmitting Morse code.

"Okay, uh... so here's the admin office." The pilot paused, a bit awkwardly. "I guess you need to—"

"Someone's here to meet me," Dar said. "Thanks for the ride." She turned and went through the door with its shiny lever handle and into the room with the windows she'd seen from outside. "Scott!"

The tall man turned and scooted her way. "There you are!"

"Here I am," Dar said. "Hope this isn't going to take long because I've got a lot to do back in Florida."

"No no, you should be back on a plane tomorrow night." Scott hustled ahead of her and gestured for her to follow. "C'mon, I got a car right outside. Team's waiting for you back at the base. We got a slot with the bigwigs tomorrow morning."

He exhaled as he held the outside door open. "I got you overnight at the lodge right near the base. Hope that's okay. You said you liked it last time."

Dar waited until they were inside the big, unmarked SUV with the doors closed before she responded. "What the hell is going on?"

"Huh?" Scott put the SUV in gear and pulled out of the parking lot. "You know what's going on. It's the sim. See what we did, Dar, we took the update you sent us, and... well, you'll see." He pulled out onto the road and accelerated. "Can't wait to show you."

Dar sighed. "How long a drive is this?"

"Bout twenty minutes." Scott reached up and pulled a pair of sunglasses out of a compartment and slid them on over his regular glasses. "J'have a nice flight?"

"Yeah, it was fine." Dar left her backpack between her hiking boots and studied the sturdy, mountainous landscape around them. "You don't want to tell me now what you all did? Save some time?"

"No," Scott said. "I can't, actually. We have to be behind the wall." He gave Dar an apologetic look. "Sorry, Dar. It's the regs."

Dar looked around the car. "Is this bugged?"

"Got it from the motor pool. Coulda been," Scott said, then glanced furtively at her. "Would you know something like that? Could you check?"

Dar rolled her head to one side and regarded him. "Not without a spectrum analyzer and I didn't bring one with me." She returned her gaze to the passing scenery, reconciled to having to wait yet more time to find out what the story was here.

Idly she took out her cell phone, suddenly remembering it's presence and turned it on.

"So, it's pretty bad there huh?"

The phone powered on, and after a moment where it seemed to stare in bewildered confusion at a functional cellular signal, it attached itself. "It's a mess." Dar flipped it to silence mode as the phone started to pick up messages. "A lot of damage, and no power in half the state."

"Yeah. I watched the news today." Scott wriggled into a more comfortable position as they paused at a light. "Did you see what happened to DC? Two feet of flood water!" he said. "The whole place is crazy freaked out. Pentagon's a mess!"

"It's always a mess." Dar thumbed through the messages.

"You been there?"

"I helped rebuild it after 9/11," Dar said in an offhand tone. "There's a punch down block there I left some of my blood on."

"No kidding?" Scott seemed amazed. "Really?"

"No kidding." Most of the phone messages were either people she'd already spoken to or numbers she didn't recognize. She called up the phone number of the reception desk and dialed it and put the phone to her ear to listen.

"Roberts Automation, how can I help you?" Angela's crisp and slightly nasal voice answered. "Oh, is that you, Dar?" She said, after a pause. "You came up on the caller ID!"

"It is," Dar said. "Kerry back yet?"

"No, ma'am," Angela said promptly. "I think she went to the office. She said she was going to the office, and you know she always does what she says she's going to do. Should I go try and use the radio thing at your place? I can try that."

"No, I'll see if I can dial the sat phone," Dar said. "If she calls in, just let her know I got here and I'm on the way to the base. Oh... ask Arthur and Elvis if they made any progress."

"I don't think so. They went to get hamburgers. They said maybe it would give them inspiration."

Dar smiled. "When they get back, tell them I did. Soon as I get Internet, I'll upload it," she said. "It might solve the problem. Have them recompile the whole assembly after I do and run the metrics on it."

There was a faint sound of scribbling on the other end. "Got it," Angela said. "I'll tell them, boss!"

"Okay great," Dar said. "Talk to you later." She hung up the phone and watched the horizon, going back over in her head the programming she'd worked on during the flight.

Then she glanced at her phone, and then fished inside her backpack for her laptop, pulled it out and opened it. "What do we have, ten more minutes? Let me see if I can get something useful done out of them."

"Um."

"Try not to go over a lot of bumps."

Chapter Thirteen

Dar felt the warmth of her laptop through the leather of the backpack pressing against her back. Her overnight bag was slung over her shoulder, and she twisted a little to keep it from hitting people as she followed Scott down the long hallway.

"It was pretty empty in here for a while," Scott said, as they turned and started down a side corridor. "Then they moved a bunch of psyops groups in here and some of the cyber guys."

"Uh huh."

"Here we go." Scott opened a door and held it, waiting for Dar to enter before he followed her inside.

It was an office suite, like a thousand other office suites Dar had entered, except most of those hadn't been buried inside a mountain. The air smelled dry and sterile and she blinked a few times as they passed a shabby looking conference room and a small kitchenette.

At the end of the hall was another door, and when it opened the smell of leather came out. Inside was a classier conference room, with new look-ing leather chairs producing the scent.

"Okay in here… did you say you needed some Internet?" Scott asked as he scurried in ahead of her. "I got a cable around here... hang on." He looked around the room. "Oh, hold on it's in that credenza…"

Dar waved her hand slightly. "I got done what I needed to." She dropped her bag against the wall and put her backpack on the table. "So, what's the plan?"

"Let me get the guys and we can do a rundown," Scott said. "Want some coffee? It's down the hall on the right... and then we can talk. The team wanted to take you out to dinner tonight. Hope that's okay?"

"Sure. Thanks." Dar watched him leave. She removed her laptop and put it on the table, and then she went back out into the hallway and found the coffee machine in the empty break room.

Kerry had switched theirs over to the single cup variety. Here there was a commercial Bunn dispenser like you might find in a hotel kitchen, and she dispensed a reasonably fresh smelling cup and mixed some cream and sugar into it.

It was very quiet in the office suite. Dar wondered if it was just a set of offices set to one side where they brought untrusted visitors to. She took a sip of the coffee and studied the room, then walked over to the slimline refrigerator and opened the door.

Inside there were the usual things you find inside corporate refrigera-tors. Mostly soft sided lunch boxes and bottles of condiment. Dar picked up one and checked the date on it, then put the bottle back and closed the door with a satisfied grunt.

She took the cup with her and went back down the hall, peering curiously into the rooms on either side of it on her way back to the rear conference room. Most had either desks or cubicles in them, and the desks were cluttered with the usual assortment of personal droppings you'd expect to see there.

A lot of trouble to go through just to fake out some random nerd. Dar decided the office space was legit, and she went back to the chair she'd selected and stood in front of it, opening up her laptop and starting it up again. She watched it while she fished inside her pack for her power cable. She unraveled it and ducked her head under the table to look for the expected surge strip nailed to the underneath.

She plugged in the supply and then connected her laptop, allowing it to charge as she folded her arms over her chest and waited, rocking up and down on the balls of her feet.

****

"Is that... hey, the repo updated." Elvis pounced on his laptop as the soft chime of an alert sounded. He pushed aside the plate on the table that held the remains of his lunch. "Let's see what's up there." He rubbed his fingers together and started pecking at the keys.

"Man, I hope she fixed that stuff." Arthur stretched his legs out on the carpet from his seat with his back against the couch. "What the hell did she do, hack the taxi to send it?"

"Phone," Elvis said. "She rigged it with a Bluetooth PAN." He glanced at Arthur. "You ever hack a taxi?"

"Sure. Last time we were in New York with Dar," Arthur said. "Had a fricken USB port in the back of it with all that stupid ad shit. Lame."

"Lame." Elvis typed, then he looked up. "What did you do to it?"

"Rerouted it and looped some cartoon porno." Arthur sniffed reflectively, studying his screen. "Cracked Dar up."

"Hahahahaha." Elvis attached to the repository and scanned the contents, the big storage segmented into all of their project scopes, the interface all ASCII on black screen, a cryptic command line that nevertheless clearly indicated to him the new files in yellow outlined letters.

Almost a hundred of them, all stamped with Dar's login and the date. He ran the script to recompile the code and waited. He whisted under his breath as he watched the small asterisk spin in place, occasionally dancing from one side to the other.

Pure Dar. He waggled his head in time with the bouncing asterisk. The bouncing was a routine to reassure the watcher something useful was going on.

It was that or waste the processing cycles to print out the compile to the screen. Not Dar's style. She hated wasting anything in her code, and it was crazy clean and almost too sharp.

Nonobvious. Everything lean and spare, like Dar herself was.

It had a lot of discipline to it, and they had all had to learn to adapt to that kind of work style because after all, Dar was the boss and she knew her shit.

"Well, it built this time anyhow!" Elvis said, after the program finished its shenanigans.

"What'd she do?" Arthur crawled over and looked over his shoulder. "Hold on, check the output. That crap's been erroring out for three weeks. I've been over it with a fricken microscope."

"Lemme check." Elvis switched to a debug screen and read out a file, his eyes and Arthur's eyes twitching in almost unison as they scanned down the lines of code. "What the hell?" He frowned, his eyebrows twisting together. "What is this thing doing now in there... in the object loop routine?"

Arthur reached over and traced a line of text with his fingertip. "What is that?" He said. "What did she do there?"

"Crap, that doesn't make any sense," Elvis said. "Look at the linked logic there, and those libraries... how is that even working?"

"Weird." Arthur returned his attention to the laptop. "Hey maybe it isn't? Run the test suite. Maybe she's messing with us." He pulled his legs up crossed under him, his straight brown hair falling into his eyes. "She coulda rigged it so it turns into a picture of an elephant or something, or makes that crazy hamster show up."

"It's a gopher. But I dunno. That guy was pretty pissed off. I don't think she'd waste our time on it," Elvis said, as he gathered the testing suite and set up the framework for it, linking a set of test data the Pharma customer had provided them. "Hey, what if the data's crap? You think maybe that's why it's not working?"

Arthur looked at him with a thoughtful expression. "You mean like on purpose? Like the guy gave us bullshit so it wouldn't work?"

Elvis shrugged. "People suck?" He started up the test. "People suck, but also, people can be dumb as shit, you know?"

Arthur shook his head. "Dar woulda caught it," He said confidently. "She's psychic that way."

"Yeah." Elvis exhaled as he watched the test run. "Well, it got farther than it did the last time so far," he said and wiggled his feet. "Let's see where this goes. Maybe it'll go all the way."

Arthur chortled a little, typing on his keyboard. "That'll be sweet."

****

Dar heard the group of them coming toward the room, the scuff and rumble of footsteps on the carpet and the opening and closing of the hallway door. She stood up to watch the entrance as shadows fell across the sill.

Scott came in and waved behind him. "C'mon, guys."

There were six of them. All male, all clean cut. All relatively young, one or two around her age and they settled into the chairs on the other side of the table as far from her as they could.

Dar smiled inwardly and remained silent. She studied each of them in casual turn.

She knew they were watching her from their peripheral vision, no one making direct eye contact. Did she know any of them? Maybe she'd traded emails.

Maybe not.

Scott came over and ran his hand through his short hair. "Okay, so let's get started," he said, then half turned. "I guess I should introduce everyone. We've probably all been on conference calls together, though."

"Probably," Dar said. She looked over at the group directly. "Hi, I'm Dar."

That got her a few smiles, Dar smiled back, She relaxed a little and uncrossed her arms. "So." She took the focus of the room. "Why am I here?"

Scott recovered himself. "What's that, Dar?"

Dar looked at him, aware he had to tilt his head up to meet her eyes. "Where I live just got hit by a Category five plus hurricane that took out most of the City of Miami, including where our offices are," she said. "I've got a list of crap to deal with taller than I am."

"Well, I know but—"

"Why am I here?" Dar cut him off. "Stop the bullshit, we're inside your hallowed halls now. I don't need social niceties. Why the hell did you drag me out here?"

Now her peripheral vision was put to good use and she saw the smirks and one or two faint nods from the gang at the end of the table.

"Ah..." Scott was taken aback. "Well, it's just—"

"Spill it." Dar let her voice lift a little in volume.

Scott caved. "Okay okay." He waved his hands and took a step back. "Take it easy!" He retreated a few chairs and sat down. "So, here's the deal. That last update you sent us, when we put it in the rig, and piped in... well it'd be easier to show—"

Dar held up one hand, then brought up both, and made a come-hither gesture with them, sharply impatient. "Keep talking," she ordered. "Just spit it out, Scott. What did you do with the code?"

He took a breath. "So, the biggest problem we'd been having with it was it just wasn't real enough, you know?" He leaned forward on the table and rested his arms on it. "We talked about it. Even when we put the 4K content in there. Anyway... the last update you did... it did something."

Dar leaned against the table. "Go on." Her voice had lowered and sharpened with interest. "What'd it do?"

"It like... the timing changed... or... look, I don't know." Scott said. "But when we put the rig on, it was like we were there. It scared the pants off me. So, whatever you did, that did that. So, we need to know... we want to know... what that was."

Dar regarded him for a long minute. Then she sat down in the chair and sat back, hiking up one knee against the table's edge. "Couldn't you just ask me that on the damn phone?" She asked, cocking her head to one side in question. "What the hell?" She lifted her hands in a plaintive gesture, palms up.

"Dar you don't get it."

She nodded at once. "Yeah, you're right, I don't," she agreed readily. "Yes, the last compile was different. I had an idea when I was at home getting ready for the storm... well, that doesn't really matter." She stopped. "But I could have laid that out for you in a text file."

"We should show her," one of the men at the other end of the table spoke up. "So, when she's in there tomorrow with the general's money guy showing off our new training system, she'll get it." He nodded at Dar when she turned her head to look at him. "I'm, Jacko, we've talked on the phone."

"Hi," Dar said. "Yes, we have."

Jacko was the technical project lead. A rough and ready looking man with a birthmark extending from one ear down his jaw. He had a slightly husky voice, and very thin lips. He nodded at Dar, his eyes closing and opening a few times before he went on.

"Whatever that thing is you did," Jacko said, "it changed the whole way that rig works. It basically ensured all of us are going to end up getting bumped three grades and be famous in a good way. So, it's a big deal."

"It's a big deal," Scott repeated firmly. "Like a really big deal. The brass is really excited about it." He nodded emphatically a few times.

Dar studied them all for a long moment, then she stood back up. "Show me," she said. "Then we can whiteboard it." She watched them all scramble to their feet, excited and eager, filing without hesitation out the door.

What had she done? Dar wondered, as she followed them, followed Scott, who seemed relieved, motioning her forward. What had she changed? She remembered writing the code. But in the chaos and craziness of that moment it was hard to remember the inspiration for what she'd done outside a notion of something that would increase the line rate performance.

Efficiency.

Not quantum mechanics.

"Can't wait for you to see this, Dar." Scott unlocked a door midway down the hall and pushed it open. "You really hit it out the park."

Dar took in a breath of cold laboratory air. "Can't wait."

****

Kerry walked out into the central space of the building and found it lit with citronella torches on all sides, and the grill was started up on the concrete pad near the door. She paused and looked around and tried to absorb all of the activity that had taken place during the day.

The bodybuilders were down near the back wall to take advantage of the onshore breeze to work out, along with a couple of the veterans who showed up to help secure the area.

Behind where the barbells were placed, there was a path leading to the loading dock. There was now a solid barrier, blocking off the access that had allowed Dar to drive Scott's RV into the center area.

Andy's crew installed a set of swinging gates, closed with a heavy brace that looked like a railway tie. The top and bottom of the gates appeared to be made from cut up telephone poles the team had inventively scrounged from the area nearby.

Well, Kerry reasoned. It's not like they weren't going to be replaced, and shouldn't those old wooden poles really be concrete anyway?

They should.

The front porch area was also reinforced. It had changed from a rather oddly casual porch to something more like a guard station. Pete's buddy Randy sat inside it, making himself comfortable to keep watch.

Inside the central area now, on the other side of it, were stacks of construction material, all covered in tarps. They were lined up against the inner wall of the long side of the office. Next to them a pop-up tent was pitched, and there was a lanky figure sprawled in a canvas chair in front of it.

Kerry remembered him from the startup of the company. One of the gang of homeless vets who'd harassed them, and now apparently had turned up with building skills and material looking to be some paid labor.

Sure, why not? His name was Mike. He'd also brought the tent and all his worldly possessions inside it and decided not to be a jerk to everyone. So sure. Kerry shook her head a little. Life moves on.

There were ten veterans around in the mix now. All of them extremely respectful to her, though they treated the security guards and Carlo's friends with casual camaraderie and considered them all part of one big...

Gang? Squad? Troop? Kerry considered. Company? "Team." She finally decided, speaking the word aloud.

Zoe came out behind her with a tray, with Pete and Hank right behind her. "Slow down there!" Hank called out. "Lemme get the table set up!"

Kerry turned to watch them, as Hank got the folding table open and hustled around in front of Zoe to put it in place so she could set the tray down as Pete got busy with the grill. On the tray were various shish kebabs and hamburgers, and under some plastic wrap were leftover sandwiches.

Pete lifted a large stock pot up and onto the end of the grill and peeled off a corner of the foil topping it. "That's gonna be a nice chili." He glanced up. "You sticking around tonight, ma'am?"

Thus addressed, Kerry came over to the pot and examined the contents, whose warming was generating a deep, spicy, beefy scent. "For a while, anyway." She winked at him. "I'm fond of chili."

"Knew you had good taste." He winked back. "Lemme go get the rice cooker." He wound his way through the makeshift kitchen area and went back inside the building.

Hank helped Zoe sort out the kabobs. "Best way to use bits and stuff," he said. "Specially that rabbit food they left us, right there, little sister?"

"Si," Zoe said, smiling at him shyly. "It will be a good dinner."

Andy and Ceci came through the door at that moment and joined them. "Any word from our kid?" Ceci asked Kerry. "I figure she'd have called someone to say she got somewhere."

"Nothing yet," Kerry said. "I tried to raise the island, but I don't think we left anyone there who knows how to use those radios."

"Nope," Andy said. "Ah do not believe we did." He looked around. "Time to take us a run back there ah do think, see all what's going on."

"Sounds good to me," Ceci said. "I'm done with sweating and the smell of days old garbage if you are."

If Dar wasn't able to get through to her sat phone, Dar would have certainly called the VOIP line at the island. Kerry nodded a little, wanting to get that reassurance. "Good idea."

It was a good idea.

And yet, there was something oddly appealing in this collection of colleagues, friends, and vagrants off the street that made her want to stay and join them in the eclectic dinner and the tale trading that she knew would follow.

Well, with the ferry... "Crap if we want to go back, we should scoot," Kerry remembered suddenly. "They said they won't run it at night."

"Hell." Andy turned around. "Hank, we all are headin off. You all done right here?"

"We're fine, chief." Hank waggled an elbow at him. "Anybody heads this way tonight's just asking for a blastin." He cocked his head to one side in a listening attitude. "Hey, I think that motorcycle fella's comin back. I recognize that engine."

Kerry was sad to miss the chili but figured there would be some left for breakfast. She followed Zoe inside. "Zoe, you sure you want to stay here? We can find room for you over by us."

Zoe shook her head no. "Oh no, Ms. Kerry, it will be fine. I have put my things up where the office is, and we are going to play dominoes after we finish the dinner," she said. "There are so many nice people here. I am so glad I came over."

The sound of the motorcycle was closer now. "That does sound like Mark." Kerry said. "Okay, as long as you're okay with staying here. I know Carlos and the guys will take good care of you."

Zoe beamed. "They are so nice," she said. "All of Mr. Andy's friends, and especially Hank." She touched her lip. "He is just like me. Did you see?"

"I did." Kerry patted her shoulder. "Okay, let's see what Mark's up to. I would have thought he'd had enough of our chaos yesterday, you know?" She handed Zoe the stack of paper plates, then went to the front door, where Andy was.

"Hey, Mr. R." Mark's voice floated in from the outside. "You met my wife Barbara, haven't you?"

What the what? Kerry went to the door and poked her head outside. "Hey, Mark," she greeted him. "Hey, Barb," she added, giving his spouse a smile. "You guys come over to just sightsee?"

"Nope." Mark removed a pair of packed bags slung over his bike. "We decided our neighborhood was getting dicey. Barb thought at least here, we got peeps," he said. "And they got fans here." He shrugged. "It really wasn't that bad here last night, once we got here and out of the cray cray."

"Got more'n that." Andy took his keys from his pocket. "C'mon, Cec. Let's get to getting and see what all them folks did back by the house." He glanced at Kerry. "We'll tell them folks to keep that boat runnin till you get there," he added. "Not all dark for a bit yet."

"I'll be right behind you, Dad." Kerry walked out and stood next to the bike. "I talked to Colleen this morning, up in Melbourne. They've got space there," she said. "I thought maybe you guys would like to go hang out there? She said she could use technical management. They have people calling with work for us."

Mark looked surprised. "Yeah?"

"That would be awesome," Barbara said. "Thanks, Kerry. I'm a little over the chaos, and it's going to be months before anyone'll come and do anything about our houses. That's what our neighbor told us today—and he's with FEMA."

Barbara was a tall woman with curly brown hair and freckles. She was dressed in a tank top and leggings under the leather riding jacket she had taken off and slung over the bike.

Kerry had met her at company parties and get togethers for years, and knew she had a high-level bank job. "They've got AC and high-speed Internet," Kerry said. "And the hotel she found has room service."

"Sold," Barb said firmly. "Can we head up there tomorrow?"

"Hey," Mark said. "What are we supposed to do with the house? Just leave everything there?"

"We can have Gus watch it for us. He'd do that," Barb said. "I'm sure Kerry would appreciate you booking more business to replace all the stuff I'm sure got canceled down here, and it'll give me a chance to work remote into our offices."

Kerry gave them a thumbs up. "Chili's on." She pointed at the door. "Zoe's there too, Mark. The shelter her family's in was getting crazy." She backed toward her car. "I gotta go or I'll miss the ferry. Think about it tonight. If you guys want to go, head on up. Colleen's expecting you."

"Rockstar!" Barb returned the thumbs up. "Kerry, you're the bomb. We'll get ourselves sorted out tomorrow and get going. Thank you! Thank you!"

Kerry waved at them as she got to the car and walked around it to the driver's side, opening the door and sliding inside into the hot interior, with its pungent smell of warm leather and the faintest trace of Dar's perfume.

As she headed for MacArthur Causeway, she saw National Guard troops assembling at Bayfront Park, apparently using Bayside shopping center as a command point.

Two large trucks were parked sideways across the road that lead out to the Port, blocking it and when she got to the turn to go east, she saw the same large trucks and a roadblock stopping progress out to the beach as well.

There was a line of cars ahead of her, and she craned her neck, but didn't see her in-laws in it. "Lucky!" She settled back in her seat and watched as several cars ahead of her were turned around amidst raucous horn blaring and flipping off and yells of incoherent rage.

Then it was her turn. She put the window down as the National Guardsman approached, his mottled camo uniform almost black with sweat. "Hi," she greeted him with a mild smile. "Long day?" She added, with more than a note of sympathy in her voice.

The guardsman looked at her with a moment of wry gratitude. "Yes, ma'am, it has been," he said. "Can I ask where you're going?"

"Home." Kerry proffered her driver's license. "Sorry everyone's being such a jerk to you."

He flashed his light on the license and then handed it back to her. "Thank you, Ms. Roberts." He had a quietly educated, uninflected voice. "I really appreciate that, especially at the end of a really crappy day."

"Anything I need to be worried about?" Kerry leaned her arm on the window edge.

The man smiled. "Not where you're going, no, ma'am. We've just had a lot of folks trying to get out to South Beach and not wanting to take no for an answer. Don't even know why. It's all a wreck out there."

"Probably that's why," Kerry said. "It's a wreck and they want to see it.

"Just people being curious I guess." The guard shook his head a little. "Got nothing better to do... or maybe they want to go out there to see what they can find ,if you... ah...know what I mean."

"Looting you mean?"

"You know it. Lot of pricey real estate out on this causeway."

Well, it was true. Kerry pondered for a mitigating factor and then had to stop, since she really couldn't... or could she? "Maybe they work out there?" She finally suggested. "We had a lot of people show up at our offices, because it was such a mess where they lived."

The guard cocked his head to one side and thought about that, in no rush to move on to the car behind Kerry's. "It could be some," he concluded at last. "But I got my orders. No one goes past here who doesn't live past here, or has official business."

"Well, I'm glad to hear it, even given the water moat we're behind," Kerry said. "But please let our deckhands through or we'll be in real trouble."

He laughed. "No, they're picking them up with the work boat off the edge of Bayside here." He pointed to his left. "You're all good, ma'am. Let me go talk to this guy yelling behind you." He took a step back and put his fingers between his teeth and let out a whistle. "Open the gates for this one!" He pointed at Kerry's SUV. "Resident!"

Kerry wasn't either naïve or stupid. She'd been born and grown up in privilege. Now she lived that way with a home on a private island, and a cabin in the Keys. And she owned an office building, and who knew? Maybe a historic homesite in Coconut Grove.

She understood, in a politically savvy way, that this gave her stupendous advantages and she understood completely she could take credit for almost none of it.

But she did question, here in the privacy of her leather seated luxury SUV, that she'd just pulled onto the ferry ramp to her private island home. She did question if it always had to be about how much money you had and who you knew.

"Just made it." The deck hand waved at her. "They told us you were coming, we held the last one for you, Ms. Kerry."

"Thanks, Juan." Kerry pulled the car onto the ferry. "I really appreciate that, though I had a cot reserved for me in our office building back there in the Grove. No power, but a nice pot of chili and some dominos going on."

"Hahaha." Juan secured the chocks behind her wheels. "Oh nah, I'm looking forward to the bunkhouse over there tonight, and get some sweet, sweet AC. I stayed at home last night. Phwwooo." He mimed wiping sweat off his brow and flinging it on the deck. "Not tonight!"

Kerry left the windows open and turned the engine off and took in the brisk ocean breeze as the ferry pulled away from the dock and started across the channel.

In the ferry cab, Juan had joined five or six others, the workers from the terminal now going back over to the island, and glad to be doing so. They would get a bunk and a meal in the marine mess, and Kerry felt they considered themselves lucky.

Lucky, like Arthur had said he felt that morning. Lucky to be comfortable and taken care of, and in that sense, privileged. Maria had said when she called her, that she felt lucky, because so many others were suffering so much, and yet she was so thankful that Kerry had made sure she was taken care of.

So, was it all about wealth and connections? Or what you did with them? Did you have an obligation to use what advantages you have in the service of others? Kerry shook her head. No, you really had no obligation aside from whatever one you created for yourself.

With a faint shake of her head, Kerry retired the subject as insoluble and turned her attention to the challenges of the day instead, and remembered an entire inbox she hadn't even had a chance to look at. "Ugh." She propped her head up with one elbow perched on the edge of the window.

But maybe there would be one in there from Dar. Her eyebrow quirked. "I'll sort newest to oldest." She told her reflection in the side mirror. "Probably makes more sense anyway. They only get angrier and might as well start with the worst of them first."

****

The lab was a clutter of cables and racks and rolling small tables with monitors plopped on top of them and connectors draped over and down to the floor.

On one side of the room, a single rack was filled with server gear that hummed loudly in a sound range that seemed geared to annoy the human ear and there were multiple air-conditioning vents overhead cooling the room to a dampish chill.

It was familiar in the extreme to Dar, but she itched to tidy it up. She knew the lab in their own office would never in a million years look like such a mess.

She couldn't stand loose cables and tangles of fiber, or stuff draped over things haphazardly.

Everyone in the company knew that. Techs carefully coiled up cables into perfectly spherical rounds, fastened by tabs of Velcro and all of the racks, test area or not, had meticulously routed connections with just the right bend radius to ensure the problem free passage of packets without any pinched or kinked impediments.

"So." Scott rubbed his hands as he bumped a cart forward. "Jocko, you got the connections done there?"

"Almost."

Dar pushed the mess aside in her head and focused on the gear instead, resting on the rolling cart in a pile of gleaming mechanical objects.

On the cart was a helmet. It looked like a cross between a flight helmet a pilot might use and an infantry helmet you might see on the ground. It was steel blue and it had long cables coming out of the back of it. It sat on what looked like a set of football shoulder pads.

Dar left her backpack behind near one of the rolling tables and picked up the helmet. She turned it around and peered inside.

It was padded, and the surface was covered in metal leads. She nodded slightly. "Looks like they're staying put now."

"Huh?" Scott peered at her. "Oh, the contacts. Yeah," he said. "That last thing you did with the little gimbles really got them solid. Haven't had one come off since."

One of the techs came over. "Can I get this ready for ya?" He indicated the helmet. "We've been using the hell out of it."

Dar handed him the helmet, then she half turned and hooked one of the rolling stools scattered over the lab with her foot and pulled it over and sat down on it. "Let me make it easier on you," she said, since the tech was on the shorter side. A little shorter than Kerry in fact.

"Ah, we got a step stool over there." The tech smiled though, as he worked. "I'm used to dealing with you tall people. I don't even mind being called Shorty. Better than what my brothers called me."

The other techs settled on stools around the lab and watched in antici-pation.

Dar watched as the helmet was swabbed with alcohol wipes, the sharp, antiseptic scent rising to her nose. She'd worn it before naturally, since the prototype was developed in her own office. Almost everyone on her team had taken a turn in putting it on and suffering the initial testing cycles.

It had given her a headache, mostly. Dar left the testing to her younger programmers. The gamers, who fully enjoyed the experience no matter how weird the programming got and concentrated on tuning the hardware level controls and interfaces for it.

Arthur tried to convince her to let him write an RPG for it, oblivious to the top secret proprietary technology they'd had to very carefully file a pat-ent on. She'd seen potential in it no matter that most of the testing data had resulted in purple triangles and block figures lurching around.

"Okay, it's ready."

The tech next to her put the helmet down, and then picked up the shoulder pads. "Let me get these on you." He stepped around behind Dar and settled them onto her, adjusting them a little. "Confused hell out of the guys out at West Point when we asked for a bunch of these, I tell ya."

"I bet." Dar let her hands rest on her knees. "But they work." She shifted her shoulders a little as he adjusted the platform, and then waited as he stepped to the side and picked up the helmet. She held her head still as it came down over her and muffled her hearing.

"They sure do and talk about a bargain." Scotts voice sounded slightly garbled. "Cheaper than those control surfaces even."

The helmet felt snug and compressed her temples. It was heavy, and uncomfortable until the tech clicked in the support onto the shoulder pads and then those took most of the weight and spread it out. She felt the faint chill of the contacts as they touched her skin and waited, as they ran the startup routine.

She heard the faint rustling as the bone conducting rings turned on and the odd sensation, almost an itch but not as the leads activated, able to send and receive electrical signals through her skin, into her nervous system underneath it.

"Ready?" Scott asked.

Dar lifted her hands in a half shrug. "Sure?"

"Okay, closing the visor." The tech reached around and slid the flexible glass cover over the front, blocking her vision. "Start 'er up."

"Starting," Jocko's voice confirmed.

For a moment, it was just dark, and she heard the techs around her shifting around, the squeaks of wheels under the stools, the rustle of fabric. She smelled the electrical smell of the room, that mixture of off gassing plastic and heated metal that was so typical of high technology.

She took a breath of it and relaxed her body as she heard the whisper of the startup crackling through the bone conductance pads and felt the padded edge of the visor as it pressed against her skin and blocked out all the surrounding light.

Then suddenly she was somewhere else. A leafy forest erupted around her, as crisply clear in her vision as reality would have been. As she took a breath, the smell of wood and moss and outside air was present. It almost made her jump, and she felt herself tense as she tried to reconcile the change.

She heard the sound of the branches over her head, and a bird. Slowly she turned her head and the vision rotated, clearly, with no pixilation. As real as any sense memory she could think of. It was completely immersive, and as she looked in all directions, it was hard to take in.

She looked down, and found herself sitting on a fallen tree, in army style fatigues, in a body outline not quite her own. The hands of it rested on scuffed knees and as she flexed her hands, she watched them move in her vision. "Huh."

"It's something isn't it?" Scott's voice intruded, excited. "You see what we mean? It's different, right?"

It was different. Dar couldn't precisely define what the quality of the difference was except to think inside her own head that it was more real. "Yeah," she answered, after a pause. "It is."

"What'd you do?" Jocko asked. "We all wondered, you know? Ever since we got the drop. Then we couldn't ask you."

"Yeah, I know. The hurricane. What did I do? Interesting question." She stood up off the stool and took a short step forward and knew she had cables behind her. She saw booted feet move on a thickly pine needle strewn ground. "It's different all right."

The clarity of the world was the equal of what she'd see with the helmet off, Dar realized. It was more than high definition. The rendering was real-time quality. "There's no lag." She lifted her hand and moved it, then moved it back. "That's the difference."

"Huh?" Scott moved closer. "What does that mean?"

What did it mean? The sim was designed to take a video scenario and build a reasonably realistic three-dimensional world out of it, using subcutaneous reactions to allow the user to experience a virtual reality. They had programmed in the ability to produce appropriate sounds and scents delivered through the electrical leads, and Dar felt it had been reasonably successful.

But as she looked around in this mock world now, rather than being aware of it being projected around her, she felt like she was actually in that place. There was a clarity and response to the surroundings that was different. A quantum leap difference that changed the experience in a way she hadn't anticipated.

A sound made Dar turn her head, and she looked into the forested distance, trying to decide if it was something she'd heard in the sim, or in the room around her and couldn't. "Turn it off," She finally said. She recognized the distraction and the urge to try and explore the experience.

The world disappeared and it was dark, just long enough for the tech to unlatch and move the visor up and out of her way.

Dar blinked, and felt a moment of dissociation that was quite disconcerting. "So." She sat there, thinking for a long moment. "What did I do. What I did was streamline the rendering pipeline mechanics."

Jocko watched her, his eyes a little squinty. "Is that... like a routine, or..."

"It's all machine code." Dar shook her head a little, conscious of the helmet still on her, the contacts now warmed to her skin temperature. "Sort of the layer below the programming. That's the tuning I was working on." She finally looked up at them. "So, yes. It's more realistic because it's more efficient. There's no lag in what your eyes see in the sim and what your brain perceives is going on."

"Okay." Scott sat down on a rolling stool and rolled over to face her. "So, this is great. It's gonna knock their socks off tomorrow. Woo hoo. All that stuff." He leaned his elbows on his knees and stared intently at her. "Here's the pitch. We take this, and we make it so we can interface with all kinds of stuff so we can train people and make em know what it's really like before they do it."

Dar regarded him. "What kind of stuff?"

"Military stuff."

"You already have sims for that," Dar said, after a moment, her brows creasing. "You have mock tanks and airplanes and whatever. I've seen them."

"No, not that." Scott paused. "Let's go talk a minute. I can't say it here." He looked at the tech behind Dar. "Take that off and put it away."

Dar felt the helmet lift up off her. She waited for the pads to come off as well, then she stood up and followed Scott out of the room. The rest of the techs stayed behind, and she was conscious of the silence as they walked down the hallway and then he swiped a card to enter a room.

A small conference room, with a round table and two chairs. When the door closed behind them, Dar felt the air compress around them and she was aware of a sense of pressure against her eardrums, soundproofing giving them privacy.

"Okay." Scott sat down, his expression now more shrewd than bland or good natured. "You're a civ. I get it, but you grew up around the military, so I know you know the deal with us."

Dar sat down and remained silent, because in fact she had no idea what he was talking about. She raised her eyebrow to encourage him to continue as she folded her hands on the table before her.

"It's not about the mechanical stuff. We can train that," Scott said, after a brief pause. "Like you said we got sims. We can put someone in a tank and teach them how to make it go. That's not a big deal. We've been doing it for years. And most of the time we got the real things to train with. We don't need sims for that."

Dar nodded, after a moment, as apparently, he was waiting for some reaction from her.

"It's the mental stuff we want to train. What it's like to pull the trigger and hit someone. What it looks like when a missile launcher blows up someone twenty feet from you." He went on. "We got tons of cam footage of guys in battle, you know? That's where that view you got is from."

He paused again and looked at her. "It's a great way to give people experience, you get me?" He waited, expectantly. "You do get it, right?"

Dar stared back at him. "You want people to know how it feels to kill someone before they have to do it," she finally said, enunciating her words clearly. "Feel it in here." She reached up and tapped her chest. "Not just watch the video."

He nodded and looked a bit relieved. "I knew you'd get it," he said. "It's all about lethality. We want to extend the contacts so you can hold a gun and feel it, and a knife, and rig it up so you can walk around with it. That's the pitch. A way to get recruits experience without them being out there having to pull the trigger the first time."

Well. It made sense. "Okay," Dar said slowly.

"Okay you can do it?" Scott asked eagerly. "You can do that, and make it be like the helmet is?"

Could she? Dar took a breath and let it out. "I have to check how that integration came together," she temporized. "Might need more processing horsepower." Her fingertips twitched, and she felt a surge of curiosity as to what the hell her code had gone and done. "We can try it, sure."

Scott sat back and smiled. "It's gonna be awesome," he said, with a sigh of contentment. "I told my boss it was gonna boot the both of us upstairs. And it's gonna be worth the bonus I told him we'd give you when you did it."

Dar smiled briefly. "Let's let me do it first," she said. "Who are we demonstrating this for tomorrow?" She asked. She knew Kerry would ask when she called her and told her whatever it was, she was going to tell her, given she didn't really know for sure what the hell she'd actually done yet.

"DOD," Scott said. "Guy in charge has a new guy who thinks he knows technology." He seemed skeptical. "Got all up in my shorts about bringing in a civilian third party to do the programming."

"Ah."

"I'm gonna enjoy introducing him to you."

Oh boy. "Sounds like fun." Dar now sat back herself. "I'll try not to get us into too much trouble."

Scott now seemed more relaxed, and almost cocky. He drummed his fingers on the table. "You like steak, right? I remember you liking steak. There's a good steakhouse down the road. I think we're due a steak and a whisky. You up for that?"

"Sure."

"Great. Let's get the team, and head out. Then I can drop you by the lodge." Scott got up and stretched, then clapped his hands together. "This is gonna be great." He walked over and released the door lock. He opened it and stuck his head outside. "Hiii youuuuu!" He let out a bellow. "Chow!"

Dar got up. "Let me go grab my backpack," she said. "I'm gonna need it."

****

The steak house was a one off. A place that had been there for a hundred years and wasn't a chain. It had a smoke-tinged ceiling and a long, long wooden bar. The tables were full of almost all men around them.

Dar checked her watch, as they sat with a round of drinks, waiting for their appetizers to arrive. "Be right back." She got up and made her way between the tables, aware of the glances that followed her as she went outside and left the murmur of conversation behind.

Outside it was just dark, and she went over to the post and rails that, she supposed, at one time they'd tied horses to. She perched on it as she took out her cell phone from her pocket, opening it and dialing the main number for the office.

She was surprised, but glad when it was Kerry who answered. "Hey," she responded, to her partner's speech.

"Hey, hon!" Kerry's tone altered from business like to delight. "Wow I was just about to try calling you. How was your flight?"

"Fine," Dar said. "I'm out at dinner with the project team."

"And?"

"And, something I did the day before the storm, when I sent them that version update did something unexpected." Dar reached up to pinch the bridge of her nose. "They are over the moon about it. Want me to extend it further. We've got a demo to the brass in the morning."

Kerry paused a moment to absorb that. "That sounds great," she said. "Doesn't it?"

"If I knew what I actually did? Sure."

Kerry chucked. "Oh, hon."

"Yeah anyway. I'm going to unpack what I sent tonight and see if I can figure it out. They do like it though, so at least there's that," Dar said, in a wryly bemused tone. "How's it going there?"

"How's it going here. Well, your father and his friends have turned our office into Fort Knox," Kerry said. "And the guys said to tell you whatever it is you did on the way to the airport worked and they sent the results out to the pharmacy company."

Dar frowned. "I should have checked it first."

"Hon."

Dar exhaled. "I know. I'm impossible," she acknowledged. "But they know better."

"But you weren't here, and we got calls from them all afternoon," Kerry said, gently. "If it's not right, it can be fixed, but at least they have something to work with. Arthur said he talked to their support guy before they went to dinner, and they sounded okay."

"Mm." Dar made a low, grunting noise.

"And it's nice to at least make someone happy. Aside from Mark's wife, who's over the moon about them going up to Melbourne," Kerry said. "Maybe you can call John tomorrow and check in with him."

"I'll check the repo tonight after I get done with this dinner," Dar said. "It's nice to be able to pick up a phone and do something reasonable like talk to you with it for a change, I'll tell you that."

Kerry chuckled. "I was going to call you, then go home and shower and just have a cup of tea on the patio. I've been here plowing through my email since I got back over to the island."

"Anything interesting?"

"Most of the yelling you already know about," Kerry said. "I did get a surprise note from Anabelle Squash at the county. She wants to talk on Monday. Maybe she can use some of the material we bought for the ten other jobs we just lost due to this thing."

Dar listened to a soft whir of wings nearby and wondered if it was a bat. "We'll figure it out," she said, after a moment of mutual silence. "Anyway, they said I'd be on a plane home tomorrow after the demo. So, hang in there and we'll work it out."

"I know," Kerry said. "We always do."

"We do." Dar felt better, just with the exchange. "Let me go get through this dinner before those guys have a couple more rounds of bourbon."

"You don't like bourbon."

"I'm not drinking it," Dar said. "So that works out. My contribution to the festivities is a Kahlua milkshake with Nutella sprinkles." She listened to Kerry's laugh, echoing softly into her ear. "That change I made... it's pretty cool, Ker."

"It is, huh?"

"If I can figure out what the hell I did, it's got promise for the gaming platform," Dar said. "Could be interesting."

"You'll figure it out," Kerry echoed her earlier statement. "But do me a favor and don't tell your coders about it until after they finish what's on their plate now? They'll never do anything else."

Dar chuckled. "True," she said. "All right. Night, Ker. I'll buzz you in the morning, let you know how it goes."

"Got it. Good night, my love," Kerry said. "See you tomorrow night."

They hung up, and Dar spent a moment regarding the rising moon over the mountains, tapping the edge of her phone against her jaw. Then she slid the phone into her pocket and made her way back to the door of the restaurant.

****

Kerry sat at the dining room table, her half-finished cup of tea in front of her along with a plate with half a banana muffin on it. She was freshly showered, and now dressed in a company polo shirt and dark green shorts and light green socks, ready for the day.

The television was on, and she was watching the early news, the just post dawn sky slowly lightening outside in a sedate pink glow.

She hiked up one knee against the edge of the table, took a sip of the tea and watched the helicopter shots of still flooded neighborhoods, shelters packed with uncomfortable looking people. And then, toward the end of the segment, almost as an offhand comment, a shot of the White House lawn where trees were down.

She'd seen that shot of the tree about two dozen times now. It didn't really surprise her. Usually when a storm came through there were a few iconic shots that represented to the world what it was like to be there.

So now this storm, Hurricane Bob, who had ripped through Florida and caused who only knew how much damage to homes and businesses, and lives, would be remembered by a shot of a tree lying across the steps of the White House with a helicopter hovering over it.

Watching the national news, she realized the country had moved on from what had happened here where she was. It was more interesting to see the amazing sight of water in the streets of DC, congresspeople wading in the streets in their suits, and the flag on the mall in tatters because no one remembered to take it down in all the chaos. That was new and different, and not just, oh Florida again.

She shook her head and picked up the half muffin with its layer of peanut butter and took a bite. Even the local reporter seemed to acknowledge it and made a somewhat snarky comment as they came back to news of the area. The ticker below the anchor scrolled off it's never ending messages of shelters, and, a new thing, personal messages.

Personal messages, because communicating was so damn hard right now. The TV station had offered to accept messages from anyone, to anyone, and put it on their ticker so that people could try to find each other and discover if friends and family were okay.

It irritated Kerry. It made her think there should be something they could do in order to… well not to fix the problems, because she realized there were things like flooded buildings that really were beyond their control. But maybe they could come up with a plan, a way to do things so next time…

The next time. In a week, it would all just be frustration and anger, and people yelling, and no one would think about what they would do differently next time. Just what they could do now to go back to normal. And then it would be lost in a flood of politicians' bluster and promises.

Well, maybe they could come up with some ideas and maybe after a while, someone would be interested.

Kerry finished her muffin and dusted off her fingertips. The sunlight came in the sliding glass windows from the patio and reflected off the ring on her finger. She got up, picked up the plate and cup and took them into the kitchen. She rinsed them before she put them into the rack to dry.

It was quiet in the condo. Andrew and Ceci had headed off some time ago to have breakfast at the mansion and then check on their boat. So Kerry was left to get herself ready for the day and whatever that had in store for her.

She could rummage around and figure out how to get the connection in the condo working, but she picked up her backpack instead, slinging it over one shoulder and clicked her tongue.

Chino and Mocha came running, tails wagging. "Ready to go to the cottage, kids?" She asked them. "Let's go see how our friends are doing there this morning, okay? Let's get some work done!"

"Gruff!" Chino was the first to the front door and when Kerry opened it, she ran out and Mocha almost knocked Kerry down.

"Hey!" Kerry closed the door and went down the steps. She walked over and down into the garage and tossed her pack into the passenger seat of the golf cart.

Chino and Mocha both jumped into the back and she turned the fob and released the brake. "Hang on, guys."

Both dogs sat down and pressed up against the back of the seat as she backed up and then swung the cart around and sent it up the slope to the road. She pulled to a halt when a string of cars came past heading toward the ferry dock in a parade of shiny well-waxed gleam.

She was glad of the pause as it gave her time to retrieve her sunglasses from the storage box and put them on, relieved to cut the early morning sun as she waited for the line of posh cars to end.

There was a lot of them. Kerry looked up and down the road as car after car went past. She finally saw the last of them, a black sedan with heavily tinted windows and surprisingly plain hubcaps she knew at once for security.

"Oh." She leaned back as it went by, then pressed the gas pedal down. "Probably the governor's buddy. Or maybe the governor himself." She turned left and went along the now empty road and glanced to her right as she caught motion to see a large crowd of landscape gardeners busy at work on the golf course.

Really? Kerry could think of a thousand other things it would be better for those men to be doing, rather than cleaning up that little 9-hole course.

Kerry pulled the cart into one of the small lots to one side of the cottages and got out. She grabbed her pack as the dogs followed her closely as she walked across the sidewalk and into the back yard of the cottage, where the satellite van was parked.

All was quiet.

Kerry walked to the double French doors and opened one of them. "Good morning, team."

Angela came into the living room area with a tray of coffee. "Hey, boss. Oh boy, I could get used to those beds, let me tell ya!"

"They're comfortable," Celeste agreed. She was seated at the table, working on a pile of message pads.

Arthur and Elvis were already on the couch, busy with their keyboards. They had plastic bottles of Coke on the table next to them and a pile of cookies. They both looked contented as clams.

They were morning people, or at least, working for the company they had become that way, more or less the same way Kerry had. She offered flexible hours. And while many of the staff took advantage of it, especially those who had to work around childcare and school classes, most of the people who worked right around Dar showed up when she did.

Just like Kerry did. Just like she always had, since she'd started working for Dar way back when. She'd check for her bosses' SUV in the lot when she pulled in, always glad when she beat her.

Well, at least until they started living together and it really made no difference. But there was something about Dar that made people want to step up and meet her mark. Kerry felt that herself from day one, and though she knew being in love with her partner was a factor, that didn't change that inner expectation.

Besides, Dar was usually mellow in the morning and her staff had learned that was sometimes the best time to approach her. "You get any feedback from the Pharma guys?" Kerry asked, as she put her pack down and got out her laptop. "Dar was asking."

Arthur glanced up and over at her. "That guy that works for them, Tony? He said he was going to call us this morning. They were doing some tests."

"Good," Kerry said. "Did those files all get transferred from our friend of the friend of the governor?"

"They did," Elvis said. "They said they'd be back."

"I'm sure they will." Kerry plugged in her machine and opened it. "Since we're the only game in town right now." She sat down to wait for the machine to present to her a desktop in some useful format. "We hear from Colleen yet today?"

"Not yet," Angela said. "It's kinda early."

Eight a.m.. "Not really," Kerry demurred.

"No." Celeste smiled, as she sat sorting pink slips of notepaper. "We always knew the day started when Ms. Roberts came in the door. Especially on Mondays," she said. "I had the early shift."

"I remember." Kerry leaned on her elbows. "It was always better to get into that mausoleum early and avoid the crowd at the elevators." She paused. "And you got the first crack at the pastalitos, of course."

Celeste chuckled. "They held yours apart." She glanced over at Kerry. "There was always a separate box. Didn't you know?"

Kerry blinked and laughed a little. "I didn't."

"Maria took care of you guys. She knew those café people and she made sure they had what you liked every morning," Celeste said. "Even if they ran out for everyone else. That and the plate lunches." She continued her sorting. "Especially the chicken imperial."

"Dar does like that," Kerry admitted. "I make it at home, but it doesn't taste the same."

Celeste nodded. "I do too. Whenever she was out, I knew I could score for lunch." She got up and brought the slips over to Kerry. "Okay, so... I think these are current customers, and these are people asking for you." She put them down. "These are some who are asking for Dar, and these... I don't know what these are."

Kerry picked up the last pile and started going through them. "Those are sometimes the most interesting," she said. "Let's see what we've got here. Angela, see if you can get Colleen on the phone. Let's get someone up there to call those current customers."

"Right you are, boss."

****

Dar walked quietly down the hall, mindful of the very pre-dawn stillness of the hotel around her. Far off, she could just hear the faintest sound of the rattle of dishes. She guessed that somewhere in some part of it some night room service waiter was bringing around a nightcap.

Or, perhaps, bringing an East Coaster like her some coffee and cereal in what was for them the middle of the night. She rode the elevator down and went into one of the more public areas, crossing an empty hall to the hotel gym.

Open twenty-four hours, and with her keycard, it was. Dar pushed the door open and entered. She took in a breath of chlorinated air from a swimming pool and the scent of spindle grease from the rows of exercise machines.

Both appealing, but Dar's target was in the back of the high-ceilinged room, a climbing wall that spread across the entire back of the facility, and one she remembered from the last time she'd stayed there. She'd woken again early, typically, and ended up so engrossed by the wall she almost missed her morning meeting.

Now she faced it again with a feeling of pleasure and sauntered over to the stand that held a block of chalk. She covered her hands with it before she approached the climbing rig.

She wanted one and pondered the idea of putting one somewhere. Maybe on the inner courtyard of their building? If she attached it to the outside of the condo it would give too much free entertainment to her neighbors.

Dar studied the hand grips and reached up as far as she could. She took a firm grab on one of the holds and pulled herself up enough to get a foothold under her. Would that be worse than giving that much entertainment to her staff?

She frowned a bit, then shifted to another set of holds and worked her way steadily upward.

A thought occurred to her. "I could build a whole jungle gym at that new place," she murmured. That would be cool." She pictured it in her head, a wooden and steel structure out in the thickly wooded area that surrounded the house, quiet and private.

She could make it modular, so she could move it around and change it.

She got to the top of the section and wondered if she should go down and then up in another area. She could see the grips she'd end up on not all that far away and without much thought, coiled her body and released the handholds she had. She shoved away with her legs and reaching out to the new ones.

Halfway there, it occured to her exactly how idiotic the motion was, but by then it was too late and all she could do was hope her grip would hold and not drop her to the floor twenty feet below.

She felt the rubber touch her fingers and she clenched them instinctively as her body collided with the wall. She swung wildly for a moment, convinced she wasn't going to hold on. Then her feet caught on two of the protrusions below her and she was able to adjust her grip.

After a moment to regain her composure, Dar started down and around this new section. One that jutted out a bit and provided her more of a challenge.

Near the floor she reached an outcrop and let herself hang from it, stretching her body out for a long moment before she released her hands and dropped the short distance, taking a deep breath.

"Lady, you are crazy."

Dar turned to find a young man in a tank top and cotton shorts nearby, with a towel around his neck. He was lithe and muscular, with curly black hair and a neatly trimmed beard and moustache. "Am I?"

"Jumping like that with no rope?" The man said, his voice rising. "With no one in here? Yeah, you are crazy."

Dar shrugged a little bit. "Seemed like fun at the time." She turned and regarded the next section of wall, which curved up and was, apparently, the most advanced part. The top part of it was higher, and the handholds seemed farther apart.

"You gonna put a harness on for that and use the belay?"

Dar half turned. "No."

The young man came over to her. "You're going to freestyle that?" He said. "I'm gonna call 911 so they can get ready for it."

It felt like a challenge. Dar felt the prickle of it tingle her arms. "I'll be fine." She reassured the man. "Don't you have something else to do?"

"With a crazy lady here about to go break her neck? No, I don't!" The man said, cheerfully. "G'wan, Tarzan. Have at it."

Dar blinked mildly at him, then she walked over and put more chalk on her hands and went toward the wall. She took the last steps at a faster pace and ended with a leap in the air. She caught two handholds as high as she could and pulled herself up.

"No, no, no... I was just..." The man yelled from below. "Crazy lady stop that!"

But it was fun. Dar got a foothold then swarmed up the wall, her body now used to the activity and well awake. It reminded her suddenly of the wall she'd climbed back on the rafting trip. That same feeling of motion and challenge.

She hadn't enjoyed it then because of the terror of the situation they'd been in, but she enjoyed it now. She made her way hand over hand up the side of the artificial cliff until she reached the top and then worked her way meticulously around the promontory to the other side.

She paused there and glanced down, to find her new friend watching her with his hands clenched in his hair in such patent horror it nearly made her laugh and lose her grip.

She wondered for a brief moment what it would be like just to let go and plummet. To land on the ground like she remembered doing on that cliff. She dreamed about it sometimes, that fall, and the tumbling in midair, and the landing like she'd had springs in her boots.

Almost. Dar imagined herself doing it. She heard the scream in her head from the guy at the base of the wall, and felt the jar of the landing all the way up into her hips.

It would be fun. As long as she actually landed on her feet and not on her head and end up getting dragged off to the emergency room.

Dar sighed. Ah well. She had a demonstration to do that was important, and so she maneuvered her way to another hold and started down the angle, depending now on the grip of her fingers to hold her against the tug of gravity.

She felt the strain across her back and was glad she'd spent the time she had over the last few months in the gym doing pull ups as she spent a bit more time in climbing around whatever she could find to climb on.

Halfway down the angle straightened, and it became a more conventional descent. She ended it with a calmly sedate hop at the very bottom. She dusted her hands off as she turned to face her watcher. "Tolja."

"You a pro?"

"I'm an IT geek," Dar told him. "Excuse me. I got a pool calling my name."

"No, seriously."

"I'm an IT geek," Dar repeated. "I just like climbing. Do you climb?" She indicated the wall behind them. "It's fun, right?"

He hesitated. "Naw, I don't mess with that," he said. "But hey, I gotta get to work. Don't let me hold you up." He backed away and gave her a brief wave, then headed toward a nondescript door in the back of the gym.

Dar watched him for a moment, head cocked slightly in mild puzzlement. His attitude had changed so quickly and for no reason she knew of.

She made her way over to the pool and pulled the T-shirt off over her head and set it on one of the brown wooden stands and added her shorts to it.

She took off her sneakers and went to the edge of the pool in her swimsuit. She dove headfirst into the water, already anticipating the cool bite against her skin.

After the climb it felt good. She swam with lazy strokes end to end in the pool for a half hour, until all the tension had wound its way out of her and she ended the last lap on her back, floating until her fingertips touched the wall.

Over her head the ceiling was tall and in the east corner of it she saw the dawn rising. The light came up over the mountains through the smoked glass panels.

She lay there just breathing for a minute, feeling the water advance and retreat over her body as she inhaled and exhaled. She felt a sense of animal comfort. Coffee, she decided and rolled in the water like a seal and glided over to the steps.

Coffee would be the next achievement of the day.

There were towels in a shelving unit and she took one as she got out and dried off. She started to hear more motion around the gym, and saw two or three bodies claim rowing machines and a treadmill. Idly ruffling her hair dry she walked over to where she'd left her T-shirt and shorts. She spotted her morning's friend standing behind one of the counters.

He faced another man, who was taller and thicker, with the air of a football coach about him. He had a finger in the smaller man's face and talked fiercely, though he kept his voice low. He glanced briefly around at the customers.

Now why, Dar wondered, was the morning being started off by someone being an asshole? She pulled on her shirt and shorts over her still damp one piece suit and sat down to pull on her sneakers. The smaller man answered, his hands up in a placating gesture, but that only seemed to make the other man point harder.

No one in their right mind would get involved with what was obviously an employer and employee issue, and yet when Dar stood up she walked in that direction, with exactly that intent and she knew it.

What was it Kerry called it? Her paladin gene? This stupid instinct to mix it up in business she had no business being involved in got her into trouble almost every time. Dar slung the towel around her neck as she approached the counter.

As they caught sight of her in their peripheral vision, both men stopped talking. The taller one turned and put his hands on the counter as she arrived. "Good morning, ma'am. How can I help you?" He asked, in a quiet tone.

Dar saw, in her own peripheral vision, the smaller man look off to one side, visibly steaming. "Can I talk to you a minute?" She asked mildly. "Somewhere a little more private?"

"Of course." He looked slightly surprised but stepped back and gestured toward the far end of the gym. "Let's go to the lounge. I think they've just brought orange juice in."

His voice had moved to a tone she characterized as customer facing fawning and she smiled in reaction. "Thanks."

Dar followed him over to a small section of the floor that was partitioned off with potted plants and dimmed lighting. There were comfortable chairs and on one side, a juice bar that was just getting set up. It smelled of aromatherapy and lemon and was empty of guests.

The man walked over and picked up two glasses of juice from a tray on the counter and came back over and offered her one. "Now, how can I help you?"

All sweet consideration and peaches and cream. Dar took the glass. "Thanks," she said. "So, I came in here pretty early, and the gentleman behind the counter out there was the only one here."

"Oh, yes?" He looked politely interested. "Seth. He's our morning setup man," he said. "He's always got some story to tell, mostly to avoid doing work," he added. "You know how it is."

"Well." Dar paused. "What I was going to tell you was, I was climbing up around on your wall there, and I think I startled him." She kept her own voice bland and mild. "Swinging around like a monkey, you know."

As she spoke, she saw his face change and go from politely interested to actually interested. "Oh really?"

"Yeah, and the thing is, he tried to stop me. I didn't want him to get in trouble on my behalf, if you know what I mean, because I didn't listen to him." Dar regarded him intently. "I don't take direction well," she added.

"Huh... yeah, he was telling me about that. I wasn't sure ..." The man paused. "You were climbing up the wall? He said you were doing it without any safety ropes and all that. That was true?"

Dar nodded and smiled at him, her pale eyes twinkling a little bit. "So, I get it was dangerous," she said. "Wasn't his fault I did it anyway," she admitted. "All in all, he took it pretty well."

He was silent for a minute, then glanced back to meet her eyes. "Ms...." He hesitated.

"Roberts," Dar supplied. "Dar Roberts."

"Ms. Roberts, that's a decent thing you just did," he said. "I was just ripping him a new one for not finishing the setup this morning. I thought he was just making up some bullshit... excuse me." His face flushed. "I'm sorry, some nonsense like he always does."

"Storyteller?" Dar asked, casually. "I get it. I've got a few working with me too."

"Never stops," the man said. He visibly relaxed and his tone became more natural. "Always making up stuff and messing with the guests... makes em laugh, but man," he said. "Anyway, I'm glad this time it was legit. I'll go tell him what you said. You didn't have to. Most don't care."

"No problem. But you know, you might want to leverage that."

About to turn away, he looked back. "Excuse me?"

"Guy makes people laugh... you must have classes and things here, right? It's a public gym isn't it? Not just for the hotel?" She drained her glass and set it down. "They have a gal at a gym I go to who makes up all kinds of stuff and teaches classes. Everyone loves em, cause it keeps them from thinking about running in place or whatever they're doing, you know?"

"Yeah?"

"They pay extra for her classes." Dar winked at him. "Just a thought." She waved and headed off toward the door. She shook her head slightly and bemoaned the frequent lack of imagination people had. She didn't regret invoking her own imagination to describe that purely fictitious scenario.

****

There was an air of nervous expectation in the room as Dar entered with Scott. The techs were already there, Jocko already heads down in the keyboard making sure everything was ready.

They were in the posh conference room this time, indicating the importance of the demo and the grade of the audience. She noticed the catering that was provided on a cart covered in starched linen against the wall.

She set her overnight bag near the wall and her backpack next to it. She saw no need now to have her laptop out and in use. She'd spent the evening last night scouring through the code and she thought she knew what happened with her change.

She had no intention of explaining it. No one in the room would understand her. Dar had spent some time as she'd eaten breakfast thinking of what she was going to say to Scott and then found he was far too nervous to listen to it anyway.

All he'd wanted to talk about was who would be there, and that she had to—be nice—to him.

Dar forbore to point out that she felt it was up to him to be nice to her, but she went to the neatly set up service in the corner and got herself a cup of jasmine tea and sat down with it. She felt relaxed and comfortable in her jeans and short sleeved shirt and now merely waited to see what was going to happen.

"Okay." Jocko finally looked up. "It's as ready as it's gonna be." He looked at Dar. "Want to check it?"

"No," Dar said mildly. "Totally trust you know what you're doing." She took a sip of her tea and wished they'd get on with it. It was already ten minutes after when they were supposed to have started, and she hoped that didn't mean it was going to be one of those days.

Scott was sweating. "They'll be here soon," he assured her. "Mary called me from the desk, and said they were coming down." He licked his lips. "Traffic I guess. You know how it is."

"It's your party," Dar reminded him. "I'm just here for the chips and dip."

That made Jocko smile, and his shoulders relaxed. "These guys can be tough," he told her, as though excusing Scott's nerves. "But you're probably used to that."

"Yes, I am." Dar smiled back at him, with just a hint of a wink. "Listen, you have a good product here and you know what you're pitching. Just relax, and let it fly," she counseled them like she would her own team. "Let your work speak for itself."

"Easy for you to say." Scott sighed and went over to fuss with the cups again.

"It's my work, so it is easy for me to say." Dar folded her hands on the table. "It'll be fine, people. Even if it doesn't work, or if it craps out everyone expects technology to do that. Relax."

Jocko made a face at her.

"I'll do the talking if it goes south." Dar almost laughed. "There's no one walking through that door who's going to rattle me. Don't really care who he is."

"You don't know this guy," Scott muttered under his breath at her.

"He doesn't know me," Dar responded crisply. "Let him bring it. I can handle whatever he pulls."

That, at least, did relax them a little and they talked amongst themselves until the door lever shifted and the door pushed open into the room, and two men entered.

One was the brass who was running the program. Dar knew him relatively well. The second was a tall, ginger haired man with a thin face and very sharp gray eyes. He was dressed in civilian clothes and she didn't know him at all.

Know the man himself. She knew the type though and had a sudden urge to kick him in the front of his pressed linen kneecaps. But she remained seated and picked up her cup of tea to take a sip as the military men around her snapped to attention.

"Where are... there you are, Peterson." The brass came over to him.

"Are you ready? We don't have much time for this." He glanced at the table. "Hello, Roberts. Good to see you."

"Hey, Charlie," Dar responded casually. "Who's your friend?"

If she'd started tap dancing, it could not have gotten a more startled response from the room, and she enjoyed it. "And you should make some time. These guys have worked their asses off for this and don't need you to be dismissive of either them or their effort."

Charles Boots paused and regarded her for a moment. "Oh, sorry." He turned to the ginger haired man. "I forgot you never met. This is Robert Haribee, from the budget oversight office." He motioned the man forward. "Rob, this is Dar Roberts. She's the one who cooked up this thing."

"Nice to meet you." Dar waited for the man to come over before she stood up and extended a hand to him. She expected and got the faint reaction as he wasn't expecting her to be taller than he was. "My company's developing this on your behalf, yes."

He gripped her hand hard, which made her smile, and then released her. "Pleasure," he said, shortly. "So, are we ready to do this?"

Dar sat back down and met Jocko's eyes. She gave him a nod. "Which one of you wants to put the rig on?" She asked crisply. "Want to cut to the chase, Mr. Haribee? Siddown on the end seat there if you do."

He absolutely just stared at her for a long, blank moment, and Dar pondered what he was thinking. She decided it was either probably, who the hell was this woman, or do these people not know who I am, or are you fucking kidding me?

She sketched him in her imagination, and added the thought bubble. Her face tensed a little as she suppressed a smile. She enjoyed the mild taunting, a favorite strategy of hers to keep others off balance and keep them from predicting what she was thinking herself.

Would he turn and leave? Tell her to fuck off? Yell at Charlie? Or take the challenge.

Abruptly, he turned and went to the chair at the end of the table and sat. "Okay," he said. "Let's do it. Should I take my jacket off?"

Ah. Dar was pleased. Nice. "Great choice," she complimented him. "Nothing I hate more than a talking head and a deck."

"If you would, sir," Jocko said. He moved the rig cart forward. "It'll fit better." The ginger haired man stripped off his sports coat and tossed it onto a nearby stand. "Okay, sir, I'm just going to get this on you. Let me know if it pinches."

Charlie sat down next to Dar. "You have balls the size of the eye of a great white whale," he said under his breath. "Anyone ever tell you that?"

"Everyone on the planet." Dar leaned back in her seat and cupped her hands around her tea. "Except my partner, who's seen me naked and knows better."

Chapter Fourteen

"So, let's see if this works." Kerry got into the passenger seat of Dar's truck, with Andy driving it. She settled back and pushed her sunglasses up onto her nose. "Oh boy, what a day."

"If they all don't touch that pole we done put up on the roof, it'll be all good." Her father-in-law put the truck into gear and they headed for the ferry. "Ah think I got that there dish focused all right."

"It'll be nice to have contact with the office. It makes me nervous, thinking of all those guys over there."

"Me too," Andy admitted. "Ah do think it would be a right thing to bring all them folks ovah here." He pulled into the ferry launch area, and waited, as two cars bumped carefully onto the car ferry ahead of them. "You all said Dar done good with that program thing?"

"She said the demo went very well," Kerry said. "She was going to meet with some suit or something afterward and said she'd try to call again before they took her back to the base and get her on some transport back here."

"Sounds good." Andy put the truck in park and leaned back, folding his brawny arms across his chest. "Ah do not know how long this here area's going to be like this, though."

"No, me either." Kerry sighed. "I don't know. I'm going to try and talk Dar into moving the whole operation up to mid-state. At least until they sort out things down here. We can't do business like this. It's nuts."

"Big old mess."

"Big old mess," Kerry echoed him. "I mean, I talked to people today. They need help. They need our services but without any connection and no power? Dad, we can't do this." She exhaled. "I have a pads worth of people willing to give me business and I can't take it."

Andy thought about that in silence as the ferry casted off and headed shoreward. "Ain't good," he said.

"No," Kerry murmured. "It's not good. I know everyone is being so good and showing up at the office. They're doing what they can to clean it up, but that's not going to let us survive as a business." She leaned her elbow on the window jam and propped her head on her fist. "At least a lot of our folks were willing to head up to Melbourne. If I can just get them some damn transport."

"Wall now, kumquat, having fuel on that there island back there is a handy thing," Andy said. "Fixing to bring that big tank they do have back and get it filled up later on." He gave her a sideways look.

Kerry looked at him. "If I have some people show up at the office with a van, can we get gas for it?"

"Surely."

The ferry parked at the far end, and they rolled off and turned left onto the causeway. It was devoid of other cars, and far off on the end, where it emerged onto Miami Beach, Kerry saw flashing lights as the sun reflected off camo trucks.

It was hot and hazy, with only some fitful breeze to stir the air. She was guiltily glad of the air-conditioning in the truck, happy to enjoy it until they reached the office. "If we get the point-to-point link up, then at least if Dar calls, they can relay it."

"Yeap." Andy nodded. "That or ah can teach one of them boys to use that radio," he said. "Ceci kept one of them little units."

"It's not that hard. I don't know what their problem is," Kerry muttered. "I mean, we're a technology company for God's sake. Just because it's analog technology it's not like it's from another planet."

Andy chuckled. "Them kids are busy in that place."

"And surely, your friends know how to use radios," Kerry said. "I mean, c'mon?"

"They do," he said. "More fun to go round and build sniper nests than yappin on the squawk like a big old chicken." He sniffed reflectively. "Never liked that."

Kerry paused in thought. "Really?"

"Didn't like hearin mah voice."

Her brows knit and she half turned to regard him, willingly distracted from the sunbaked tarmac. "I love listening to you talk," she said, after a moment's pause. "I always have."

They pulled up to the line of cars waiting to go through the roadblock and Andy gave her a sideways look, his grizzled eyebrows quirking slightly. "Say what?" He said. "Ah talk like a hick from the backwoods, which is what ah am."

Kerry regarded him and smiled. "Exactly."

"Scuse me?"

"Exactly. You don't pretend to be anything other than what you are," Kerry said, after a brief pause.

The barrier lifted and Andy was distracted by having to drive past it.

Kerry seemed to realize there was more explanation needed. "When I first met Dar, what struck me about her was that she was so honest. It was really strange at first, you know? All my life I'd lived in a family and in an environment where everyone around me was all...part of a game."

Andy grunted.

"You had to think about what people said because it never really was what it sounded like," Kerry said. "There was always some kind of agenda."

"Dar ain't no innocent, rally," Andy said, as he paused before turning left to go south.

"Oh no, that's not what I meant at all. Dar has all kinds of strategy in that head and its always light years past where anyone's expecting. But when she says something, it's just what it means. There's no hidden message."

"Ah."

Kerry smiled. "At the beginning I would ask her, what did you mean by that, Dar? And she would look at me with this weird expression, like maybe she'd accidentally answered in a foreign language or something and she'd say, "What do you mean what do I mean?""

"She tells you straight," Andy said. "That is a true thing." He nodded. "No messin round."

"Its why people didn't, and still don't, like dealing with her. She never lets people down easy, you know? You ask a question and you better the hell want to hear the answer because that's what you're getting." She gazed out the window, a fond smile on her face. "It's a relief."

"Relief?"

"A relief," Kerry said. "I can ask her something like, hey, what do you think about me dying my hair purple? And she'll say, Kerry, you'd look really stupid with purple hair. I never have to worry about what she's thinking. It comes right out."

"Ain't no games."

"Ain't no games," Kerry echoed him. "You always know where you stand. So, when I met you, I knew where that came from because that's exactly what you're like too."

He smiled, just a little. "Got my ass in trouble mor'n once.," he demurred. "And Dar too, growing up."

"But it's such a blessing."

He digested that as he drove for a moment. "Ya'll really want to make your hair purple?" He finally asked, tentatively.

"No. I'm a faux anarchist. It was radical for me not to have bangs." Kerry said. "Did you not see my family's reaction to my tattoo?"

"Ah do remember that." Andy chuckled, as he pulled into the street where their office was and dodged the still rotting piles of garbage, and cars that had been swept into the fronts of buildings by the storm surge.

They went past a National Guard truck parked along the side of the road and two more behind it, then into their parking lot.

All of the debris had been moved out of the yard, and the trees that had been down, or dropped limbs, were trimmed back and looked relatively tidy. They parked and got out. "Lemme go get some of them boys," he said, "to get this dish from the back here."

He headed toward the front door, which was standing open, and Kerry heard the sound of a saw going from inside. She stood out by the truck for a moment and studied the building and then drew in a breath and exhaled. She felt the sweat start as she walked up the path.

The porch, with its guard post seemed unscathed, and the post itself was empty though there was a folded blanket inside it, and a water pot.

Unlike the previous day, when it had mostly smelled musty and moldy, today the inside smelled like freshly cut wood. She looked down the hall and saw two sawhorses set up, and caught the scent of bleach. There were four men standing at the end of the passage studying some paper.

Did she know them? Kerry scooted through and went out the back door into the central space, deferring the question for later. On the back porch, she stopped and looked around, a little startled at the activity.

Half the area had been turned into a construction workshop. They were using Hank's Humvee as a work platform and the single gas grill had turned into an outdoor kitchen, with no less than three larger grills in a semi-circle, including one that was set up as a wok.

"Ah! Hello, Kerry." Sasha popped up behind her and put down a cooler. "How are you? The kids invited me to move my kitchen here. Okay?"

"Um. Sure." Kerry sidestepped out of the way. "Must be safer for you here than in the street, right?"

"You got it, and got me customers here always hungry," Sasha said. "It was good, you know, with the army but they told me I shouldn't be out there early, late, nothing I might get kilt. You know? They were good, they were nice, liked my sandwiches, but not around at night."

"Got it." Kerry stuck her hands in the pockets of her shorts. "So, what's been going on around here, Sasha?"

"Here?" Sasha paused in the midst of removing a bag of chopped meat from her cooler. "You got the only good stuff going on the whole area. Guys are here fixing things.   Everything else on the block is dead as a fish." She put the bag on the makeshift worktable. "Nobody's coming back here, anytime soon."

No. Kerry had felt that too, as she walked from the parking lot into the building. The atmosphere of desolation and destruction were sobering. "Yeah, I talked to the insurance adjusters when they were out by the sailing club. They said the owners were just looking to cut losses and sell."

"Oh yes?" Sasha perked up and looked around at her. "You got their name? Maybe I buy. My brother can bring his fishing boat here." She looked speculatively at the back of the facility, where beyond it was the road and then the club. "Make a restaurant."

"That would be awesome," Kerry said, after a startled moment. "No one really used that sailing club anyway. Dar thought they were laundering money through it."

There was a knock against the doorframe behind them, and Kerry turned to find a National Guard lieutenant there, his regulation green cover in hand. She studied his face but didn't recognize him. "Hi, there."

"Hello, ma'am." Thus recognized, the lieutenant came forward. The patch on his chest said—Galahad—and Kerry got a sudden mental image of him on a horse with a sword. "My captain told me to come in here and have a chat with you all."

He was probably in his mid-thirties, and had a rusty red crew cut. "Sure," Kerry said. "What can we do for you, Lieutenant?"

"So, we were looking for a place to set up a command point. He thought maybe we could ask you if we could set up in your parking lot out there." Galahad pointed vaguely over his shoulder. "You're a little in the corner here, it's kind of a good spot."

National Guard camping in the front yard? "Would you be here all the time? As in, at night?"

He nodded. "Yes, ma'am, we've got a generator with us. They asked us to patrol down here. There's been a lot of criminal activity, with people breaking in and stuff."

"Absolutely you can take over the parking lot," Kerry said. "As you can see, I have a number of staff taking shelter here. It would ease my mind to have you and your team around."

Unexpectedly, he smiled, a wholehearted and genuine grin that creased his sunburned face and almost made Kerry blush. "That's awful nice of you, ma'am. We saw you all had a generator and all that here yourselves, and it kinda felt like it was a safe place for us to be too."

Andy arrived from his inspection. "Lo there," he greeted. "What all we got goin on here?" He came up to stand next to Kerry.

"Lieutenant Galahad, my father-in-law, Andrew Roberts." Kerry made introductions. "The lieutenant wants to set up camp in our parking lot, Dad," She said. "We seem to be strategic."

A darkly humorous expression appeared on Andy's face. "Do tell."

The guardsman took that at face value. "My captain asked me to come ovah here and ask if we could put our trucks and our tents over in that lot there, sir," he said. "We been asked to set up a command post. Patrol down here, and make sure folks don't get all crazy." He tilted his head a bit. "Crazier than has been, I mean."

"Ah see," Andy said. "That all right with you, kumquat?"

"Definitely," Kerry said. "The more guys guarding my peeps the better." She winked at the guardsman. "Will you tell them where to put things, Dad?"

"Surely." With a casual gesture, he indicated the entrance. "Let's get you boys all settled out there."

"You bet. Thank you, ma'am," the lieutenant said to Kerry, with a courteous duck of his head. "We really appreciate it." He put his hat back onto his head and adjusted it absolutely straight, then followed Andrew out and back through the building hall.

Kerry regarded them, then turned and regarded Sasha. "That is good, right?" She asked. "Having the National Guard outside?"

"More customers," Sasha said, nodding briskly. "Yes, very good. Soldiers always hungry." She went back to her bag of chopped meat and opened what appeared to be an art portfolio leaning against the table, removing a plastic cutting board and a neatly wrapped package of knives.

"You'll be a franchise by the time we're done here." Kerry abandoned her to the grill. She walked along the outside edge of the central space and headed toward the Humvee, and its makeshift woodshop. "Hell, we might end up a dozen franchises ourselves."

****

"Boy it's hot, isn't it, sir?"

Andy regarded the shorter man. "Always is round here," he said. "That part of where you all want to set up?" He pointed at the south end of the parking lot, where it angled to run along the side street. "Need to leave this here bit clear."

"Where that driveway is?" Lieutenant Galahad said. "That where you all are putting your cars at night? That's smart, sir. Don't leave nothing out here in the dark."

"Had them some trouble the other night," Andy said. "Got some of mah old Navy buddies bunking in there." He eyed the guardsman carefully. "Fellers who can take care of themselves," he clarified. "Don't mess round with them, you all."

The lieutenant nodded solemnly. "Yes, that's what my captain said, sir. He said he saw some veterans around here, and talked to one of them, named Pete last night." He glanced over his shoulder at the building. "It's your building, isn't it, sir? Has your name on it, and all?"

"Ain't," Andy said. "B'longs to mah kids. "Weren't going to let it get torn down, kids got a lot built into it."

They walked together across the lot, toward the front street where two large guard trucks idled, the back of one of them revealing a lashed down generator, and a dozen already sweating uniformed figures. The lieutenant lifted his hand and pumped his fist, and they paused as the trucks rumbled into gear and pulled into the lot.

"Totally get it," Galahad said, with a satisfied expression. "We got to take care of our own, right, sir?" He walked over to the lead truck as it arrived near the front edge of the lot, and guards piled out of the back of it and moved into the shade from the few still standing trees.

Andy watched them with a faintly furrowed brow, as the lieutenant pointed and indicated directions, outlining with the edge of one hand the entrance to the path that led through into the center of the building with care. The second truck arrived, and one of the doors opened, letting an older man emerge, dusting his dark cap off on the leg of his uniform pants before he set it on his head.

Andy stayed where he was, just watching. "That there's brass," he commented to himself. "Don't change no matter what the service."

The older man talked to the lieutenant for a minute, then he turned and headed toward where he was standing. Behind him, the soldiers started removing wood planks and boxes of supplies, quickly starting to cover the open ground.

It was steamy hot and overhead clouds started to gather on the fringe of the sky, and as he stood there waiting for the guard brass to make his way over, Andy saw a large open back truck with a battered city logo pull up next to one of the garbage piles.

Six men jumped out, all dark skinned, all drenched. They pulled on thick canvas and leather gloves as they approached the pile. One of them pointed toward the busy guardsmen, then waved at the piles and yelled an order. As he watched, they started loading the garbage, dripping and stinking, into the back of the truck.

"Good, they done got here." The captain walked up and looked over his shoulder. He watched the truck as well. "Bout time." He held a hand out to Andy. "Ah do believe your name is Roberts," he said. "Jerry Dodge. My family comes from the same part of Alabama as yours ah do think, down by Ozark."

"That's right." Andy took his hand and they gripped and released. "You all the feller that helped out one of mah kids t'other day, out west of here?"

The man smiled. "I sure am," he said with confident good cheer. "Spunky young lady. Might have figured she'd lead me on back here to this place." He indicated the office building behind where they were standing. "Recognized the name. Figured had to be the same's she told me."

"Yeap," Andy said. "Glad to have you all round here."

"Glad to have you all at our backs," Dodge said, frankly. "Gotta say we've been doing more policing than rescuing in these here parts. Didn't realize it was like that." He reviewed the setup. "Anyway, let me go get us all set. Have time for some coffee later?"

"Ah'm sure."

Dodge gave him a brisk nod, and headed back over to the trucks, and the busy soldiers. Andy exhaled as he watched him retreat. "Ah do believe," he said, to no one in particular. "That man done thinks he knows what ah think," he mused. "And he surely does not."

He turned and headed back to the office, silently shaking his head.

****

"All right, in here." Haribee pointed at a door, and then stiff-armed it open. He moved inside and held the door for her to enter.

Dar followed him inside the room and went to the table. He closed the door behind her to block out the noise of the hallway beyond, where rooms full of some kind of training were going on.

It was lunchtime and she was hungry. She took a seat behind the table and hoped this conversation was going to be brief, and that whoever drove her back to the air base knew where a Wendy's was.

Now that the demo was over, and apparently a success, her mind moved back to the challenges they faced back in Florida. She wasn't really in the mood to listen to some BS lecture from some government lackey.

Maybe he sensed that. Haribee slid into the chair opposite her and leaned on his elbows. His air of detached aloofness, for the moment a least, gone. "Okay," he said. "That was something."

Dar interlaced her fingers and cocked her head slightly to one side in a listening attitude. She decided the statement didn't require a response and more was to come.

She knew he'd been impressed. One look at his face when they took the helmet off had been enough to show that. Even Scott relaxed along with the rest of the techs in the room when he turned and stared at them all in silent, evident, astonishment.

Now he watched her with a sense of barely held interest and eagerness, totally at odds with his original attitude and so Dar wondered what it was that was on his mind.

"Know what I think?" Haribee said abruptly.

"I'm about to," Dar said, in a dry tone.

For whatever reason, that made him smile. "I think you surprised the hell out of me. That was all those gadget heads claimed it was. Congrats. That doesn't happen often around here," he said, briskly. "I'm more used to looking at loads of crap duct taped together with vague promises."

Dar nodded. "Tech's like that. Sometimes you can get away with it."

"Yeah?" He eyed her. "So, when was the last time you did that?" He waited, seeing her smile. "Don't answer. You don't have to. I had my office find out who the hell you were when they said you were flying in here for this. I figured it was either they wanted someone to explain it to me, or someone to take the blame if it flopped."

"True on both counts. Figured it was easier to show than tell."

"You have an interesting file on you. A lot of people in a lot of places have crossed paths and come away with all kinds of opinions that mostly boil down to you being a damned useful person if something needs to get done, so long as you agree it needs to get done."

Dar nodded again. "Fair assessment."

"It doesn't mention that much about the fact you're some kind of engineering genius," he continued. "You have to go to the US Patent office for that."

Really nothing to respond to for that, so Dar didn't. She just sat there in silence.

"You don't talk much."

She cleared her throat a little. "I haven't had any need to yet. You've only asked me one question and then told me not to answer it." Her eyes watched him alertly. "Glad you liked the demo. Assume that means it'll continue to be funded, great news for me. Anything else you want?"

"Uh huh." He laced his fingers together. "All prickles and edges. That's what someone said, and they were right. Lucky for me I don't care about that."

"Okay," Dar agreed amiably.

He cleared his throat. "I'm sure this'll do whatever it is these yokels are planning for it. Train new troops? Okay, whatever. Makes good press. No issues for me. Budget's not even that significant. But when I'm not running around collecting a paycheck for giving my opinion on government spending in the real world, I fund businesses." He paused. "Specifically, high tech startups."

Dar waited.

"I know a market when I see one," he said. "That gizmo, shined up and put out there, is a gaming gold plated winner. You must know that. "You do, don't you?"

"The thought." Dar leaned back in the chair and regarded him. "Had occurred to me, yes. In that, it would be interesting to see if someone wanted to market it. Easier for me to sell it to one of the big console makers."

"Why?" He asked. "Why lose out on all that money? For what, for royalties? Two bucks on every game? When you have it all? C'mon. It'll take years for any of those guys to adapt this to their system. They're too big. Got too much invested in their own platforms."

This was actually going in a direction Dar was totally not expecting. She hadn't bothered to deep research who would be at the demo, because at the time to her it hadn't really mattered. She'd been in the presence of government oversight hacks before.

True, though she also acknowledged silently, there hadn't been much time or access to data for her to check anything in the last couple of days. So, she pondered his speech a moment, considering the statement carefully, evaluating the potential truth in it.

There was truth, she decided. This was someone who knew what he was talking about in the same crisp, confident way that very often she herself did, and knowing it in herself. She could see it in him. Was it the whole truth? Partial truth?

Extremely good acting?

"Possibly," Dar finally said. "But it also means I don't have to invest in marketing and manufacturing. That's something my small company doesn't do, along with mass market distribution. We do custom solutions."

She paused, then an eyebrow twitched up. She waited to see where that would lead.

He nodded in comprehension. "You're right on with that. So, let's not waste time, either mine or yours. We've both got better places to be than a moldy conference room in some government rockpile."

He wrapped his hands together firmly and met her eyes. "So, here's the pitch," he said. "Let me bring this all together. I know people in both marketing and manufacturing. I'll build a shell company that we can use as an umbrella to make this thing."

Really unexpected. Dar drew in a somber breath and regarded him.

"We can't waste time. This is going to be hot," he said. "I know all about confidentiality. I also know one of these kids is going to spill this to his buddies over beer, if they haven't already."

He was probably right. Dar had considered that herself after seeing the demo, had mentioned it to Kerry in their conversation. "Probably," she acknowledged. "But we have a lot of things on our plate right now."

"Like?" he asked. "This?" He indicated the room.

"No. My office just got hit with a Category five hurricane," she said dryly. "It's in South Florida."

"Move it," Haribee said, at once. "You don't want to put anything like that down in that cesspit anyway. No talent down there. It's got lousy weather issues, lousy local politics. Only plus is no state income tax. Wait to retire there. Move it here. Plenty of good office space, a lot of talent coming out of the colleges, and..." He studied Dar with intent, impersonal regard. "You look like you enjoy the active outdoors. I love it here for that."

Dar thought about her encounter with the climbing wall that morning. "It's nice," she said. "And I have a major customer nearby." She looked around the room. "I'll think about it on the way home. I have to discuss it with my partner."

"Call them."

Dar felt a bit like she was in a new car showroom, she smiled briefly. "I can't." She shrugged a little. "There's no cell service in half the state. That's why Scott was having a nervous breakdown setting this up." She opened one hand and made a come-hither gesture at him with two fingers. "Gimme a number I can call you on and we'll talk."

He didn't want to. He wanted to close the deal. She saw it in the lines of his athletic body and the shifting motion. She held herself still and calm and projected an air of take it or leave it at him with what she hoped was the right mix of interest and caution.

It didn't really matter, in the long run. She wasn't going to commit to anything with him without discussing it with Kerry. No matter how much prospective cash was on the table.

Maybe he knew that. He reached into his back pocket and pulled out a very thin billfold. He removed a card from it and tossed it over the table at her. "Don't waste time," he said. "I'd like to pull this together fast for a next Christmas campaign."

"All right." Dar picked up the card. "Maybe I can send a team to work out here when I get back. They'd probably like the break from heat and rain, and they can get Scott's checkpoints nailed down." She paused. "And start up this new project."

Haribee grinned. "That's the ticket." He slapped the table with his hand and stood up. "Today's been a worthwhile day for me, Roberts. Thank you. I don't get many." He turned with no further speech and left the room at a brisk walk. He left behind the faint scent of linen and men's cologne.

Dar glanced at the card, then stuck it in her back pocket with a faint shake of her head. "Oh boy," she muttered, into the empty room. "Has been a day hasn't it."

She contemplated going in search of Scott, but just as that thought made her stand up, the door opened and he entered. He wore an expression of enormous relief on his face, a bubbly jubilance showing in his motions.

"He's really happy," Scott said. "Thanks, Dar. It was great." He flopped down into the chair Haribee had just vacated. "I was kind of surprised, you know? That he wanted to get into the rig. That was bold of you to ask him."

"Fastest way." Dar folded her arms. "Seemed like a sharp guy. I wasn't in the mood for a dog and pony."

"He's a..." Scott paused. "He's tough. One of those guys who's the smartest guy in the room all the time. If he wants your opinion, he'll give you one. That kind." He eyed Dar. "But he liked you."

"Mm." Dar's pale eyes twinkled just a little. "I've been accused of being that kind myself y'know," she said, but in a mild tone. "So maybe it takes one to know one."

Scott took a breath, then stopped, looking uncertainly at her.

"You all would have done fine without me," Dar reassured him. "All he needed to do was see it. Glad he thought it was worthwhile. He's not going to cut your funding." She started over to grab her bag. "Can I get a ride back now? I'm sure ten thousand things have gone to crap back home while I've been out here enjoying having electricity and Internet."

"Take you myself," Scott said. "I called the base, they said they've got something going that direction in about two hours. Time for lunch?" He added, in a hopeful tone. "Got a little place on the way that's got great barbeque."

"Sure." Dar got her backpack on and slid the strap of her overnight bag over her shoulder. "Lead on."

"No definitely, he's happy." Scott opened the door for her and followed her outside into one of the many, similar hallways with their cryptic wall plates and school color painted walls. "He greenlit us to go forward. The team's over the moon!"

They walked down the long passageway and out the front entrance, emerging into a beautiful early autumn day that featured clear blue skies and dry, sweet smelling air. "Nice day," Dar said as they walked across the pavement toward the parking.

"Yeah it is. Too bad you can't stay a few days, gonna be great weather over the weekend." Scott pulled his keys out of his pocket. "My buddies are trying to get me out to do Pikes Peak. Now that we got good news, I might be talked into it."

Dar got into the passenger seat of his SUV and set her bag and backpack down between her feet. "Lot of folks do stuff outdoors here I guess."

"Sure. We've got a little of everything here. Hiking, fishing, rafting, hunting, you name it." He glanced at her, as he paused before turning out onto the main road. "Skiing, kayaking, you know." He turned and headed off down the road. "Rock climbing."

Dar spent a brief moment thinking about that. "That lodge has a climbing wall in their gym."

"Oh, it does. A lot of folks belong to that place. They have tournaments sometimes. It's a great wall," Scott said. "Did you try it?"

"Yeah," Dar murmured. "I noticed it the last time I was here, so I gave it a go this morning." She regarded the passing scenery. "Pretty entertaining."

"Guess there's not a lot of that down by you?" Scott hazarded.

"No mountains, no. I suppose some gyms have walls," Dar said. "Mostly water sports down there. Deep sea fishing, surfing, wave boarding, diving, that kind of thing." She paused thoughtfully. "I spend a lot of time in or on the water. I'm a scuba diver."

"Oh yeah?" Scott said, in a surprised tone. "You have a boat?"

"I do." Dar folded her arms over her chest. "Matter of fact that's what I used to get our server stack back up and running after the storm came through. Brought them over to where I live, where there were generators and a satellite truck."

"Wow." Scott glanced quickly at her, then at the road. "On a boat? That sounds crazy."

"It was." Dar regarded the scenery out the window, and the towering mountains in the distance. "But you do what you need to do in that kind of circumstance."

They were both silent as Scott turned and headed off on a side road heading north. "What was it like being in that storm?" He asked suddenly. "I saw the news reports, but most of what they showed just looked like a big wet mess."

"It was a big wet mess. But it also came with hundred and sixty knot winds," Dar said. "It's a gigantic tornado, just slow. It's coming at you at maybe ten, maybe six, maybe 20 miles per hour and you see it coming for days. It's literally like being in a slow-motion train wreck."

"Oh, Lord!"

"Then when it finally gets to you there' a lot of wind, it's loud," Dar continued. "Things are breaking and getting thrown around all over the place. Then if you're in direct path, you get into the eye and the wind stops and it's very low pressure. You feel your ears pop and all that."

"And then the wind starts coming from the other direction when you come out of the eye, and it's loud and full of banging and roaring again. Can last for an hour, maybe more coming right over you. If you're lucky you're in a place that's built for it." She sighed. "If not, you can get your roof pulled off and the walls blown out around you, or twelve feet of water blast through your yard."

"Why in the hell did you stay there?" Scott spluttered. "If you can see it coming, why not just leave?"

Why? That really was a damn good question. So many of her neighbors hadn't. But some had. They'd all of them, all of the people who lived on that island had the choice, the means, the ability to just leave and go somewhere else, and watch, from afar.

She and Kerry could have taken the programming team and come here. She could have challenged the programmers to wall climbing efforts after they'd finished coding for the day. They could have taken hikes and just watched CNN like the rest of the country had.

Her parents could have taken their boat, with its oversized engines, and gone pretty much anywhere.

Why did they stay? It hadn't even been a question in her mind until they were in the middle of it and they all realized just how ridiculous it was that they hadn't decided to go elsewhere.

"Good question," Dar finally said. "I don't really know." They pulled into the lot of a wood and stone building that featured a long shed behind it full of split logs and a steady plume of smoke curling from a large pit in the back corner.

"Seems crazy." Scott reached ahead of her to open the door to the restaurant. "I saw those news interviews. My goodness! People wading through the water, all those people dead! They should have all left!"

Dar sighed. "It's not that simple." She followed him over to the ordering counter. "Some people can't. The shelters can't handle their needs. Some want to stay with their pets."

"Pets?"

"Dogs and cats, and potbelly pigs and goldfish and whatever." Dar glanced at the board. "Rack of ribs and a root beer." She turned to Scott. "Some have no cars, no way of getting anywhere." She paused. "I, apparently, am just a stubborn idiot who decided to stay in my house on an island on the edge of the Atlantic."

"My goodness."

They took their trays and claimed a wooden benched table, with simple wooden poles holding up rolls of paper towels and squeeze bottles full of four different kinds of barbeque sauce. Scott promptly picked up two of them and squirted them in tandem on his chicken.

He hummed under his breath. "First time in weeks I can eat in peace and not have a stomachache," he said. "Damn I'm glad we're past that."

Dar picked up a rib and took a bite, finding it well cooked and tasty, even without the lurid mixture of sauces that Scott was now also applying to his French fries. "Those guys really hassle you?"

He put down the sauce and picked up a drumstick, twisting it free of the half chicken he'd ordered. "You don't get much chance, in our area, to get on a project that gets you in the spotlight, y'know? Well, sure, y'know." He took a bite of the chicken and chewed it. "If he'd tanked it, and he could have, we'd all go back to the grind and carry that with us. You know, there goes that guy that was on that stupid killed dead project."

Dar did know. "Yeah, I get it," she said. "I'm glad it worked out the way it did. It was a win for us too. Now we can start on the next set of deliverables."

Scott looked around, but it was early, and there weren't many other people in the place yet. "Might go even faster. I got a call from my boss not ten minutes after we were done in there. They want to show this off for the quarterly video show. I gotta make a speech."

He grinned, almost maniacally at her. "I can't wait to send a copy to my mom."

If they did end up moving some folks out here, Dar decided as she toasted him with her rib and a wink. She would pitch the takeover of the whole team as an outsource. Would they want to leave the military and come work for her?

She finished the rib and took a sip of her root beer. Perhaps they would.

****

Kerry tipped her head back and watched as one of the LAN techs, wearing a harness, stretched his arms up as high as they would go and pushed the dish they'd brought up as near the top of the metal pole strapped to the side of the building as he could.

"We're going to have to ground that to earth," another of the LAN techs said to Kerry. "Lightning hits it and it'll end up right in the server room."

"We don't want that," Kerry murmured. "Though right now there aren't any servers in there, or anything else really."

"No, ma'am, just the racks. We got everything else out of there, but there's a lot of copper in the floor still, and if someone was in there it'd light em up."

"Well, that's what that second line is, the ground, so we should be covered." Kerry paused. "Miguel, be careful!"

"Yes, ma'am," Miguel called down, as he kept the dish at the desired height while he tightened the bolts with a wrench. "I'm tied in good here!"

"Okay got it tight," Miguel called down. "I'm gonna throw the cable down." He stuck the wrench in his back pocket and edged over along the tile roof to where the coil of thickly rubber coated strands were lying.

He nudged them with his foot and held onto the pole with one hand to keep his balance. He booted the coil off the roof and it tumbled down the inner side of the building. Then he went over to a second coil, this one of bare metal, and booted that off as well. "There's the ground!"

"Got it!" The second LAN tech yelled up. "I'm gonna run it into that window."

Pete smoothed the ground along the pole. "I got this," he said. "Found a railway spike we can use for it. I'll weld it."

"How's the roof look, Miguel?" Kerry shaded her eyes and watched him. "Still look okay up there?"

Miguel went up several steps to the peak and stood there with a foot braced on either side. "There's still those couple broken tiles," he said after a minute. "Looks okay otherwise. New skylights look good."

"Good job!" Carlos called out, from his position. "You all done?"

"I'm gonna hang out here in case we need to adjust the dish," Miguel called back and sat down on the peak to let his legs sprawl out along the slope. "Gonna be a nice sunset, with those clouds."

Kerry paused and looked around. It already was a little brighter inside, with the replacement of the two big skylights over the stairwells, that no longer had black tarps pasted over them. Now the holes in the roof were filled with square, sturdy aluminum and glass coverings, the inside edge showing fresh caulking still in need of paint.

She smelled the freshness of it. The tang of uncovered wood and the chemical scent of the caulk. As she walked along the hall, the surface of the floors were shades lighter, a sanding machine standing now silent in the corner near the stairs.

"Y'know," one of the veterans, whose name she'd heard but forgotten, came over, wrapping a cable around one arm. "You should leave these floors alone."

Kerry regarded him. "Not sand them?" She asked.

He shook his head. "Sand n'reseal em." He gazed at the wood. "Don't put no carpet back on it. Nice grain."

Kerry studied the floor. "Would it sound stupid to you for me to say I can't because I have dogs here that would slide on it?"

He didn't answer for a long minute. Finally, he cleared his throat. "No that don't sound stupid," he said. "Just never something I'd think of right off." He regarded her with bright, hazel eyes. "It's just pretty wood."

"It's beautiful," Kerry agreed, with a smile. "Maybe we can put down a central piece of carpet and leave both sides   natural."

"Jute maybe," he replied thoughtfully. "Natural and could be inset like. Look nice too."

Jute. "I'll look into that." Kerry spotted the LAN tech pop his head into the hallway and wave at her, at the same time memory belatedly surfaced. "Thanks, Bill," she said. "It's a great idea."

He lifted his hand in acknowledgement and moved off, slinging the cable he'd coiled over the sanding machine and walked out the door into the central area. Kerry stood in the empty hall for a moment, and then walked along it to the inside room where the radio was.

Inside, the LAN tech was adjusting the phone precisely on top of the switch. He turned as he heard Kerry enter. "I powered up the switch and its booting." He went over to the window and began to route the cable down the wall.

"Thanks, Mike." Kerry regarded the device. "No way we nailed the point-to-point on the first go. That's a long distance."

"It is," Mike agreed. "But it's pointed in the right general direction anyway." He tacked down the last bit of cable. "Let me get my laptop and see if I can ping the other side." He trotted out. "Get that to start anyway."

Kerry went to the window and leaned on the sill, the air from the courtyard brushing against her, a warm humid mixture of construction and humanity and the sharp bite of the spices Sasha was using in her wok.

Across the way she saw Andy standing in the shade of the building, arms crossed, talking to Pete, who had his welding helmet on with the shield tipped up, the welding wand clasped in one hand as it cooled.

A brief breeze brought her the scent of it, the odd, spicy smell of the welding and from beyond that a hint of the sea.

"Okay, let me connect up." Mike returned and put a laptop down on the table, plugging a console cable into the switch. "Is Ms. Roberts coming back soon?"

"On her way right now," Kerry said. "I'm about to head out to the airport to get her." Kerry remained leaning on the windowsill. "You need her for something?"

"No, ma'am. Mark was just asking before he left." Mike started typing into the keyboard. "What IP... oh there it is." He rattled the soft touch keys. "Wait, it needs a gateway, so let me just..."

The phone rang and startled them both. Kerry actually jumped. "What the..."

They stared at the phone that continued to ring, until Kerry finally reached over and picked it up. "Hello?" She answered tentatively. "Kerry here."

"Ah hah!" A voice said in triumph. "They were right, how bout that!"

"Hey, Angela." Kerry gathered her wits. "I guess it's working?"

"Holy crap." Mike regarded his screen. "Yeah, it's pinging clean!" He glanced at the window. "That's a freaking miracle from Baby Jesus right there."

"No kidding," Kerry muttered.

"The kids saw something in something register or something," Angela told her. "And they said the thing you put up was probably up, and they were right!" Angela sounded triumphantly pleased. "So, this is great! We can talk to you guys!"

"I guess you can." Kerry and Mike exchanged bemused looks. "Well that's great. How's it going over there? I was about to head out to the airport to pick up Dar."

"Oh great!" Angela responded. "Now what did that remind me of... what?" She muffled the receiver briefly. "Oh right! Sure, so that guy came back here, you know? The guy from yesterday? With the thing, whatever it was, the boss did?"

Kerry stared at the phone in bewilderment. "Um... what?"

"That guy. The big guy, with the attitude."

"That entire island is full of big guys with attitude."

"Yeah, sure, but it was that one guy and he sent those kids over, and the boss did something for them with that box."

"Oh. The governor's contractor guy," Kerry said. "What did he want?"

"Dunno, said he wanted to talk to the boss. I told him she was out of town. He started cursing at me. Mrs. R ran him out of here. But he said he was gonna come back. Anyway, we also heard from the drug guy, and they want to talk to you."

Kerry sighed. "Okay, do me a favor and call the Pharma guys back. Tell them I'll call them as soon as I get back from the airport." She checked her watch again. "I gotta go. Glad this thing's working, give it a ring if anything else happens, and hopefully someone'll hear it and answer."

"No problem. What about the governor's guy?"

"Tell him next time it's lucky its only my mother-in-law chasing him not my mother, the Senator," Kerry said, firmly. "We'll talk to him when we get back there."

"Got it. See ya later, Kerry."

Kerry put the phone down. "What number is this phone?" she asked. "Please don't tell me it's mine."

"No no no...It's a spare," Mike said. "I configured it to use the one we had in the server room. Nobody knows it except HPE and CenturyLink. The guys probably just saw it register in the online portal and told her which one it was. It's a dial in direct, though. You can call it."

"More importantly, you all can dial out from it," Kerry said.

He nodded briskly. "Oh yeah, for sure now, that it sees the portal. You know, maybe I can talk to Mayte and we can add a survivable gateway here for the next time this crazy stuff happens."

Kerry regarded him. "That's not a bad idea," she said, after a long pause. "But I'm pretty sure we have a long list of things to make better for next time, like alternate power sources and a satellite dish on the roof."

Mike looked at her. "Mark was saying maybe we'd all move, like up to Melbourne or... wherever. You think we will?" he asked. "I know he and Barb headed up to that office the support team's at."

"We'll do what we have to in order to keep the business moving forward. I don't' know..." Kerry hesitated. "I'm not sure what we'll do long-term because I know Dar's pretty attached to this area."

He nodded again. "I'm kind of a nomad, doesn't matter to me but I know a lot of folks here have a lot of family around and kids in school and all that stuff."

"Yeah, I know." Kerry sighed. "Okay, let me figure all that out when we get back. I don't want Dar hanging around at that airport too long, someone'll grab her and she'll be rewiring that control tower if I don't pick her up."

Mike scribbled something on a pad. "This UPS battery here'll last to power this switch until they boot the generator," he said. "And that'll recharge it then. Sound okay?" He looked up at Kerry. "We took over the tech support room and moved the desks around. Those cots Mr. R brought over were great."

Kerry rested her hands on the back of the chair he was sitting on. "Is your family okay, Mike? I think I missed asking you yesterday."

He smiled at her. "My family's in Iowa. So yeah I'm sure they're fine," he said. "It's just me here. I moved down cause I was going out with a girl who ended up going out with someone else."

He scratched his nose, which had freckles over the surface of the skin. "I actually live in a duplex in Doral. It did fine, but man it's boring when you ain't got nothing to do but look at the paint peel, you know?"

"Got it." Kerry said. "I was by myself when I moved down here at first too. I would have probably cleaned my apartment six dozen times by now if I was still where I was then," she said. "Anyway, I'll be back in an hour. Tell anyone looking for me where I went."

"Yes, ma'am," he said cheerfully. "We got some Korean barbeque on tap for tonight. One of Carlos' buddy's a cook at Shizo's down on Brickell. He got here this morning and hooked up with Sasha." He got up and left the phone with its small display sitting on top of the switch. "He brought a barrel of kimchee with him."

"Oh boy." Kerry followed him out of the room and into the hall. "Glad we got the National Guard at the front door cause the smell of all that's going to attract everyone for five square miles."

"It's true," Mike said. "It's yummy."

She went outside and down the front sidewalk, the view toward the main street now blocked by tents and trucks all painted Army green. Along with the buzzing rumble of a large, truck mounted generator.

The Guard had made sure there was a clear path from the front of the parking lot out to the street, but she noticed that they had also planted a small tent on the far side of the driveway as though including that path under their watch.

Kerry got into the driver's seat of the truck and moved it up so she could reach the pedals. She started up the engine and backed out of the lot. The street, she noted as she pulled out past the Guard encampment had been cleared of garbage, and the soldiers had set up barriers around their tents and trucks and had mounted a watch.

The young man standing there, rifle in hand, waved at her as she turned.

Kerry waved back, then paused and rolled down the window, leaning her arm on the warm surface as he walked over. "Hi."

"Hello, ma'am," the soldier greeted her, his crew cut under a green peaked cap, and his eyes hidden behind sunglasses as hers were. "You going for the day?"

"No," Kerry said. "I'm going over to the airport to pick someone up. Are you all..."?

"We're going to be here all night," The soldier said. "We took down all the license plates back in that lot there, so they'll be let in if they come and go. No problem, ma'am, and we know to clear anyone else with the folks inside. All good."

"Thanks."

The guard glanced around. "Would you like one of us to go with you, ma'am? To the airport? There's some dangerous roads between here and there, though you look like you've got good clearance with this vehicle."

Kerry smiled. "I think I'll be okay, long as I get on with it before it gets dark. See you in a bit. I think they're cooking barbeque in there." She indicated the office building. "I'm sure you all are invited."

"We smell it, ma'am." The soldier grinned. "Don't you worry." He gave her a thumbs up, and Kerry returned it, then she rolled up the window and started out along the street, heading for the highway.

****

The cargo flight landed with a jarring bounce, and Dar cautiously opened one eye as she heard the big engines going into reverse, ready for the noisy, bouncing flight to end.

"Sorry about that," the pilot in the seat ahead of her said. "We're pretty heavy."

"No problem." Dar opened her other eye and watched the airfield flash past out the front window of the C-17 Globemaster, just glad to be on the ground again.

She was the fourth person in a four-person cockpit, the two pilots busy ahead of her and the loadmaster relaxed in his seat as he waited to start the process of unloading the full load of relief supplies behind them.

It was a rough and cramped ride. The spare seat not really intended for someone of her height. She couldn't wait to stand up and get out of it, though she'd found the inside of the cockpit interesting and enjoyed watching the process of flying the plane.

But now it was near sunset. The big cargo craft taxied off the long runway and rumbled toward one of the huge hangars where lines of trucks stood by. Two large portable pole lights were already on to light the area for work.

"Where are we staying overnight?" The copilot asked. "Not in a tent, are we? It's still ninety some degrees out there and it's almost night."

"They got power in there," the pilot pointed at the airport, "Ops told me they got bunks for us, and a mess." He steered the big plane up to a mark on the pavement, and then shut down the engines. "There we go. Hope it wasn't too bad a ride for you, ma'am."

"Nah." Dar unbuckled the four-point harness holding her to the seat. "I've had worse. That was a lot of rough weather though."

"Out flow from that damn storm." The pilot shook his head. "Big mess. They still don't' have power here and I heard they may not for weeks! he said. "Jesus!"

"Probably not." Dar got up and ducked through the door and climbed down the steel stairs that dropped to the bottom of the deck and gave access to the entrance hatch.

With the engines off it was already getting hot. She retrieved her overnight bag and laptop from the bin near the door and waited for the pilot to come down to open it up. "Thanks for the ride."

The pilot came over to stand next to her. "No problem. Charlie, run the checklists willya?" he called up over his shoulder. "I'm gonna let our passenger out."

"Doin it," the copilot called from the cockpit. "Look out, back door's cranking."

There was a lot of noise around them suddenly, the cargo hatch at the rear of the plane opening up and its ramp grinding groundward. The door near the cockpit opened up with a crinkly pop that came with a rush of damp, hot, Jet scented air.

The pilot swung the door downward and extended the steps built into it and walked it down to the ground. He pulled sunglasses out from his pocket and put them on as he peered into the setting sunlight. "Nice sky."

Dar climbed down after him and followed as he walked along a marked path along the planes parking position. She exchanged nods with the technicians and unloaders who came to swarm over the C-17.

"You expecting to be met here, ma'am?" the pilot asked, as the sound of a helicopter landing clattered past them. "They're not really operating."

"Yes, and I know," Dar said. "I have someone picking me up."

"Well, that's good. I'm glad you didn't expect a taxi or something. I was here overnight day before yesterday and nothing's working around here."

"That's true." Dar waited for him to open the door that would let them into the concourse and off the tarmac. "I've got it from here," Dar said. "Thanks again." She shouldered her bag and took a turn down another hallway, heading toward the civilian part of the airport.

The pilot stopped, then he shrugged. "Okay, g'bye." He waved. "Guess you know what you're doing." He shook his head and went in the opposite direction.

Dar ignored the comment. She let her sense of direction take over and maneuvered through the winding halls, passed offices and people in uniforms with an air of determination that made them quickly step out of her way and not ask her any questions.

She got through the last door and then she was back in the darkness of the airport proper. Still full of mold and mildew. She thought she might have seen a rat scuttling along as she went through the silent security tables in the gloom and headed for the front doors to the terminal. She heard the sound of leaks dripping on the floor just in time to slow down and not slip and fall on her ass.

The water on the floor felt slimy, and smelled worse, and Dar put a hand out to keep her balance as she moved from the floor to the carpet. She then walked along the wall full of boarded up windows until she came to one of the sliding glass sets of entrance doors.

They were locked. She set her overnight bag down on the terrazzo, she listened to the whining clunks as the activators in the floor pads tried to open the doors, separating them in the center just slightly.

Hmm. She got her fingertips around the edge of one of the sliding doors and hauled back on it. She got it partly open and set off an alarm. "Crap." She winced at the loud siren that made her ears buzz, unable to budge the glass any farther.

"Stop! Hold it right there!" A loud, male voice sounded at a distance behind her. "Stop! Hey! Who are you?"

"Nope, not today." Dar squeezed through the partial opening with a determined grunt, yanking her bag along after her as she emerged into the overcast dusk. She ignored the footsteps and the yells behind her as she got to the curb and away from the front of the building.

She looked up and down the drop off area, dirty concrete lit in lurid orange pink and full of powerless shadows. The lane in front of her was crowded with emergency trucks and vans and the military.

There was really no reason for her to confidently expect Kerry to be there but at the end of the drive, behind the parked government cars and security vehicles, engine idling, there was her truck and she turned and headed for it, with a grin of relief.

"Stop!" Behind her she heard the crack of the door opening all the way and leather soled shoes against the concrete. "Hey!"

Kerry put the truck in gear and came rocketing forward. She nearly sideswiped one of the security vans as she intercepted Dar's path and rode the wheels up onto the pavement. She then turned on the high beam lights to blast them into the eyes of the chasing guards.

Dar reached the truck and opened the door as the guards came to a halt. They threw their hands up and yelled in outrage.

"Just go," Dar said as she slid in. "No going back inside that building tonight for me."

"No problem, hon." Kerry put hammer down and rumbled over the road divider and the guards dodged out of her way as she headed down the wrong way entry. "It's been that kind of day. Hang on."

"Hanging." Dar grabbed the door strap as they zoomed down the on-ramp and hoped they weren't going to come face to face with a squad of National Guard coming in the opposite direction. She held her breath until they reached the bottom of the ramp.

Kerry stolidly went up and over the divider again as she had the day before and they bumped down onto the luggage level and a clear path out of the airport. "At least it was clear yesterday." She swerved around the cars and trucks parked there for safety, and then onto the exit road leading east.

"Oh yeah." Dar turned and shoved her bag into the back seat. "Good job."

"Good job picking this truck instead of a sports car, hon." Kerry changed lanes and headed off onto 836. She waited until she was on the highway, then glanced to her right. "How was the flight?"

"About as good as a jump seat in a cargo plane would be." Dar shifted the seat backward and extended her legs. "What's up here?"

Kerry exhaled. "What isn't? Well, mostly nothing is actually, except we got the point-to- point link up just before I came out to pick you up."

"Nice," Dar said. "Good work. That's a long throw." She rested her head against her fist. "Got an email I managed to read overnight from the guys at Pharma. They want to talk about the contract."

"They called the cottage," Kerry said. "I figured whatever it was could wait for you to get back. Didn't sound promising."

"No." Dar sighed. "I should have checked that code. They probably want to cancel."

Kerry reached over to pat her on the leg. "Is what it is, hon. Everyone did the best they could. If that guy doesn't get what we're going through here he's not worth it as a customer." She glanced to the left as they crossed over I-95 and spotted a rolling blockade full of police lights and sirens to stop traffic. "Uh oh."

"That's not for us is it?" Dar eyed it drolly. "I didn't figure they could get that in place in that short a time."

"And on the wrong highway. No. Probably some government derp," Kerry said. "Which reminds me, your friend from the other night wants more favors."

"Jackass."

"Your mother went after him. He was being mean to the staff."

Dar covered her eyes.

"Toldja, it's been one of those days." Kerry had to smile regardless. "But you said the demo went well?" She watched Dar out of her peripheral vision and saw her shift and half turn, a hint of a grin tugging at the corners of her lips. "How well?"

"It went well," Dar said. "I stuck the helmet on the government bean counter's head."

"Oh, Dar." Kerry started laughing. "Was that nice?"

"Hey, he liked it." Dar chuckled. "More to the point, he greenlit them moving forward. So that contract's safe, at least."

"Yes!" Kerry danced a little in her seat.

"Even more to the point, he's an angel investor. Interested in taking the concept and putting it into a gaming rig." Kerry turned to look at her, jaw dropping slightly. "Ah ah ah. Eyes on the road. Even if we're the only ones on it."

Kerry jerked her attention back to the highway. "Holy bananas, Dar!" she blurted. "Are you serious?"

"I am. Let's wait till we stop so I can tell you all the gory details without the risk of us running off the road." Dar watched the darkness creep over the landscape, tiny islands of light in isolated spots. And oddly, one section of the highway lights coming on for about a block length. "Any chance of a Kahlua milkshake?"

Kerry moved right to the offramp that would take them down to ground level. "Well. It's possible by the time we get back to the office, they'll be making and selling Kahlua milkshakes, so you could be in luck."

"Huh?"

****

It was almost dark, the low, lingering dusk of the subtropics that threw everything into shadows by the time they got back to the street where the office was.

"What the hell?" Dar sat up as they turned the corner.

"Oh." Kerry observed the sulphur lights that illuminated the National Guard camp. "My friends from the other day needed a place to set up station. I figured having the guard outside our door wasn't a bad thing."

"Does the guard know not to mess with my dad and his friends?" Dar asked, in a quizzical tone. "That could get exciting. Not in a good way."

"Yes, they do," Kerry reassured her. "They're being very nice and asked permission to park in our lot, which we all know they had no real reason to ask for."

"True."

They pulled into the parking lot and paused as Kerry rolled down the window and waved at the guard. The same tow-headed man who'd been there when she'd left. He waved back and gave them both an easy grin and a thumbs up.

"Well." Dar sat back and folded her arms as they pulled past the encampment and into the back half of the lot. "Okay."

The office building had lights showing in multiple windows, and as they parked and opened the door, the sound of generators rumbled in counterpoint to some far-off thunder.

There was a brief snatch of music on the air, and the onshore breeze also brought the smell of spices and cooking meat. "Something smells good," Dar commented. "Are we stuck here tonight? The ferry probably stopped running."

"I'll call over there when we get inside," Kerry said. "I have no idea what the rules are today, since a whole crapload of some kind of brass went off the island this morning. I don't figure they'll force the governor to sleep in a shelter, but hey. You never know."

They walked side by side up the sidewalk. "They clean up here?" Dar looked around. "That big pile of debris is gone."

"They did. I guess they started that part going here in the city."

The door to the office was open to allow the breeze in. The lights were on at the receptionist's desk, and in the conference room and as they entered the office, they could hear many voices through the open center door into the courtyard.

Kerry glanced at Dar, who looked slightly bewildered. "There's a lot of people here, hon. Don't freak out."

"Our people?" Dar asked, a trifle uncertainly.

"Our people, some people we know that aren't our people, some people we know from the area, some people I don't know, but I think your dad does, and some people who just showed up to work on the office," Kerry said. "Like I said, it's been a day."

"Um."

"Just go with it. One of them is Sasha, and she brought her kitchen." Kerry gently nudged her. "And I'm hungry."

"Sasha from the Pho place down the road?"

"That Sasha, yes, and some friend of Carlos who's a Korean chef."

"Oh." Dar paused for thought. "Yum."

****

They ended up carrying sturdy Chinet paper plates upstairs into Dar's office, along with cups of Thai iced coffee. "Put those down here," Dar said. "Lemme go get a light."

Kerry set her plate and cup down on Dar's desk and then she went over to the window and opened up the shutters that had blown shut from a random gust of wind. It allowed a breeze to come in and she sat down on the bench seat to look outside for a moment and enjoy that.

Kerry turned at the sound of Dar's footsteps and watched her come back in with a roughly teardrop shaped candle casting a warm golden glow up to highlight her face. "That's a nice candle."

Dar came over and set it down on the windowsill. It had a glass roundel that blocked the wind and lit up the small area nicely. "It's a hurricane candle," she said. "Appropriate."

"Is it really?" Kerry inspected it, while Dar went over and retrieved their dinner. She brought the plates over and then returned for the cups.

"It's designed specifically for hurricanes?" Kerry asked.

"Not really, no." Dar handed her a cup and then sat down next to her and extended her legs across the floor and crossing her ankles. "But the sides keep the breeze from blowing the candle out." She took a forkful of the spicy scented mixture on her plate and chewed it. "Mm," she said, after a pause. "That's good."

"Sasha was talking about buying the sailing club and turning it into a restaurant," Kerry said. "I thought that sounded like a great idea. She really can cook."

"She can," Dar said. She glanced over her shoulder out the window toward the shore. "That'd be kind of awesome. "

"I told her that," Kerry said. "Meantime, I told her she's welcome to hang out here."

"Ready made customers, with the Guard here."

"That's what she said."

Dar ate a few more forkfuls. "I'm still a little weirded out by how full of people this building is. I'm not sure I get it," she said. "I mean... I'm glad, stuff's getting fixed but..." She looked over her other shoulder at the inside of the building and shook her head.

"It's weird," Kerry said.

"It's weird."

"I talked to Zoe today, about it. You know, I wasn't really that cool with her hanging out here overnight. But she told me something interesting."

"Mm?" Dar leaned back against the windowsill and watched Kerry's expression in the candlelight, seeing some tired introspection there. "This is her tribe." She guessed after a moment's quiet pause.

Kerry looked up, a trifle startled and their eyes met. "She didn't say that but... "She paused. "She meant that I think. Yeah. I mean, she has... she only has work in common with some of the people here and nothing in common with some of the people here, but she feels safe."

Dar chewed for a minute in reflective silence. "Well." She took a sip of the iced coffee and swallowed the spicy Korean pork mixture. "Carlos and his gang are here, and Dad and his guys. It's safer here than almost anywhere, and now we got the guard over there."

"True, but it wasn't that." Kerry forked up some of the barbeque. "She said at the shelter, everyone was just angry. Just bitching, you know?"

"Well." Dar moved her shoulders in a slight shrug. "It's understandable."

"Yeah sure, I would be too. But here they're not. It's not comfortable, but everyone is just sort of...I don't know. It feels like safe shelter to them," Kerry said. "I'm flattered. I mean, people just show up here with useful skills and building materials and start rebuilding our walls, you know?"

"I'm sure they're expecting to get paid." Dar's eyes twinkled a little. "Let's not get crazy altruistic."

"No, I know." Kerry chuckled softly. "I don't know. It just touched me, seeing that," she said, in a wistful tone. "I talked to Maria this morning, from the cottage. Tomas is doing well. Now her worry is, if they release him, what she's going to do. They can't live in that house."

"Not with him in a cast in any case," Dar said. "Can we send them up to Melbourne?"

"She doesn't want to go. I asked her. She's got a lot of family down here, and they've been visiting, but they're all in shelters."

"Hmm. So I guess going to Colorado would be out then," Dar mused. "She could set up the satellite office they asked me for when I was there."

"What?" Kerry cocked her head a little to one side, intrigued rather than startled. "By the base?"

Dar cleared her throat a little. "The angel investor lives there. He suggested we move the company there. Said it had good office space and a good local workforce." She set her now empty plate down and hiked a knee up, lacing her fingers together around it. "Thinks he can pull together the resources to launch this thing and market it in time for next Christmas."

Kerry studied her face intently. "Would you actually do that?"

"Would we actually do that?" Dar countered. "This is our company, not mine."

Kerry put her hand out and touched Dar's arm. "Didn't mean it that way," she said. "I was just remembering asking you if we'd consider moving and you were right away, like no way."

It was odd, and intensely intimate, this candlelit conversation, as though the darkness provided an unseen clarity.

"I know I said that. But was that me just being an asshole?" Dar asked, moving her head in silent conciliation. "What makes sense, Ker? If this guy can deliver what he says he can, that takes this to a whole other level."

Did that matter to them? Kerry put her plate down on top of Dar's and set her ice coffee down next to it. "That must have been some change you made." She shifted the conversation slightly. "We should look at what all our options are, sweetheart. If that's the right thing to do, we'll know."

Dar smiled in response, her body relaxing. "It was one of those things where after I found it, I was like…" She bit her lower lip a little. "Huh. It's a new way of addressing hardware."

Kerry's brows lifted.

"I'm not sure what made me write it that way but... I mean, it seemed obvious once I saw it," Dar said. "It's really cool. Arthur and Elvis are going to lose their minds when they try the new code." She looked up at Kerry, from between some slightly overlong hair obscuring her eyes, and grinned. "Guess I got lucky typing away there on my keyboard waiting for Armageddon."

"The hell with them. I want to try it." Kerry laughed. "Maybe this damn storm did someone some good." She lifted Dar's hand up and kissed the knuckles. "Good job, hon, and you know it's not luck."

They both paused, as the sound of yelling voices echoed softly through the air. "Tell me someone isn't causing trouble." Kerry sighed, exasperated. "Jesus Christ."

"Around here with that platoon outside?" Dar stood up and pulled Kerry up with her. "C'mon, let's see what the hell's going on."

****

Everyone heard both the shouts and the rhythmic steps on the stairs as Dar and Kerry came down them.

"Lord." Andrew stood at the bottom of the stairs.

"What do you figure, Dad?" Dar asked.

"Ah do not know." Andy skulked ahead of them to the door and through it, and Dar and Kerry both noticed the automatic in a holster at the small of his back. "But ah suppose we're fixing to find out."

"People would have to be nuts to cause a problem around here," Kerry said as they went out into the night and found the space between the front of the building and the National Guard camp empty and quiet.

The sounds came from past the military camp, and it occurred to Kerry that there really was no reason for them to even get involved.

"Why the hell are we out here?" Dar conveniently read her mind and spoke her thoughts aloud. She put her hand on Kerry's back as they sped up to catch the rest of the gang already streaming toward the noise. "Do we not think the National Guard can handle a street mob?"

"We don't know that it's a mob," Kerry said, in a reasonable tone. "And I agree with you, but here we are." She could now see the soldiers up near the edge of the road, and beyond them a reasonably large crowd of people. "Oh. Okay. Maybe it is a mob," Kerry conceded.

"Maybe it is," Dar said. "I guess it's better to know what the hell's going on." She and Kerry caught up to the line of people who had emerged from her office, and saw Hank and Pete come up behind the ranks of them, rifles cradled in their arms.

"C'mon." Dar took Kerry's hand and started forward, firmly pushing people aside as they made their way through the crowd. "Let's figure this out before someone gets shot."

"Right with you, hon." Kerry was glad enough to follow Dar through the path that hastily opened, and they ended up right next to Carlos, who had gotten to the front of the gang. "Hey."

"Hey." Carlos just stood and watched, as the crowd surged against the line of soldiers. "Glad those guys are here. That's a lot of people."

"What do they want?" Dar asked, aware her father had stepped up next to her. "Any idea what's up, Dad?"

They were just at the back end of the guard camp, where the halo of their lights spread but all the attention was focused on what looked to Dar like about a hundred people who were in the road in front of the camp. Some of them held torches.

"Are those tiki torches?" Kerry murmured. "Someone do a run on Pier 1 before the storm?"

"Home Depot carries those." Dar used her height to her advantage to study the crowd. She moved forward a few steps to get a better look.

The group of people were a mixed lot, from what she could see, but mostly men, and all of them angry. They yelled at the guards in angry Spanish.

"Let me go see what's going on." Dar started forward and after a second Kerry caught up with her. They walked up the road past the perimeter of the National Guard camp, aware from the sound of footsteps behind them they were not alone, their little gang was behind them.

Kerry sensed the crowd's agitation, and as they came up to the crossroads where their parking lot turned into the road, the guard captain came out and started speaking to the group as one of the sentries hurried over to meet them.

"Oh, hang on ladies, hold up there," the sentry said. "Just hold off back of the road there. Don't want you to get mixed up in this."

"It's our parking lot." Dar moved past him. "We want to know what's going on here."

Kerry gave the sentry a brief, sympathetic smile as she scooted past him, and her cadre of ill-assorted weightlifters, nerds and armed veterans followed. "We'll be fine," she reassured the man. "Really."

Dar walked past the barrier fence that had been thrown up around the encampment and crossed over to where the captain stood, a bullhorn in one fist. On either side of him were young, slightly overwhelmed looking guards, their automatic rifles held ready in front of them.

She identified one problem immediately. The crowd yelled in Spanish, and the captain didn't understand even a word of it. He told them over and over again in Southern inflected English to disperse, and move away from the camp, and most of the crowd didn't understand any of that in return.

She slid past the right guard and tapped him on the shoulder.

He jumped and turned around. The guard with the gun whirled and took a step back in surprise. "Who..." The captain then glanced past Dar, and saw Kerry standing there with her hands behind her back, a bemusedly humorous expression on her face. "Oh, ah..."

Dar offered a hand. "Hi. I'm Dar." She gestured behind her. "I think you know my partner, Kerry."

The captain turned fully around and focused on her, blinking a little in surprise. "Oh right! Sure! Of course, I couldn't really see ya... ah, ladies you probably don't want to be mixing up in this here."

"Mind if I help you out with these people?" Dar didn't wait for him to connect the dots. "They're asking for water and ice." She held up a hand to the crowd who'd been edging closer. "Hold on, let me talk to him," she said, in Spanish.

The captain recovered his composure. "Right... okay, ma'am I can understand that, but see, we don't have any water, or ice here," he said. "I've been trying to tell them, if they need provisions, they need to go on up to that downtown location near to the seaport." He made a vague gesture northward. "We can't do nothing for them."

Dar held her hand out for the bullhorn. "Gimme."

After a pause, he handed it to her. Dar half turned, bringing the bullhorn up to her lips. "These guys are just soldiers. They don't have supplies," she told the crowd in Spanish. "Place with water and ice, is Bayside."

The nearest of the crowd, a tall, grizzle haired man with a ripped T-shirt rolled and tied around his head like a headband threw his hands up. "What do you mean? We were downtown. They told us to come here!"

Dar repeated that in English to the captain.

The captain shook his head. "I don't know anything about that, but take a look." He turned and spread his arms out, indicating the camp. "We got some tarps, sandbags, and tents. That's it. We had a truck full of water, but they told us to send it over to Bayside."

"They sent all their water to Bayside," Dar told the man, who had now come up next to her.

He cursed. "We have nothing," he told her, in Spanish. "The water is out in Doral, where we live. Not even so that we can boil it. Nobody thought that would happen. We have chlorine to treat it, you know?"

"Sure," Dar said quietly.

"Evaporated milk for the babies, we can't use it." The man looked at her, his eyes a little on the desperate side. "Cup of soups, rice, nothing."

Kerry eased up on the other side of Dar and listened in silence. She guessed what was going on by Dar's body language. After a moment, Carlos came up and joined them.

"They need water." Dar turned to the captain. "They have busted pipes or something where they live. They've got no water left."

The captain nodded. "I get that. I don't have any."

Kerry cleared her throat. "Could we call over to Bayside and see if there's some there before we send these folks over again? It must be super frustrating to go back and forth." She had her hands in her front pockets and her tone was mild.

The trick with Kerry was, Dar pondered, she always sounded so kind and reasonable you just wanted to agree with her because to disagree with that kind, interested, sincere engagement, by definition, made you unreasonable and feel like a jerky jerk.

The captain looked like he wanted to disagree, wanted to tell her, and Dar, and all the people standing there that this was not his problem, and go back to having his dinner or whatever it was he'd been doing.

But he was also a smart man, and the words had time to be absorbed and reason won. "Why, sure," he responded. "We can do that, sure. That's a good idea, Ms. Kerry."

Kerry smiled at him.

"Jackson, give them folks up to the north a call on the radio, wouldja?" The captain directed a tow-headed woman standing nearby. "Find out if they got any supplies left."

"Yes, sir." The woman trotted off.

"They're calling over there to see if they have water," Carlos told the nearest of the crowd, in Spanish. "My bosses gotcha," he added, confidently. "Don't worry about it."

"This is how we get into this stuff isn't it?" Kerry shifted her hands from her pockets to behind her back, clasping them together and rocking a little on the balls of her feet.

"Yes," Dar said. "What are we going to do if they don't have any?" She turned her head and regarded Kerry. "Now that we're in it?"

Kerry eyed her in silence.

"Run a hose from our building?"

"We're not sure our water is any good, Dar," Kerry replied, in a mild tone. "They're boiling it to drink and cook."

The captain nodded at her. "That's smart. Can't be too careful, with all the pressure loss."

"They had loads of water in the Cargomaster I flew back here on," Dar told the captain. "Over at the airport. They were unloading it."

"Ten, twelve pallets of it," Dar continued. "So, you could send someone out there to pick some up."

"Maybe." The man said. "But it's likely marked for someplace though. Seems like everyone's looking for supplies." He glanced around and then back at her. "Not like you all are, with the boiling. I bet your folks have antiseptic tabs, too." He looked pointedly at the crowd. "I been over in there. You all were prepared."

"No, I think..." Dar turned. "Is the water bad, or off?" she asked in Spanish.

"It is off," the man answered readily. "No pressure, nothing."

"That's what I thought." Dar turned to the captain. "It's off totally. They can't boil or chemical it. Probably a busted main."

"Well," he said, with a tiny shrug. "You're supposed to have a three-day supply, y'know."

Kerry sighed. She'd heard that a lot lately. Not only from the soldiers but on the television from frustrated government spokesmen, repeated by the television anchors. "Gallon jugs," she murmured.

"Yes, that's right." The captain nodded at her. "Big old jugs, like they sell in the supermarket. We stock up on em every year, round these times. We don't get many storms, but when one comes it's a big old mess in our parts." He looked past Dar. "Ain't that right, Mr. Roberts?"

"Ain't be there for a long time," Andy replied. "What all we're gonna do here for these folks?" he asked. "They got kids at home."

Hank came up behind him, cradling his gun, silent and listening.

"Sir." The tow haired Jackson came back. "They're all out sure enough in Bayside, and supply said the load that came in on the plane is heading up to Aventura."

"Well, that's too bad then." He turned. "Sorry about that, all. They just don't have any, and we don't either. Maybe the next load, coming in tomorrow morning."

Kerry thought about what they had in the office, and kept silent, knowing their couple cases of sixteen-ounce water bottles wouldn't do much. "What are they supposed to do?"

"Wait," he said. He gave her a small, brief twist of his lips. "Close the gates up, we're done here." He turned and walked back into the camp, as the guards rolled shut a hastily erected chain link fence gate that now also had a line of soldiers behind it, holding guns.

"Asshole," Andy called after him.

Both Kerry and Dar grimaced, as the man turned to stare at him. "Okay." Dar turned and faced the man and the crowd. "They don't have anything to give out. None of the water that came in today came here, and

Bayside's out, like they told you."

"Jesus." The man looked exhausted, his face hollow. "No one will help us."

The crowd murmured, at a loss.

"Can't you go to a shelter?" Carlos asked. "There's three of them over that way."

"They are full," the man answered simply. "We went too late. Everything's too late."

Kerry tugged Dar's sleeve. "Can they try the big base on the north side of Doral?" she asked. "The one where I was? I bet they have water. They had piles of stuff there, Dar."

"Southcom?" Dar mused. "They probably wouldn't be amused if a crowd showed up there."

"How bout I rev up the Vee and take some of them over there and see," Hank offered. "Can't hurt to ask, can it? You'll go with us, huh Andy? Them boys'll listen to you."

"I'll go along to translate," Carlos said. "That's a good idea, head over there with maybe that guy, and the other one there, and find out," he said. "And Mr. R's right. That guy could give a shit and he's an asshat."

"Be right back." Hank turned and trotted off toward the building, holding his rifle in both hands. "See if Zo wants to go," he called back over his shoulder. "Nother translator."

Dar turned. "So." She walked over to the crowd. "Some of my guys want to ride over to Southcom down on 41st and see if they've got anything there. You up for that? They can take a couple people," she asked him in Spanish. "Then if they've got some, everyone can go over there."

Two of the nearest men had come closer and were listening to her. "You think they have some?"

"They might," Dar said. "We don't know, but there isn't any here."

"Why not try?" the first of the men said. "Yes, I will go. Of course. Why not?" He held his hand out. "I am Henry," he said. "This is Juan, and Maikel, my friends and neighbors." He clasped Dar's hand firmly. "Thank you for helping us out."

Kerry put her hands back into her pockets. She wondered if sending a Humvee with a roof mounted machine gun full of armed veterans and desperate residents was really the best idea on the table. She glanced at Andy, who had turned his back on the guard camp and folded his bare arms over his chest. "Pissed you off, huh Dad?"

"Some bitch." Andy frowned. "Ah do not care for that—don't give a shit—attitude," he said. "S'what they get paid for, this kinda thing."

"It's a humanitarian mission," Kerry said. "Yes, I get it."

"Don't matter if them people are being jackass. Got their homes wrecked, family's hurting." Andy glowered out at the crowd. "How'd he like it if it was his kids not eatin?"

Well." Kerry cleared her throat a little. "I understand what they're saying, about why didn't these folks prepare, you know? Why didn't they have jugs of water and things like that. But, of course, it doesn't matter. They need help."

"Xactly."

Kerry smiled. "Dar gets her crusader gene from you."

Andy turned around and faced her. "Say what?"

A loud horn sounded behind them and they both turned to see the Humvee headed their way, with Hank at the wheel, and just visible, Zoe in the passenger seat, eyes wide as baseballs. Behind it, Hank hauled his landscaping trailer, empty of anything but some coils of rope.

"That'll do it." Andy stepped forward. "C'mon, boy." He tapped Carlos on the shoulder. "Let's go find us some jugs." He got into the front of the Humvee next to Zoe, and Carlos piled into the back with Henry and Juan, as the crowd cleared out of the way to let them get out onto the road.

Dar took a step back as well, next to Kerry who slid her fingers into the back of her shorts. "Should we..."

"No," Kerry said, firmly. "They've got a better chance of not having anything weird happen if we're not there." She waved at the truck as it trundled off. "Let's go get more kim chee." She started backward, tugging Dar with her. "And just be glad your mother isn't here."

Chapter Fifteen

It was warm and sticky inside the office. Dar perched on the window seat and took advantage of the breeze coming off the water, listening to Kerry in her own office talking to two of their techs. The hurricane candle was flickering sedately on her desk, providing an amber glow.

It had been a very long day. She really wanted to just go home and get comfortable and not worry about finding water for people or what to do with mad customers and irate government contractors, when it would be more fun to think about the AI rig and its potential.

She wriggled her shoulder blades, getting them into a more comfortable spot against the window frame and watched the clouds gathering, covering the moon and casting the exterior into utter darkness, that she could nevertheless pick out dim outlines in.

"Um... uh... Dar?"

Dar looked up and over at the door to the inside of the office. "Over here." She responded. "Catching a breeze."

"Oh, there ya are." Their LAN tech entered. "There's a phone call for you?" He said, tentatively. "I think it's your mom." He added. "Well, I mean, yeah, it's your mom. I mean, she said so."

"Ho boy." Dar got up and followed him down, then sat down and picked up the receiver. "Hello?"

"Ah, Dar."

"Hi, Mom." Dar rested her head against one fist. "What's up?"

"The governor's moron won't leave us alone. He has this file he wants sent, and won't take no again from me," Ceci told her. "I told him you're not here, which is visually evident since you're not a midget living in that big black rolling case, but he doesn't care."

"Well, I'm not there, so he can just..." Dar said. "Wait, hang on." She put the phone down and went back down to her office and picked up her backpack. She brought it back with her to the room.

She sat down, pulled out her laptop and put it on the table. "Where the hell is my cable." She rummaged inside the sack. "Damn it."

"Are you asking me?" Ceci's voice emerged tinnily from the receiver. "There's a pile of cables here, not sure what you want done with them."

Dar glanced up and put the phone on speaker. "No, sorry. Talking to myself. Did he leave the file?"

"No."

"Is he there banging on the door? If he is tell him to give you the file and have Arthur stick it into a laptop and mount it." Dar watched her machine boot. "I can get to that router from here and send it. It's late enough for the rest of them to have keeled over in their bad wine."

Ceci chuckled softly. "Hold on. He's probably walking around in a circle outside cursing and checking his watch. Let me go see."

Dar logged into her machine and connected it to the switch on the desk. She connected to the island and rummaged around in the router, tweaked some settings and applied them.

"Dar?"

"Right here where you left me," Dar said.

"Okay, the governor's friend is hustling back to his bodega. He's going to send either Thing one or Thing two back over with the file."

"Yay."

"How's it going over there?" Ceci asked.

Dar studied the small digital screen of the phone. "Do you really want to know?" she said. "Did they tell you they have the National Guard camped in front of the door?"

"Your father did say." Ceci chuckled. "He doesn't really care for them. They're from back home, he said, and apparently they're prouder of that than he is."

"Well." Dar exhaled. "A bunch of people showed up and they wouldn't give them the time of day, so now he really doesn't like them."

"Uh oh."

"He and Hank took off in that Humvee and headed over to Doral to find water."

There was a brief silence. "For the guard?"

"For the people." Dar rested her chin on her fist. "Hey, the government liked my program."

"Hold on. Is your father going to get into trouble?" her mother asked. "Trouble as in you're going to have to go bail him out?"

"No, we didn't go with them," Dar reassured her. "I'm sure they'll be back with a load of water, along with two dozen pizzas and a case of beer, none the worse for wear. Unlike if we'd gone, where we'd have ended up having to modify a Martian spaceship and I'd be calling you from the moon."

Another silence. "Well, Paladar, that is actually pretty likely the truth. So, they liked your thing huh?" Ceci asked. "Is that the artificial insemination program you all were talking about?"

Dar started laughing.

"Was that funny?"

"They probably would have really liked that. Artificial intelligence. Yeah," Dar said. "Project's moving forward. So at least we'll get paid for it."

"Oh well that is good news," her mother said. "The kids here can't wait to try whatever it is you did after hearing it went well. They need a helmet? They keep talking about a helmet."

"I have it here," Dar said. "Tell them I'll bring it back with me and they can run it tomorrow." She shifted a little. "How's it going there? People still yelling?"

"Wait, I hear the minions coming, hold on."

The hold music came back and Dar got up and walked across the hall into the server room and opened a metal cabinet mounted on the wall. Inside was a large square case and she lifted it out and took it with her back into the radio room. She set it down on the floor before she resumed her seat.

There was still hold music playing, and in the distance, she could hear a soft rumble of thunder. The breeze coming in the window brought with it the far-off smell of rain, and sea, and the air was so full of moisture she could almost feel it condensing on her tongue.

"Okay!"

Dar jumped, as the phone music stopped and Ceci's voice came through the speaker. "He got the file?"

"The kids have it, and it's in the laptop, and the laptop is sitting here," her mother dutifully reported. "Everyone is standing here, expecting you to do something to turn it into a circus clown or I don't know what," she said. "Hey, listen, they also told me they're running the ferry all night tonight, because the government people are still out there."

"That's great news." Dar remoted into the other laptop and examined the thumb drive in the port. "Twice the size of the last one." She frowned. "It's going to take forever." She set up the transfer then she paused, and as she had the other time, she pulled up a file editor and glanced at the file.

Names, names and addresses, and brief descriptions of damages and... Dar studied the records in silence for a long minute, scanning the list of them. "Hang on." She got up and left the radio room, walked down the hallway and back to her office and through it, through the interconnecting door into Kerry's.

"Hey, hon." Kerry was seated behind her desk, a candle planted on its surface, writing on a pad in the candlelight. "Where were you? I wondered where you went."

"They're running the ferry all night. Want to wrap it up here after Dad gets back and go home?" Dar perched on the edge of her desk. "I was just talking to my mother. That jackass contractor has another file of names for me to send."

'Sure, I do." Kerry sat back in her chair. "So that guy's back huh?" she said. "You don't want to do it?" She looked up at Dar and watched the faint candlelight outline her profile. "Just because he's a jerk? At least that other guy brought decent empanadas."

"I saw all the names he's sending. Whole list is from the Gables, Miami Beach, Aventura, Doral... every high rent district," Dar said, bluntly. "There's no names on there from North Miami or Sweetwater or any place else."

"Does that surprise you?"

"Why wouldn't there be damage reports there?" Dar asked. "There has to be thousands of claims... you saw those houses out by Maria's."

"I'm sure there are. But that guy?" Kerry gave Dar a wry look. "He's there to take care of the people who donate big to the politicians, hon. He's taking care of who he's taking care of. C'mon." She put one hand on Dar's knee. "Everyone else has to wait for the adjusters to get here, if their insurance company even bothers to send them and doesn't just write the state off."

Dar looked at her.

"You saw the damage. This storm's going to run every private insurance company out of here. They can't pay all those claims, and I was talking to Zoe before. There are a lot people who fully own those homes and didn't have insurance."

Dar folded her arms. "That's incredibly unfair," she said flatly. "Those people don't have third homes to fly off to."

Kerry nodded. "You're absolutely right. But if you're thinking of not sending that file, or sending it to Taiwan, it won't change what he's doing. He'll just send it some other way and the same people will get the same special treatment because that's kinda how it works."

Dar's eyes narrowed dourly, but she remained silent because she knew, and she knew Kerry knew, that Kerry was right.

As though in acknowledgment of that, Kerry leaned forward, using her other hand to give Dar a pat on the calf. "He's a jerk, hon, but the planet's full of them, y'know?"

"I don't like it," Dar finally said. She stood up off the desk and ruffled Kerry's hair, then headed back out toward the radio room and muttered under her breath as she walked.

Kerry put the pen she'd been writing with between her fingers and studied the empty doorway. She took the time to just sit and feel the intense love she felt for Dar in that moment.

It wasn't that Dar wasn't a realist, she was. She knew perfectly well how the world worked. Kerry had perhaps a bit more cynical worldview caused by her upbringing, but not by much. Dar just really didn't like blatantly visibly unfairness. She championed the underdog as naturally as breathing.

But of course, Dar had never in her life considered herself in any sense an underdog in any situation. Her assumption, always, was that she would achieve whatever it was she was after and any roadblocks she had to move out of her way were just incidental problems to be solved. She never took any of them personally.

With a faint smile, Kerry stood up and went to the door. She crossed the hall and rambled down the steps to the first floor. She paused to look outside and peered past the guard camp in hopes she would see the Humvee arrive, hopefully with its trailer of water.

Instead, she saw a single, lone guard soldier coming toward her, a young man with a rifle slung over his back. Kerry went out onto the porch and stood there.

"Hello, ma'am?"

Kerry smiled briefly at him. "What's up?"

"Ma'am, there's a person who's asking to come back in here. Says she knows you all, but she's got no ID or nothin," he said. "My lieutenant said to hold her there. Maybe one of those locals is just trying to get past us."

Kerry shrugged slightly. "Sure, let's go see who it is." She motioned him in the direction of the camp. "If they're asking for me, chances are it's legit."

She walked alongside the soldier down the path and across the front part of the parking lot, where Dar's truck was parked. A gust of damp, cooler air rustled the trees on either side. "Rain again."

"Yes, ma'am," the soldier said, a touch mournfully. "That's what they told us."

"Well, it cools the air off."

They walked along the barrier the soldiers had put up and into the pools of light from the generator serviced pole fixtures. As they did Kerry heard her name being called.

Startled, she looked up and past the soldier and shaded her eyes from the light. A slim figure stood just outside the National Guard camp. She was dressed in a T-shirt and jeans, a sturdy backpack on her back. The figure waved at her.

"Mayte!" Kerry yelled in response. "Is that the person?" She asked the soldier. "She definitely belongs here."

"Yes, ma'am," the man said. "I guess so if you know her." His voice sounded doubtful.

Kerry reached the gate and found Mayte there being blocked by two armed soldiers that she herself walked past without hesitation. "What are you doing here?" She opened her arms and they exchanged hugs. "How's your dad? They were putting that cast on this morning when I talked to your mom."

Mayte looked at her, then glanced at the guards and hesitated.

"C'mon." Kerry easily interpreted the look. "And guys..." she addressed the guards, who watched her with furtive, sideways looks. "If someone asks for us by name, just let them past. I've got another dozen people out there I haven't heard from."

Kerry steered Mayte back along the road and left the soldiers behind, without waiting for an answer. "Sorry they stopped you. They're a little clueless," she said. "They're from Alabama and nothing here makes much sense to them."

"Ah, Si." Mayte relaxed. "They talked like Dar's papa."

"Same part of the world he's from."

"So, yes," Mayte continued. "Mama is still at the hotel next to the hospital, but I thought I would go out and see what I could do about our house, you know?"

"Sure," Kerry said. "But can you even get over there? I saw on a news report it was still flooded in those parts." They reached the door and she ushered Mayte through and into the building. "As you can see, things are pretty weird in here too."

Mayte glanced up and down. "Oh, it is not so bad in here." She sounded surprised. "Is it new already?"

"Sort of." Kerry pointed at the central door. "I can explain better out there." She walked out onto the porch and paused. About a dozen people were gathered around a small hibachi. One of them strummed a guitar.

"Some people in the area are doing some work for us." She indicated the construction area.

Mayte stopped and looked around. "Oo!" She made a surprised exclamation. "Do we know these people?"

"We do now," Kerry said cheerfully. "So anyway, you were saying about your house?"

"I cannot get there." Mayte turned to face her. "I tried to go, but they have fenced off the whole neighborhood. I found one of my neighbors, he said all the people were taken out."

Kerry nodded. "Makes sense."

Mayte stuck her hands in her jeans pockets. "And then I..." She glanced around and then back at Kerry. "There is nothing to do at the hotel. You just can watch the TV all the time and it's depressing. "So, I told Mama I was going to try to come here."

Kerry's pale brow lifted. "She was okay with that?"

"No." Mayte grinned ruefully. "She was not okay at all, but I am here. Papa is doing fine, and they are treating him and Mama very nicely. I told Mama it would be better if I came here and tried to help you."

"That's kind of what everyone's said so far," Kerry said. "I even had a few of the folks from ILS show up and we put them to work. Celeste is over at the island helping my mother-in-law hold the fort down there. Arthur and Elvis are on the island coding."

Mayte's eyes widened. "Wow."

"Zoe and Carlos are out with my father-in-law and some of his friends trying to find water for those people out there," Kerry continued. "I just sent Mark and his wife up to Melbourne so you're in good company. But it's not too comfortable here, Mayte. We do have some generator power, but no AC."

"That is fine, Kerry." Mayte smiled. "It is better than all my family, who are in the shelters. It is not good there. I knew if I came here, then one of my aunts would come and stay by Mama and use that room. The rest of them are full and it will be better for her, you know?"

"Got it."

Footsteps sounded on the floorboards behind them and Kerry turned to see Dar emerging from the hallway. "Hey, hon, look who's here."

Dar came forward, dusting her hands off, a look of satisfaction on her face. "Hey, Mayte," she greeted the younger woman. "Come over to join the gang?"

"Hello, Dar," Mayte said. "Si, I did. I cannot believe all the things going on here." She looked around the yard. "Mama was right. She said at least if I came to here things would be happening." She half turned again.

"You said Zoe was... what was Zoe doing?"

"There's a crowd of folks outside who need water," Kerry said. "So... the National Guard didn't have any, and we thought maybe there would be some over in Doral. So, they took a truck there to see if they could bring some back. There's some water pipes broken nearby I guess."

Mayte regarded her with a bemused look.

"Yes, the National Guard should be doing that," Kerry didn't miss a beat. "We shouldn't even be involved, but here we are."

"Here we are," Mayte agreed. "We are always finding the trouble."

"Let's introduce you to everyone." Kerry clapped her on the back. "Since you'll be in charge when we leave." She hooked a finger through the belt loop on Dar's jeans. "C'mon."

"Do I want to be in charge of things?" Mayte asked, doubtfully. "I am not really sure what is going on."

"Neither are we. Just roll with it."

"Ay yi."

****

Dar heard the sound of the Humvee returning, the rumble of the engine drifting in through the window as she stood in Maria's office looking out into the night. "Ker?"

"You called?" Kerry entered behind her, wiping her hands off on a neatly torn piece of paper towel. "What's going on?"

Dar pointed, and obligingly Kerry came up next to her. They stood side by side as she looked out across the parking lot. "They're back."

Past the halon lights of the National Guard, past the front of the lot where a scattering of their cars were parked, the headlamps of the oncoming vehicle were visible, and as the Humvee came slowly to a halt near the entrance to the lot they saw the trailer behind it was piled high with boxes.

"Good job, guys." Kerry smiled and gave Dar a rub on her back. "Should we go meet them and give them a hand?"

"Is it safe for us to do that? Shouldn't we stay here in case the crowd suddenly turns into zombie Figment dragons?" Dar asked, in a serious, concerned tone. "Or a tidal wave comes up?"

Kerry eyed her in silence.

"Tinkerbell shows up and turns them all into giant schnauzers?"

"Dar." Kerry covered her eyes with one hand, her shoulders shaking.

"Sorry. I'm tired, and hot, and it's been a long, weird day," Dar admitted. "If Tinkerbell did show up, I'd pay her to twinkle us into our bedroom."

Kerry gave her a comforting arm squeeze and kissed her on the shoulder as they sucked in the faint, slightly damply cool air coming in the window.

They watched as the crowd, who had settled down to wait across the street from the guard enclosure, got up and approached the truck. Carlo's distinctive, dark, crop haired head came poking up out of the top hatch.

Pete came up behind them and peered past Kerry's elbow. "Hey lookie there. Looks like a successful mission. Hot damn. Now we can close up the shop and get some shuteye."

"It does look that way," Dar said. "Kerry and I were just keeping our distance, so it stays chill."

Pete laughed. "You all do attract the weirds." He turned. "I'm gonna go help em out, then we can get that rig back in the gates."

"We do attract the weirds," Kerry said. "C'mon then, Dar. I just finished making some leftover nachos."

"Mm. Nachos."

Kerry glanced at Maria's desk. "Oh, wait, let me grab this. Mayte was looking for it." She picked up a slim leather portfolio tucked neatly into the organizer on the desk. "She must not have seen it under there."

"Maria's little black book?" Dar mused. "Woulda thought she'd taken it with her."

"She took a copy home," Kerry assured her. "But she didn't grab it on our way out of the house naturally and she gave Mayte a list of things she wanted done now that she's here."

"Sounds like Maria." Dar smiled gently. "Glad she's got the time to think of that stuff."

"C'mon." Kerry took hold of Dar's elbow and guided her back out into the hall and down to the small second floor kitchen, where there was a shallow bowl on the counter, gently steaming. "Three different kinds of barbequed meats and leftover taco cheese."

"Mm." Dar inspected the dish, and picked up a chip, which had a beefy, cheesy blanket over it. "Did you just get bored?"

"It's almost eleven p.m.. I just got hungry." Kerry took a chip herself and went over to stand near the window that faced the same direction as Maria's office did. She watched idly out the open panes as Andrew got out of the truck and came around to one side. Hank joined him.

It all looked orderly and calm. Kerry heard Zoe's piping voice, and then she saw Carlos duck down, and come back up holding Zoe by the waist. He boosted her up and sat her on the roof of the truck near the machine gun. "Zoe's taking all this really well."

"What, nerdly Armageddon?" Dar was content to stay where she was and enjoy the snack. "Does she have a choice?"

"Well... sometimes your dad's friends take a little bit of adjusting to. Zoe just took it in stride."

"Sure." Dar went to the tiny refrigerator and took out a can of soda, put in to cool down while they powered a little of the office from the generator outside. "I think she likes Hank."

Kerry remained thoughtfully silent for a minute. "Likes as in likes? Or likes as in…"

"She think's its cool there's someone else here who's like she is," Dar said. "Probably not many people around her like that, you know? And he's funny."

"He is funny, and a little random," Kerry said. "I think he acts crazier than he is?" Her voice lifted a little in question. She turned to see Dar watch her, munching in silence, one eyebrow slightly raised. "Or maybe not."

"He's a good guy," Dar said. "Dad wouldn't bring him around if he wasn't."

"No, I know that. Let's get our stuff, and get ready to head home, soon as Dad's done there. Okay?" She picked up the dish and they made their way back to their offices, sharing from it.

It was damp, and warm inside, and Kerry was happy to pick up her backpack and zip it up. She slid it onto her shoulders and went over to douse the candle still burning, blowing it out gently.

She went to the door between her and Dar's office and stuck her head inside and watched Dar in the act of picking up her notepad and putting it into her pack. "Any word from Richard, Dar?"

"No," Dar said. "I put my phone on the AP they have down the hall and picked up messages. Nothing." She looked up thoughtfully at Kerry. "Not sure how I feel about that. I forwarded all that crap about this building to him."

"Hope he's okay."

Dar slung her pack over her shoulder, and then gestured to the door. They walked together and Dar snagged the nacho bowl before they went out into the hall. "I'm sure he's fine. It's possible he tried to call the office, tried to call my cell, didn't get an answer and didn't want to leave a message."

"True," Kerry said. "Give me that, let me..."

"Ah ah ah. I got it." Dar walked down to the kitchenette and came back a minute later, sans dish. She licked her lips and winked at Kerry. "You should make that again."

"Not sure I can get that mixture of leftovers again, hon, but I'll try."

They walked down the steps, past the little nest that Pete had vacated near the top of them and down through the lower hall to the closed front door. Kerry pushed it open and they paused. The front porch guard station was also empty. "Guess they went over to see what was going on."

They walked across the dark frontage to the front of the lot. Dar opened the back door on the truck to toss her bag inside."

"C'mon." Dar closed the door and started over, holding out her hand and clasping Kerry's as she joined her. "Should be safe enough unless a unicorn or something shows up."

"Don't invoke things," Kerry mock protested. "You know, when I was at Hunter's Point, I was thinking about getting you a horse if we lived there."

Dar was briefly silent. "A horse?"

"You know, four legs? Large pointed head?"

"What made you think of that?" Dar seemed slightly bewildered yet charmed. "There's room there but... is that going to go with the flock of sheep?"

Kerry chuckled. "No, the shed we took shelter in had an old horse stall in it." She linked arms with Dar as they got to the front of the lot and stopped. They watched the organized process as Carlos directed the crowd in Spanish.

The trailer held a lot of boxes, and next to it Andy stacked one heavy box, and two lighter ones. He stepped back as some of the crowd came over to claim them, some with wheeled moving dollies, others just hefting the boxes to their shoulders and retreating.

Retreating where? Kerry wondered. They walked away, off to the south, down Main Highway and, she supposed, to whatever transport that had brought them there, parked down the road past where the police had blocked it. They'd seen that coming in.

Hank was on the back of the trailer. He shifted the boxes forward as Andy portioned them out. The two men who had gone with them helped him, with brief, frequent, satisfied nods.

"What's in there?" Kerry whispered.

"Big box is four-gallon jugs of water. Little ones are MRE's," Dar said. "At least, that's what Carlos is telling them it is."

"Wow."

"How big a horse could we keep in there?" Dar suddenly asked.

Kerry stared at her in some bewilderment. "What? Oh!" She bit off a laugh. "It was the size of a one car garage. Does that tell you?"

"Oh!" Zoe spotted them. "Ms. Kerry! Ms. Dar!" She scrambled down from the roof of the Humvee and popped out the side door. "It was so wonderful!" Then she looked past Kerry and let out a squeal. "Mayte!" She ran past them to greet her friend and they burst into rapid Spanish chatter.

Behind their barricade, several of the National Guard watched them, but seemed unwilling to either help or hinder what they were doing. There was no sign of the guard captain, but the tow-headed lieutenant who had come in to ask for space was seated on the hood of a truck nearby.

Hard to tell from their expressions what they were thinking. Kerry resisted the urge to go over and find out. She stayed next to Dar, hooking her thumbs into her shorts front pockets as Dar rested her elbow on her shoulder. The crowd's attitude had shifted now from angry despair to calm and waited their turn to come up to the trailer.

"This was so the right thing to do, Dar," Kerry said, after a moment of silence. "Why wouldn't they want to do it? Why did we have to?"

Dar shrugged. "Hey, Zoe." She turned and addressed the two younger women. "How'd it go out there? Where'd you get all this stuff from?"

"Oh!" Zoe came over with Mayte right behind her. "It was very good," she said. "We went to where you told us to, Ms. Kerry, to the big place near the airport. There were many many people there," she said. "And Papa

Andy went to the gate and explained what we needed, and they let us in right away and gave us all those boxes."

"Just like that?" Kerry asked.

"Si." Zoe nodded. "Just like you said they would do so," she said. "They were very happy to have us to come get them, I think? There are so many things there it was nice for us to come and take some for them," she added. "They thanked Papa Andy over and over again."

"Sure." Dar rolled with it. "I think a lot of people maybe can't go to where the supplies are, and they're waiting for them to come to them."

"Si," Mayte now spoke up. "That is exactly what they were saying at the hotel where we were. The floods are so bad, and flooded the cars, and all the things."

Now the trailer was almost empty, just the boxes left for the two men who had gone with them, and those men stood next to Andy and Hank. They shook hands, with Carlos rapidly translating in both directions. The men took hold of their boxes and hoisted them to their shoulders, their body posture triumphant and proud.

"They are so happy," Zoe said. "To be able to take this back to their family."

Dar watched them go, and as they crossed in front of the National Guard, both of them made a very American rude gesture with one hand, before they went out of sight and out of the light into the shadows.

"Wall." Andy stepped down off the trailer. "That there was a good old night."

"Good job, Dad," Dar said. "Ready to go home?"

"Ah am." He pulled off a pair of worn leather gloves and stuck them into the back of his waistband. "Get this here inside before anybody else done come and wants something."

"That was good." Carlos also looked quite satisfied. "Those guys out in Doral were pretty cool, too. They were all like, oh, you need some water and meals? No problem! C'mon in!" he said. "So, I don't know what that jackass in there's problem was." He pointed to the guard camp. "They told us if they'd known we needed water and stuff, they'd have sent a truck."

"They were right grateful," Hank said. "They liked my rig." He patted the side of the Humvee. "I asked them what the jack was wrong with these guys here, but they didn't know em."

"Nice." Pete materialized on the other side of him. "Gimme the keys if you're gonna yap out here. Let me pull this thing inside." He held out his hand and without comment Hank handed over the small animal skull keychain he kept the starter key for the vehicle on.

Pete got behind the wheel and they all stepped away from the truck, as he started up the engine and headed it down the driveway toward the office.

"C'mon." Andy pointed after him and they all strolled along in the truck's wake, until they reached Dar's truck. There, Andy, Dar and Kerry paused, and the rest hesitated.

"Good job, people." Dar leaned on the hood of her truck. "I know for sure those people appreciated what you did tonight like crazy."

"It was good," Carlos said, with a smile. "Pissed off the guard guys though." He didn't seem regretful. "And I'm glad those people got what they needed and not an ass kicking cause they coulda."

"True that," Hank said.

Kerry turned and pulled the small portfolio from her back pocket. "Here, Mayte, I found your mom's book in her desk." She handed over the item. "We'll be back in the morning."

"Maybe tomorrow we'll have cell back," Carlos said. "Maybe more folks'll show up."

"I will see if I can use that phone to contact everyone." Mayte held up the book. "That is what mama told me to do first, check off who we know about. She has that in here, all the home information for the people, with all the other things she keeps, the vendors and the phone numbers and everything."

"Old school." Carlos smiled. "C'mon guys, let's go inside before it starts raining again." He patted the hood of the truck. "See you guys tomorrow."

They got in the truck and watched as the oddly assorted gang moved off toward the building, a faint burst of laughter coming back to them on the breeze through the open window on the passenger side of the car. Dar started up the engine and adjusted the seat, with a sigh.

"Another very strange day," Kerry said. "But I'm glad that all worked out, Dad."

Andrew stretched his long frame out across the second seat in the truck and draped one arm over the back. "Wall." He paused. "Ah am some glad it did my own self." He watched out the window as Dar drove past the guard camp. "Ah do spect we'll have us some tussle with them folks though."

"Maybe they'll realize we saved them a lot of trouble." Kerry half turned and leaned on the back of her seat. "We did, y'know? Those guys were all kinds of pissed off and we fixed that."

"Dad called him an asshole in front of his men," Dar said, as she turned onto the main road and headed north. "He heard you."

"Yeap. Meant him to," Andrew said, unrepentantly. "Folks should not spect to not have jackassery made a note of, and that man was some fool and ah do not care for no fools."

Kerry regarded him. "Well, he did give me a ride," she said, in an almost apologetic tone. "But yeah, even when he was out there near where Mayte and Maria live, he didn't really have any helpful vibes. He wanted to get out of there."

"Jackass."

"Well, they didn't have anything that would help, Dad."

"Same story," Andy said. "Ain't got, ain't got. Kerry, we didn't get nothing neither, but we went and got. All that man could find was excuses." He frowned. "That bit got mah mad up."

"Yeah, I know." Kerry leaned her head against the headrest and watched Dar's profile as she drove. "But you know, I think everyone they send here does at least want to help. Most of the time either they have no clue what's going on, or they're not prepared for what this place is, you know?"

"Jackassery."

Dar turned right and drove up to the checkpoint, now seemingly built up a bit more with a sturdy barrier that closed the causeway except for a space large enough to allow one vehicle. And there were now tents set up with air handling units stretching out and supply trucks parked nearby.

She opened her window and pulled out her wallet, waiting for the guard to come over. "Feels like Checkpoint Charlie."

The soldier walked over to the car. "Can I help you, ma'am?"

Dar handed over her license. "Going home."

He glanced at it, then handed it back. "We just had a VIP movement there, ma'am. Go on, but you might get held up at the terminal." He stepped back and motioned at the tented control area near the blockade. "Have a good night."

"A VIP movement." Dar drove through the opening and out onto the causeway. "Guess the governor's back."

"Gov'mint." Andy said dourly. "All them movements gen'rlly involve a head or somesuch kind been mah experience."

"Hope it's just that," Kerry said. "That's usually what they say when they're moving around the President." She sniffed reflectively. "As if we really need that Ringling Brothers scenario right now."

Dar gave her a sideways look.

"If he's here, sure hope he doesn't have my mother with him."

****

Kerry stood at the kitchen window and looked out over their small backyard and garden, past the seawall and out over the Atlantic Ocean.

Today it was a mild, lightly ruffled green. The sun was just over the horizon bathing the outside of the condo with warm pink light.

A soft ding distracted her and she went over to the toaster and removed two corn English muffins. She set them down and applied a round sausage patty and piece of Swiss cheese to them before she picked up the wooden tray they were on.

Kerry maneuvered through the living room and went into Dar's office. She set the tray down on the desk and then walked over to the window.

On the couch nearby was a wood file, and around the bottom of the window was a thin layer of whiteish gray dust. Dar leaned over the back of the couch and pulled a cable over the edge of the sill from the outside.

Kerry watched as her beloved partner routed the cable into a newly cut trough in the wooden windowsill then slid the window shut.

The condo's alarm system issued a satisfied sounding beep as the window seated, and Dar reached up to close the locks that would keep it in place. "There."

"Nice job, sweetie." Kerry gave her a little scratch on the back.

"Thank you." Dar got up and backed away from the couch, routing the cable around to the small table next to the window that now had a small switch on top of it. "If the kids at the office can keep their phones online, why can't we?"

Kerry chuckled. "Eat your muffin. It'll get cold."

Dar sat down behind her desk and picked up half of the muffin and took a bite. On the desk was a capped thermos, and she picked it up to wash down her mouthful.

Kerry took a seat on the couch with her own breakfast. "So."

"So." Dar paused in her chewing. "Is it Saturday?"

"It's Saturday," Kerry confirmed. "Does that mean something?"

"Not really." Dar's expression shifted slightly. "Except it defers calling Pharma." She regarded her quiescent computer at her elbow. "Guess maybe the answer to that is in my inbox."

"Might be," Kerry said. "Worse case, he's canceled our contract. What's best case?" she asked, after a brief pause. "As long as we're talking about it."

"Best case?" Dar looked slightly intrigued. "You mean, if lightning struck twice and I did something unexpected on that plane flight and revolutionized the pharmaceutical industry without planning to?"

Kerry nodded as she chewed.

"Can we not think about that?"

Kerry shrugged expressively.

Dar leaned over and turned on her computer. Then she got up and went over to the small table, coiling up the cable from outside neatly, fastening it with a piece of Velcro, and plugging it into the switch. She then picked up a rounded square almost white piece of equipment and set it on top of the switch and connected an ethernet cable into the front of the now blinking front panel.

The access point blinked, as if in sympathy.

Dar went back to her chair and sat down. "We can bring over a phone from the cottage," she said. "Keep everything in here so when our service comes back up, I don't have to screw around with rewiring everything." She eyed Kerry. "You mind?"

"Do I mind what?"

"Not having connection upstairs?"

"Oh." Kerry paused. "I'll just bring my laptop in the living room, hon. Signal'll reach from here."

Dar smiled. "Or work from my couch."

"Or work from your couch," Kerry said. She got up and collected the platter. "I'm going to go run over and grab one of those phones so we can just take some time to sort things out from here. Want more coffee?"

Dar held out the thermos. "If you're making some."

"I am. Probably we'll need it when the investigative team returns." Kerry took the thermos and went back out through the living room, it's interior unusually quiet due to the lack of the two dogs that were usually running around in it.

Andrew and Ceci had taken them out for a tour of the island. Kerry could only imagine what stories they were going to come back with, and she resisted the urge to turn on the television to the island channel to pre-empt the tales.

****

Dar regarded her inbox and tried to consider a sorting model that would produce anything other than bold faced exclamation points.

When everything was urgent, nothing was. A well-known corollary for anyone who had ever done anything in the realm of operational systems, and Dar certainly had. In the world of prioritization, you had to start some-where. Even in situations where everything seemed like it was the most important thing.

Which, when you had customers, was everyone. No one sent her emails that thought their work, or their request, or their deliverable was less important than anyone else. No one was dropping her a note just to say hey.

Dar finally decided to sort by non-company email to top, then by date, then exclude repeat senders with the same subject. This produced one long page of things for her attention, and she grunted in satisfaction as she adjusted her chair., She paused and then got up and went around the desk, studying it.

Kerry entered, carrying her backpack. "What's wrong? Not working?" She watched Dar's profile. "Not working the way you want it to?"

Dar grinned briefly. "I want to stand up," she said. "I got used to that desk in the office." She shooed Kerry ahead of her. "G'wan, go grab the phone. I'll get some boxes or something."

"Gardner's are outside. Maybe they have some crates." Kerry stood in her way long enough for them to gently collide, then remained as Dar turned the gesture into a hug. She took a breath full of the clean smell of Dar's cotton shirt and the hint of their soap. "Wish it really was Saturday."

"As in, hey let's go out on the boat for a dive Saturday?" Dar kissed the top of her head and rocked them both back and forth a little. "Yeah, me too. I was thinking about what it would be like if we could take a ride down to the cabin, check that out."

"Too much to do," Kerry said, in a mournful tone. "But thanks for reminding me I have to call the management people down there and see if we've got something left to check." She disengaged reluctantly and slid the other strap of her backpack onto her shoulders. "If we stay here today, maybe we can compromise with a sunset from the hot tub."

"Mmhum. You're on," Dar said, She walked Kerry to the door and opened it, then watched her go down the stairs and turn into the parking garage under the condo. "Oh, hey wait, Ker," she called. "Hang on."

She went out and down the steps into the underground space. "Take that helmet over," she said. "The kids want to test that code change." Dar went over to the truck, opened the back door and hauled the rugged case out and walked over to the cart.

Kerry leaned on the awning supports. "I want to see it," she said. "They have everything they need there to hook it up?" Dar nodded. "Vroom." She waggled her eyebrows as Dar got out of the way, and then slid behind the cart's steering wheel and turned it on. "I bet it's cool."

"It's cool," Dar assured her. "Tell them to use the explorer sim with high res."

Kerry grinned and gave her a little wave as she backed the cart and then sent it up the ramp, giving the horn a little beep beep on the way.

****

The door to the cottage flew open as Kerry put the parking brake on, with Arthur and Elvis almost colliding in the opening as they fought to get outside.

"She's got it!"

"You got it!"

Arthur won the struggle and bolted for the back of the cart and grabbed the handle of the case. He yanked it off the back of the cart and grunted as it hit him in the knees. "Ouch."

"Hey, take it easy." Kerry laughed, as she got out of the cart. "It's not going anywhere."

"No, but we talked to Scott and he won't shut up about the sim," Elvis said, as he moved out of the doorway to let Arthur carry the case inside. "A bunch of people have been here already this morning looking for you."

"Me?" Kerry followed them inside. "Morning?"

"Hey, Kerry." Angela was already seated at the table, pads and pens and folders of paper surrounding her and her laptop. "Boy we've been busy."

Celeste was in the corner amidst a pile of cables, sorting them and coiling them up. She looked up and waved as Kerry came inside and set her backpack down. "The governor was here, looking for you, ma'am," she said, as though this happened to Kerry every day.

"What did he want? Did that file not go through? Dar said it did." Kerry paused by the table.

"He didn't say anything about that." Elvis looked up from the case he was kneeling next to. "He and some goon showed up and just said they wanted to talk to you."

"Nice."

"Want some coffee? They just refilled," Angela said. "They brought over some fancy waffles for breakfast. They were great."

"They were great," Arthur agreed. "They had that Nutella stuff in them."

Kerry winced a little. "For breakfast?" Then she shook herself. "What am I saying? I'm the one who makes chocolate chip pancakes at my house." She paused. "I just came over here to pick up a phone. Dar got our place connected."

"No problem." Celeste got up and went to the gear cabinet. "The guys have been teaching me about all this stuff. It's pretty cool." She picked up one of the IP phones and a round of cable to go with it. "Do you need a power adapter?"

"No, Dar has a POE switch." Kerry accepted the device, which she slid into her backpack along with the cable. "Thanks. Easier for us to be able get calls transferred there and not have you folks having to take all the messages." She paused, then pulled the phone out of the bag and checked the sticker on the bottom.

"One of the spares from accounting," Elvis said, without prompting.

"Great." Kerry put the phone back in the bag. "We ran payables before the storm and no one on the face of the planet is calling our accounts receivable department this week." She zipped up the bag. "Now. Let's see what this revolution Dar created is all about."

Arthur grinned, as he pulled out the helmet and an incongruous set of football shoulder pads. "Sweet."

Elvis was busy with his laptop, periodically glancing up at the rack of servers. "Glad like crazy we have this here and not up in the cloud," he said. "Wouldn't want to try this over that satellite."

Kerry went over and sat on the couch. She rested her elbows on her knees as she watched the two programmers setting up the rig. "You're really excited about it huh?"

"Man." Elvis nodded his head, typing furiously. "I can't wait to see it."

"Me either," Arthur agreed. He connected the cables into the helmet. "Who gets to go first?" He looked up at Elvis, and then after a beat of somewhat awkward silence, they both looked over at Kerry. "You want to go first, Kerry?"

Kerry was charmed. "Tell you what. I'll go last. Then it'll be fresh in my head when I go report back," she said. "Go ahead and flip for it."

Elvis grinned, but shook his head. "He's the gamer." He indicated Arthur. "Get in, bro. Let's see what this thing can do."

****

Dar typed contentedly, her body relaxed behind the somewhat make-shift arrangement she'd made of her desk, with a set of wooden boards and some concrete blocks between them. Some construction flotsam and jetsam agreeably, if somewhat confusedly, provided to her by the landscaping team.

She had lifted her screen up to standing height using two blocks and two boards and put a lower shelf in to hold her keyboard. Her chair was pushed back against the wall out of the way.

The mail wasn't as horrific as she'd imagined. She'd answered at least a dozen that were just customers and random people she knew sending notes of concern, asking how they were doing, how had their house held up, that sort of question.

A note from Alastair to check in, and one from Hamilton Baird of a similar nature.

She clicked on the next one, from Gerry Easton.

Dar! Need to talk to you about that thing we talked about before you went on your own! Know you've got a mess down there, but call me!

Dar pondered that. "That thing we talked about." She lifted her hands up and spread them. "Sure, Gerry. When I get a phone that works, I'll call you." She typed out the same into the response and sent it on its way then went on to the next message.

A knock at the door to the condo made her look up in irritation. Who in the hell would be knocking at her door?

Guest Services maybe.

With a sigh, she headed around the desk and out of her office. She crossed the living room and went to the entryway and opened the door. She pulled it inward and looked out. A man in his mid-forties or so, with short, neatly cut black hair with a sprinkling of silver at the temples stood there.

He had a Rolex watch, and was wearing leather boots. New resident? "Hi."

The man studied her briefly. "I'm looking for Dar Roberts."

"Congrats. You found me." Dar stuck her hands in her pockets. Was he a random rich friend of someone who didn't like her? Someone who knew the sleezy contractor who wanted his own files sent somewhere?

Maybe someone renting a nearby condo who wanted a cup of sugar?

No, Dar mused sadly, not asking for her by name. "What can I do for you?"

"My name is Jason Billings," the man said. "I'm the director for communications for the State of Florida."

Definitely not cup of sugar. "Okay." Dar took a step backward, and gestured. "Want to come inside?"

He followed her in, and she shut the door. "What can I do for the state of Florida?" Dar asked. She indicated one of the plush leather chairs. She took a seat in the other and waited for him to join her. "I assume you're here with the governor? We saw the police blockade when we came home last night."

"I am," Billings said. "The governor's brought a group of specialists down here to see what can be done to start recovery operations. I'm sure you appreciate the need for that."

Dar nodded. "I do," she said. "It's a mess."

"It's a mess. That's a good way to describe it, and a lot of it's my mess, because the biggest issue we have is that no one can communicate. Most of the cellular towers are still down. Most of the power is still out. No one can talk to anyone else because we're all using different radio frequencies."

"Reminds me of 9/11," Dar said, as he paused. "We didn't learn much. At least after Andrew, we made people build decently for a few years at any rate."

He regarded her quietly. "No one likes to spend money on infrastructure. It's boring and never wins you points with the voters. No one cares if they have redundant power and underground cabling when it's time to vote."

"Until they're in this kind of situation."

"Even then. People are mad while they have no power, and they're flooded. But soon as the power's back on, and the ground's dry they're out there hustling to scam their insurance company and laughing at the government," Billings stated, flatly. "You can't even make people keep three days of beanie weenies in their house for an emergency."

"Some do."

"The ones who don't, yell the loudest about what crap we all are," he said, bluntly. "Sorry, not a fan of the unprepared public."

Dar merely nodded, assuming there was no advantage to her in telling him off. "So, what can I do for you?" She repeated her request. "I've got some beanie weenies in the closet."

He sighed and leaned back in the chair. "Sorry about that, Ms. Roberts. I spent the whole damn day out there yesterday with the governor and got my ass handed to me every two miles." He paused. "My father's best golfing buddy 's Alastair McLean."

Dar started laughing in pure reflex. "I just got an email from him asking how things were going. I should have known he was involved somewhere in this." She relaxed, though, since if that was the source of his information on her, at least she knew why he was here.

At least he was not going to be a jackass to her. Alastair would have warned him about that.

He nodded. "So let me not waste your time. We need someone to help us get communications going here and build a plan to put things back together, so it works better the next time. I want to give you a contract as a consultant to help me."

Dar blinked, startled silent for a long moment.

"I heard what you did in New York, from Uncle Al." He said, after the silence had gone on long enough to be uncomfortable. "The whole story. So at least this time, I promised him you'll get paid for it."

****

Kerry was silent for a very long minute after the sim ended, trying to absorb it. Finally, she pushed the eye shield up and looked at the eagerly waiting young men, who had, with great effort, stifled their reaction and waited for hers. "Holy shit."

"Ha Ha!" Elvis danced as he sat on the couch. "I thought you were gonna say that!"

"That is super rad," Arthur said, and nodded in a grave, but emphatic sort of way. "I mean it's like I want to just crawl in that thing and live in it, kind of awesome." He glanced at the server, then back at her. "It's gonna rock the world."

"Oh yeah," Elvis agreed. "Can't wait for Dar to come over here and show us what she did."

Kerry sat back in the chair she was in, that she'd sat down hard in as the reality of the virtual world she'd gone into had become breathtakingly overwhelming. "Swear to God I could smell the forest we were in."

"Programming." Arthur nodded. "We put that in the last sprint. But not the..." He waved his hands around incoherently. "That thing. That new thing."

"So cool." Elvis eyed Kerry. "You ready to come out of it?"

Kerry smiled and gestured him forward. She suspected her two employees were going to get exactly zero sleep and spend the night exploring this new facet of their project. "Much as I'd love to look around more, damn, I've got stuff to do."

She held still as Elvis undid the catches that locked the helmet to the pads and lifted it clear of her head. She imagined she could still hear the sounds of birds and crickets that didn't exist here in the cottage around her.

Wow.

"Cel, you want to try it?" Arthur half turned. "It's so cool."

Elvis lifted the pads off her shoulders and Kerry stood up.

"It really grabs your head, doesn't it?" Elvis asked. "You keep thinking about it after it's over."

"You do," Kerry had to agree. "It plays over again in your mind." She glanced over at Celeste, who was hesitating. "It's okay," she said. "Though I should have you sign all our NDA paperwork." She half turned. "Can you print out a set, Angela?"

"Sure." Angela pecked at her keyboard. "None of that helmet stuff for me. Last time I tried it I threw up for an hour." She glanced up at the programmers. "Not that you asked me or nothing."

"What does that mean?" Celeste asked. "The paperwork?"

It occurred to Kerry she'd been assuming, without thinking, that Celeste might want to remain and be a part of Roberts Automation, and not go back to ILS. Which seemed pretty arrogant, now that she sounded that out in her head.

Kerry felt a bit sheepish. "Sorry about that," she said. "I should probably back up a step. I know you stopped by just to hang out, but I had Colleen put you on our payroll. You want to come work for us?"

Celeste blinked at her. "Seriously?"

"Toldja." Arthur rolled his eyes.

"I don't do any of this stuff," Celeste said. "And honest... with those guys you have there, you don't need me and Frank for security."

"Right now, we have no idea what we need," Kerry said, frankly. "You want to be here? We need people who can just pitch in and do anything."

Celeste looked down at the pieces of cable in her hands. Then she looked back up at Kerry. "That wasn't why I came," she said. "I just wanted to feel like I was doing something useful."

Kerry nodded. "I have an entire building of people over on the edge of Coconut Grove who showed up there because they wanted to do something useful. I don't even know who some of them are, but if you want to stay, you've got a spot. Your choice."

Arthur looked at Kerry from between his shaggy bangs. "Sure, she wants to stay," he said, with a somewhat bewildered expression. "You want to, right?"

Celeste was momentarily silent, considering. "I do," she said, in almost a tone of surprise. "I'd like to learn how to do some of this stuff. I think it would be more fun and a lot more interesting than guarding a glass door."

Elvis chortled and shook his head. "We can write a bot to do that."

"Great. That's settled then," Kerry said. "So now, on to the NDA. It's to protect some of the special things we're working on. It means you can see them, but you're not allowed to tell anyone about them. I signed one."

Elvis chortled again. "Dar didn't."

"Well." Kerry eyed him. "She's the one who's inventing them. Wouldn't be much point."

"Is there a point to you signing?" Arthur asked. "I mean..."

"Not really. It just set a good example," Kerry said. "Dar makes a point of never being a good example." She grinned and put her hands on her hips. The two programmers laughed along with her.

"Cool. I'm in." Celeste put the cables down and came over to the table, where Angela collated a set of printed papers from the small printer. "I mean, who even knows what's going to happen around here, right? Seems like a good time to get a new set of skills."

A time of change. Kerry suddenly flashed back in her mind to the night she'd hit submit to send her resume to Dar, where it had seemed the same to her. No idea what was going to happen, and a great time to get a new set of skills.

A mental dialog that had been complete logical fabrication, even in the silence of her own mind, because if Dar had offered her a job flipping pancakes in the executive grill, she'd have taken it.

Maybe Celeste wanted that kind of change too. "Well then, welcome," she said. "Let me get this phone back to the house and see what trouble my other half's getting into, while you enjoy our little contraption there. Which is..." She exhaled, with a shake of her head. "Freaking amazing."

"Freaking amazing," Elvis repeated with satisfaction. "We're gonna be on a billboard."

"In Times Square," Arthur confirmed. "Like right above that ticker thing.

****

Dar closed the door and paused to shake her head in some bemusement before she retreated to the kitchen and obtained a glass of milk. She stood at the window and looked out as she sipped it. The gardening team looked to be about finished with their work cleaning out the debris from the yard. With a slight clearing of her throat, she put the glass down and went to the door, opened it, and walked down the steps.

The gardeners spotted her and paused as she approached. They waited warily as the supervisor edged in front of them and stood between her and the rest of the group. "Good   morning," he greeted her politely.

Dar came to a halt. "Hi."

"Is there something wrong, senora?" the man said.

Dar recognized him as one of the men who maintained the golf course. "Nothing," she said, in Spanish. "You guys just did a kick ass job out here, and I wanted to say thank you." She looked around at the yard, which was now completely free of debris. "It was a real mess."

He relaxed a little. "Everything is a big mess," He said, with a brief smile. "So much to be done."

"My father says that every five minutes," Dar said.

"But it gives us work. We hope for good overtime," the man continued. "And right now, we need every moment of it."

He paused and looked at Dar.

It took a second, but she caught the clue. "If you want to come by here when you're done, we could use some extra work here," she offered. "Cash basis."

All of the men who stood behind him, looked at her and smiled in unfeigned appreciation.

"Make my partner happy to have her garden back," Dar continued. "So just let me know."

"Of course," The supervisor said. "We were going to put some plants in around the big house tonight but maybe..."

"Hundred an hour?" Dar offered, her hands in her pockets. "If you get us the really nice plants, two hundred."

"We will be here," the man promised, at once. "It will look very nice, for sure."

Dar gave them a thumbs up, and then made her way back to the steps, and started up them as her ears caught the sound of the front door opening, all the way on the other side of the house.

She slipped inside and closed the kitchen door, as Kerry came into the kitchen from the other direction. "And?" Dar asked, seeing that faint, almost wondering, smile and the shake of Kerry's head. "Like it?"

"Dar." Kerry came over and put her hands on Dar's stomach. She leaned forward and stretched up to kiss her. "That was like nothing I have ever seen in my life."

Dar put her arms around Kerry and returned the kiss. "It's cool," she said. "Glad you liked it."

"I did. The kids are over the moon with it." Kerry reached up and cleared a wisp of hair out of Dar's eyes. "So, thank you, my dearest love, for being the genius you are."

Dar's face twitched a little, an almost grimace. "No need for that. It was just an off chance," she demurred. "Anything else going on there?" She changed the subject. "Did you trip over the government nerd on your way up the steps? He was just here asking me to take over the restoral effort on behalf of the State of Florida."

"Abu... what? Wait... what?" She looked behind herself and then back. "No, I didn't see anyone... wait, he asked you to what?"

"Want some milk?"

"Dar, hold on. Did you say the state wants to...what do they want you to do?"

"I want some chocolate pudding," Dar placidly responded. "Can you make chocolate pudding?"

"Of course, I...wait a minute, hold on." Kerry started laughing helplessly. "Dar!" she gripped Dar's arms and shook her insistently. "What the hell did you just say?"

"Yes?" Dar chuckled in reaction. She rested her arms on Kerry's shoulders and gazed at her. "Turns out the guy who runs comms for Florida's father is an old buddy of Alastair's," she said. "He wants to hire me as a consultant to help them get their act together."

Kerry stared her, brow fully knitted, in a long moment of perplexed comprehension.

"Yeah, no. As in I told him no," Dar responded to the unsaid words. "I'm not going to do that. Been there, done that, not going to spend my time yelling on behalf of the governor. I have better things to do." She leaned forward and kissed Kerry again. "Like that and getting some chocolate pudding."

"That will just end up being thankless." Kerry slid her arms up and wrapped them around Dar's neck. "Just like the last time, no matter what they say."

Dar nodded. "Agreed." She casually wrapped her arms around Kerry. "That's in fact what I told the guy, along with how much of my own chaos I have to sort out here. That's a full-time mind suck."

"It is."

Dar made a low, grunting sound of approval.

"Good decision, hon. Kerry gave her a quick hug, then released her. "Nothing much going on over at the cottage. I brought a phone back."

"I feel it." Dar patted the backpack on her back.

"Which I'm going to plug in and see if I can give Maria a call. I'm going to try and talk her into taking Tomas upstate. Colleen got space in one of the residential resorts there and there's room."

Dar turned her around and guided her back to her office. "Don't forget my pudding."

"Dar."

"You said you could make it."

$$****$$

Dar finished typing and looked up, as Kerry entered. "You know what I should have done? I should have bought out that damn satellite scamster."

"To get all the bandwidth?"

"To get all the bandwidth," Dar confirmed. "What a pain in the ass."

Kerry perched on the edge of the desk and watched Dar type for a minute. "Mind taking a break? I think I'd like you to try and convince Maria."

"Won't go, huh?"

"They're releasing Tomas tomorrow," Kerry said. "I told her to see if they can keep on staying at the hotel there, but she says they have so many people who need rooms she doesn't think they can."

"He needs medical care." Dar stopped typing and leaned on her makeshift keyboard shelf. "What does she want to do, try to go back home? I thought you said Mayte tried that yesterday." She focused on Kerry. "I heard on the news this morning they're looking at having to pump out some areas."

"They don't want to leave home."

"They can't live in their home, Ker. That makes no sense."

Kerry nodded. "I know, but you've known her longer, and sometimes that pragmatic logic comes better from you than from me."

Dar considered that in silence, then nodded. "Okay." She moved around the back of the desk. "Trade. Just got an email from Richard, g'wan and read it."

"What does he say?"

"Don't know. Haven't read it yet." Dar walked along the cable laid neatly on the floor and followed it out into the living room to the comfortable chair and low table Kerry had dragged over to work from.

Kerry waited for her to move past then she took Dar's place behind the desk, standing in the makeshift cockpit her partner had constructed, all full of the scent of concrete block and wood. It was workable though, and now she stood there quietly and looked at the big, slightly curved monitor full of gray on black text.

Hey, Dar!

No luck getting in touch with you! Been trying for days. But I guess it's as much of a mess down there as I see on the news. Want you to know that storm even blew down a tree in my front yard, so I can't even imagine what it was like to be where you are.

I did see in the news that your island did well, and it's where all the fancy people are staying, so at least there's that. Glad that you and Kerry and your folks did all right, or I assume you did all right based on what I know.

So on to business.

I sure hope that property did well in the storm, because I hate to tell you, but it's yours.

Kerry paused, and took a breath, surprised by the surge of happy excitement at the words. She took a breath to yell the news to Dar, then paused as she heard Dar's low voice outside the door, already on the phone, apparently talking to Maria.

She went back to the note instead.

Hate to tell you, because I saw what the damage was down there, and if that's damaged, because of its historical status you have no way to restore it and since it is protected, if it was damaged, you're responsible for it and we might be looking at a lawsuit over it because you didn't protect it.

I've reached out to them on your behalf, and I have a call later today with their legal department. I'll let you know how that goes, but if you have any intel for me on what the status is down there send it over. They are not happy at all with the way the transfer of ownership was done, and there could be trouble there too.

On a happier note, I got your text about the office building and started working on that. That's a more interesting problem because it's free and clear of encumbrance to my surprise, and based on the location, that's a valuable piece of property.

First thing I checked was the property taxes and got a pleasant surprise in that they have a grandfather clause from way back and at least you lucked out there and are covered. I've reached out to the insurance company as well on your behalf and got that rolling for you.

Between you and me, there's a lot of panic in those insurance guys. So, whatever you do to improve the facility, put up tarps, whatever you need there, keep every damn receipt!

"Have we kept any receipts?" Kerry mused. "Are there receipts for random piles of construction material that just mysteriously showed up in our yard?"

I hope the team down there did all right. Let me know when you get a phone hooked up to something so we can talk real time, and I'll have some info back from the Historical Society later on today. Be safe!
Richard.

Kerry reread the note again, finding it a little hard to suppress the urge to immediately get Dar and get in the truck and drive over to Hunter's Point, and get a look at it in daylight. Take a camera, and get some pictures, and send them over to Richard.

They had so much else to worry about.

Dar appeared in the door to her office and leaned against the jam. "Doesn't want to go," she said, briefly. "How's the news from Richard?"

"We have a new home," Kerry said. "Which we may or may not be able to do anything with and might be served a lawsuit over but here we are."

"Figured."

"Richard wants all our receipts for what we did for the office."

"Did we keep receipts?"

Kerry nodded as Dar's question echoed her own thoughts. "He wants to call you," she said. "Let's send him back the phone number here so we can get all the details." She retreated from behind the desk. "Have you said anything to him about the AI rig?"

"Not yet." Dar remained where she was. "Know what I want to do?" She asked, after a brief pause where they simply looked at each other.

"Yup. Let me get the keys to the truck."

"We can stop by the office on the way back," Dar theorized. "Maybe there's some receipts there."

"Maybe." Kerry headed past her out into the living room. "Maybe there's a Walgreens open where I can get a package of pudding mix. I don't have any gelatin here, Dar."

"Came in number 10 cans back in the day," Dar said.

"Along with the peanut butter?"

"Yep."

****

The drive down to the Point was uneventful, except for groups of residents in the streets, some with children's red wagons or shopping carts being pulled behind them that had multiplied in the areas between the turn-off to the beach and the southern parts of Coconut Grove.

There weren't many signs of troops, or police in the area. Dar paused at a four way stop to tip her sunglasses down and regard their surroundings.

"Not getting any better."

"Not really," Kerry said.

Dar drove through the intersection and continued along the road that had a lot of debris on its surface, and in two places, fallen trees, blocked their progress.

Dar slowed and looked around, vaguely remembering the area from the other night. Now it was full daylight, though, and she could see better. "We went through there, I think." She pointed at a corner of the crossroads, and a small gap between fallen power poles and a fence.

"With the Humvee?" Kerry's voice lifted a little in skepticism. "Oh boy." She took a grip on the grab handle over her door. "That must have been a blast at night in the rain."

"Yeah, it was idiotic. So here we go." Dar directed the truck to the sidewalk and up onto it. She squeezed past the bus bench and along the fallen tree blocking the road. "Then we saw that wall and I figured out where we were." She rocked down back onto the road and then they were going alongside the mentioned stone structure.

It was visibly old, and built of limestone and coral. Some parts of it painted with graffiti and the occasional crater where someone had veered off the road and crashed into it, and the corner of it they passed then ran east out of sight behind a lot of trees.

"Does that go all the way to the water?" Kerry wondered.

"No idea," Dar muttered. "But I suspect we'll find out soon enough." She indicated the gates at the bend just in front of them. "There's the entrance."

They parked in front of the gates, up on the sidewalk and out of the roadway and met in front of the truck, pausing to regard the tall wrought iron portal newly re-wrapped with a thick, sturdy metal linked chain.

Dar put her hands in her pockets. "It's a..." She paused. "It's kinda over the top," she said, a touch sheepishly. "Y'think?"

Kerry stood next to her, arms folded over her chest. "It's totally over the top," she agreed readily. "C'mon. Let's see if that smaller door is open because I'm not sure I want to have to break in again."

"I jumped over the wall," Dar said. "Didn't have time for all that chain stuff. So, if it's locked, I can pull the truck over next to the wall and we can hop over that way."

"Let's hope we don't have to." Kerry patted her on the back. "All we have to show we own this place is an email from some lawyer and I don't really want to have that conversation with the Miami police department today, my love."

"No, me either." Dar followed Kerry over to the small alcove. "We were in here that night, and my dad was saying he could smell the gas from Mark's motorcycle."

Kerry paused and turned around and looked at her. "What?" She twisted around and reviewed the alcove. "We just pushed the bike through here. It wasn't in here that long."

"Yeah. I know but he said he could," Dar said. "But it didn't really matter because I knew you were here." She edged past Kerry and started to examine the small gate, with its locking mechanism. "And anyway, it made sense." She took hold of the gate and then yanked it toward her.

"B..." Kerry paused. "Oh, with that thing." She waved vaguely at the side of her head.

"Yeah," Dar gave her a sideways look then she winked at her. "That thing."

Then she shoved the door outward and it opened, with a protest of rusty hinges. Dar looked out over the entryway. "Let's snoop." On either side of them, the wall ran along the edge of the road to the left and the right past their vision.

"Let's." Kerry glanced down the length of the wall that bordered the road and tried to fit in the sunlit view with her memories of that night.

Then it had seemed all darkness and formless shadows. The daylight revealed it to be full of tattered plants and ground cover, somewhat wild looking. A row of scrub pines ran along the length of the wall, but set back from it about the width of their truck.

The entry gates guarded a path leading away from them made from old inlaid pavers, and easily seen were the marks from the Humvee as it shoved pieces of rock out of the way. In some places the pavers themselves were broken. "That'll need to be fixed," Kerry said.

"Yeah, that truck's a brute." Dar touched one of the broken pavers with the toe of her boot. "Couldn't really see any of this that night. Just looked like gravel."

The paver path led forward through a stand of trees, and as they entered the stand they paused. "Manuel thought this was kind of a shame, it blocked the view of the house," Dar said, as they stood together for a long moment, just looking around. "But I liked it."

"What did Hank call this?" Kerry asked. "A hammock?"

The area was thick with trees, some with red, peeling bark, and others with white, forming a lacy canopy swaying in the light breeze. The branches that had covered the ground the other night were gone, and through the leaves they saw a rambling, variable ground.

Under the trees they could see ferns. "Hank mentioned ferns," Kerry said. "It's..." She looked around. "Interesting," she said. "Different."

"Natural." Dar gestured to the path, and they started walking up along it. There were many places where it was overgrown with weeds, and black with dirt and algae, but it appeared mostly intact and someone had kept the edge moderately trimmed.

Two or three minutes' walk and they passed a side branch. "That's where the shed was," Kerry said, pointing. "Where we ran to get out of the rain." She turned off onto it and Dar caught up to her, their footsteps made a soft, scuffing sound on the ground. "It's so quiet."

"Probably not when life's normal." Dar took in a breath. "You can smell the water," she said as they walked down the path and under the tree canopy, where now the shed could clearly be seen. It was also built of stone, with a tarpaper paneled roof.

"Yeah, I could that night," Kerry said. "Even with the rain and everything."

In the light, it was water and weather stained, and the boards creaked as they took the two steps up onto the overhung porch where they'd parked Mark's bike. As at that time, the door was open, and Kerry pushed it ahead of her and they went inside.

It smelled of gasoline and mulch, and old wood, just as it had. "That's what I thought was a horse thing." Kerry pointed to the side. "Tell me if I was right"

Dar went right over to the area and inspected it, going around the half wall and standing in the center. "Oh yeah," she concluded immediately. "It's even got feed bins, there. Cracked and useless, but that's the only thing they could be." She went over to the outside door and examined it.

With a tug, she drew back the sliding latch on the top half of the door, opened it and peered outside. "Nice out here on this side. There's a ramp." She noted. "And a trail, I think."

Kerry came over and peered out. "Where?"

"There." Dar pointed. "You can see the rocks lining it." She closed the top and latched it. "Cool." She regarded the inside of the horse stall. "Yeah, I can imagine a horse in here. Maybe they left it out, and let it roam around. Plenty of space." She glanced back out of the half wall. "You all were in here?"

"We were," Kerry said. "There's an oil lamp there. Mark lit it. We were just glad to be out of the rain." She gave the   railing an affectionate pat. "It's a nice shed."

"It is." Dar nodded. "C'mon. Let's go check out the house."

They walked out and went up the path again to the main roadway. "Mostly dried out," Dar said, as they walked along. On either side of the roadway was a grassy sward, before it merged into trees again. "Damn good thing those guys kept mowing the lawn."

"No kidding." Kerry shaded her eyes. "Are we going uphill? It felt like we were, going toward the house."

"Yes," Dar said. "I think it's built up on a limestone ridge." She looked between the trees, to her right. "Is that a... I think I hear water over there."

"We should make sure it's not a broken pipe," Kerry said.

"No kidding."

They detoured off the road and across the grass into the thickly forested area beyond it. They found a path among the trees and followed it until they halted at a roundish depression in the rocks filled with water, here under the trees shaded a murky dark amber.

"Is that left from the storm?" Kerry studied it. "No, look. There's a flow there. Maybe it is a broken pipe."

"Doesn't smell like chlorine." Dar went to the edge and knelt. She stuck her hand in and cupped the water, then brought it back up to her face and sniffed it. She then stuck her tongue cautiously in it. She mouthed the results, a surprised look on her face. "Thought that would be brackish at best. It's fresh."

Kerry came over. "Maybe he built it as a pond and filled it? It's nice, with all the trees hanging over it. I could imagine myself on a bench over there, reading a book." She pointed to one side of the pond, where there was some clear space, speckled with green and amber sunlight. "I like it."

"You know who else is going to like it?" Dar stood and shook the water droplets off her fingertips. "Our dogs."

"They like water," Kerry agreed, wryly. "You know, now that I think about it, it would be nice to sit out here and work when it's a little cooler. Can you cover this area with WIFI?"

Dar chuckled softly. "Sure." She studied the small pool. "I think it might be a spring, coming up from underground."

"That's cool," Kerry said. "I bet the birds love it."

"Bet they do."

They went back along the ridge to the road and continued on around the bend to the right, and then to the left that finally gave them a view of the house. This side of it included the access to the kitchen they used.

They stopped to regard the view facing them.

The architecture was utilitarian and functional. There were no embellishments, just square lines and straightforward building techniques. Most of the walls were built with the same stone technique as the outer ring wall was.

"I'm glad there are no gargoyles, Dar." Kerry said, after a long pause. "No weird statues or things anywhere." She looked around. "I guess the guardians aren't on duty today."

"Guess not," Dar said. "Maybe they cleared out after that night, Ker."

"Mm. Didn't read them that way, but maybe."

They walked up the steps to the kitchen door and tried it, but it was locked. They backed off from the concrete porch and walked along the back of the house to where the porch started on the left-hand side.

There was a small set of steps up, and an entryway that was worn by time and footsteps, up onto the broad, wooden porch that went along the side of the house. And here, in the light they could see the plant and algae stains on the walls and floors.

It was empty, but Kerry could easily imagine it with a table or two, and some comfortable chairs to sit on. The boards of the porch gave a little under their weight. They moved forward and lizards flew in every direction. There was a scent of old wood, and dirt and recent wetness around.

Halfway to the front of the house the view on their left cleared of the last of the trees, and the bay appeared, a mostly calm vista with a few boats on the horizon.

A fresh breeze came up off the water and made it almost pleasant in the shade.

There were tall, paned windows along the wall, and as they passed one Kerry looked to her right, into the inside of the house. She paused and went to the window and put her hands on the sill. She peered at the interior, at the hall with its stairwell up to the second level and its high ceilings, all painted in the same bland, off white.

Dar came up next to her and watched over her shoulder. "Big inside."

"It's like a blank canvas," Kerry said, after a long pause. "Dar, did he live in it like this? It's just a big white box inside. Unless that kid came and emptied this place all out. What do you think?"

"Could have. We can ask the rangers," Dar said. "I noticed that too, seemed like someone came in and repainted to get it sold. I mentioned that to Manuel. He thought so too." She paused. "So how would you restore that?"

"How would you?" Kerry mused. "I mean, if you don't have any of the original stuff, would there be a point? Have someone create replicas? I've been in historical houses. The fascination is seeing the actual things people lived with in those times."

"No one really wants to live in a museum of fake antiquities," Dar said, somewhat bluntly. "I don't."

"Do we have a choice if we go for this?"

"There's always choices," Dar said. "C'mon."

They walked around to what was the front of the house, which overlooked the deeply sunken pool, and the multilayered deck and the stone steps going down to the coral and wood dock.

Because the house was on a point, and this was the curve of it, their horizon was mostly open water across Biscayne Bay, facing Key Biscayne. "They didn't get the full storm surge here," Dar said, after a moment's silence. "The Key took the brunt."

They walked down the steps to the pool. It was half full of green, murky water and the deck was covered in debris. "That'll take some work," Kerry said. "Let's see what the dock's like."

There was an air of neglect here that wasn't as apparent in the rest of the property. Dar led the way carefully across to the edge of the stone verge. Another stretch of steps led downward to the dock level, but these had broken edges, and were covered in algae.

The dock itself seemed in battered, if okay condition. From where they were standing, they could smell the acrid richness of seaweed and the salt from the sea.

Kerry enjoyed the breeze, content to stay where she was as Dar navigated her way down the steps to inspect the piers safety. Several boats were out in the channel, but they were far away enough that their engines were inaudible. She could only hear the wash and slap of the tide against the rock wall.

She looked down, thoughtfully. Then she turned and looked up at the house, it's lower level at least ten or twelve feet higher than where she was standing.

"Looks all right." Dar climbed back up to stand next to her, dusting her hands off. "Literally just rock. Only thing its good for is parking the boat, if we want to, and tying up. There's some iron cleats sunk into it." She glanced across the channel. "Have to pick up gas over at the marina there."

There was a stone bench at the edge of the deck, and Kerry went over and sat down on it. "A little shorter run down to the cabin. It's a lot of work though." She removed a small camera from her pocket. "Was it like this back here when you looked at it, Dar?" She took some shots of the exterior.

Dar joined her, and they watched as two boats cruised by, one with the blue flashing lights that indicated some kind of officialdom. The other was a sturdy work boat, a cabin cruiser with a heavy set of visible radar and a half dozen men in khakis and golf shirts onboard. "No water in the pool," Dar said. "But yeah, looks pretty much the same. "

The boats slowed and then the one with the light started circling, while the other puttered around in a roughly square pattern. "What do you figure, Dar? Are they looking for a sunken boat or something?"

"They're sounding." Dar watched them. "So, they're looking for something."

"Something like a body something?"

"No, not with a depth sounder." Dar leaned back and folded her arms. "Maybe someone dropped something there. It's too far off to be a car or that sort of thing." She paused thoughtfully. "Sunken boat maybe."

"Mm."

They turned and regarded the outdoor space. It was, aside from the stone platforms, devoid of any decoration. There were no plaster fountains, or dolphins or anything. Just... "Like inside," Dar said. "An empty slate. I wonder if there's anything that shows what this place looked like when he lived here" Maybe we can research it once the libraries open up again. Might be in the Main library off Brickell. They have a big Florida history section."

"Is this going to be crazy, Dar?" Kerry asked, suddenly. "What if we can't do anything at all here? What if we can't even put in air-condition-ing?" She kicked her heels gently against the rock. "I guess we can..." She fell silent.

"We can build a tent platform and put a tent up." Dar said. "And get a swamp cooler."

"Dar."

"Let's see what the actual historical designation is." Dar smiled gently. "Is it the house, or is it this homestead? There's land enough here to build whatever we want if we can't live in that big thing." She patted Kerry's knee. "Relax until we know."

Kerry shifted and regarded her with interest. "Explain that a little."

"What was declared historic? His house? The pool? The dock? Or the entire property?" Dar said. "That'll outline what can be done. What are they protecting?"

"Huh."

Dar gestured. "There's nothing particularly historically interesting here, Ker. Old man Hunter was a character, but he wasn't anyone who was taught about, or did something that was notable. He just owned this place and was a cantankerous bastard. What is it they want to save?"

"Huh," Kerry repeated. "I figured he was famous, as in, I could go down to the Herald and do research on him kind of famous," she said. "I had a note to do that before the entire half of the state got pressure washed and I haven't had time to use our three bits a second access to look at anything."

"Far as I know, he was just known for annoying the local tax collector, and anyone who wanted to develop this point." Dar stood up. "Let's keep exploring. Maybe we'll find a treasure map," she said. "Maybe we can build a high-tech tree house over in those woods."

Kerry amiably followed her, as Dar picked her way across the debris strewn deck and past the green, murky pool. They left the water behind and walked around to the south of the house, along a path of crushed shells bordered by old, scuffed half pavers.

It gave their footsteps a gentle crunch, a bit like breakfast cereal. The path led away from the bay and into a thick stand of trees, winding between two ridges of moss and fern covered rock. It was odd, and uneven. There were dips and trenches all along the ground, with moss covered trees full of feathery red bark and thick leaves, only a little stripped from the recent storm.

"You know what this reminds me of, Dar?" Kerry said. She stopped and looked at the trench to her right. "Weirdly, but a little?"

"Coral."

Kerry turned. "It does, doesn't it? It's like a reef, but above ground." She turned around in a circle. "What is this?" She asked. "I don't think I've ever seen nature like this anywhere."

Dar went over to one of the ridges and sat down on it. "It's part of the Miami Rock Ridge." She slid her boots out and studied them. "It's a line of topology that goes from the top of the keys up to the county line. There are only tiny bits of it left showing in places here in the east. Wainright Park has some of them. I remember seeing it when I was there for some picnic or something."

Kerry sat down next to her. "It's a little jungle like." She touched one of the ferns. "It makes most of the land sort of..."

"Unusable unless you flatten the ridge, grind it down to the ground like they've done to the rest of it around here. It's limestone." Dar rubbed her thumb against the rock. "And... at one time, in the past, it really was part of the ocean floor." She looked around at the quiet surroundings. "If I scraped the top of this, we'd find sea fossils. Miami Rock Ridge was what it sounds like, it was a ridge. It's about twelve to fifteen feet above sea level," Dar said. "So, the house there, it's built on top of the ridge. He left the rest of it." She glanced around, and then up at the canopy, visibly shredded and thinned by the storm. "Natural, I guess."

Kerry got up and wandered farther on the path. "You said there were mangos here." She paused and looked up at a tree. "And... avocados?"

"And gumbo limbos, but I don't think you make gumbo from them." Dar smiled. "This is old Florida. This is what it was, before all the development. Just swamp and plants and nature."

It was hard to imagine. Kerry turned around in a circle again, then she climbed up onto the limestone ridge and walked along it and stepped over a small gap that held a thick puff of ferns. "I think this is cool," she said. "I like it, Dar. It's really kind of unique."

"Reminds me of some places down south I used to camp in, when I was small," Dar said, with a smile. "All gone now. I drove through the area when I was doing work down there. Condos." She leaned back against a tree pole, a tall pine with horizontal branches.

"What are these?" Kerry found a small, green leaved bush tucked behind a line of the red barked trees. "Baby oranges? Do they grow up to be big oranges?" She looked enchanted. "Fresh squeezed orange juice from our own tree in the morning?"

Dar hopped up onto the ridge and walked over to look past her at it. She started laughing.

"What's funny?"

"Those are kumquats."

Kerry stared at the small, round fruits on the bush. "Those are kumquats?"

"Those are kumquats." Dar searched among the leaves. "Careful, it's got thorns." She found a mostly ripe one and removed it from its stem. Then she took a bite of it and handed the rest over to Kerry.

"You eat the skin?" Kerry watched her chew and nod. Then she put the half fruit into her mouth and bit down. Immediately, she regretted it. "Oh, crap, Dar," she mouthed, caught between wanting to spit it out and her ingrained manners. "It's sour!"

With a grimace she swallowed the tart, tangy substance and breathed in, getting an intense wash of citrus across the back of her throat. It made her eyes tear, and she half turned, giving Dar an outraged look.

Her partner stood there innocently, licking her lips. "They're great on pizza."

"You're toast." Kerry bolted for her, hands extended to give her a pinch.

"They're not bad on toast, either." Dar hopped out of range. "C'mon, can't you imagine those as a jam?"

Chapter Sixteen

"You know what?" Dar climbed back into the truck, still perched on the sidewalk. "People were told to have three days supply of things in their house."

"It's been three days." Kerry closed the door on the passenger side, twirling a reddish leaf, newly fallen, between her fingers. "So now what. Is that what you mean?"

"That's what I mean." Dar started the engine and reached up to take her sunglasses from their holder and slid them over her eyes. "You know what we need?"

"Combuses." Kerry smiled briefly. "Oh lord I remember those showing up." She paused, suddenly, as Dar rocked the truck down off the sidewalk and onto the road.

"Huh."

"Huh?"

"No, was just thinking of something," Kerry murmured. "They need to start getting things open again, Dar."

"Portable kitchens. Food trucks. Why can't they?" Dar asked.

"Probably no one thought of it," Kerry said. "Which is a damn shame, because let me tell ya, they could be roaming around all over the place making an absolute killing right now." She propped her head up on one hand, her elbow on the car jamb. "Why didn't Sasha think about that?"

"Sasha's probably kitting out Scott's Airstream right now to go mobile." Dar found a side street and turned down it. "Let's see if there's a route that doesn't involve me going up on the sidewalk." She went west a block and turned north again, down a street that was filled with branches, but no full trees.

Kerry looked thoughtfully at the neighborhood they were rolling through. "Is this all really on top of that ridge thing you were talking about?"

Dar was silent for a few minutes. "Actually, I think it is." She sounded slightly surprised. "Which makes sense, I guess. We had surge, but not much flooding by the office and in that area," she considered. "That reminds me, I guess we should see if our lamented landlord had flood insurance."

"Wouldn't he have to?"

"Not necessarily."

"This is one of those Florida things, right? Because this whole state is practically flat as a pancake. Everyone should have to have flood insurance, Dar. We have it at the condo."

"Sure. It's an island. We have it at the cabin too," Dar said. "But both the island and our cabin are in an official flood zone. If you're not, you don't have to buy flood insurance."

"That office is a block from the water."

"But you have to go down four steps and it slopes to the parking lot." Dar turned back onto the main road. "I never thought about it until right now. Our first floor can see the roof of the sailing club."

"Wait. You mean our office is on this thing too?" Kerry sounded incredulous.

"Or built on top of a trash pit. Could go either way around here."

Kerry pondered this as they navigated Main Highway, which now had a lot of cars on it, moving slowly through the lightless four way stops. "I think I'm getting to really be fond of this Miami rock ridge, Dar," she said. "Even though I literally just heard about it."

Dar chuckled.

"So, I'm guessing where Maria lives isn't on this ridge," Kerry said, then paused, her eyes opening wider. "Hell, it's in a hollow behind it, isn't it?" She said. "I mean, if there's a ridge, by definition what's not that is in a valley, right?"

"Apparently. Though honestly it's not something I ever really paid much attention to," Dar said. "I'm not really into geology I just knew about the ridge because of a report I had to do for… " She paused. "High school biology maybe? Something about frogs."

"Frogs?" Kerry frowned, distracted. "What do frogs have to do with it?"

"Habitat. They live in the water and on land. Ask my mother."

"Your mother?"

"My mother. She had to go and kick the principal around because they thought I copied it from the Encyclopedia Britannica and my father was deployed at the time," Dar said absently, as she studied the street they were moving slowly along. "Yeah, all dry here."

They slowed to turn into the parking lot, and the National Guardsman on duty moved out of the way to let them through. He lifted a hand in brief acknowledgement, nodding when Dar returned the gesture.

"Seems okay," Kerry said. "Maybe they figured we really did them a favor?"

"Maybe."

Dar parked the truck and they got out. As they walked toward the front door to the office, Kerry appreciated the slight rise to the ground, and the uneven cast to it with new eyes. She hadn't really thought about it at all, but now she could see it, and the dip and trench in front of it that she always figured was on purpose.

Was it? She resolved to find some material on it once things got more normal. She caught up to Dar and slipped her arm through Dar's and clasped her hand.

They walked up the steps to the fortified porch and through the open door, where the sounds of some kind of sports report echoed.

Everyone was in the central space, the office itself was absolutely empty. There was no work going on in the lower hall, and the upper hall was silent. "It's Saturday here, I guess," Dar said.

Kerry nodded. "Good. Everyone deserves a break. Even us."

They walked through the hallway and out the back door and paused on the threshold and watched the activity outside.

Sasha was seated in a director's chair behind the now four grills and one portable cooktop, next to a refrigerated case that had a cable running from it to a square black box nearby that had a quadrangle of spread panels pointed up at the sun. "Hey hey!" She greeted them cheerfully.

"Solar panels?" Kerry pointed. "Are those solar panels on that UPS?"

"My brother brought them," Sasha said. "He's looking at that club there." She made a vague gesture toward the water. "Tear it all down, a mess! But he likes the dock, yes? He has his boat tied up to it. One of those boys, he said you had a phone call, Kerry."

"Not surprising. Was it from the island? I don't think we gave many people that number," Kerry said. "Never mind, let me go up there and see what that's all about. I'll just dial back from the caller ID." She turned and went back into the building. She went down the hall and into the room they'd put the radio in. The phone was still there, and she checked the history to find the last caller.

****

The inner yard was busy. Beyond the barbeque pad, and the Airstream parked next to it there was a group of mixed veterans and bodybuilders, with a few nerds thrown in playing baseball. It was a very short field, and there was more crap talking and laughter than serious play, but it sounded like fun.

"That soldier was here," Sasha said after a short silence. "Looking for you I think maybe. His whole bunch was here buying breakfast from me."

"He's pissed at my father." Dar came over to examine the solar panels. "I bet he wants to talk about that," she said. "This is a great idea." She indicated the panels. "We should get more."

"Stupid man then," Sasha said. "But I gave him a sandwich. He liked it." She regarded the panels. "You want? No problem. Let me tell my brother. He said he was going to get a big bunch sent to here from Vietnam."

"He could make a killing." Dar stood up. "We should get solar panels on the damn roof." She looked up at the building. "I bet we have enough footprint." She looked at Sasha. "You just take everything for granted."

Sasha smiled, ruefully. "Yes yes. You think the power, the air-conditioning always there." She looked around. "But we're doing pretty good here, you know?"

"Yeah," Dar said. "Well, let me go find out what the army wants." She turned and walked back through the building and out the front door.

A gentle puff of warm air hit her face as she went along the sidewalk and she was conscious of the sun as it striped her body coming through the branches of the trees around the office.

The leaves covered the ground and she heard the faint crunching her hiking boots made as she walked over them. She was glad, despite the heat, that she was wearing jeans and a collared shirt for this unexpected visit.

The captain was likely going to be a jerk. She was likely going to end up being an asshole to him, and she was self-aware enough to know that was more effective when you were not distracting things with animal physical presence.

Which she had. Dar wasn't blind to that.

Dar understood that she really had no responsibility over what her father had said. He was his own man and had his own views. She would no more have told him to hold them off than he would in the reverse.

Besides, she agreed with the sentiment. The guy had been a jerk to the crowd, no matter how nice he'd been to Kerry. She settled her attitude around her and went to the gate of the encampment, ready to deal with whatever was presented.

The guard recognized her, and willingly went to go find his captain at her polite request, apparently glad enough to get out of the sun that was baking the tarmac covered area.

Dar remained near the entrance and gazed idly around at the camp. The guard soldiers were all busy, moving around and mostly stocking boxes from a large 18-wheel truck into the back of smaller vehicles. Everyone was sweating, their uniforms dark with moisture.

It all seemed orderly, no one even gave her a sideways look and Dar relaxed a little, shifting her thoughts to the property they'd just come from. She pondered the possibilities of just how much trouble and heartache they'd opened themselves up for there.

Probably a lot. The more she'd looked at the house the more she'd realized there were going to be issues with the two of them trying to use it in the short, or even the long term. What with the legal entanglements that probably now existed around it.

And yet. Dar thought about the trees, and the pond, and all that space and she couldn't do anything but smile. Just walking around there had made her happy, and while she never would have considered buying a horse, the idea that Kerry had made her even happier.

She imagined, for a moment, coming there to the shed and finding a horse in it, and felt her face break into a grin. What kind of horse, she wondered, figuring without question it would be a pretty one with a soft nose.

"Ma'am?"

Dar jumped a little and turned, to find the guard who'd gone off standing there. "Hi." She focused on him. "We ready?"

"Yep, c'mon with me." The man gestured and turned, and headed off, clearly expecting Dar to follow him, which she did.

Dar was ushered into a tent at the back of the encampment, and as she entered the plastic lined door, she felt a puff of—not cold, but cooler air. At the back of the tent was a table, and on either side were smaller ones covered in what looked like radio gear.

The captain was behind the table, and now he looked up at her.

"My staff told me you were looking for me," Dar said. "What can I do for you?" She removed the sunglasses she was wearing and tucked them into the collar of her shirt and stood there waiting for his response.

"I was," the captain said. "Sit down."

For a moment, Dar paused, as though considering remaining standing, and then she took a seat on the folding visitor chair he'd put in front of his makeshift desk. To one side of it, there was a corrugated hose about a foot in diameter, and that was producing the cooler air. The pretention of it made her lip twitch.

She folded her hands, interlacing her fingers and stared at him, until he looked away.

"I just want to get something clear between us," he said. "About all this high and mighty stuff."

Dar remained staring at him, and he avoided her eyes. "You and I have had about two minutes of conversation and none of it was anything other than random Spanish translation about water," she said, in a deliberate tone. "Is this about last night?"

"We have a mission here. It doesn't involve pandering to unprepared residents," the captain said, flatly.

"Okay," Dar responded in a mild tone. "No one forced you to pander to anyone. We did it ourselves because we could. Seems to me like that should satisfy all around."

He stood. Dar remained in her seat. "I have done all I can do to help you. You had no reason to call my brass and get them involved."

Dar's brows creased at once and her face tensed into an expression of bewilderment. "Excuse me?"

"No, I don't excuse you." The man was furious. "Telling my bosses, we're a bunch of hicks? That we don't know what we're doing? Bold words, coming from the likes of you." He leaned forward. "Maybe I should tell all them people what you are."

Dar's brow remained creased. "What I am?" She asked, in a puzzled tone. "Those people, in the building there?" She pointed at the office. "You going to tell them I'm gay? They know." She now wondered what the hell was going on. "No one cares."

"That you all, you bleeding hearts, you're the granddaughter of a Grand Dragon," he said. "They know that? They think you're all let's be fair and equal?" He lifted his hands up. "Preaching all that be good to your neighbor mish mash?"

Dar stood up. Then she put her hands on his fake desk and leaned forward, making him abruptly straighten to move back rather than go nose to nose with her. "They wouldn't care any more than I do about some guy I never met who my dad turned his back on when he was sixteen," she said. "Or did you think I didn't know?" She leveled her eyes at him. "That the game? Shame me on it?"

"Well makes all that lefty spouting a lie, don't it?" he said, after a long pause, his anger replaced with sudden uncertainty. "Wasn't sure your old man told you. I heard he didn't get on with his pa." His head jerked. "But you know what I'm talking about. You don't believe all that we're all the same BS. No way you do. Not coming from where we come from."

Dar stared at him for a long moment. "Do I believe we're all the same?" she finally said. "No. We're all different. But what color we are, or where we were born or who we sleep with doesn't matter in what we bring to the table as an individual."

He stared at her, visibly working that out.

Dar helped him out. "Bigotry is stupid and a waste of time," she said. "Exceptional people come from everywhere."

"A hundred generations of my family thinks that's BS," he said, bluntly. "And there's a lot more of us, than of you, thank the Lord."

"My father was right," Dar said. "You are an asshole, and what's worse, you're a stupid one." She removed her sunglasses from the neckline of her shirt and shook her head. "I'll do us both a favor and not tell him we had this conversation. But for the record." She put her sunglasses on. "I didn't call anyone about anything last night."

"I'm sure you didn't."

"I didn't," Dar repeated. "But now I just might." She turned and went to the door, thrusting the flap open and nearly bowling over a young guardsman standing just outside as she strode toward the gate.

****

Kerry put the phone down and sat back. She picked up the pen on the desk and twiddled it between her fingers. "Hmm." She pondered the scribbling she'd scrawled down, then paused as she heard the distinctive sound of Dar climb the stairs at the end of the hall.

Always at a jog trot, not enough weight to be one of the guys, but with a power and energy she immediately recognized. She got up and went to the door and stuck her head out as Dar reached the top of the steps and started her way.

She was pissed. Kerry emerged all the way out into the hallway and prepared herself to deal with whatever it was that had ticked her partner off. "What's up?"

"Stupid moron." Dar came to a halt, her nostrils flaring a little bit. "I'm going to kick their asses out of our parking lot."

Kerry reached out and put a hand on Dar's stomach. "Hold on. What happened?" she asked. "I thought it was Dad he was mad at. Isn't he? Let him be, Dar. If he's dumb enough to mess with him, he'll end up with his head planted in his ass on the corner out there."

Dar took a breath and released it. "Someone called that moron's boss and told him he was being an ass."

Kerry nodded. "Good for them. He was. Why is that a problem?"

"He thinks it was me."

Kerry hooked a finger into one of Dar's belt loops. "Let's get some coffee," she said, and they retreated to kitchenette. "Does he think it was you because of what Dad said?" She took out two cups, while Dar leaned against the wall, arms folded. "And I mean, who cares?"

She poured coffee into the cups and looked back over her shoulder at her glowering companion. "What on earth did he say to get you so upset?" She handed Dar a cup, waiting for her to take it before she picked up her own.

"He wanted to know how the granddaughter of a Grand Wizard got off calling him a bigot."

Kerry paused in mid sip, absolutely still, staring at Dar over the rim of her cup in utter silence for a long moment. Then she put the cup down on the small table, covered in carefully clipped and wrapped bags of potato chips and pretzels. "He fucking said what?"

The reaction seemed to mollify Dar. "He threw it at me like he was going to tell everyone, and it would matter." She took a sip of the coffee. "Jackass."

"He actually said that?" Kerry leaned forward against the table, still incredulous.

"He actually said that."

"What did you answer for that?" Kerry straightened up and put her hands on her hips. "Did you tell him... what did you tell him?"

"I told him my father was right. He was an asshole, and what's more, he was a stupid one," Dar dutifully reported. "And that while I didn't call anyone about him, now I might."

"What did he say to that?"

"No idea. I left." Dar gave herself a little shake, as though settling ruffled feathers. "It's just bullshit. Ticked me off." She started investigating the bags. "Oh... Fritos." She unclipped it and removed a handful of the chips, crunching one contentedly. "What was the call?"

Kerry sat down on the nearby stool. "Hold on, let me finish being seeing red level mad," she said. "Of all the completely idiotic things for that bozo to pull out of his ass. What a piece of trash." She felt almost lightheaded. She looked up at Dar who stood next to the table, watching her with bemused concern. "What an absolute piece of trash."

Dar put down her coffee and came around behind Kerry and put her hands on her shoulders. "Total," she said. "When he first started hinting he was going to spill something about me I thought it was that I was gay. And I was like, boy are you late to the party."

That brought a short, almost barking laugh from Kerry. "Our staff you mean?"

"Everyone around here."

"Yeah, no one's asked me if we're sisters in a while." Kerry leaned back against her. "Jesus, that's so... I mean, why would it even matter, Dar? He's your grandfather. You never even met him. You can't change who he was."

"I can't change being gay," Dar replied simply. "Wouldn't want to." She wrapped her arms around Kerry. "But I guess from his world view, blood matters."

"It doesn't." Kerry said, softly. "But you know, my father believed the same kinds of things. He wrapped fancy language around it, but it was all about that," She said. "All about hate, all about how everyone who wasn't exactly you or your kind were bad, were evil."

"Were going to hell," Dar finished for her.

"That too," Kerry said. "But you know, that was never part of the dialog, Dar. We were never pitched that going to hell line, we were just told we'd be thrown out of the family and when all you know is your family, that's even more terrifying than hell."

"Didn't want to be an outcast."

"No." Kerry paused, and then she twisted around in her seat to look up at Dar. "Did you ever feel like that, Dar?" She watched that strong profile shift a little, as her partner thought. "Like you didn't want to be the outsider? Wanted just to be... normal?"

Normal, meaning conventional. Not gay. Traditional. A Christmas card that had a man, and a woman, kids, a pious, solemn engraving with a clear, undisputed place in the world.

She met Dar's eyes, knowing the truth even before her partner spoke.

"Me?" Dar smiled suddenly and engagingly, a roguish twinkle appeared in her eyes as she shook her head. "Nah. I was always the outsider, Ker." She looked fondly down at her. "The most normal thing I ever did was marry you."

Utter truth, and Dar both lived that truth and was totally comfortable with it. She enjoyed being a unicorn, albeit that her unicorn manifestation would have a pirate patch over one eye and go around biting people on the ass.

Kerry had endured a different history. She was glad, though, that Dar didn't have to carry that burden and reckoned she, herself, would come to that lived truth eventually.

"Heh." Kerry released her anger. "What a derp that guy turned out to be," she said. "We should kick them out of our parking lot. Being there might give us a bad name," she added, then moved on. "So, the call. The call was one of my prospects, telling me they were going to kill their project for now. I don't blame them; it was a sales gig."

"Don't blame them either."

"They did like my pitch though," Kerry said. "It was a weird one.

They wanted to open up a sales office that could service all three counties but not have to have their salespeople travel."

"Eh?"

"Anyway," Kerry went on. "I pitched we set them up with a back office in Miramar, and then three traveling tricked out mobile homes, bring the sales pitch to the customer but with a sat service so their people could work."

Dar was momentarily silent. "Wow," she said then, her eyebrows lifting. "That's a great idea, Ker."

"I know." Kerry grinned. "They would have gone for it. But..." She lifted one hand and made a vague gesture. "Anyway, I'll have to call the mobile rental agency and cancel the hold I'd put on three of them. Bummer." She leaned against Dar again. "So that's zero clients except for the government that's going to be any net new. Maybe that Colorado office really does need to spin up, huh?" She exhaled. "If we want to keep making payroll."

Dar was silent for a long minute. "I'll send Mark out there," She said. "And call that agency, but don't cancel them. Have them deliver those things here."

"Here?"

"Here, and have them set up service for them. We'll use them to let people live in them while things are getting done here. Maria and Tomas can use one," Dar said. "They can't live in that house, but they can live in there and go back and forth."

"Holy crap, why didn't I think of that?" Kerry said. "I didn't even remember about that pitch until they called me."

"Call them." Dar gave her a bump. "Fast, because everyone in South Florida's going to be thinking of that if they already haven't."

"On it." Kerry hopped up off the stool and strode out of the kitchenette, leaving Dar to finish her coffee and a handful of Fritos.

****

Dar stood talking to Carlos in the courtyard, the long shadows of early evening striping it when the sudden vibration against her hip made her jump and let out a faint squawk.

"What?" Carlos whirled, jerked out of absorbing the tale of Dar's interaction with the guard captain. "What's wrong?" He searched the area quickly.

"My damn phone." Dar dug her cell phone out and inspected it. "Holy crap I have signal."

"What?" Carlos turned and cupped his hands to his mouth. "Hey, everybody! Cell's back!" He turned back. "Lemme go get mine. I left it upstairs." He moved quickly toward the door. "Progress!" he yelled and lifted both hands into the air.

Dar nodded, as she watched her phone sync it's messages, with a somewhat wan, but apparently sufficient two bars of radio power. She turned to see Kerry sprinting out of the door and held the phone up. "Look!"

"Wasn't expecting that!" Kerry said, her own phone in her hand. "Wow!"

"Mixed blessing." Dar inspected the message counter. "There's one from Richard. Let me call him and see how it went with those lawyers." She selected the number and hit the dial. "Call Colleen and tell her the lines are up again."

Kerry glanced up, actually in the act of doing that very thing, but Dar had half turned and covered her other ear, as the crowd in the courtyard came together, everyone checking their phones.

She sat down on one of the camp chairs as the phone was answered. "Hey, Col!"

"O... wh... oh!" Colleen responded. "It's you!" She sounded immensely surprised. "They said there wasn't going to be phones down there for another week! We were just talking about that, me and Mr. Mark here."

"Not sure where the signal's back, but we've got some here at the office now," Kerry told her. "Not surprising since we're not that far from city center." She stretched her feet out. "How's it going? You all at the hotel today?"

"Calls are going fine, and so far, the call center customers are happy," Colleen said. "We've got the place set up pretty nicely, but I have to say the team misses being back there."

"Do they?"

"They do," Colleen said. "Even though it's a mess there, and we're comfortable here, it's not home." She paused to listen to something. "No that's right, Mark, we haven't had time to really look around much, but still."

Kerry pondered that. "Well, they can't really do much here, even if we've got some cell back and there's a generator around the corner power-ing some stuff in the office and we have..." She glanced to her left. "Some solar panels."

Colleen laughed. "Surprised Dar hasn't fixed up a hydro engine over there by now. Anyway I think the folks here have been talking to the folks down there and they've got a case of the FOMO's," She said. "Had two of them ask me yesterday before we left that office when we could go back."

"Huh," Kerry said. "Let me talk to Dar. It's so crazy here, Col. And we have no real way to keep the phones up. I don't know how stable or perma-nent this cell signal is."

"I told them it'd be a couple weeks at least," Colleen reassured her. "So don't you worry, there, madame, they're not going to start a caravan just yet. I just wanted you to know how they felt, and now if the phones are back ... oh wait you said you didn't have city power yet."

"No. So our company is being run from a shoestring out on that island that could honestly go down any minute. If I was going to do a caravan, I'd do it in the other direction." Kerry sighed. "Col, we can hold on like this for a little while, but there's a ton we can't do."

"Hold on," Colleen said. "Mark wants a word."

Kerry waited for the phone to be transferred and glanced aside to watch as Dar paced slowly back and forth, under one of the trees. The gathering twilight in the courtyard, and the rich, vivid orange of the sun still visible on the roof marked the end of the day, and in that she could also feel a cooler breeze coming from the water not far away.

She was surprised to find she felt comfortable, sitting there.

"Hey, poquito boss."

"Hey, Mark." Kerry focused her attention on the phone. "What's up? You guys doing okay up there?"

"Barbara's super happy. She's got a desk all set up in our office and an Internet connection, and air-conditioning. Her company's happy with us," Mark said. "I've mostly just been grabbing calls since I got here."

"People bitching?"

"Some," Mark said. "Got some calls from those guys in Brazil wanting to know what was going on. They were supposed to kick off on Monday." He paused. "Wasn't really sure what to tell them."

Kerry closed her eyes. "What is it they need... oh, that was the new support team, wasn't it? They were supposed to onboard this past week."

"Yeah. We told the sourcing op to hold on because of the storm. I tried to call them to find out if they still have those guys lined up, but I couldn't reach em, like anyone else down there. Maybe now that you're back up though..."

"Crap." Kerry exhaled. "Okay let me review the scope for them and see what options we have."

"Sorry, boss."

"Not your fault."

"No, I know," Mark said. "We just had a lot of stuff going on."

"Yeah."

"I can try to find some folks up here?" Mark ventured. "We can just set them up in the office where the rest of the team is, y'know? I think ... maybe not here in Melbourne but maybe closer over in Orlando we can find some people with that skill set, the cloud guys."

Kerry pondered that. "Damn, I'm torn. It's a great idea, but we went through a great round with that team from here, and I thought they were a really good fit for the customer. It's going to take weeks to get back to that point with new people."

"Well—"

"No, I know. Do it." Kerry gently cut him off. "At least, get that in motion, and either way let's get an area set up for them up there."

"Got it." Mark sounded more confident. "And I'll call that guy back on

Monday and tell him we've got a plan," he added. "We'll figure it out."

"Dar's going to call you and talk to you about a startup office in Colorado," Kerry said. "It's all tied up with that new advance they made with the AI platform she's doing for the DOD."

Mark was momentarily silent. "Wow," he finally said. "They want us to open an office there for that?"

"No, she'll explain it. Someone else is interested in using it for something else," Kerry said. "it's kind of..." She hesitated. "Um..."

"On the Q. Got it." Mark cut her off this time. "Did you like it when you got to try it? I heard you did. The kids down there won't shut up about it."

"I did." Kerry drew in a breath and exhaled. "It's really something else. I get what the big deal is."

"Cool. Here lemme give you back to Colleen. It's awesome you guys are back online. We'll try to hold the fort down from here, Kerry. Don't stress."

"Was I stressing?"

"Sounded like."

She consciously cleared her throat a little and acknowledged there were people in her immediate circle who now knew her well enough to know that, just from her speech. "I'll do my best, Mark. We just found out this morning it turns out we did get that property in the South Grove."

"Oooh boy."

"Yeah, like we needed that complication. Anyway, get some rest, and tell Col I'll call her tomorrow. Just wanted to let you all know we had some service back."

Kerry hung up, and let the phone rest against her thigh. She idly watched the people, in random groups, check their phones, or talk on them.

It was strange. When they'd been so cut off, it seemed like they had time to deal with whatever it was that was happening. Now that she knew they weren't, she felt like she was now aware of time ticking, of things left undone.

Of people's expectations they were maybe going to let down.

Dar came over to her and sat down in the camp chair next to her, her phone clasped in her hands. "Considering taking a weed whacker and going to find the closest cell tower and sabotage it."

Kerry eyed her, eyebrows raised.

"Historical society legal team is driving down and wants to meet at the Point tomorrow," Dar said. "Apparently we're legally responsible for any changes that were made to the property since they received the affidavit."

"Dar, that's ridiculous. We just took ownership."

"Richard agrees, which is why he's on his way here with another legal buddy of his to help us." Dar sighed. "He seems to think these people are kinda on the wingnut side."

"Great."

"On the other hand," Dar continued, extending her hand out between their chairs. "It's the end of the day, it's Saturday night, and I'd like to take you home and go to bed with you."

Kerry took her hand. "You're on." She forcibly dismissed the anxiety that had started to crash over her. "Let's go. Tomorrow's another day."

"Tomorrow is." Dar stood, pulled her up, and led her toward the door, leaving the busy courtyard behind them.

****

The breeze off the water was acceptably cool, enough to make the warmth of the hot tub both comforting and comfortable. Kerry stretched her legs out and relaxed against the smooth side wall, glad to simply wait for Dar to pour some wine from her seat next to her.

The sky ahead of her was dark and the Atlantic Ocean just the rush and rumble of waves. Below, in the garden, she heard the muffled clanks and rumble of speech of the men working in the glare of the outside lights, invisible past the edge of the patio half wall.

Dar handed her a glass of wine and leaned back at her side. "There."

"Where did your mom say they were going?" Kerry asked, after a sip of the chilled pale beverage.

"Fort Lauderdale," Dar said. "Something to do with the Coast Guard. I didn't really ask for details." She tipped her head back against the edge of the tub and regarded the invisibly cloudy sky. "They said they'll be back on Monday."

Kerry nodded. "So, the storm is now rolling over New York," she mused. "But it's only a Cat one. Or is it just really a Northeaster?" She took a sip of wine. "I saw there's flooding in Manhattan. I'm pretty sure we walked in some of those tunnels they were showing."

"We were."

"Glad we're not there now," Kerry said. "Based on that news report, it's more chaotic there than it ended up being here."

"Me too." Dar slid closer and pressed her shoulder against Kerry's. "I can imagine all those tunnels filled with water."

Kerry pondered that. "Can rats swim?" she asked. "Because that would be terrible, wouldn't it? There's a hell of a lot of them down there."

Dar turned her head and looked at Kerry. "If they can't, they'll probably just take over the subway cars and ride uptown. But yeah, I think they swim. The ones here do." She took a sip of her wine, and exhaled.

The sound of the bubble jets were soothing, and the smell of the chlorinated water familiar. There was a pot of soup warming on the stove inside for their dinner, and the promise of a peaceful night ahead of them.

Somewhere, off to the east, thunder rumbled, but it was far away, as was the lightning on the horizon. Chino and Mocha were curled up on the couch inside. For the first time in days, it seemed okay to just sit back and chill.

It was awesome to have it be quiet, and sort of normal. Kerry wiggled her toes and felt the jets against the bottom of her feet. She set her glass down and rested her head against Dar's conveniently nearby shoulder.

"Surprised we ended up having signal here," Dar said.

Kerry eyed her. "I'm not," she said. "A, we have power, B, the governor's here, and C, money talks."

"Well, that's all true."

"Too bad it's just voice service," Kerry said. "I mean, it's better than nothing, but it would be great not to have to deal with that satellite anymore."

"Yeah, I'm sure they cut off data because they've only got one tin can and one string up." Dar slid down and enjoyed the jets pounding against her back. "Better than nothing though."

It was. Kerry finished the wine in her glass and floated quietly for a few minutes, and then pushed herself up and swung her legs over the side of the tub. "I'm going to make sure the soups not bubbling over." She slid down to the tile and picked up one of the two towels nearby and draped it around her swim suited body.

She slid the glass doors open and went inside and felt the brush of the chill air against her skin. She crossed into the kitchen and took the cover off the soup and picked up a wooden spoon stirring it experimentally. "Looks good."

She turned on the convection oven to toast the bread and started a pot of tea going, then went over into the bedroom to exchange her suit for a worn T-shirt.

Chino lifted her head and watched her as she returned, ears perked. Mocha was dreaming, his front paws twitching and soft grunting yelps came from between his lips. "Hey, kids," Kerry said to them, as she went by. "It's nice to have a quiet night, huh?"

Chino barked gruffly.

She went back to the kitchen and studied the toasting bread, then glanced out the window to watch the gardeners at work below. It seemed like they were almost done. Kerry was charmed to see the improvement, even more so when Dar diffidently admitted to her machination of it.

Plants in the yard—frivolous. And in the long run of things, unimportant. Yet the orderliness of it did in fact make her feel better, regardless of how insignificant it was in the broader view. And thinking of Dar pausing in her work to meticulously arrange for it made her smile.

She heard the glass door slide open and looked to the left as Dar's tall form appeared in the opening to the kitchen. "You know what?"

"What?" Dar tucked her towel in and folded her arms across her chest and leaned one shoulder against the doorjamb.

"You are the best." Kerry came over, stretching up and giving her a kiss on the lips. "I love you."

Dar responded with a pleased smile, and she returned the kiss. "Back at ya, Ker." She paused, and rested her forehead against Kerry's. "No matter the craziness of the world, we got this."

"We do."

Dar kissed her again. "Let me go change. We've got a night to ourselves and I'm damned if I'm not going to enjoy it. "

Kerry gave her a pat on the hip and sent her on her way, and then turned back to the preparation of their light meal.

****

"Everything going okay there, Mayte?" Kerry sprawled on the couch in Dar's office, aware of the sound of the kitchen door opening and the hustle of toenails on the floor outside.

"Yes, it is quiet," Mayte said. "Some people came by here, and they were looking for you and Dar. I took down their information and sent a note over."

"Hmm."

"They said it was important. Something about your new house."

"Oh boy." Kerry sighed. "Well, it can wait for Monday. Nothing's going on there tonight or tomorrow, I can tell you that."

"Si, I told them, but that made them upset. So, I asked them what they wanted, you know?" Mayte said. "To see if I could help them but they said it was private." She sniffed audibly. "I think they didn't want any help."

"Some scam, probably." Kerry stifled a yawn. "Okay, thanks, Mayte. Everyone comfortable there? Those soldiers didn't cause any problems, did they?"

"Oh no. They have not come here," Mayte said. "Zoe told me that Hank has told her they were told to stay away from us."

Kerry had mixed feelings about that. She didn't really want to have an antagonistic relationship with a large group of armed people, but on the other hand, they were being led by a jerk and probably some of them were of the same mind. She didn't really want them around her people either.

"Good," she said, briskly. "Just so you know, they kind of had a mix up with Dar earlier."

Mayte chuckled a little. "Si, we heard about that. Some of them told us because they could hear it, and we know the boss of them is mad at us because we helped those poor people. Carlos called them some names," she said. "And Hank was telling everyone about how these people should not be bothering Dar because she will kick them."

Kerry took a breath to dismiss the idea, then paused. "Well, that's true," she admitted finally. "But they shouldn't bother Dar for a lot of other reasons. Or any of us. We did the right thing."

"Yes, we did that. Zoe was telling everyone all about it and she told the news person who was here too."

"News person?" Instinctively, Kerry leaned over and looked out the door toward the television, where the governor was holding what appeared to be a press conference.

"Si, they came here because they heard about the water. Someone told them," Mayte said. "I think I am becoming good with talking to reporters."

Kerry could well imagine it. "Okay, I can't wait to see where that ends up. But you all stay clear of the soldiers. We don't need any more trouble."

"Okay, no problem," Mayte said. "We will leave them alone, but some of them are upset because they liked very much the food from Sasha, and I think they will come here anyhow. Some of them are not bad, I think so?"

"I'm sure that's true, Mayte. Just be careful," Kerry told her. "And hey, I have a surprise for you all tomorrow that I hope's going to work out. And maybe after that we can convince the soldiers to move along."

"Oh, yes?"

"Yes. I'm going to wait to see if it works out before I say anything." Kerry smiled. "I don't want to get anyone's hopes up. But I think it will really help. And, by the way, we do have cell signal out here. So, if these phones go down, you can reach us that way."

"No problem, and everyone is very glad they can use their phones now," Mayte said. "I was talking to Mama before, and Zoe was able to talk to her sister. It makes everyone feel better, you know? To know things are okay."

"Like I do right now." Kerry grinned. "Okay, you guys go have fun, and we'll see you tomorrow. We have to go by our new place, and then we'll be over there and maybe we'll have some good news for you." She paused. "And your parents."

"Oh, yes?" Mayte repeated the question, which was now audibly a curious question. "Mama told me the doctors said yes, they will let Papa go out of the hospital tomorrow. I told her it would be good for her and Papa to go out to where Colleen and Mark are, but she won't listen to me," she added mournfully.

"No, me or Dar either." Kerry commiserated with her. "Your mom's a stubborn woman. But we'll see what we can do for them. Cross your fingers it all works out."

"Okay, Kerry, have a good night," Mayte said. "We will see you tomorrow."

Kerry hung up the phone, then got up and went into the living room just as the kitchen door opened and Dar came back in, with both dogs in attendance. "They done?"

"Done." Dar came over and extended a hand to her. Between her fingers was a flower. Kerry leaned over and sniffed it delicately, with a smile. "Looks a lot better than it did this morning."

"It sure does." Kerry took the flower and walked over to one of the bookcases. She selected a large book and opening it. "Let's see." She settled the flower between the pages and closed the book. "Remember I put that at Chapter 4, will you?"

She put the Modern History of Computing back on the shelf. "We attracted news attention again, according to Mayte. Someone came by about the whole water thing."

"Nice." Dar rolled her eyes. "Wish I knew who kept poking that bear," she muttered. "Didn't think there were that many people around that night to see what happened, unless you count the folks needing water."

"And some random dudes came by looking for us about something to do with the Point." She looked up to see Dar make a face. "Yeah, I know. I told Mayte to just leave it all alone and go to bed."

"Great idea." Dar took her by the shoulders and turned her toward their bedroom. "Let's go do that."

"Let's." Kerry allowed herself to be nudged toward the room, where she could see through the door the waiting comfort of bed and the cool tones of the walls.

She could already smell the scent of clean linen, and the wood of the new corner dresser they'd recently put in, and from behind them the lingering hint of lemongrass from the soup they'd shared.

Dar pulled her T-shirt off over her head and paused to fold it neatly, setting it down on the dresser, her tall body outlined in the dim lamplight.

Kerry took off her own shirt and detoured into the bathroom and half turned to check if the sunburn she'd gotten the other day had faded. "Hah."

Dar slid in behind her. "No peeling," she said. "Nice." She ran her hands over Kerry's shoulder blades, and then gently kissed the back of her neck. "Wonder what happened to your pilot. Think he hung around with those guys out west?"

Kerry turned and slid her arms around Dar's waist. "Depends how much they offered." She looked up and studied the pale blue eyes watching her. "I hope they treated him good. He did us a good thing, bitching all the way through it. "

"He did." Dar kissed her, then reached out to shut off the bathroom light as she backed toward the bed, her arms draped around Kerry's shoulders. "Bitching or not."

They paused by the edge of the bed and kissed again. They stood there in a light embrace that shifted as they started to explore each other, and thoughts of airboats and their troubles evaporated.

They slid into bed, and Dar untangled one arm long enough to reach out to turn off the light that plunged the bedroom into darkness, save only the faint stripes of moonlight coming in through the not quite shuttered closed windows.

****

The next morning dawned bright, with only a scattering of clouds in the sky. The air was full of moisture and even the early morning sun shimmered against it.

Dar had just put their backpacks into the truck when she heard the crunch of footsteps on the drive behind her. She stepped back to see who was coming.

"Morning," the stocky, middle-aged man coming toward her said, shortly.

Oh great. Dar turned and waited. "Morning, Jim," she responded just as shortly. "You just get back?" she added, not really thrilled with having the island's developer coming at her so early on a Sunday morning. Their relationship, always strained, had been positively negative the last few months.

He nodded and came to a halt at the bottom of the driveway. "Landed about an hour ago." He glanced around, then back at her. "God damned mess. Airports a wreck."

Warily Dar came forward, detecting a note of reluctant cordiality she hadn't expected. "It is," she agreed. "We did pretty well out here though. No doubt at all your people knew what they were doing." She offered the compliment at face value, and in fairness because it was utterly true.

His body posture shifted, and he relaxed visibly. "Yeah, team did a good job. Only place in the tri county that was prepared and got through it." He paused. "Don't want to keep you. Just wanted to stop by and say thanks for helping the team out that first day there, and with the cabling and everything."

"No problem. Was glad to do it. And it helped me out too, that last part," Dar said. "More or less my usual line of work."

"I know that's your area," Jim said. "And I know we don't see eye to eye a lot, but I wanted to come over here first thing and tell you how much I appreciated you doing it."

Dar paused a moment, honestly quite surprised at the stolid sincerity in the man's tone. "You're welcome," she responded.

He nodded again. "Anyway, let you get on your way. Thanks again and give your family my regards." He lifted a hand, turned, and jogged back up the slope toward the road.

Kerry emerged onto the porch as he left and now stood on the top of the steps, hands on the balustrade. She looked down at the entrance to the parking. "What the hell was that?"

Dar spread her hands out. "He came to thank me for fixing his cameras," she said. "And I guess, for setting up the sat."

Kerry reached behind her and opened the door again to allow Chino and Mocha to emerge and bustle past her down the steps to where Dar stood. "Well okay then." She closed the door and locked it. "That's some way to start the morning."

"Maybe it's a sign." Dar put her sunglasses on and went around to the driver's side of the truck. "At least it's a positive one."

Kerry opened the back door to let the dogs jump in, then got in the passenger side. She held up her other hand with her fingers crossed.

****

Dar was about to park the truck up onto the sidewalk in front of the gates but realized as she got close the gates were actually unlocked. The large chain and padlock missing. "Huh." She pulled the truck to a halt and popped the door open. "Be right back."

She walked over to the gates and pulled them open one leaf at a time, noting the marks in the wrought iron and the bent portion from their visit the other night. Then she went back to the truck and climbed back into the driver's seat. "Maybe it's another sign."

Kerry had her camera out, and she idly took a picture of the open steel portal. "Someone expecting us?" she wondered, as they slowly pulled through and onto the paver lined path beyond. "Should I get out and close them?"

Dar pulled the truck to a halt and looked around for a long minute, but the area was devoid of any obvious life. "Yeah," she said. "They're blocking the sidewalk. Hate to have someone do a header into them, those suckers are heavy."

Kerry got out and went back to the gates and pushed first one closed, and then the other. She looked around for the chain and lock, but it was nowhere to be found. "Huh." She echoed Dar's earlier comment and returned to the truck. She climbed back inside. "Lock's gone."

"I saw," Dar said. "Maybe Richard called ahead."

Kerry checked her phone. "No signal here," she said. "Who would he call? A bird? Maybe the eagle scouts just figured they'd see who showed up if they left them open."

"Doubtful." Dar put the truck in gear, and they trundled slowly on. "What do you think, kids?" She asked the two dogs, who both had their heads stuck between the front seats and peered around with great interest.

"Growf." Chino pulled her head back and then went over to the side window to look intently through the glass. "Growf!"

They drove through the trees past the garden shack, and through the second wooded area until they saw the house ahead of them. "Ah hah." Dar pointed. "That's who opened the gate."

Parked near the entrance to the garden was Hank's Humvee, with its trailer loaded with what looked like cases of water.

"Well at least he left the gates in one piece this time," Kerry said. "Wonder why he's here?"

Dar shrugged. "I think he said that night he wants to be our gardener," she said. "Maybe he's rethinking that with all this foliage?"

They stopped near the Humvee and opened the doors. Kerry pulled open the back door to allow the two, now wildly curious and excited, Labradors to jump out. "Here we go, guys."

"Growf!" Chino looked around, then went nose down to sniff the area.

Chino spotted a squirrel, and galloped off toward it, ears flapping.

Kerry came around to the front of the truck to join Dar and they watched the two dogs race around in a frenzy of discovery for a minute. "This must be so cool for them," Kerry said. "They've never been any place like this."

"Whole new world." Dar draped her arm over Kerry's shoulders. "C'mon. Let's go see if we can find Hank."

They walked past the Humvee and then onto the stone pathway that led through the delivery area, and then past the empty garden to where there were steps that led up to the kitchen. There was no sign of anyone, but when they mounted the steps, they saw the kitchen door was open.

"Mysteriouser and mysteriouser," Kerry said.

"Mm."

Dar pushed the door all the way open and they entered. Inside was a passageway, in the same wood paneled whitewashed motif they'd seen elsewhere in the house. To the right was the entrance to the kitchen and they turned into it.

It was quiet, and clean and empty. All the evidence of coffee makers and supplies removed, and the area carefully dusted off. Light streamed in from the tall, bubble glassed windows that provided a mild and diffused visibility.

The kitchen was large. It was obvious that it was intended to be a workspace. There were built in storage shelves, all wood, all custom, all in the same bland whitewash color. The long table on the inside of the room was butcher block.

"That table is expensive," Kerry said, as she roamed around the space.

"Is it? It's pretty." Dar studied it. "I like it."

"Me too."

The light fell on the table from the windows. Around it were the short, mid height square wood stools they'd sat on and she briefly imagined a group of people there preparing some large amount of food.

A workspace, Kerry found herself thinking again. Like the kitchen had been in her parents house. Not meant to have the family sit in. "Did he have big parties? Seems like he meant to."

Dar had her hands behind her back, and she stood in the center of the room. She looked around with interested curiosity. "Like a hotel kitchen or something."

"Something."

They moved from the kitchen back into the hallway that then widened into a double width space lined on either side with built in cabinets.

Kerry paused and took hold of the iron handles of one and tugged it open. It moved reluctantly, the wooden doors stiff and a little swollen from the humidity. Inside were shelves of a good depth, but they were completely empty, and their surface had no markings on it.

"Painted these to sell the place?" Dar said, over her   shoulder. "Doesn't smell fresh."

"No." Kerry thoughtfully closed the cabinet.

They walked on to the end of the hall, where swinging doors opened up into the large spaces beyond. Here, today, in the light they were almost overwhelming in their bland, high-ceilinged reach.

There was nothing architecturally graceful about the house. Kerry walked across the stone floor, whose surface was matte and had a grain to it. It was built square, the windows tall and well fitted. They let in a lot of light but the lines had no curve to them, and there were no moldings anywhere.

Just good, solid workmanship.

Kerry went to the doors at the back and opened them, finding a set of doors to the outside.

Dar came up behind her. "We came in that way. I thought it was the front door, but it's not really."

"No." Kerry looked around. "Well, maybe it is. It's an entry foyer. You come in and then can go right upstairs, or into the room here. I guess this was the living room." She glanced behind her. "Yeah, there's a fireplace."

The staircases on either side of the end of the room were the only pop of color. The treads a warm, honey colored wood, and the bannisters an inky black wrought iron. "What's the upstairs look like?" Kerry paused, next to one of them.

"A lot of empty rooms," Dar said, after a moment's pause. "We were a little short on time. I just skated through them."

"Ah." Kerry started up the steps. "Well, since Richard and gang aren't here yet, let's take some time to look."

They got to the landing and found a narrower set of steps continuing to the third floor. Kerry glanced at them, then proceeded along the corridor. There were two large inside rooms in the center. "These'd make good offices."

"No windows." Dar made a mild protest. "I think there are some on the third floor, with portholes. I think I like natural light better when I'm working."

"Yeah, me too." Kerry closed the door to one of the inside rooms and they walked on, then turned into an inside hallway that had medium sized rooms on the outside that when they were opened up, proved to be what were meant to be bedrooms.

All empty. All with the same whitewashed wood paneling. Here they had wooden floors though, that matched the stair treads. There were no closets, and the wood had been removed from the windows outside to allow the light to come in. "I see what you meant by lots of rooms," Kerry said.

"Mm." Dar made a sound of agreement. "I like the floors."

"We're going to have to put in ten thousand rubber backed scatter rugs," Kerry said. "But I think the stone floors downstairs are not slidey enough to need them."

They walked along the hallway and found at the end, a corner that turned into a hallway that went the width of the house. It had a large entry with double doors in the center of it. The inside of the wall had more of the cabinets.

Kerry opened one. "Oh. A walk-in closet?" She sounded surprised. "A walk-in cabinet?"

It was a large space meant for storage, and on either side of the inside wall of the space there were brackets that held old, belled, glass lamps. The walls of the space were lined with shelving. The edges of the shelves had a wrought iron bar that allowed a wood and iron ladder to slide along it to give access to the higher ones.

"Nice," Dar said. "The master suite's on the other side here."

Kerry closed the cabinet and then stood back as Dar opened the double doors opposite. A blast of light illuminated the inside hall from the floor to ceiling windows inside. "Oh, wow."

Like everything else, it was completely empty, but the room spread across the width of the side of the house and faced the water. Here, unlike the bubbled glass on the first floor, the glass was clear. It allowed an unimpeded view of the water, and the curve of the point.

The sun outside poured in the glass in a slanted wash of light, and here the floor was a beautifully inlaid pattern of light and dark wood boards.

The view of the blues and greens of the bay, with its lightly fluffy chop was stunning. Kerry could easily imagine waking up to it.

"Nice, huh?" Dar said, rocking up and down on the balls of her feet.

"Very." Kerry turned and gave her a hug. "It's amazing."

Dar smiled. "Yeah, seeing this kind of sealed the deal for me," she said. "That and just… all the space."

Kerry released her and went across the room to another doorway and looked inside. "Well, they had indoor plumbing." She eased inside the large bathroom, which had a big, square stone lined bathtub inside it, and cast-iron pipes.

A stone shelf sat under a bare wall, with spaces and pipes for a big sink.

There was an alcove off to the inside, and she looked inside, to find more cast-iron piping, standing ready. "Does it go to a septic system, Dar?"

Dar regarded the unfinished bathroom, apparently waiting for its toilet and sinks. "Given when they built this, it was either that, or… "She glanced over toward the water. "Have to have this place really checked out. Can't be that far from city sewer hookup."

Kerry turned and leaned against the door to the toilet area and folded her arms. "Would chickee boo have removed the fittings, Dar? Or did they maybe just…" She trailed off. "Seems weird."

"Seems weird," Dar agreed. "Maybe they were in a really bad shape and she had them pulled out. Or cracked, the porcelain."

Kerry nodded. "Yeah, that could be. Anyway, I'm glad to see there's pipes so at least we know it's possible," she said. "This is a big room." She regarded the bathroom, which had some built-in cabinets in the wall. And along that wall a long stone bench to sit on.

"It is." Dar studied the bathtub. "Now I'm wondering if we're going to be able to do anything as simple as putting a shower in."

"Oh." Kerry regarded the space. "Hmm."

"Mm."

They walked back out into the bedroom and looked out of the window at the battered, weathered pool deck and its algae and mold covered surface. "Oh, Dar." Kerry sighed. "This is going to be such a pain in the ass."

"It is," Dar agreed. "C'mon. Let me show you the rooms upstairs and we can go find Hank. Hopefully, Richard's here too and the wingnuts. Let's get all the bad news on the table at the same time."

"Happy Sunday."

Chapter Seventeen

"It's a great piece of land." Richard Edgerton was seated in the back seat of Dar's truck. "I mean, seriously. I checked out the satellite shot of it when you told me about the place, Dar, and to find this size property in this area relatively undeveloped… my goodness."

"We haven't even explored all of it," Kerry said. "Though by now probably the dogs have."

Both dogs were laying down in the grass, in the shade, visibly wet and in Chino's case, covered in mud that turned her cream-colored coat almost brindle. Both had their tongues lolling, but if there was a look of contented delight that could be expressed by a canine, they had them.

Dar had the air-conditioning in the truck running and she and Kerry were half turned in their seats in the front to face Richard. He was dressed in a short sleeved khaki shirt and slacks and loafers, with sunglasses perched on the top of his head.

Richard checked his watch. "The historical, or as I referred to them to my buddy yesterday, the hysterical society people should be here in the next couple of minutes. Jason is over at the county government building to see what documentation he can dig up on this place."

"Are they hysterical?" Kerry asked. "Or just passionate."

Richard grinned briefly at her. "I should be used to pedantic people, shouldn't I? I'm a lawyer, and a son of a lawyer, and a grandson of a lawyer. My whole family's either in the legal trade, or college professors." He chuckled. "Anyway, I just found these folks very impenetrable, in their area of expertise."

"Ah. Not sure there's much for them to get excited about here," Dar said.

"Well, that's their point, you know? That everything just gets wiped clean like it did in the thirties, and there's no respect for the past," Richard said.

"It got wiped clean in the thirties because it literally was wiped clean. Big ass storm came in and scoured the whole area," Dar said. "Wasn't anyone's fault."

"Anyway," Richard said. "They're livid, and I mean livid, that apparently the young lady who sold you this place did like that storm and wiped out everything in the house and threw it all away. Her view was, it's hers, and she's got the right to do what she likes with it."

"You spoke to her?" Dar asked.

"Of course, I did. I mean, I did the paperwork on the deal. She was glad enough to talk to me about it," he added. "She said it was nothing but a mess, and she had a company come in and just empty it all out, bout a month ago, before she put it on the market."

"Well, I can see the point," Kerry said. "Did she even know about the historical designation?"

Richard nodded. "Sure, she did. Didn't care," he said. "She told me it was just a government scam, and she was sure you'd figure a way around it."

"She's an ass."

"Well, Dar, from a strictly financial, hardheaded viewpoint, I get it," Richard said. "She thought the old man had done that just to screw her over, and she was determined she was going to get what she could out of the place before everyone figured it out." He paused. "Which she did, with you all."

"No wonder she took the deal, no questions asked," Kerry mused. "Dar, you must have been like an angel sent from heaven to her."

"She really didn't have much respect for the old man. Got nothing against you two, by the way. Said she wished you well with it," Richard said. "So, at any rate, those folks from the historical society are just fit to be tied. I did talk them off the edge of trying to hold you responsible, though. Thanks to the timestamps on the pictures, you sent me from here before the storm, it's clear who was the culprit."

Kerry leaned back against the window. "So where do we go from here? Does it make sense to try and recreate what was inside that house? If they just use modern materials, how is that even interesting?"

"Well, here they are, so we can ask them." Richard pointed out the passenger window, to where a light green Prius pulled up behind them on the path. "Try not to get all crazy with them. I just got them talking like adults with me."

He opened the door and slid out.

Dar put her sunglasses on and shut the car off and opened the driver side door. "That doesn't sound promising. What do you bet me our dogs growl at them."

Kerry chuckled briefly as she got out on the passenger side and shut the door. She put her hands into her front pockets as they waited for the three people in the car to sort themselves out and join them. "Let's be positive, Dar. Maybe we'll get lucky."

The three people got out and walked over. Two men, one tall and bearded, with a little stoop to his walk, a second shorter. The third was a woman with frizzy brown hair and huge eyeglasses. The men were dressed in cotton twill pants and tucked collared shirts, and the woman had on an ankle length skirt of many colors and a peasant blouse.

Dar came around the truck to stand next to Kerry, content to allow Richard to move forward and greet the newcomers and handle the pleasantries. They stood in the shade and it was tolerably breezy, the leaves on the trees all around them rustling.

Kerry allowed her attention to wander a bit when she spotted several butterflies amongst the bushes nearby. They were yellow and blue, and some red. They flicked in and out of the beams of sunlight coming down through the trees.

"So, folks. Let me introduce you all to these ladies, Dar and Kerry Roberts, who are the new owners of the property." Richard led them over, and Kerry felt Dar's elbow come to rest on her shoulder as they neared. "This is John Siward, Larry Rogers, and Mitzie Higglebotham."

"Hi," Kerry said. "Nice to meet you. Dar remained silent next to her. "Thanks for taking the time to come down here on a Sunday."

The taller man nodded at her. "Can we go inside and take a look around?" He pushed his glasses up on his nose. They had a bit of fog on them from the heat. "We kind of understand what happened here but we want to see for ourselves what the situation is."

"Sure." Kerry gestured to the kitchen door that they'd left standing open. "After you."

The man nodded jerkily at her. "Thank you." He gave Dar a sideways glance, but Dar merely kept her position, eyes hidden behind her dark shades. "Excuse us," he muttered, nervously.

Kerry waited for them all to pass by, then she gently poked Dar in the ribs. "Stop that."

"Me? I didn't do anything." But Dar smiled and took her elbow off Kerry's shoulder and slid her arm around them instead. They followed the group back up the path to the back door.

****

Dar opened the door to the pool and deck and walked out into the breeze off the water. Behind her, she heard the discussion continuing, but the stuffiness inside the house had started to get to her and she halfway seriously considered just jumping off into the water.

The bay water, not the green, algae covered storm leavings in what could be, if given the opportunity, a nice pool. There was only about four feet of the murky sludge and Dar wasn't really in the mood to break an ankle.

She went down the layered steps past the pool and over to the edge of the point. She sat down on the grass covered rock ground and dangled her legs over the wall and listened to the swirl and rush of the water against the land.

To her left, there were trees and foliage to the edge of the water that blocked the view in either direction. To her right, the point sloped around to the south giving her a view of the far offshore of Key Biscayne across the channel.

To the south there were more houses, but she couldn't see them, and there were more to the north, but she couldn't see those either.

She felt a little bad about leaving Kerry to hold up their end of the argument, but she figured she'd been very close to telling them all to just kiss her ass, and that wouldn't have done anything positive for anyone.

She heard doggy toenails behind her and turned to find Chino and Mocha trotting toward her. They looked ridiculously pleased that they had discovered her sitting there. "Hey, guys."

They collided with her, and Mocha rubbed his face on her back, bringing the smell of damp dog fur and mud with him. "Are you having fun?"

Their tails were wagging, but that, she knew didn't really mean that much since they were typically wagging constantly, reflecting the mild, happy disposition of their breed.

They did like the place, Dar decided. It was large and had endless ground and trees and plants and animals to explore and there was a naturalness about it that appealed, she felt, to them the same way it appealed to her.

She turned around and looked up at the house, its entrance elevated over the deck and allowed herself to feel the irritated annoyance at the stubborn, intractable attitude of the people from the society, who seemingly could only see the situation from one point of view.

Chino licked her ear, and she glanced at the dog, almost getting another lick right on her eyeball. It made her laugh in reflex, and she reached over to give the animal a scratch behind her ears. "Thanks, Chi."

Mocha stretched out on the ground next to her and put his head on her leg, watching a seagull as it coasted above the water, searching for fish.

****

"You haven't really answered my question," Kerry said, for the tenth time. "Do you have records of what this property looked like so it could be restored?"

She sat behind the kitchen worktable, on one of the square stools, her legs extended out and her arms crossed over her chest. "I don't think we're going to get anywhere arguing about how this happened. We weren't here. We have nothing to do with it."

Richard Edgerton nodded. "Exactly."

The woman from the society, Mitzi, looked frustrated. "You really don't understand," she said. "We had very little contact with Mr. Hunter before he passed. We'd just started to collect information about his life, and the property."

Richard took a breath to answer, but Kerry stood up. "You don't understand," she let her voice lift and take on an edge. "It doesn't matter how we got here. What matters is, can it be restored or not." She put her hands on the table and leaned forward. "So, either put your documentation down on this table, or get the hell off my land."

There was a small silence when she finished, as everyone stared at her.

"Not kidding," Kerry added, crisply. "I appreciate the frustration here, but I have to deal in the world of reality. And that world says if you want me to do something you have to give me data to do it with."

"Well, you have to get it from his family!" Mitsi stated. "That's not our responsibility!"

Richard leaned back against the kitchen counter and folded his hands. "His family states they have no documentation on anything to do with the property," he said. "I asked."

"Someone has to know," Mitsi said. "You have to find them. I can only tell you what the rules of the society are."

"Then I guess we have to find a legal route to have those rules revoked," Kerry said, calmly.

Just then, there were footsteps in the back passage, and then a tall figure appeared in the doorway, stopping short and looking at them in somewhat startled surprise. "Oh."

It was one of the rangers they'd encountered the previous visit. He had smears of mud and foliage all over him and was wearing a tool belt. "Sorry I..." Then his eyes fell on Kerry and he relaxed a little. "Oh, it's you."

"It's me," Kerry agreed. "Hi, John. Sorry for the unexpected intrusion," she said. "These are some folks from the historical registry, and our lawyer, Richard Edgerton."

Richard lifted a hand and waved.

"Oh, hi." John gave the historical trio a brief glance. "Didn't mean to interrupt. We were just working on some of the plants... that fella that came with you dropped by and brought us some water. Nice guy."

Kerry smiled. "Yes, Hank's a great guy."

"I'll just come back later." John started to move backward.

"Hold on," Kerry said. "You might be able to answer a question for all of us, matter of fact." She moved around the table and went over him.

"Sure." He halted in the doorway and waited, furtively brushing the bits of bark and moss off his arms. "If I can?"

Where to start? Kerry studied him. "We're having an argument, because these good folks here issued a registry for this place based on its historical value."

John paused, then nodded, with a faintly confused look. "Okay."

Kerry paused herself to consider how to ask the next question. "When Mr. Hunter passed away, what was done to this place? What did his granddaughter do, in terms of, moving things in and out, furniture, that sort of thing."

The three people from the historical society listened with interest. "Who is this?" Mitzi asked. "Does he work for the property?"

Kerry held up one hand. "Let him answer."

"I'm not sure what you mean," John said. "She came in, sent a big company in here to clean up. We worked with em. Lot of stuff got dragged off."

"What about from the house, here," Kerry asked. "Did they take any pictures? What it looked like before they cleaned up?"

"Here?" John seemed surprised. "No need to do much here, ma'am." He looked around. "Wasn't nothing in here. Old man never lived in the big house here." He gestured to the kitchen. "Used this, just a bit, but Minnie didn't care for it, my dad said."

Kerry stared at him. "What? He didn't live in the house?"

Mitzi came over. "That's crazy. He built it, didn't he?"

John nodded. "Oh yeah, he built it. Him and maybe... I don't know... ten other guys. They built it themselves, for sure. He just never lived in here. Nobody did. That's why there ain't nothing here, nothing upstairs, neither. Didn't even put fixtures in."

Kerry held a hand up again. "Wait," she said. "You mean it just looked like this?" She gestured vaguely around. "Just empty rooms?"

"Yes, ma'am. They came in and swept, you know? Mopped the floors and put some paint up on one wall that had some stains and all, but cept that, it's always just been empty." He looked around a moment. "The cleaning, y'know... that was stuff on the grounds. Busted up stuff, and a couple old cars and stuff."

Kerry looked at Mitzi. "No one came here to see what was being registered?"

Mitzi was stunned silent. She turned and looked at her two companions, who looked back at her, wide-eyed.

John looked at all of them. "You want to see where he lived? Him and Minnie?" He asked. He turned to Kerry. "I guess it's yours now, but we hid it from that kid. Didn't' want her to send them to clean that place out."

Kerry blinked. "Of course, we would," she said, after a pause. "Lead on."

"Sure." John gestured toward the back hallway. "C'mon." He walked out, and they followed.

****

Dar noted the work boat was back. She observed the lightly scuffed hull come around the edge of the point and return to the area she'd seen them searching the last time, motoring slowly around in a circle over a specific location.

There were divers onboard this time, and Dar watched with interest as they prepared to go overboard. She felt just a bit envious of them. She could see, now that they were closer, this wasn't a police boat. There were three men aside from the captain and the divers who were dressed in business casual.

"Gruff." Chino's ears cocked, as the boat dropped its anchor, and a short time later, the engines cut off as the boat swung into the line of the current and they pushed a dive ladder overboard.

"Wonder what they're looking for, Chi." Dar kicked her boots idly against the seawall.

The divers rolled over backward into the water and went under, a faint flush of white foamy bubbles coming to the surface in their wake.

The men on the boat stood there talking, and after a minute, Dar saw them point at the edge of the shoreline, on the other side of the pool deck from where she was seated. Curious, she got to her feet and dusted herself off, then she walked down the edge of the seawall toward where they were working.

She reached the edge of the point, the dogs at her heels, and watched as one of the divers came up, holding on to the dive ladder as he took off his mask and spoke to one of the men.

Then one of the other men looked up and spotted her.

Dar folded her arms as she watched that man, tap the shoulder of a second and point at her, and then the third man gestured for the diver to come up on deck, then knelt and banged a dive weight against the dive ladder still extended into the water.

"I sure hope that's not a box of cocaine and I'm now a witness, Chi," Dar muttered, as it became obvious the men intend to cut short their dive and move in her direction. "Maybe I should have stayed inside." She sighed. "What do you think? Six guys versus me and two dogs?"

"Gruff." Chino sat down at her side and watched the boat.

Well, it was broad daylight, Dar reasoned. And if they got really saucy, she could... She paused thoughtfully. Well, she could do something. "I could call my lawyer to be a witness, I guess."

The boat's engines turned over and a minute later the bow was headed in her direction. With a sigh, Dar sat down on the seawall and put an arm around the dog on either side of her and waited, as the boat came close and then turned so its starboard side was even with where she was. "Hi," she called out.

"Hey!" One of the men leaned on the railing. "How'd you get in there!" He pointed at the land.

Dar cleared her throat. "I bought the property," she yelled back. "Came with a set of keys."

That seemed to cause a huge spurt of excitement, and all three of the business casual guys were now at the railing, while the divers were on the other side, pulling off their gear. "You what?" The first man yelled. "For serious? You the owner there? For real?"

Dar nodded.

They exchanged a lot of inaudible, yet visually excited conversation between the three men. The boat's captain just leaned on his console, watching the tide, and the distance of the boat from the shore.

"Hey, can we come talk to you?" The first man finally yelled at her, cupping his hands. "Can we ask you something?"

"This could end very badly." Dar told the dogs. "But what the hell." She lifted her voice. "Dock over there!" She pointed at the boat dock to one side. "I'll meet you down there." She got up and started for the pier, as the boat curled around in a circle and headed in the same direction, in a slow, rolling rumble.

****

They walked along one of the paths through the foliage, going south from the house in a direction Kerry didn't recall her and Dar exploring yet. There were tall trees and rock ridges on either side of the track and the ground was well worn as though many had used it in the past.

"Not very attractive, the planting," Mitzi commented. "It would be a lovely garden, if you took all those rocks out."

Kerry, who was behind John, saw his back stiffen and she saw his hand close into a fist.

Interesting.

"This is actually part of the Miami Rock Ridge, and a hardwood hammock," Kerry said casually. "It's part of an endangered ecosystem." She turned her head toward Mitzi when she said it, and when she turned to face forward again, she saw John look over his shoulder at her, with a huge grin on his face.

"Oh," Mitzi murmured. "Like the Everglades, I guess."

"Nothing like the Everglades," John muttered, but not loud enough for her to hear.

Kerry heard, though. "We realized the other day that our offices over north in the Grove were on a piece of it also." She told him. "It made a lot of what we saw, with what areas were flooded make a lot more sense."

"Yes, ma'am," John agreed. "It's special."

"I really like it," Kerry said, raising her voice a little to make sure the others could hear her. "And Dar loves it. She grew up down south where there was some of it, and now it's gone."

"Thought she was born in these parts." John glanced back at her. "Talks like it."

They walked between a thick stand of pines, half of which were leaned over against each other and one that was lying down completely with its roots sticking up in the air. "Wind," John said, briefly. "We were going to work on replanting that one next."

The path crossed a circular area, with a stone firepit in the center, made from carefully fitted rocks, whose interior was stained a deep black from long use. John led them to the right after that, and they walked along ground that was littered with dead leaves toward a gap that was blocked by a gate made of what looked like twisted vines.

John pushed it open and walked through and then they were in a small clearing. On the other side of the clearing was a hut.

It was made of wood, it's walls covered in tree bark, and had a thatched roof, and to one side of it was a wooden rack that was about six feet high, and half falling down. The hut itself seemed intact, though there were patches of thatch laying on the ground nearby.

"It's in here." John went to the door of the hut and pushed the bead curtain that formed its door aside. "Go on."

Kerry slid past him and entered. She walked into the hut far enough to let the rest of them follow her and then stopped and just stood there. She looked around at a completely unexpected interior.

It was the size, really, of a one car garage, only square. On one side there were two wooden platforms, with wool covered mattresses on them, and tucked around them were beautifully knit blankets with still bright colors in them.

Next to the platforms were stools constructed from wood sticks, their seats padded with more brightly knit wool covered pillows. On the walls were pieces of string art, like spiderwebs made from tiny colored pebbles strung on some kind of twine.

The walls were wood planking, well fitted, the joints caulked with a lighter colored substance. The roof was held up with sturdy posts and the vertical ones had hooks set in them that held up bags and sacks in both cloth and some hair-colored animal skin.

Near the beds was a table, full of writing implements and stacks of paper, and two lines of colored ink. On the top sheet of paper, Kerry saw an illustrated bird, in watercolor. "Oh, wow," she murmured, briefly imagining Ceci's delight on seeing all of it. "Look at that!"

"The man who owned this property lived in here?" One of the two men who had accompanied Mitzi said, in a disbelieving voice. "In this century?"

There were gas lanterns hanging on hooks, and a small gas stove on the other side of the room, with a set of tin pots and a wooden box with some worn lettering on it.

"This is where he lived," John said. "He liked it. He spent a lot of time drawing the plants and birds and things." He looked around. "This is where he lived with Minnie. "There's a path outside, goes over to a spring. He would sit out there all the time."

"I've seen it," Kerry said. "This is beautiful." She walked over behind the table and found a wicker chair there with a comfortable looking set of pillows on it, and imagined him sitting there, painting.

The top sheet had dust over it, but even through it she could see the clarity of bird's form, and it's pert, intent eye looking at her. She glanced up over it at John, who watched her with bright eyes, and a smile. "He was a good artist."

"He was really into nature," John said solemnly. "We got one from him, of a squirrel he gave my dad in our house on the wall."

She looked at Mitzi. "You found your history. Here it is." She gestured around at the hut. "Isn't this amazing?"

There was a brief, awkward silence. Then the taller of the two men removed his glasses and cleaned them on the tail of his shirt. "Okay." He looked up and over at Kerry. "Let's go sit down and talk. We need to make a deal."

****

Dar walked down the stone steps to the dock, noting it was high tide, and the water was only a foot or so from the bottom of the pier. She stood there with her hands in her pockets and watched the workboat make its way in. As it closed with her, she pointed at the cast iron cleat sunk into the stone and extended one hand for them to toss a rope ashore.

The captain gave her a little wave of understanding and called back to one of the two divers, who stood on the deck in his wetsuit, the top portion peeled down off his shoulders and hung behind him.

The diver walked up to the bow and picked up a coiled line. He waited for the captain to maneuver close, and then threw it shoreward.

Dar caught it, and got a wrap around the cleat, pulling it in as the boat approached and tied it off with casual expertise as the hull bumped against the pier.

The diver stepped off the aft as the captain tweaked the engines and brought the back end in, and then he tied the aft rope to a second cleat.

Two of the men in business casual scrambled off the boat onto the pier and came over to her. Dar knew at once they were in technology.

They had that nerdly engineer look though no one had a pocket protector. The men all wore glasses, and they had expensive watches on their wrists. "Hi there," she greeted them amiably. "What can I do for you gentlemen?"

One of them extended his hand readily, with a card in it. "Hi! Thanks for letting us land!" He said. "Specially out of the blue like this. We won't take much of your time we just have a few questions for you." He took a breath. "I'm Charles Depant, and this is Joe Evers. We work for a company you probably never heard of called Level 3."

Dar glanced at the card, then back up at him. She slid the card into her pocket and extended a hand to him. "Dar Roberts," She said. "And I have heard of your company," she added, with a wry anticlimax, as they both reacted to her name.

They both just stared at her for a long, silent minute, with a shocked reaction somewhere between startled and delighted.

Dar looked from one to the other. "So that's going to make this conversation a lot shorter, right?" she asked, with a brief grin. "Cuts out a lot of explanation."

"Oh boy yes," Charles finally spluttered. "I had no idea... I mean...I have to admit you are the very last person on the planet I expected to meet on this dock today." He belatedly took her hand and shook it, then relinquished it for Joe to do the same.

"What he said." Joe just nodded. He was taller than his companion, and had a long, somewhat mournful face. "But yeah, that sure makes this a shorter ask," he said. "So damn I'm glad it was, and regardless, it's nice to meet you finally."

Dar nodded. "Back at you. So now what's the story here?" She asked. "What's on the bottom there, fiber?"

The captain shut off his engine and sat back in his chair, and the two divers found a shady seat and drank cans of energy drink, idly listening.

"We got two trunks down there. They go into the NAP. NAP's gotten feet of water flooding it and we can't get near there. We want to bring the trunks up on shore, and we need an easement to our Biscayne South ring, it's about a block west," Charles said, launching right into it. "Of the front of the property, I mean. Cross the road."

"Where does it go now?" Dar asked. "Along the coast?" She glanced to her left.

Charles nodded, then rushed on. "All the way north, then west. No one was able to get any utility grant on this bit of land here, so it lands about a mile up," he said. "But the onshoring path there's totally trashed. Snapped the trunk, picked the darn sealed repeater up out of the water and it ended up wrapped around the Metromover pylon. Whole thing has to be replaced, and we've got to rerun everything."

He paused. The boat captain, who'd been listening, just shook his head and said something to the divers, who also laughed. "You'd save us a ton of time and money letting us bring it along here."

The Level 3 guys looked at Dar expectantly.

Dar turned and looked at the seawall thoughtfully. "Buried?"

Charles nodded. "Sure. My predecessor, one back, tried to get this done here, trench, relandscape, the whole nine yards but the owner wouldn't even talk to him. Didn't want any part of it. Not for any price."

"Yeah, I bet," Dar said. "Tell you what. Put in a ring splitter and give me a couple line rate 10G ports off it, and you got a deal." She put her hands in her pockets and cocked her head, one eyebrow lifting as she tossed the metaphorical ball into their court.

Charles eyed her. "No easement tax?"

Dar shook her head. "Getting service in here'll be more than worth It to me."

"We'd have to bring power down," Joe said. "Have to be two trenches for that."

"Even better," Dar said. "I'll take a tap off that while you're at it. Can you bring in a 440 line from the street?" Dar asked. "Not much service of any kind out here." She glanced around at the house. "We just bought it, about a week ago," she said. "Right before the storm came through."

"Bold," Joe said, solemnly.

Dar shrugged. "Got a good deal on it."

Charles stuck his hand out again. "Put her there, Ms. Roberts," he said.

"We'll be able to get the whole government service back up in a month shorter time than we promised. You'll be a hero," he said. "I'll be a hero. We'll get to stay in a hotel with air-conditioning. Hot damn my life just got a half ton better."

Dar shook his hand, but grimaced. "Leave my name out of it, wouldja?" she asked. "I've got them asking for favors already and I don't have time to mess with them."

"Oh sure, no problem." Joe turned around. "Hey, Gus, we can bring it onshore here! Grab some measurements and I'll radio home base."

The third business casual man gave him a thumbs up, and a big grin. He grabbed an over the shoulder bag made of canvas with a company name blazoned on it and hustled over to the side of the boat. "Nice." He stepped up onto the dock. "I knew today was going to be lucky. I told you, didn't I?"

"You told us," Joe agreed. "Over stale Rice Krispies and powdered milk at breakfast."

Dar took a step back to let him pass and leaned against the seawall. "There are dogs up there."

The third man stopped and looked back at her.

"Labrador Retrievers," she reassured him. "Just don't let them knock you over."

Relieved, he continued up the steps at a trot. After a slightly awkward pause, Charles and Joe followed him, leaving Dar behind on the dock.

The captain and divers looked at her with some interest. "You one of these techy people?" The boat captain asked. "Seems like you understand their jabberwocky."

Dar came over to the side of the dock. "These fun to drive?" she asked, pointing at the work boat. "What are those, two seventies?" She looked at the engines. "Twenty-one feet? What's the draft?"

The captain leaned on the side of the boat. "What the hell are you?" he asked bluntly.

"Boat handler," one of the divers said. "You saw her tie up the bow." He looked up and winked at Dar. "Bet you dive."

Dar's eyes took on a twinkle. "Matter of fact I do."

****

Kerry led them back to the house, and the kitchen, and as they reached the steps to the back door Hank caught up to them and followed them inside without any invitation. "Hey, Hank."

"Hi, there," Hank said. He was in a work coverall in blue camouflage. With his worn military boots, scarred face and the visible handgun in its holster in the small of his back it was obvious he both startled and discomfited everyone who didn't know him.

"Glad you're here," Kerry told him. "This is Hank, he's a friend of the family." She indicated the work stools around the table. "Sit."

John stayed behind, muttering something about planting as he disappeared into the brush once they left the homestead, carefully closing the vine gate behind them.

The society group settled on one side of the table, while Kerry, Hank and Richard took the stools along the wall on the other side. Kerry put her elbows on the table, folded her hands together and pinned her gaze on the taller of the two society men. "You were saying?"

Larry Rogers, the taller man, cleared his throat. "Let me put the cards on the table," he said. "This property has been of interest to many for a long time. It's large, it's in a valuable spot in the county, it could be worth a lot of money."

Kerry deliberately misunderstood him. "What does that have to do with its historical significance?" She asked. "That's what we're here to talk about, aren't we?"

"Of course," Mitzi said.

Larry shook his head. "No."

Hank giggled softly under his breath.

Mitzi looked at Larry. "What are you talking about?" she asked. Their third companion just kept his mouth shut, his elbows tucked close to his sides, hands resting on his knees.

Rogers hesitated briefly. "It's a question of the value," he said. "Look we want all of us to come out ahead on this, don't we? There's some potential for this to be very lucrative if we work together on this place."

Kerry sat back, straightening up. "I'm not sure I understand. From my perspective, what I want is to be able to live on the land. That's what comes out ahead for me. What do you mean by lucrative?"

A little more confidently, he nodded. "I get it. Look you bought this place as is." He glanced around. "As is, it's not worth a hill of beans. We can't draw people in to look at anything here because there isn't much."

"Draw people in?"

"That's where the money is, Ms. Roberts." Rogers was a little condescending. "No one wants to come see empty structures and mud huts. We need to make this place a 19th century Florida showplace. Fix up the house. Put in period looking furniture. Make a beautiful garden. Put in a café on the water. You see?"

"Turn it into Fairchild Gardens?" Kerry's brows lifted.

"Sure."

"Larry, no." Mitzi seemed scandalized. "This isn't a theme park!"

"Of course it is." He eyed her. "Let's cut out the sanctity of our history, Mitz. That went out the window when they expected us to make a profit." He looked back at Kerry. "We're not protecting things just to protect them and leave them moldering. This place could make a good pitch. It's a good location, and we could do a deal with the local hotels to push it."

"But there's nothing really historical here but that hut," Kerry said, slowly. "Or are you suggesting that we create an old Florida fantasyland here for people to come see?"

Rogers nodded. "That's what I'm suggesting," he said. "No one's going to want to come to just see that hut. But we can pitch you some funding to fix the place up, put in gardens, and facilities, bring in services. We can rig the commercial codes. Then we set up packages, and most of the profits come to us until all that's paid back."

Kerry regarded him somberly.

"You really don't have a choice," Rogers said. "You can't do anything with this place. That's why we were told to issue the certification."

"Were told?" Richard spoke up, quietly.

Mitzi and the other man, John, stared at Larry.

Larry nodded. "C'mon people," he said. "This is just a black hole, from a monetary perspective. No one could buy it and develop it. But if we did what we were asked..." He stared at them. "And we were asked... and make it historical we could make money from it. Us..." He indicated the three of them. "And the government of the county, who needs those taxes."

Richard took a breath to speak, but Kerry reached over and covered his hand with her own. "No, we're not going to do that," she said, in a calm tone. "I'm not going to live in a theme park, we're not going to bastardize this beautiful place for tourists."

"You really don't have a choice," Larry told her. "Look I know it's a shock and all—"

"There's always a choice." Kerry cut him off gently. "So, you can leave now, and we can continue this discussion through legal briefs."

Richard nodded in satisfaction. "Glad I was here to hear that," he said, in a pleasant tone. "Saves some time."

With a shrug, Larry stood up. "It'll cost you a lot of money, and you're going to lose in the end. Suit yourself." He turned and left the kitchen and headed down the hallway. In a moment they heard the door open and close.

Mitzi looked across the table, with a stunned face. She looked at the other man, then back at Kerry. "I'm sorry," she finally said as she stood up. "For what it's worth, I thought that little place was fascinating and I..."

Her words trailed off. "Come on, John." She tapped him on the shoulder. "Let's go."

The other man stood, and finally spoke. "You know, Larry's right," he said, with a twisted little grimace. "His uncle's a county commissioner."

The two of them left, without further comment and for a long moment it was silent in the shadowed, warm, whitewashed kitchen.

Kerry smiled briefly. "Well, that was fun. I should have probably told them just how little it matters to me that they know a politician." She sighed. "Given my mother's a senator."

"And I'm a lawyer," Richard said.

"And I'm a crazy man with a gun," Hank piped up. "And they really ain't had to deal with the real powerhouses of the family yet, cause Dar could probably get up into their computers and make em forget this here spot ever was."

"That's actually true," Kerry admitted, with a wry grin "But don't suggest it to her yet." She turned her head and looked at Hank. "So why are you really here?"

"Found us a primo spot to put a still in," Hank said at once. "Got them boys real interested in Andy's family recipe from that last little run up here."

Kerry gave him a thumbs up.

"I knew I liked you right off." Hank smiled his sweet, slightly twisted smile.

"Should we go find Dar and fill her in?" Richard said. "I think I heard those dogs barking out there somewhere." He stood up and dusted his hands off. "This is going to be one hell of a mess."

"We should." Kerry also stood up, gently nudging the stool back and out of her way. It was going to be trouble, and it was probably going to be expensive, and yet, it was good to know the worst of it. "We'll start doing stuff here anyway. I don't really give a crap about those guys."

Hank chuckled.

"You know, Kerry... "Richard began. "Maybe let me do some research first?"

Kerry shook her head and led them out of the house. "Really no point. Dar's not going to go for that plan no matter what research you do, so we might as well just move on."

They walked outside. The historical society's car was gone, and as they went around the side of the house toward the water, they spotted Dar and the two dogs coming back toward them.

"Did it rain while we were in there?" Richard asked, in a puzzled tone. "Dar's soaking wet."

"So are the dogs," Kerry said. "Not sure I even want to ask."

Dar met them at the corner of the pool deck and was, in fact, completely drenched, her cotton shirt and shorts plastered to her body. "Found out who those guys in the boat are," she said. "You work things out with those guys?"

"Told them to get off my land," Kerry said and put her hands in her pockets. "Who were the guys?"

"Level 3."

"Oh really?" Kerry's eyebrows rose. "That's a little unexpected."

"Really." Dar casually folded her arms over her chest, the sunlight sparkling on the water droplets on her tanned skin. "So, are we in deep legal crap with them?" She asked Richard. "Cause I just told L3 they could trench from the edge of the water there to the road." She looked from Richard to Kerry. "Twice. But I figured buried cables weren't going to be much of an issue. Are they?"

"Probably," Richard said. "You might want to ask Kerry what their deal was. I'm still shaking my head. Anyplace around we can get a sandwich? I need to see if I can find some signal and see how my buddy's doing at the archives."

Dar reached up to run her fingers through her wet hair. "Let's go back to the office. Got food and signal there," she said. "You can tell me what happened, and I can tell you what Level 3's going to do here."

"Deal." Kerry paused. "Do I get to hear why you're soaking wet?"

"That's a whole other story."

"Do I want to hear it?"

****

The wet dogs, wet human and Kerry drove back north along the coast with Richard following them in his rental car. Kerry could smell the rich, mineral tang of sea water so she wasn't surprised to hear they'd ended up diving in and hey, it was a hot day so why not?

"So, they wanted to show me where the junction box was in the bay, so we moved the boat out to take a look at it," Dar said. "I went over the side with a mask and a tank to check it out, and the dogs freaked out."

"Thought you were drowning?" Kerry guessed, easily picturing their loyal pets jumping to the rescue. "Are you heroes, kids?" She glanced back in the back of the truck, where both damp dogs were lying down on the leather seat, tongues lolling. "You'd think they'd be used to that from the cabin."

Chino barked in response.

Dar glanced in the rearview mirror at her. "No idea. They ended up swimming out to where we were, and we had to drag their furry asses back onboard before they went paddling after a pelican."

Kerry chuckled. "So, they're bringing their main line onshore across our property?" She asked. "And you traded that for a big pipe and power?"

"Uh huh."

"You're such a rock star."

Dar eyed her as they paused at a four way stop. "Ker, that took exactly zero brain cells to agree to," she drawled. "C'mon." She directed the car forward. "Key point to that being, they have emergency power for that interlock, and it puts us on the priority grid."

"Underground."

"Underground," Dar agreed. "What do you think about putting solar panels on the roof of the house? That's a big surface."

"Not sure those society folks would appreciate that. But I like the idea," Kerry said. "I like the idea a lot. We should do that at the office too. What about... "She glanced reflectively behind them. "Could we put up a windmill?"

"Oh, that'd be popular." Dar laughed.

Kerry chuckled as well. "Can you believe that historical guy pulled that, though?" She shook her head and exhaled. "That kid was kinda right about it being a scam."

"This is Miami. Of course, I can believe that. You always have to suspect a scam when local politics is involved. Google Miami Rapid Transit if you don't believe me," Dar said calmly. "But now I want to go back and see that little house."

"Huh." Kerry frowned, her arms folded over her chest. "This could be a huge mess, Dar."

"Let Richard worry about it," Dar said. "Meanwhile, let's see if your RVs showed up yet and figure out what we're going to do with them." She got in the right-hand lane so they could turn onto the street that their office was on.

"Not much I can do anyway." Kerry sighed. "It is what it is, Dar. And they actually thought we'd go along with that plan."

Dar just laughed again.

"Wait till they hear about our bootleg hooch."

"That might actually be more historical than you think."

****

There was a conspicuous lack of the National Guard camp when they turned and saw the office. The entrance to the parking lot was open and unimpeded.

"Well." Kerry hitched one knee up. "At least we have room now for the RV's."

Dar picked a spot near the three large vehicles speckled in tree shaded sunlight. They looked sleek and clean. "Have to admit I'm glad the National Guard is gone." She glanced at the front half of the parking lot. "At least they left it tidy."

"Me too. I wasn't really looking forward to another confrontation today." Kerry opened her door. "Let me go see if you have any dry clothing upstairs."

Dar got out and opened the back door for the dogs to jump down. "It's sunny. I'll dry." She riffled her fingers through her hair to put it in some kind of order. "There are the guys who dropped those things off." She pointed with her elbow at four men in gray shirts and black pants, talking to Carlos and Mayte.

They walked over to the six of them, the dogs trotted at their heels. A moment later Richard caught up to them after parking nearby.

"Signal." He held up his phone. "I was able to get hold of Jason. He managed to get some info for us, he's headed over here right now."

They met up with the RV delivery men, and Carlos and Mayte.

The deliveryman nearest was already holding out his hand. "One of you Kerry Roberts?"

"That'd be me." Kerry returned his clasp. "This is my partner, Dar, and our lawyer Richard Edgerton." She half turned. "How's it going here today, people?"

"Guard left." Carlos jerked his square jaw toward the lot. "Didn't say anything to me, but I think some of their guys talked to Sasha cause they came over to get breakfast."

"Hope she charged them double," Kerry said. "We're glad they're gone."

"Good riddance," Dar confirmed, with a nod of her head.

"So, Ms. Roberts, we have your three RV's here," the RV deliverer said. "I set up every other day service for em, including fuel. Just remember to turn em over to charge the batteries." He glanced around. "Don't suppose you'll get a power hookup any time soon... but we'll pump out the washrooms and restock supplies, and of course fill up the gas tanks."

"Thank you." Kerry smiled. "You all must be really busy."

"You're lucky you had these reserved. We're all out as of tonight, most of them on long term rental. Had to hire a half dozen guys to do service. Boss said, it was an ill wind that blew nobody good, but it sure did good for us," he said. "And we've got our own fuel supply."

"I signed the papers for them, Kerry," Mayte said. "They are very nice."

The RV men waved and left, walking over to a beat up looking open topped Jeep and climbed into it.

"Sasha inside?" Dar asked, waiting for Carlos to nod. "C'mon Richard. Let me get you a sandwich." She pointed to the office, and they walked toward it.

"Change your shirt!" Kerry yelled after her. She saw Dar lift a hand in response, then turned her attention back to Carlos and Mayte. "What a day," she said. "So, now these RV's. C'mon."

"Was it raining at your new house?" Mayte asked. "It did not rain here."

"No," Kerry said. "Dar jumped into Biscayne Bay to look at something." She glanced at them, who nodded as though this was an unsurprising statement. "Been quiet here?"

"Oh yes," Mayte said. "Very nice."

"Real quiet," Carlos confirmed.

They walked over to the three large vehicles, parked at the front of the lot. Kerry went to the first one and opened the door. "They should all be the same." She walked up the steps into the RV.

It had a plush seat for driving that reminded her of the one she and Dar had driven across country. Behind it though, was a space that was designed somewhat for business. It had two slide outs, and a table that folded out and down, with cabinets behind it for storage and a folding wall that separated the section from anything aft of it.

Kerry went over and opened the folding door to look behind it.

There was a bathroom on the left, and on the right, a compact kitchenette with a mini fridge. Past that, two small sofas facing each other as part of another slide out and in the very back a bunk room with two lower single bunks and two upper bunks that were folded up out of the way.

It was utilitarian, but it smelled new and clean. Kerry turned inside the bunk room and faced them. "So."

Carlos stood behind Mayte, his hands braced against the entry door to the bunk room. "What was the idea here, boss?" He asked. "Those guys said you grabbed these before the storm."

She turned and faced them, leaning against the edge of the folding door. "I did. It was part of a pitch to a client," Kerry said. "That's now on hold, but I had these reserved, so here we are." She looked at Mayte. "You think your mom and dad would be able to use one of these?"

Mayte blinked, then she looked around and behind them, then back at Kerry. "To stay in here?" She asked. "Oh yes!" She nodded vigorously. "They could manage it, yes I think so."

Kerry looked past her at Carlos, who smiled back at her, a deep, kind smile that made his dark eyes twinkle with understanding. She winked at him.

"How about I drive this thing over to the hospital with ya and pick em up?" he said. "That work, Mayte? We gonna be able to pitch it to em, or do we need to bring Dar with us?"

"Oh no, no I think it will be okay." Mayte broke into a relieved grin. "It is perfect, you know? If they must go to the house, they can go and see, but it is safe. Kerry, it's amazing. What a good thing to think of!"

Kerry smiled. "It was Dar's idea," she demurred. "Having them sent here. That out of the box brain of hers didn't take more than five seconds to bring it up." Her eyes went to Carlos. "Her idea was, one for Maria, and two split for some people here so they can get some comfortable rest."

Carlos nodded confidently. "I figured, girls and guys?" he suggested. "One bus for each I mean."

"There are more boys than girls," Mayte said. "That is not fair."

"Most of the guys are cool with their tents," Carlos said. "Probably won't want to bunk here unless I force em to."

Kerry chuckled. "Okay, I'll leave it to you guys to sort this out. Let me go find Dar and see what trouble she's gotten into in the ten minutes we've been talking to each other." She hopped out of the RV and headed for the building. The rumble of rock music greeted her as she neared the door.

As she mounted the steps to the porch, a puff of warm but not hot air came out of the open door, and it had the smell of Korean barbeque and charcoal on it. "Hope Richard likes spicy," she said as she entered the main hall and paused.

The conference room was on her left, and she noticed the supplies had multiplied and branched out, now including soap and cases of toilet paper along with the boxes of chips and peanut butter and cookies. On the opposite side of the hall was a second, smaller conference room but that had been left empty, its windows and door open to aid in ventilation.

She walked past the reception desk, it's surface empty and clean, and then took a look in either direction, where the walls had received an initial coat of plaster. She could smell the slightly musky scent of that, along with freshly cut wood.

She crossed the hall and went out the back door into the central court-yard, where she realized the sound of music wasn't from a radio. It came from four men and one woman near the weightlifting benches playing instruments and singing.

There were fifty people seated in the grass listening. Kerry counted perhaps thirty that she knew.

Dar stood on the cooking platform next to Sasha and Richard was seated on one of the coolers, eating a sandwich.

Kerry walked over to them, as a song ended, and everyone clapped. "Mayte thinks the RV's going to work out. I told her and Carlos to drive over to the hospital in one of them," she said. "They're basic inside, but there's decent space for a couple people."

"Good deal." Dar took off her sunglasses and tucked them into the collar of her shirt. "Tell Ker what the guard told you, Sasha," she prompted. "Before the concert starts up again."

Sasha was seated on her padded wooden stool from her shop. "Nice boys," she said. "Some of those kids. They sent the whole bunch of them out to the Everglades. Didn't want to go. Rather stay here where it's dry, and no mosquitos."

"I can imagine." Kerry glanced up at the canopy that had been put up over the grilling area, providing a nice pocket of shade. To the left, a solar powered fan gave them a breeze. "Well, I'm guessing they can do more to help out there than hanging around here."

"Some big shots came and sent them," Sasha said. "Everybody's sure it was this one." She pointed her thumb at Dar. "They said Dar told their big man she'd do it." She studied Dar with one raised eyebrow. "Yes?"

"I did say that," Dar said. "But I didn't do anything. By the time I got home the hot tub was more interesting than assholes."

"Let them think you did." Kerry patted her on the back. "Having people be scared shitless of you is great leverage sometimes, honey."

Dar rolled her eyes, a puckish grin appearing. "Anything for you," she said. "Let's just hope he doesn't decide to show up here tonight and make trouble."

"Ah, don't think so." Sasha waved off the suggestion with one hand. "Maybe they come to have barbeque." She winked at Dar. "Maybe so."

"I know they were good customers, Sasha, but I'm kind of glad they're gone," Kerry said. "Hopefully they can help out some people out there like they were supposed to here and are too busy to haul their asses back across the county to mess with us."

Dar turned to face Sasha. "Did you say your brother ordered a ships worth of solar panels?" she asked suddenly. "Containers of them?"

Sasha eyed her. "You want talk to him?" she suggested shrewdly.

"You buy them, put them here? Good for solar. Nothing blocking." She got up and pointed in all directions. "No big buildings, right on east coast."

"Yeah," Dar agreed. "Here, and on our new place. Same angled roof surface and sun exposure."

"Now, Dar." Richard swallowed hastily. "Hold on there, not sure you can do that, with that society agreement."

"Don't care," Dar told him. "Figuring that out's your job. We're going to move out there and start working on the place, and when you need us to come testify, call." She nodded a few times. "Be right back." She took her sunglasses out and put them on and stepped off the concrete pad and into the sun, heading toward the group.

Richard looked at Kerry, who had her hands clasped behind her back. "That's really not a good idea."

"Oh yes, I know, and actually Dar knows that too," Kerry said. "But we're going to do it anyway. We talked about it on the way back here. She figures, with what that skanky guy said, there's money and politics wrapped around it and at some point, someone's going to want something we can trade it all off for."

"Like what?" Richard took a bite of his sandwich and chewed.

"Technical services. Consulting," Kerry replied. "How to get around having your Internet sniffed." She winked at him. "Our promise not to call random people in the government we know and cause trouble for them, or have Dar figure out how to route all their political donations to PETA."

Richard chewed thoughtfully and swallowed. "Can she do that?" He watched Kerry nod, her eyes twinkling. "Well, that gives me something to work with anyway." He shook his head, but with a smile. "You two certainly keep me busy these days."

"Funny, Dad says that too." Kerry smiled back. "I think he went off somewhere on the boat to get away from our crazy for a day."

Her cell phone rang. "Excuse me." Kerry removed it from her pocket and walked to the end of the concrete before she opened it. "Kerry here."

"Ker!" Mark's voice had a faint echo to it. "Wanted to give you an update on the Brazil issue."

Brazil issue? "Oh! Right," Kerry said. "Sorry, we're having an exciting day down here with our new place. What's up?"

Mark exhaled.

"Not good, huh?"

"Well, there are folks up here who speak Portuguese, and there are folks up here who do high tech," Mark said. "Problem is I'm having some trouble finding both in one person."

"Mmm."

"Not saying I can't do it eventually. I found two guys," Mark said. "But not in time for tomorrow morning. And we need to kit them out with an image for that client. It's going to take me at least another week for it."

"Be easier if we could do it here," Kerry said.

"Hella."

Kerry pondered that. "I can't see that happening, Mark. I mean, I'm sitting here thinking – what if I can find the resources here and get them over. Then set up one of the RVs with a satellite dish and use some of the PCs from the office. We don't have to get them connectivity."

"Uh huh."

"Still don't think we can do that before nine a.m. tomorrow morning." Kerry sighed. "Finding the resources being the hard part, because I have Dar for the second and the PC LAN team here for the last."

"I can keep trying," Mark said. "What RVs are those?" He asked, belatedly. "I saw on the news they were talking about getting FEMA trailers down there."

"We have three commercial RVs," Kerry said. "Long story. But anyway, let me talk to Dar and see if she has any other ideas. She's been batting a thousand so far this weekend."

Mark chuckled softly. "Since I've known her," he said. "But anyway, I'll call the guy tomorrow morning and tell him we're going to have to delay the start. I don't want to bullshit him. He's a good guy. Colleen said she'd call with me, so the guy knows we're trying."

"Okay," Kerry said, after a brief pause. "Not really much in the way of options right now. Let's see what he says. Maybe he'll agree to hold off a week." Even saying it made her grimace, despite the fact that Kerry realistically knew that a natural disaster was something outside their control.

Natural disaster was, yes. Response to natural disaster was something they had to get better at. She was fully conscious that they'd done a piss poor job of planning for bad things to happen. All the customers who'd been calling them had every right to be angry.

"Not fun," Mark said.

Kerry exhaled. "A lot of opportunity for learned lessons," She said. "Let me know when you call him, no matter what he says. Dar and I will call him afterward and apologize."

"You got it." He hesitated. "Things there okay?"

Kerry turned around, scanning the area. Dar was over talking to the brown-haired bearded man with the guitar slung over his back that she now recognized from the small bar down the street. She thought about the challenges with the property, and the customers, and smiled. "Things are good here, yeah," she told him. "We'll get through all this Mark and we'll end up better for it."

"Barb said the same thing to me at breakfast this morning," Mark said. "Anyway, talk to you later. We're going to take a ride up to see Cape Canaveral. Talk to you tomorrow."

Kerry closed her phone and turned it in her hands as she pondered, watching the shadows start to lengthen. She walked back over and sat down on the bench next to Richard, still chewing his way through his sandwich. "Crazy world."

He wiped his lips. "Tell you what, Kerry," he said. "We're only given one life to each of us. Might as well be as interesting as it can be, you know?"

Sasha nodded vigorously. "Yes, yes. Take everything and use it. No worries."

Which, Kerry reflected, was what Dar would say if she put it to her. "Yep." She extended her legs in front of her. "We'll figure it out." She shrugged off the worry for the time being. "It is what it is."

****

Pete walked around the internal courtyard and paused every ten feet or so to light the tiki torches planted in the ground near the walls. The smell of citronella was strong and mixed with the scent of charcoal and cooking food, and the odd waft of toasted marshmallows from the small hibachi.

The sky in the east was already black, and the last streaks of light with their mellow pink and purple tints in the west were fading.

Kerry perched on the hood of Hank's Humvee, arms braced behind her as she listened to the circle of the staff around the front of the vehicle talk about the day.

Hank had the driver's seat of his rig tipped back and was asleep, his hat over his face, his clothes almost black with soil and debris from his long day of work at the Point.

Several large racks of ribs were in the largest of the barbeques and they smelled amazing. There was a pot of baked beans on the smaller grill and a plastic square container of coleslaw waiting nearby.

Where, Kerry wondered idly, did the ribs come from? There were no supermarkets open anywhere, and no restaurants, and yet, there seemed to be an endless supply of fresh food here.

Where the hell was it coming from?

Zoe came over with a pitcher of iced tea and offered her a refill of the cup she had clasped in one hand. "Miss Kerry, I have to tell you, Mayte was so excited to see the truck houses." She filled Kerry's cup. "Mayte said we could stay in one of them."

"All true." Kerry smiled. "You guys deserve it. I think Carlos and some of his friends are going to use the other one."

Zoe nodded.

"Zoe." Kerry leaned closer to her. "Where are we getting all our supplies from?"

For a moment, Zoe looked puzzled, her brows drawing together. Then Kerry held up her cup in question. "Oh!" she said. "You mean, the foods and things."

"The foods and things. Yeah," Kerry said. "I know some things must have come from Sasha, but not those ribs? And I saw all the stuff stacked in the conference room."

"I think some of the people who came here, brought the things they had," Zoe said. "And some of the people who are Papa Andy's friends brought us some cases of things. I think they had been frozen? So now we have to cook them."

Kerry's eyebrow quirked up a little bit.

Zoe waited, watching her expectantly. "It smells good, yes?" She finally asked.

"Smells great," Kerry said. "Barbeque is something I've never been able to cook. Never really had the time."

"No, me either." Zoe leaned against the Humvee. "My papa has a box, you know? For the lechon. That takes many hours also, and we only do it for special times. It is nice here, to get to try different things."

A movement caught Kerry's attention and she glanced to her right as Dar came through the door, her hair slicked back and damp, and wearing a blue company T-shirt a little too big for her, its sleeves rolled up to expose her biceps.

A moment later she came around the side of the Humvee and joined them. "Hey, people."

"Feel better?" Kerry asked.

"I felt fine before," Dar said. "But since the shower's up there, and I got the water filter installed, I thought might as well." She leaned against the car. "At least we're getting use out of that box of sample shirts that sales guy sent us."

Kerry could smell the clean, sharp scent of soap, and the newness of the cotton of the T-shirt. "She studied the dark blue material. He did a pretty good job," she said. The company logo was embroidered on the upper left chest, and a larger image was printed on the back.

"He did," Dar said. "And the water doesn't smell like chemicals any-more."

Kerry reached over to untangle a bit of her hair from the shirt collar. "Where did we get a water filter?"

Dar shrugged. "It was on the worktable upstairs."

"I think someone brought it this morning," Zoe said. "I saw it when I answered the telephone. I think Carlos said he was going to see if someone could fix it."

Dar winked at her. "Someone did. I remembered I had my toolkit in that cabinet in my office. Had the right size wrench for it."

Of course, she did. Kerry had to smile. "You know, this is nice." She indicated the central area. "A little medieval, but nice."

The band members finished playing another set and were seated around the hibachi, where not only marshmallows, but a bottle was being passed. Everyone looked relaxed, and there was laughter on the light breeze that drifted across the grass.

"It is," Dar said, after a thoughtful pause.

"Yes." Zoe nodded. "Mayte said it would be good for us, and it is true." She hesitated. "It feels nice to be here." She felt the pitcher. "I will go see if there is more tea. Would you like some, Ms. Dar?"

"Sure."

Zoe trotted off to the large coolers, two of which now had cables running from them to the large battery pack that was connected to the solar panels.

"I feel like staying here tonight."

"You think we should stick around?"

They both spoke at the exact same time and then laughed. "You've been wanting to hang out here all week," Dar said. "But yeah, with the guard gone, I'm twitching a little. We should stick around." She watched the ring around the hibachi. "I'll go in and send an email to the guys over on the island, let them know."

"Works for me." Kerry rested her elbows on her knees and clasped her hands together. "I wish I'd thrown one of our overnight bags into the truck, though."

"Check out the conference room," Dar said, dryly. "Most of what we need is probably in there."

Kerry leaned over and whispered. "Where is all that stuff coming from, Dar?" She watched the shadows shift as Dar frowned. "Should we ask?"

"Where do you think it's coming from?" Dar whispered back. "You think they're raiding the Costco down the road?""

"I don't know! What do we do if the cops show up here if they did?"

Dar considered. "Offer them barbeque and beer," she said. "No one's going to much care about a couple of boxes of toothpaste and some toilet paper, Ker." Her expression became thoughtful. "Wonder if they managed to pick up a big can of peanut butter."

"It's kind of illegal."

Dar nodded. "It is, and I wouldn't have agreed to it if they'd asked me, but they didn't ask me. And I'm not going to call the cops and have them get involved in it either," Dar said, in a practical tone. "For all we know someone went out and bought the stuff. It's not like we pay minimum wage."

Kerry thought about that. "Well, that's true," she mused. "Let me ask Mayte when she gets back." She slid forward and got off the hood of the Humvee and landed with a little thump on the ground. "Let me go check out those supplies. I'll send the email out to the guys. Enjoy the music." She leaned up and gave Dar a kiss on the lips. "Be right back."

She walked around the truck and went into the office, going across the hall and into the front conference room, noting that Pete had started setting up his guard post nest on the porch. That made her pause for a moment. Was he twitchy too?

Better safe than sorry. Kerry turned her attention to the supplies. She examined the boxes, but they were plain brown boxes. There were no tags or labels on them, though they did seem to be the kind of thing you'd find in a warehouse store.

Basic, but functional and she took her selections and put them into a small, empty box while she put everything else back into place. She picked up the box and went upstairs with it.

It was very quiet on the second level, everyone was outside in the yard, and she walked through the outer area of her and Dar's offices aware of the sound of her own footsteps on the newly sanded wooden floor.

Kerry went into her own office and put the box down on her worktable and turned around to regard her space. Then she went next door into Dar's office and stood with her back to the window, considering.

Then she went back into her office and went to her storage closet, hunting around inside of it for anything she could use to make their night comfortable.

For obvious reasons, she was somewhat short on things like pillows and blankets, but given the temperature of the office they probably wouldn't need the latter anyway.

Kerry paused, thoughtfully. The couch in Dar's office was wide enough for both of them, and quite comfortable.

Didn't change not having a change of clothes. With a shrug, she continued pushing aside various boxes of supplies and then paused. She saw something dark on the floor in the back of the closet. She removed the flashlight from her pocket and turned it on, shining it into the space.

It was a raincoat. Kerry knelt on one knee, reached inside, and took hold of the slick fabric. "Could have used this. Don't remember sticking it in...."

The fabric slithered around her knees as she looked past where it had been shoved and saw a rounded surface of scuffed leather beyond it. She resisted the urge to slap herself on the forehead. "Jesus, I totally forgot about that."

"That" was a leather duffle bag, with a handle on the end fastened with brass hardware. She grabbed the handle and hauled it toward her as she backed up. So intent on her mission, she didn't hear anything behind her until something cold and wet hit her in the back of the neck. "Yahhh!"

She whipped around, to find Mocha staring wide eyed at her, his nose the culprit. "Mocha!"

He sat down, then after a pause, licked his lips. "Burf."

Kerry had to laugh. "You scared the hell out of me." She chuckled, then turned back to her prize. "But it's okay, honey. Look what I found!" She pulled the bag and half turned so it was between them. Mocha agreeably sniffed the bag, and his tail started wagging.

"That solves a lot of problems." Kerry stood and picked up the bag. She moved over to put it on her worktable. She unzipped the double zipper on top and opened it up. "Yes, it does."

She then took the box with its assorted bottles and things and went back downstairs with it.

****

Dar had settled into an incongruous plastic Adirondack chair that suited her long legs. She cradled the cup of tea, Zoe provided, in her hands. She tasted it and found it to be mint and refreshing. Pete came into the cooking area and opened up the barbeque. Nightfall had brought the temperature down just enough to be bearable.

Chino laid down next to her, and regarded the courtyard, tongue lolling idly. "Have a fun day today, Chi?" Dar reached down with one hand and gave the dog a scratch behind her ears, which caused her tail to thump on the ground.

The door to the Humvee opened and Hank emerged. He spotted Dar and ambled over to her, dropping into a camp chair at her side. "Hey, junior."

Dar grinned tolerantly.

"Them kids out there are all right," Hank said. "A little boy scouty, but I figured they'd be okay after they asked me about the shine." He eyed Dar. "You all know that little pond there, that's spring fed," he said. "Comin up from the aquifer I figure."

"I tasted it. Thought it would be brackish, but it wasn't," Dar said. "It's so close to the bay."

"Nope." Hank shook his head firmly. "Took me some chemical readings. Pretty decent. Got some dissolved limestone and all that you'd spect."

"Sure."

"Drinkable," he said. "I told them we could use it for the hooch." He paused thoughtfully. "What'd you think about that little hut thing."

Dar set her cup on the arm of the chair and then folded her hands on her lap. "What do I think. I don't know that I think anything about the hut," she said. "It's just the bare essentials you need to live in, I guess."

"I like it," Hank replied. "I think that fella was a little sideways but that's all right. I'm a little sideways too." He winked at Dar. "You gonna keep them kids on there? They want to stick around. Made a point of tellin me cause I guess they figured I'd make a point of telling you. Which I now done."

"Hmm."

Hank let her think about it, glancing up as Zoe came over with her pitcher of tea. "Hello there, little sister." He accepted a cup of the tea with a smile. "Why thank you."

Would she? Dar considered. The property was more than big enough to need some people around to do things to it. Things she didn't know that she wanted to do herself, though the thought of getting a riding mower was kind of fun. "What do they actually do in real life?"

Hank chuckled.

"No, I mean... they do something to make a living for themselves, right?" Dar asked. "I mean, they're not stupid guys."

"Most of em do stuff like work at hardware stores, that kind of thing,"

Hank said. "Sorta blue collar boys. None of em been to college. Just got out of high school and their after-school jobs went full-time I guess." He crossed his military boots. "Like me. S'how I ended up in the Navy. Got tired of bagging Publix."

Zoe sat down next to him on one of the small beach chairs. "My mama likes Sedanos, but I was saying to Mayte just before, I like Publix better," she said. "My brother works there as well. He makes sandwiches in the deli."

"Now that's a job." Hank grinned at her. "I coulda done that. Skipped out on all the mess of the military." He glanced over at Dar, who silently pondered, a faint crease between her eyebrows. "But those are pretty decent guys, junior. Got good hands, good hearts."

Dar's pale blue eyes fastened on him. "You want to come run them?"

Hank remained silent and watched her face. He put his hands behind his head and leaned back, his eyes narrowing a little bit.

"We have no idea how to take care of a property like that," Dar said, after a long pause. "And it needs a lot of care."

"Well," Hank said, slowly, thoughtfully. "I'd come and do for you whatever you want, Dar." He shifted a little bit in the chair. "I just don't know how much I'd like running folks. Not sure I'd be any good at it, y'know?"

Dar leaned on the arm of the chair nearest him, her eyes twinkling a little bit. "No, I wasn't either," she admitted. "Actually, I figured I'd rather get everything done myself. It was easier than trying to explain myself to everyone all the time."

Hank made a spectacle of looking all around the courtyard, and at the office building, and then looked at her with an expression of disbelief.

"Eventually I figured it out," she said. "Sort of. Kerry's a lot better at it than I am." She picked up the cup and took a sip of the tea. "Think about it. Let me know."

"Hey!" Pete let out a yell. "Bring that table over here. We got a lot of ribs to plate!"

The group around the hibachi got up and came over. Two of them detoured over to where there was a stack of folding tables on the ground. They picked up the top one and brought it over and set it up near the concrete pad.

"Get another one of them," Sasha directed, a large metal bowl in her hands. "Need a place for the dishes."

"C'mon." Hank got up and gestured to Zoe. "Mess call."

Dar was about to get up and help when she saw Kerry come through the doorway, with Mocha in attendance and a big grin on her face. She waited for her to come over to hear what had made her steps so jaunty.

"Hey!" Kerry dropped to her knees on the ground next to Dar's chair and leaned her forearms on the arm of it. "Do you remember what we were doing when we heard about this damn hurricane?"

Dar peered at her with a bewildered expression. "Should I?" She eyed

Kerry in question.

"We were planning a trip down to the cabin," Kerry said. "We were going to take the boat to the sailing club dock, then leave from there last Friday, and head on down. Then you looked at the weather channel and said…"

"I said, oh crap. Yeah, I do remember that but—"

"Do you know where I ended up tossing our go bag?" Kerry arched her brows, her eyes a soft honey color in the light from the torches. "Because I packed it on Thursday morning and brought it to work with me?"

"Ah!" Dar's eyes lit up in comprehension. "You left it here."

"I left it here. So, we're covered." Kerry half turned to watch as everyone came over across the grass to the tables. "So now we can relax and enjoy ourselves." She exhaled in contentment. "I think they're going to do more music after dinner. This is going to be fun, Dar."

Dar leaned back and folded her arms. "It's going to be something." She sighed. "At least it doesn't look like rain."

"Shh."

Chapter Eighteen

Dar walked down the hallway, carefully unrolling a lurid orange extension cord along the inside wall. She gave the cord a twist as she released it so it would lie evenly and straight on the floor.

It was dark, and quiet now outside. Chino was beside her. She idly sniffed at the cable in her role as canine escort. Her dark toenails made soft clackety sounds on the wood and, as usual, her tail gently waved back and forth.

On the other side of the floor, the techs were squirreled into their space, and the varied temporary residents were bunked down outside in trucks and tents. For some, pallets under the stars by choice.

Carlos and Mayte were still out and about. Dar and Kerry helped Zoe settle her things and Mayte's into the second of the two RV's after Zoe's failed effort to turn the RV over to them.

The third RV now housed Pete and Randy, and they'd reserved space for Carlos when he got back. Pete had moved the RV to block access to the front of the office and had named the vehicle "Outpost West." He and Randy had moved long canvas covered cases and other various paramilitary gear into the rig and were rummaging around it in thinly veiled delight.

Dar ran the cable under the door to Zoe's area, and patiently continued along the wall toward her office door, her bare feet making almost no noise.

Inside the office, the mellow glow of candlelight shown, and as she approached the inner door, Kerry stuck her head out and smiled at her. "Hey."

"There you are." Kerry stepped back to let her inside. "It's really not too bad in here."

"Gets a breeze off the water." Dar finished her obsessively neat laying of cable down and coiled the remainder of the hundred-foot length in a perfect circle next to the small box fan near the couch. She knelt and plugged the fan in, and it obligingly turned.

"Nice," Kerry said. "I had fun tonight."

"Me too." Dar stood up and dusted her hands off. "Kinda think that Carlos and Mayte should be back, though." She frowned. "Or at least called if they were going to hang out near the hospital."

"Well." Kerry took a seat behind Dar's desk and picked up the mug of hot chocolate that steamed gently on it. She took a sip. "I tried calling their cells, but naturally it just fast busied."

"Naturally."

Chino went over and curled up in her bed. Mocha was already in his. He sat up and watched them, a tiny tip of his pink tongue displayed between his teeth.

It was very dark and silent outside toward the water where the windows faced. There was a decent breeze blowing, and they heard the rustle of leaves, and at the back of that the faint wash as small waves hit the seawall that protected the edge of the bay.

It was an onshore wind, and there was salt on it. Dar went over to the window and sat down on the built-in seat under it, leaning back against the edge of the sill and looking out over the neighborhood. "We are the only thing with any life around here."

"We are." Kerry rolled the desk chair over next to her. "I'm glad we stayed."

Dar smiled and reached out to pat her on the leg without looking. "Damn good ribs," she said. "That's a pretty broad-minded group out there. Some of them surprised me."

"That one ex-marine in the back, what's his name, Buddy?" Kerry asked. "He has a degree in microbiology. Has no interest in using it. He likes just doing odd jobs."

Dar's face quirked into thoughtfulness. "Might be more interesting. Different things every day."

Kerry moved her hand to cover Dar's and folded her fingers around them. "They're good people out there. I'm glad they showed up. Even that veteran who messed with Scott. He turned out okay."

"He did." Dar exhaled. "While I sat out there and listened to that band play, I thought about all the cool stuff we could do with this building. How cool it could look. We never really thought about changing it."

"Wasn't ours to change. I was going to work some reno into our rental contract but..." She lifted her hands with a little laugh. "But now we have to pay for everything."

"We would have ended up paying for it one way or another anyway." Dar let her head rest against the wall. "Maybe I should think about going back to that guy from the state and taking that contract. Numbers he was talking about could cover all of this."

Kerry regarded her thoughtfully. "Instead of going after more new accounts?"

Dar nodded. "Until we get this all back together." She looked at Kerry. "If he's still interested. They need the help. You heard them on the news. It'll give us the capital to make things bulletproof so we don't have to be stressed like this again."

She watched Kerry think, her brows contracted just a little. She reached out and tweaked her nose. "Think about it. Who even knows if it's still an option."

"I will think about it," Kerry said. "That's an interesting thought because it's a no cost contract for us. They're just buying your brain."

Dar regarded her with a slight grin. "Isn't that what you said you'd do? Sell my brain?" She stood up and held her hand out. "Let's get some rest. It's been a long ass day."

Kerry got up and rolled the chair back behind Dar's desk. She paused with her hands on the back of the seat, her fingertips pressing a little into the sturdy webbing that it was made of.

She watched Dar walk to the side table where she'd put their go bag, her tall form outlined in the golden candlelight. "Not sure we can do that and the game thing at the same time, hon," Kerry said, leaning on the chair. "They kinda both need your focus."

Dar unzipped the bag and removed their bathroom kit. "They do." She tucked the kit under one arm and turned to face Kerry. "I'd rather go for the sure thing. The gaming rig has too many questions around it," she said, matter-of-factly. "We can still open up a small office there, to deliver the military contract."

It made absolute logical sense.

But.

"That game console has bigger potential," Kerry said. "That could really be a breakthrough."

She understood at a root level how much more exciting it would be to see that come to fruition, and to be honest, how much more interesting it would be for Dar to do.

Dar's eyes, a colorless tan in the light, met hers. "I realize that."

"Not only that, but you could also lose those kids," Kerry said. "They're so excited about this."

"Then we find more kids," Dar responded calmly. "Bottom line, Ker, we have to do what makes sense in order to deal with the cards we got right now."

Kerry walked around the desk and went over to her, feeling the distance between them like sandpaper on the skin. As she closed, she saw Dar's head tilt, and the faint smile appear on her lips. She bumped up against her in gentle affection.

The warm candlelight brought an intimacy with it, and Dar lifted her hand and gently cupped Kerry's face, acknowledging the moment. "If it's meant to be, it'll happen," she said, with a simple certainty. "But it's not going to happen tonight."

"No." Kerry leaned into the touch. "Let's wait for tomorrow. No telling what that's going to bring to the table with our usual luck."

Dar chuckled, a low, musical sound. "No kidding." She patted Kerry's check gently. "Anything could happen with us here. Let's get some rest before it does."

"Let's."

****

Dar wasn't sure what woke her up. She just went from full asleep to full awake in a breath, her eyes opening into the darkness of her office. She blinked a few times to focus and quietly lay there, just breathing as she tried to figure out what was going on.

It was dead quiet. Next to her on the wide couch Kerry was still deeply asleep, curled on her left side, her left arm draped over Dar's body.

They were using the go bag as a pillow, with half of its contents removed it was soft and comfortable.

Nearby, the dogs were asleep in their beds, undisturbed.

She stretched her hearing outward, detecting a few faint creaks of the building, and the soft whirring of the fan, wafting room temperature air over her.

Past that, she heard the generator outside with its incessant rumble.

All seemed peaceful. Dar let her body relax, and decided it was just the strange location that maybe stirred her awake. With a brief twist of her lips she closed her eyes and tried to compose herself back to sleep.

The couch was reasonably comfortable, and after all when Kerry had chosen it for her, it had been with the odd nap in mind to begin with. The furniture was more than long enough for Dar's height, and wide enough to really be more of a daybed than a couch.

With thick pillows in place, you could sit on it, but with the pillows tossed aside it provided a nice resting place, even without air-conditioning to relieve the muggy heat.

Dar felt her body relax, and she started to drift off again, when from outside the window, on the water side of the building she heard the sound of a branch breaking.

Her eyes opened again. Quietly, she rolled off the couch and stood up and moved over to the window on noiseless bare feet as she leaned against the built-in seat and peered outside.

It was very dark. There were some clouds overhead covering the half-moon but after a moment her eyes adjusted to the shadows and she could make out the shapes of the bushes and trees at the back of the building and the wall that enclosed the property.

Between the wall and the building, she saw something moving. Something the size of a person and in a stealthy kind of way that made the hairs on the back of her neck prickle. She watched for a moment more to make sure she wasn't imagining it, then turned and walked swiftly back across the office and out the front door.

She was dressed in a ratty long T-shirt and cotton shorts to sleep in, and she felt the breeze coming in from the open front door, as the door to the courtyard on the inside was open.

Maybe that wasn't smart, leaving it open, regardless of the RV parked outside. Dar moved onto the porch and paused, only her eyes moving as she scanned the outdoors between the building and the vehicle where it was dark and quiet.

She wondered what time it was.

The inky darkness around her lightened a bit, as the moon came out from behind the clouds, but with the guard gone, everything past it, everything toward the road as far as she could see was blank and dead and as she took a breath of the warm night air some internal instinct warned her of something just not right.

She got to the RV, but before she knocked on the door, she went around the front of it and looked past into the parking lot. She saw that the second RV had been pulled up close to the first, and the third, that Carlos and Mayte had gone off in, was still missing.

The parking lot though, save the front line of it where her truck was parked, was empty.

She turned and looked back at the office. Through the open windows on the lower level, she saw some faint glimmers of light, flickers that indicated candles to make the load on the generator as minimal as possible to save on fuel.

The top level on this side was all dark.

She looked at the edges of the building on either side, but it was full of foliage and bushes, the tough scrubby plants that had protected the building from the wind in the storm.

Was she just being goofy?

Did she really see someone in the back, or just imagined it?

She stood by the RV, one hand on its side, for a long moment indecisive. Then caution took precedence and she moved over and raised her hand to knock on the door when very unexpectedly it opened outward, and Pete appeared.

He was fully dressed in dark camouflage and had a dark cap on his head, covering his silvery hair. He carried a semi-automatic in one hand. "Hi there," he said. "I heard you were an early riser, but this is what we used to call o dark whatthehell."

Dar smiled briefly. "I heard something," she said. "I think I saw someone in the back."

Pete reached behind him and rapped softly on the inside panel of the RV. A moment later Randy slunk down the steps, carrying a shotgun. "You were righty tighty, Whitey," he told him. "I was having a cuppa at that nice little table inside watching out when you came out the door," he said. "Randy thought he saw someone go down that side street."

Randy nodded, a short, thickset man with caramel colored skin and somewhat jerky, nervous movements. "Let's go see."

"Right. Since we have boots and guns, let's do that, and you go back inside?" Pete told Dar. "Might just be a vagrant, smelling that barbeque smoke we painted the area with."

Dar eyed him thoughtfully.

"Please?" Pete went on. "If something happened to you while your daddy was gone, it'd kill me before he did."

"I'll go get dressed," Dar said. "Go on, I'll check out the inside and make sure nothing more than that damn cat got in."

She turned and went back toward the building.

Pete sniffed reflectively. "Apple didn't fall very far from that tree." He cocked his handgun and turned his cap around. "C'mon. Let's go scare the crap outta whatever dipshit's wandering."

Randy fell in behind him. "Hope it's a dipshit. Not some fuckin yahoo."

They got to the edge of the building and Pete pointed right and tapped his chest, then pointed left and pointed at Randy. They split up and started around both sides.

Dar re-entered the building and halted as she spotted Mocha and Chino coming down the steps toward her, their toenails echoing softly on the wood. Behind them at the top of the steps Kerry stood, scrubbing a hand through her hair as she looked down at Dar.

Silently, she spread her hands out in question.

Dar motioned her down, resigned to an early start to their day and hoped like hell that was all it was going to be.

****

Kerry got to the bottom of the steps. "What's going on?" She whispered. "What's wrong?"

Dar put her hands on the banister. "Not sure. I thought I… no, I did see someone in the back. Pete's checking it out."

"Well, at five a.m. it probably should be checked out," Kerry said. "Should we get dressed in case we're about to be under assault?"

Dar glanced down. "Probably. I should put some shoes on at least."

They both trotted back up the steps and went into the office. As Dar went to the table to grab a pair of jeans, Kerry stepped over to the window to look out.

"Maybe not stand in the open window, Ker?" Dar said, fastening the buttons on her pants. "No idea who has guns out there. At least our guys do."

"Mm." Kerry retreated. "Can't see anything anyway." She came over to claim and pull on her clothes. "Yeesh what a way to wake up."

Dar took her boots over to her desk chair and sat down to put them on. "Where'd the dogs go?"

"They stayed downstairs." Kerry perched on the couch arm to pull on her sneakers. "Okay. Let's go see what the hell is going on." She stood up and paused. "Should I go get the shotgun from the truck?"

Dar looked up. "Is it in there?"

"Yup."

"I'll go." Dar got up and headed for the door. "Probably be more useful than the pocketknife I'm carrying."

Kerry followed her. "I don't know, hon. That was pretty useful against that mountain lion."

"He didn't have a rifle."

They clattered down the steps, and now there were two more people coming in from the courtyard, one of Carlo's lifting buddies and Hank. "Hey early risers, what's the rush?" Hank said, stifling a yawn. "This how you big time corporate raiders operate?"

"Dar saw someone sneaking around the back," Kerry said. "So...."

"Got it." Hank whirled and started back toward his truck.

The lifter nodded. "Guys were saying maybe there'd be trouble. Lemme go get a bat or something." He retreated, and as he did, they heard the murmur of voices outside as the campers stirred.

"Maybe we should shut the door," Kerry suggested, as Dar started for it. "Don't dawdle."

In response Dar broke into a run as she jumped off the porch and landed on the ground. She launched herself forward toward the edge of the parking lot.

Kerry watched her, then remembered the other RV, and looked around for it. She spotted it up near the building. She started toward it when she saw motion in her peripheral vision and stopped. She turned to see shadows heading toward them from the road. "Dar!"

Dar had just reached the truck when she heard her name. She yanked the truck door open and dove under the back seat.

Kerry stood still for an instant, then turned and bolted back into the office. She let out a yell as she reached the inner door. "Everybody look out!"

Hank was already barreling toward her, his gun cradled in his arms and a sidearm strapped to his chest. "Move out the way, shortie!" He dodged past her and was out the door and down off the porch in a rapid thunder of boots on wood. "N'get yer butt down on the ground!"

It was far too dark to see much. Kerry hesitated, trying to peer through the shadows. Then she cursed and ran back into the building and into the conference room to grab a large flashlight off the table.

Bodies rushed past the door on the way to the front, and she let them pass then ran after them, going to the edge of the porch and turning the light on to beam it across the yard and toward the parking lot.

****

Dar got her hands on the shotgun and pulled it out from under the seat, more concerned with someone else grabbing it than intending to use it herself. She slid out of the truck and slammed the door behind her with one elbow, the gun held in front of her.

She turned to find a melee in the yard, yells and grunts and silence as men came pouring out of the office to engage with the line of figures dressed in dark clothing, their faces and heads covered and obscured.

Dar paused for a moment, then ran along the edge of the lot and through the bushes, to where Kerry stood with her flashlight illuminating the fight. "Get inside."

"I want to see who these assholes are," Kerry said. "Tell you what, you take the light and I'll take the gun," she said calmly, as she reached out one hand for the weapon. "They're not interested in us, they're busy, Dar."

They were behind the makeshift guard post and Dar had to agree that no one seemed to be paying them any attention. She handed over the gun and took the flashlight, twisting it to its brightest setting and aiming it into the eyes of the hooded attackers. "This is nuts."

"This is nuts," Kerry agreed, as she inspected the gun and then chambered a round. She turned and rested the muzzle on the shelf in the shack built apparently for just that purpose. It provided a slot to aim out of. "You figure these are those guard guys?"

"No idea," Dar said, busy with her light-based assault that was having some good effect as the attackers threw up arms to block the beam. "No one's shooting."

The scuffle in front of them was surprisingly quiet, but already it was obvious the attackers were overwhelmed by the locals.

Pete applied a short bat to the head of the figure he was opposing, and he went down, then he scrambled and rolled away and let out a shout. He got to his knees and then to his feet and broke into a run toward the lot.

He was followed by a flood of other dark clad bodies, apparently obeying an order to retreat. The men from the office let out yells of derision, and Hank stooped to pick up a piece of rock from the ground and threw it after them, hitting one of them on the back.

Dar tipped the flashlight up as their crowd started to return from the fight. "That was idiotic."

Their team was visibly exultant as they came back over, obviously pleased with the result of the fight.

"Morons!" Pete said, as he dusted his hands off and examined a scrape along his wrist bone. "What a bunch of dipshits. Nice work with the light, junior."

Hank took a nose count. "All good here," he said, as Kerry unchambered the round she'd gotten ready in her shotgun. "What'n'hell was that?" He asked as they gathered at the porch. "Guess they figgered they'd catch us sleepin."

Pete scratched his eyebrow. "Almost did." He indicated the guard shack. "Front door was wide open. They'd have gotten inside more than likely if junior here hadn't come flying out to go hunt em barefoot in her underwear."

"You were out here." Someone pointed out. "What the hell, Pete?"

"They came in the back," Dar said, in a quiet, even tone. "I saw them between the back wall and the building." She paused briefly. "I heard them through the open window in my office."

Everyone fell silent, and looked at Dar, who stood there, with the flashlight clasped in her hands, pointing at the ceiling of the porch, a splash of the light outlining her face.

"So, we probably should make sure that doesn't happen again," she said. "I'm not sure what their thought was coming in here, whether they wanted to do mischief or if we were in real trouble." She handed off the light to Pete. "I'm going to go pull my truck into the middle there. Someone open the gate for me."

"I'll check to make sure Zoe's okay," Kerry said. "It's almost dawn."

Sobered, the dozen men who had run out meekly went back inside.

Hank settled behind the guard post. "I'll hang out here."

"You two, come with me," Pete said. "Let's take a look around the back, make sure no one's lingerin round." He took the light in one hand and started off, with the other two at his heels.

Kerry watched them go, as Dar stepped off the porch and headed toward the truck. She exchanged glances with Hank. "Creepy."

'Dipshits," Hank replied. "All of them were just messin, Kerry. Weren't serious to fight, you saw em." He sniffed reflectively. "I figure they were just sent over here to scare us. Didn't even have no long guns or nothin with em." His evaluation was calm and professional. "Lucky for em Andy wasn't round here. He'd have broken them in parts."

"Mm." Kerry tucked her shotgun under one arm and walked down the steps. "Let's hope you're right."

****

Dar angled toward the truck, it's outline easily visible to her in the darkness. She reached the sidewalk and started around to the driver's side as she dug the keys to the vehicle out of her front pocket. The incursion of the attackers concerned her, and she went over the events in her head as she walked.

She rounded the front of the truck and then halted, as she found two men crouched behind it. They were dressed in the same nondescript dark clothing as the others had been and stared up at her from behind their face masks, hands clasped around black batons.

Dar felt her body react in utter instinct, and she shoved the keys back into her pocket and moved into a defensive posture, spreading her hands apart and leaning forward above her center of balance as the two men started to stand up.

One raised the baton he was carrying and without thinking, Dar shifted and kicked it out of his hand, glad she had her boots on and hadn't tried that barefoot. The baton went flying and now full of adrenaline she kicked out again and caught the man in the chest and sent him sprawling backward on the tarmac.

The other one scrambled up and reached for her and Dar caught his hands in her own and then let her hold slip down to his wrists as she lunged forward. She crashed into him and slammed him against the truck.

She was taller than he was, and about the same weight and the energy that coursed through her was ferocious and aggressive as she slammed against him again. He tried to yank his hands loose and kicked out with one boot that just missed her shin.

Behind her, she heard footsteps running and the scramble of dog toenails coming in her direction, but she took advantage of the position she was in and brought one knee up to nail the man she had a grip on in the groin.

He squealed like a pig and sagged in her grip. She heard the sound of motion behind and turned just in time to see two large animals rush up in the darkness and issue hideous sounding growls, bustling to get between the remaining man and Dar.

The man threw his hands up and stumbled back. "Hey! Don't hurt me! C'mon! Got mah hands up!"

Dar could see his eyes, wide and fearful. "Chino! Mocha! C'mere!" she ordered, as Hank, Kerry, and one of the weightlifters came barreling around the front of the truck.

Hank threw his gun up to his eyeline and threw the safety off. "Fuck'errrrrrz!" He let out a yell, then paused, as they took in the one man with his hands up, and the other curled in a fetal position on the ground. "Well, now hell, junior."

Chino and Mocha came over to Dar, tails wagging in the pre-dawn humid air.

"What happened?" Kerry was a little out of breath. "Holy crap, Dar!"

"They were hiding behind my truck," Dar said. "I think I surprised them. They sure as hell surprised me." She went over to the truck and opened the driver's side door. "Bring them inside. Maybe we can find out what the hell this was all about."

Two more veterans showed up behind Hank, weapons drawn.

"We got it." Hank flipped the safety back on his gun. "C'mon, dip-shits." He went over to the one still standing and grabbed him by the bicep. "You heard the lady. G'wan get moving before she just decides to keep on keeping on with your dumb ass selves."

The weightlifter and one of the veterans each grabbed an arm of the man on the ground and lifted him up, half carrying him between them as they marched back toward the office.

Kerry went around and got into the passenger seat of the truck and let out a squawk as Mocha jumped up into her lap. "Mocha!"

Dar regarded the scene, then opened the back door to the truck to allow Chino to, with far more decorum, jump in. Then she got in herself and started up the vehicle. "It's almost dawn. I probably should have just left it here."

"Gives us a minute to stop freaking out." Kerry had her arms around Mocha and now she exhaled. "Because I don't mind telling you I'm freaked out."

Dar chuckled and backed the truck out of its spot. "Zoe okay?"

"Slept all through it," Kerry murmured. "Though I might have slammed that RV door on her hand when I realized you were over here fighting with something."

Dar chuckled again. "Let's see what those guys say." She drove along the side road toward the back entrance to the building. She turned on the truck's lights to show the makeshift gates in the process of being pushed open to let them inside.

"Did you get hurt?" Kerry asked, suddenly.

"No." Dar guided the truck through the gates toward the area where Hank's Humvee and Pete's Jeep were parked. "Hank was right. Those guys weren't really serious."

"Then what the hell?"

"That's what I want to ask them." Dar pulled in behind Scott's RV and parked. "Was it just something stupid, in which case since we have a lot of people here with weapons, and they knew that, it was really stupid, or ... "She turned the engine off and regarded Kerry. "Or what?"

Kerry eyed her back, from behind Mocha's head. "With us? They could be extraterrestrial cat people, Dar," she said. "They seemed really scared of our Labradors."

"Well, they were growling." Dar looked from Mocha, to Chino who was had her head between the front seats, drooling on the console. "And they are pretty big." She opened her door. "Let's go see what we can find out."

Kerry sighed but opened her own door and urged Mocha to get off her legs. "Do I want to find out? I mean... it's Monday. Could that mean it's anything not horrible?"

"Probably not."

Kerry got out of the truck and closed the door behind her. As the eastern sky morphed into pinks, the sun peeked past the buildings between them and the water and sent a few errant spears of light through the windows on the far side of the courtyard.

****

Kerry picked up two of the breakfast sandwiches, fluffy eggs inside pieces of baguette with some lettuce, grilled tomato and Swiss cheese tucked inside. "Let's go see what our unexpected visitors have to say for themselves."

She put the two sandwiches on a plate and navigated her way through the inner entrance to the office, where the construction workers were setting up their tools and sawhorses and the smell of plaster wafted.

She walked past the reception desk and into the left side conference room, where Pete and one of the weightlifters kept watch on their two attackers. The two men were seated at the table with their head coverings removed, nervously waiting. Dar was sat down in her preferred seat, and Kerry took a chair next to her and passed over a sandwich.

The two were young. They were both sandy haired and freckled, with a splash of sunburn across their cheeks. One was still bent over, with his elbows on his knees and periodically he stared across at Dar with a look of suffering. Kerry thought they were perhaps in their early twenties.

Kids.

"So." She set her plate down with its edible burden. "Can I ask what the hell you people were doing here?"

Dar was content to let her talk. She took a bite of her sandwich after carefully removing the lettuce from it and depositing it on Kerry's plate.

The other boy, who was sitting straight up in his seat, cleared his throat. "We were told to come here, ma'am." He admitted. "We was told, we left something back here, and we were supposed to try and get it back."

"In the middle of the night?" Kerry asked, in a mild tone.

"Figured it was safer," the boy replied. "Just to check the grounds, like."

Kerry finished a mouthful of breakfast as he spoke, and now she swallowed and wiped her lips with the paper napkin she'd set next to the plate. "So let me get this straight," she said. "You got sent here, to a place that your people in charge knew had armed military veterans inside it, to search the grounds in the middle of the night and they thought it was a good idea?"

"Yes, ma'am," the boy acknowledged, in a somewhat mournful tone. "That's what we was told to do."

"Dumbass," Pete said, from next to the doorway. "Coulda got your ass shot."

"Probly hurt less," the second kid said, in a strained voice.

"I been shot," Pete told him. "Woulda hurt more. Lasts longer, that's for sure, than a set of bruised balls."

Kerry dusted her fingers off. "Are you seriously telling me that no one thought just coming over here and knocking on the door in daylight wouldn't be a better idea? Just asking if you left something?" She leaned on her elbows, studying the two kids. "C'mon."

"What was it?" Dar finally spoke up, staring at the two of them. "What were you all supposedly looking for?" She got to her feet and both of them flinched. That made Pete smile. "Cough it up, because we need to tell the police, I'm about to call, what you were after."

The kids exchanged looks. "Ma'am, we don't know," the one she hadn't kicked said in an earnest tone. "They just told us to go with the older guys, and help. S'why we were hidin there, behind that there truck. We were waitin for everybody to settle down then we were gonna run off."

The other nodded. "We didn't want to be part of nothing," he muttered. "Whole thing here's been just garbage for us." He looked up. "Don't call the cops on us, huh? We didn't do nothin. We just want to get out of here and go home."

Dar studied them with narrowed eyes, ones they refused to meet. She glanced over at Kerry, who observed in silence, her fingertips steepled and touching her lips. Then she looked over at Pete and the weightlifter guard, also silent.

Dar's lips quirked. "Get them some breakfast," She finally said. "Let me go think about what to do with them." She turned and walked out. After a moment, Kerry followed.

****

"Not a good way to start the morning."

Kerry accepted the cup Dar held out to her and they settled together side by side in camp chairs under a tree in the courtyard lawn.

"No." Dar extended her long legs out and braced her elbows on the camp chair arms. "Stupid kids."

"Mm. They're lucky it was you that found them," Kerry mused. "All the rest of us had guns and knives and baseball bats and teeth and I don't know what else." She shook herself briefly. "Damn lucky."

Dar smiled briefly. "Guess that kid I kneed doesn't agree with you," she said. "You buy the story they *forgot* something?"

"Not in the slightest."

"No, me either."

"I don't believe that's the reason that whole gang was here," Kerry said. "It might be what they told those kids though. Let me talk to them. See if I can find out a little more."

"Mmm," Dar said softly.

"We're not going to turn them over to the cops, are we?"

Dar made a face, her nose wrinkling up.

"Should we even report this to the cops?" Kerry wondered. "I mean, they have so much crap going on, would they even come over here and talk to us about it?" She gazed across the courtyard. "Ugh."

"Depends on if we offered them barbeque," Dar said dryly. She studied the open space, where people were starting to work on construction tasks and the veterans were gathered in one corner, perhaps discussing the morning's attack.

"Let's not call the cops," Dar said. "I'm not in the mood for them. Only damage wasn't to us anyway."

"True. Let me go talk to those kids," Kerry said. "Then let me get to my inbox. Are you going to call the Pharma guy?" she asked, looking sideways at her. "We've pushed him off long as we can I think."

Dar sighed. "Yeah," she said. "And I better call that VC. Tell him... I don't know. Push him off too."

Kerry reached out and patted her on the arm. "I'd offer to do that for you, hon, but they're just going to want to talk to you anyway." She took her coffee and stood up. "Let me go find out where the heck Mayte is, what's going on with Maria, what our people upstate are doing, and take a damn shower."

"Be right behind ya." Dar finished up her coffee as Kerry threaded her way along the concrete pad, pausing a moment to speak to Sasha before she moved on into the building. "Damn I wish this whole mess was over."

With a sigh, Dar pushed herself to her feet. She paused to watch sunlight turn the courtyard gold, and beams showed dust and gnats in equal portion. "Monday," she added, aloud. "Yuck."

Zoe came out carrying a pot of water that she set down near one of the grills and paused to wave at her and smile.

Dar waved back, before she headed toward the building, and her stuffy, dusty office, and her phone calls.

****

Kerry took the time after her shower to replenish her coffee and stir a bit of powdered creamer into it as she stood near the window and pondered her strategy.

The shower, the water lukewarm from its transit through pipes near ground level retaining the heat from the previous day had at least been wet, and she felt somewhat ready to face the day despite its nerve-wracking start.

She was dressed in a company polo shirt with its sleeves neatly rolled up and khaki carpenter shorts, as close to business casual as she could cope with given the lack of AC.

She picked up the cup and went down the hall to the conference room where the two guardsmen were just finishing up the two large breakfast sandwiches they'd been given, along with a dish of tater tots and cups of coffee.

They paused in mid chew as she entered. They looked alarmed.

Kerry smiled at them and took a seat with her coffee. "Keep on." She waved casually at them. "I just want to have a chat."

Pete and the weightlifter, who had remained near the door, kept up a casual stance against the wall.

"Thanks for the chow, ma'am," one of the two men said. He wore a patch on his chest that said—Boone. "It's real nice of you given all what happened."

Kerry leaned back in her chair with her coffee cup. "I have to say that we normally have a great relationship with the military, you know?" She indicated Pete with one thumb. "So, it's kind of sad to have what happened this morning happen, because I don't really understand why."

The two just chewed and looked at her in silence.

"I mean, you all couldn't really have been here to find something you left behind, could you?"

The two exchanged quick looks.

"That was awfully dangerous," Kerry said. "For everyone."

Boone, who was the luckier of the two and only had a bruise on his wrist to show for his efforts, eyed her and licked his lips. "Didn't mean no one to get hurt, ma'am," he said. "We got moved out, you know? We got sent to a real bad place."

Kerry rocked forward and put her cup down. "Now, you can believe this or not believe it. But we had nothing to do with that." She said. "I know people said Dar called someone, but she didn't."

"Somebody done," the other guardsman said. His patch was blank, and he was still hunched over a little, leaning his elbows on his knees. "We were just here doin what we were told to do, is all."

Boone nodded. "All of them folks got hot up before, wasn't our fault."

"Like we couldn't go off and do nothing," the other man said. "And man, we didn't want to, all of them people so nasty and rude and yelling at us."

Kerry thought about that, considering it from the soldier's perspective. "They were upset and angry," she said.

"Not even talking like us," Boone said. "Couldn't even understand what we was saying, and it's in our country, you know?" He looked up at Kerry. "Why'd they want us to go do for them, they ain't even take the time to learn English?"

"You all are from a part of the country where people speaking more than one language is not that common, I guess." Kerry regarded them gravely. "Here, a lot of people do, so it's not as critical, I guess, for people who come here to learn English."

"That ain't' right," Boone said, in a heartfelt, sincere tone. "You all come here, want stuff from us, you should learn to talk to us. Not the other way round."

The other man nodded in agreement. "So yeah," he said. "Cap'n said we could come back ovah here, give you all a scare like." He looked across the table at her. "Just a payback, you know? Cause we were done dirty."

Kerry was aware, in her peripheral vision, that Pete rolled his eyes, and though he didn't say it, she could imagine him thinking the words— grow the f- up—. Because she, herself heard that same internal echo. But the young men's resentment was real, and sincerely felt.

It was not by any stretch of the imagination an isolated viewpoint. She'd heard those same words from her father on many occasions, and viewed through the eyes of these young people she felt it was an unfortunate, but valid internal outrage.

"I understand what you're saying," She finally said. "When I moved here it was a big adjustment for me. I wasn't used to having to deal with a large number of people around me that I couldn't communicate with. It was hard." She saw them both nod, just a little, and their body tension changed, and relaxed a bit, their shoulders under the dark fatigues dropping. "And I chose to stay. You didn't have a choice."

"Yes, ma'am," Boone said. "We're just here cause we were asked to help, and we got screwed."

Kerry nodded, and put her cup down and rested her hands on the table. "Okay, I get it," She said. "So, since we're here talking, and you seem like reasonable gentlemen, let me share some thoughts with you. "

"Ma'am, you all always been nice to us," Boone said. "You seem like a straight up lady."

"We can debate that because a lot of people would tell you I'm not a straight anything," Kerry said, dryly. "But here's the deal. The reason you all think we called someone on you is because Dar told your commander she might have to after he threatened to tell everyone who her grandfather was."

"Say what?" Pete said, and started to laugh. "Oh my God. Did you tell Andy?"

The two guardsmen looked puzzled. "Sorry, ma'am?" Boone said. "What does that got to do with nothin?"

"No," Kerry said to Pete. "Andy's father, Dar's grandfather, is Duke Roberts, from Alabama. You might have heard of him." She swung around to focus on the guardsmen. "I think you all do come from around there."

The two guardsmen stared at her over the table, eyes wide, mouths open in perfect little O's of astonishment. "For real?" Boone finally said, in a tone of amazement.

"For real," Pete interjected. "Andrew B Roberts, Duke's oldest boy."

Boone let out a low, breathy whistle. "Do say," he murmured. "Oh... now hold on ah did hear about one of them—"

"Going for the Navy," Pete concluded the statement. "Andy did, cause he hated that man, and son, if I were you, I wouldn't mention that old jackass to him if you want to stay upright." He crossed his booted feet and cradled his gun comfortably. "He doesn't mess around."

Boone looked at him seriously. "Ah won't hear bad stuff against Cap'n Duke, sir," he said. "Wouldn't be here if it hadn't been for him. He paid out for my mama to get a doctor when me and my sister was being born and it was a rough time for her."

The other man nodded. "Gave his shirt off his back for folks," he said. "Don't know what argument his boy had with him, but he done a lot for a lot of people round our parts. Drove em down to nothin, really, though lately now they got their old house fixed up some."

"Yeah, he took care of folks. Long as they were his kind," Pete said, implacably.

"Sure." Boone looked over at him. "Don't know what's wrong with that? Took care of his own. Least somebody did. Don't know why you all think e'vrybody's due everything just cause. What did them people the other night do to help themselves? Just gimme all."

"You all are here to help them," Pete said. "The hell you all are thinking."

"Well then, sir, them should talk nice to us, and use our language," Boone said. "That all's what we're thinking."

The conundrum gave Kerry a headache. Mostly because there was internal logic to it from these kid's perspective and she could, save the difference in the language and the idiom, hear most of her family say just the same thing.

Sad, and not a little exhausting. "I guess, I just feel like if you can help people, you do, like us giving you guys a ride, and a meal, even though you tried to hurt us," she said. "It's just the right thing to do."

"Well," the other guardsman said. "I guess we all just think different, ma'am."

Kerry propped her chin up on her fist. "I guess we do." She glanced at Pete.

"C'mon, kiddos." Pete straightened up. "Let's go for a ride." He gestured toward them with the rifle. "I gotta go pick up some barb wire now in case any more critters get ideas to come mess around with us."

The two guardsmen got up obediently and walked out, ducking past Pete with little nods of acknowledgement. He rolled his eyes behind their backs and followed.

"Thanks, Pete," Kerry called after him.

The weightlifter came over and sat down in one of the seats the men vacated. "That was some crazy talk," he told her. He was tall and had beautiful creamy brown skin, with a slightly overgrown but closely cropped tightly curled dark hair. "Was I hearing that? They're just right out racists? They said all that out loud?"

Kerry sighed. "You know, Larry, I think it's more complicated than that," she said. "When you live inside a culture where everyone around you looks, and acts, and believes like you do, it's really easy to assume, to really believe inside your mind, that it's right and natural."

"Hey no, they got brains in their heads. They got the Internet. They don't live inside a plastic bag, Kerry. C'mon now." Larry shook his head. "I seen people like that all my damn life, looking down on me and treating me like a lower life form cause I ain't white."

"You know, it's easy for me to agree with that," Kerry said. "Because I grew up inside a society where that ideology, though not said quite that openly, was the norm." She pondered. "Still is, and I obviously made other choices."

"And you all are gay," Larry said, casually.

"Yes, so that's a part of it right? When you're not quite in the group, there's more reason to think outside it," Kerry said. "It's easier to put yourself in someone else's place when you've had to deal with that in your life I guess." She paused. "The one who really walked out of the box just because he decided to was Andy, Dar's dad. He had every reason to let that be his pattern and he just didn't."

Larry nodded a little bit. "He's a different kind of guy."

"Yeah, I don't really know how he got to that place in his head, you know? That young." She shook her head a little. "He just said, Nope. Not gonna do that. Not me," she mused. "In fact, he said, I'm going to find me a pagan, vegetarian witch and get us hitched just to extra special drive everybody out of their ever-loving minds."

Larry smiled. "I really like Mrs. R," he said. "He's a lucky man."

"He is." Kerry looked past him out the window, where she saw Pete trundling out along the road in his Jeep, the two guardsmen along with him. "Wish there were more like him. He's the right kind of different."

"Y'know." Larry smiled a trifle. "One of the reasons I started lifting, aside from liking how I looked and what it felt like, was because it gave me something to have people stare at past my color." He paused, considering that. "And I get pulled over less."

"Ah," Kerry murmured.

"Least now, if they see me driving my nice car around, they all assume I'm some rich guy's bodyguard," he said. "So, I kinda wish there were more folks out there like him too."

They sat there briefly, in silence. "We kinda live in a messed up world," Kerry finally said.

"We kinda do," Larry agreed. "But right now, I got a nice place to lift, and some cool folks to talk to, so today... today's a good day." He winked at her and stood up. "Even if it started out whacked."

He sauntered out, twisting his broad shoulders so they would clear the doorjamb.

Kerry stood up and looked at the wide-open windows letting in the warm, moist air, and shook her head.

****

Dar made sure all the jalousie windows in her office were propped wide open, and the shutters were out of the way to allow whatever breeze there was a chance to come in. She sat down behind the desk in her web weaved chair and pulled out her cell phone.

From where she sat, the construction in progress wasn't overwhelmingly loud. She heard the baseboards being cut downstairs, but upstairs the plastering was going on quietly.

Dar opened her desk and took out a contact book. She flipped the pages until she found the one she was looking for. She glanced at her watch, then typed the number into the phone and held it up to her ear to listen.

Should she have checked in with Arthur and Elvis first? She hesitated, but the line was picked up and it was too late to worry about it.

"Dect Pharma, John Deland speaking."

Dar took a breath. "Hello, John. Dar Roberts here. Emerging from hell."

A momentary silence. "Oh, damn! I wasn't expecting a call from you," John spluttered. "Been watching the news, figured it was a miracle you all got done what you did last week, seeing all those floods and blackouts and everything!"

Dar felt her internal tension relax just a trifle. John's voice didn't sound angry or agitated as it did the last time she'd spoken to him. "Well, there's a story around how that got done, but you said to call, so here I am. How's it going?"

"Really good, Dar. I have to admit to you, I never thought we'd get here, but that last submission really seemed to pull things together," John said readily. "We've been testing since we got it. My guys have a bunch of things they want as enhancements, but so far, so good."

Dar felt somewhat nonplussed. "So, the integration's giving you back the answers you're looking for?" She asked, after a slight pause.

"The test ones? Sure are," John said in a satisfied tone. "Listen, Dar, I'm sorry I pressed you so hard about it. It's just been so tough for us this year. This really looks like it's going to let us move ahead a little bit. Charlie said he took a copy of our real database and put the program against it. It found a few things already we're looking at." He paused. "Can't say more than that. IP you know."

Dar chuckled a little. "John, I wouldn't know a word about what you all are doing anyway. Not my gig. Hope it works out the way you want it to. Give us a list of the enhancements you want. I'll get the guys to work up a quote for you on them."

"Don't worry we will!" He responded. "But... I saw video of that area by you, Dar. Are you all floating on the tops of your roofs working off cell phones or something? How in the hell? Or did you move folks out of the area like you said you might."

"We sent our support folks up north." Dar relaxed into her chair. "I had the server stack moved to the island I live on, and we set something up there with a satellite rig. We've got generator power out there."

"Oh! Huh. Sounds easy," John said. "Well, great to hear from you, Dar, and thanks again for making that date for us. I knew we could depend on you. I'll let you go now, I got Charlie in my doorway and he looks excited."

"Talk to you later, John. Tell him hello." Dar hung up the phone and let it drop to her leg, as she looked around her office in bemused surprise. "Son of a bitch."

Mocha lifted his head from the couch they'd slept on, his tail thumping gently against the leather.

She picked up the phone and dug the card out of her slim wallet, typing it in. "Let's see if our luck holds, Moch. Maybe it'll be an okay Monday after all."

****

Kerry had one hand on the stairwell railing about to go up when she heard, through the open front door, the sound of a large vehicle approaching, its tires crunching on the dead leaves in the parking lot, engine rumbling. She paused and went to the door and peered out.

"Ah." She made a relieved sound. "About fricken time."

"What's up?" Hank appeared literally from nowhere at her side. "Oh, the last bus is back." He watched it approach. "Wasn't that supposed to stay with somebody?"

"It was, but after they left it occurred to me they probably didn't have a way back." Kerry acknowledged. "I mentioned that to Dar, because we also realized they probably didn't have a way to call us because Carlos and Mayte left their sat   phones here."

"Sweet planning."

"Well. There was a lot going on. You know how it is." Kerry walked out onto the porch. "C'mon, let's see what the deal is. Hopefully they have Maria and Tomas in there and we all get to say hello."

"Right behind ya." Hank ambled after her willingly, and they walked together down the sidewalk toward where the big RV moved across the lot to where Dar's truck had been parked.

Carlos was behind the wheel and he waved as he put the brakes on. The RV rocked to a halt and the door popped open, with Mayte right behind it. She came down the steps closely followed by her mother, who let out a squeal.

"Aiiee! Kerrisita!" Maria was dressed in a University of Miami sweatshirt and jeans and was in high spirits.

Kerry smiled in reaction and waved. "Hey!"

They met near the RV and Maria threw her arms around Kerry. "I have been telling everyone how you are amazing!"

Carlos climbed down out of the RV. "Hey, boss!" he greeted Kerry. "Sorry we took so long! We had some adventures. Hey, Hank."

"Us too." Hank grinned briefly at him. "Hello, ma'am, I'm Henry," he said to Maria, who had turned to look at him in question. "I'm a friend of Andy's."

"Yes, Mayte has told us everything and how all the people have come here." Maria released Kerry. "Tomas is resting in the so nice bedroom. Dios Mio, Kerrisita, this is an amazing thing." She took Kerry's hands. "Please you come and see him."

Of course. Kerry willingly followed Maria into the RV and glanced around as they came up into the living area. There were a scattering of supplies on the sideways mounted table and the inside smelled strongly of Cuban coffee, which made her smile.

"I was amazed," Maria told her, as she led the way back past the divider and through the kitchenette. "I could not imagine there was so much inside when Mayte told me about this."

"Yeah, we got lucky," Kerry said. "I see you got the important stuff." She grinned as they passed the small hot plate, with a silver, black handled coffeepot on it.

"The people at the hotel were so nice," Maria said. "One of the people there, they went out and found a little bodega and brought us back some things for us, for this."

They moved back into the bedroom, where Tomas was laying on one of the lower bunks, his leg propped up on pillows, reading a Spanish language book. He looked up as they entered and then smiled. "Ah!" He put the book down. "The Angel is here!"

Kerry held a hand out. "Hello, Tomas! How's the leg?"

The bedroom was neat and tidy, the lower bunk opposite had a bag and some folded shirts on it. On the small table at the very back of the RV there was a stack of folders and paperwork from the hospital.

Tomas himself was dressed in a T-shirt and shorts and was freshly shaved. Nearby, a basin with a washcloth and shaving supplies sat on a built-in bench.

"It is okay." Tomas indicated the limb, encased in fiberglass, which extended from his foot up to just over his knee. "The doctors put some things inside of it."

"Metal things," Maria said, standing behind Kerry. "Some things, I think, that Dar's papa also has."

"Ah." Kerry nodded. "Plates," she said. "You look a heck of a lot better than the last time I saw you." At the side of the bed was a wooden box. On top of that was the utter normality of a Styrofoam cup, with a coffee-stained plastic cover and a small stack of tiny plastic thimble sized containers.

"I will go find Dar," Maria said. She patted Kerry on the back. "Sit down, Kerrisita. I will soon return." She indicated the other bed, then trotted back out, leaving them alone.

Kerry felt this was likely by design. She sat down and rested her elbows on her knees.

"Would you like a Cafecito?" Tomas offered. "I am so glad we came here to see you. I have been thinking in my head what I would say to you when we met again."

Kerry knew better than to refuse. "Sure," she said. "I never turn down a good cup of Cuban coffee."

Tomas twisted his upper body and poured out the small cup and handed it to her. "I know you will say this was nothing for you to do," he said, after she took it. "I have spoken to Maria, and she has said this, that it does not seem amazing to you what you did."

Kerry sipped the inky, pungent, strongly scented beverage. "You mean, maybe I think renting an airboat to come find you and all that is not a big deal?" she said, after a moment of silence. "After living with Dar and doing the things that we do for all this time, no, that didn't really seem amazing. In fact, it didn't even really seem unusual." She paused again, and then smiled. "Maria knows that. She knows us."

"Si." Tomas also smiled. "She said to me, when we were at the hospital, that everything was not surprising to her. The doctors, and the nurses, they thought this was very exceptional, however. Because you know, Kerry, many people are not   like that."

"But a lot of people are," Kerry said. "And... you know... I like being able to look in the mirror, and believe it when I say to myself, I did the right thing."

"You are an angel."

Kerry shook her head. "No," she said, "I'm not, but I like to think I work to stay on the side of the angels. I think of that when I make those choices." She regarded the small cup, then glanced over it at Tomas, who sat quietly watching her. "And you know, I have to live up to Dar, right?"

Tomas laughed. "When Maria first was going to work for Dar she came home and said to me, Tomas, I have a job with a very unusual person," he said. "Maria said, many of the others there told her Dar was a demon, a devil, you know?"

"Oh, I know. They told me the same thing." Kerry's eyes twinkled. "But I'd already fallen for her, so it really didn't matter to me."

"But Maria said, no no, she saw God in this person," Tomas finished, making Kerry's jaw drop. "So, like you, yes? She knows every day she is on the right side."

The RV rocked a little bit, and Kerry glanced through the door to see Maria returning, with Dar's tall form behind her. "Speaking of," she said. "Anyway, I'm really glad you're feeling better, Tomas. I just wish your house had fared as well as you did."

"We are here." Maria moved all the way into the little sleeping area and cleared the way for Dar to come in behind her. "Isn't this nice, Dar? The men who helped us go from the hospital liked it very much."

Dar ducked her head a little bit to enter. "Hey, Tomas," she greeted the man casually, then set her hands on her hips as she looked around the small sleeping room. "It ain't the Hilton, but it's all right," she said. "Probably better not to have a lot of space to cover right now."

Kerry patted her knee. "Sit, hon. Before you hit your head."

Amiably, Dar took a seat next to her.

"So now," Maria took a seat on the tiny stool at the very back of the RV, "what has been happening? Mayte has told us some few things, but I am very sure there is more things for us to hear about."

Dar chuckled.

Kerry cleared her throat. "Oh boy. Where do I start."

****

"So Fifty-fifty," Dar said.

"Huh."

They were upstairs in Dar's office, alone. "Remind me to send a kudos to the kids," Dar added. "That update they sent to the Pharma guys, it did what it needed to."

"Without you inspecting it?"

"Without my obsessive nitpicking, yes," Dar said. "They did a good job."

"Maybe you're rubbing off on them." Kerry was seated near the window, hands braced on the bench seat, her back to the warm breeze coming in off the water. "I like that idea. We need more of you."

"Hrm." Dar looked a little gratified, regardless of the grunt. "But no answer from the VC," she said. "Hey, I said I would call. I called. I left a message." She shrugged. "I'm not going to worry about it. Maybe he's kiteboarding or something. He said he was into that."

"You were going to push him off anyway."

"I was. It's not good timing. We can't focus on that, and it needs focus," Dar said. "We need to get this back online first, and make sure we can handle one of these damn things the right way the next time."

Kerry nodded. "You're right," she said. "I mean... Dar, you're always right."

"I am not, or we wouldn't be sitting here sweating," Dar reminded her drily. "Anyway, I'm glad Tomas feels better." She changed the subject. "That RV worked out."

Kerry smiled. "I know they're worried about their house though. Maria's been trying to get through to her insurance company, but it's been nothing but busy signals."

"Not surprised," Dar said. "Maybe some of the guys can ride down there tomorrow with them and see if they can get near it." She watched Kerry nod in agreement. "Where'd we end up with the Brazilians?"

Kerry snapped her fingers. "I knew there was something I was forgetting to call Mark about." She got up. "Thanks, hon, let me go check." She headed for her office. "I kinda think if he didn't call it's not great news," she said, over her shoulder as she walked through the door that linked the two rooms.

Dar remained where she was, the room mostly cast into shadow as the sun started to trend to the west, sending spears of warm, rich sunlight through the windows across the hall.

In the outer room, Zoe was busy with messages and the LAN techs had run a cable down into her office for a phone. Dar heard her speaking softly into it, the light scratch of a pen against paper going as an undertone.

The construction was going on, the sound of drills and saws, driven by the battery powered UPS in the hallway, interrupted the relative quiet at unexpected intervals. And the smell of plaster and paint came and went.

She wished the whole damn thing was over already.

It was so damned inconvenient and uncomfortable.

"Dar." Maria came into the office, holding her cell phone. "A very strange thing has just happened."

Dar regarded her. "Stranger than what?" she asked. "Pretty much everything's been strange for the last week, so this should be a doozy. You finally get hold of your agent?"

Maria sat down in the visitor chair across from Dar's desk. "He has not called." She frowned. "But a person just did make a call to our number. They said they were from the government." She paused. "Do you think this is a scam thing, that we heard on the news about?"

"Maybe. What did he say?"

"Something about a program, and he needs to talk to us about it," Maria said. "I don't know about any program. Tomas says, he doesn't know either. Could it be something to help because of the flooding? They want to send some papers. I gave them the efax thing Mayte set up for us."

"Sure," Dar said. "Might be some FEMA help or something."

"But we did not ask for this," Maria said, in a puzzled tone. "How did they know to call me on this phone?" She held up her cell phone. "It is my phone from the office. I did not take the one from our house. It was not working and there was no battery anyway."

Dar's lips twitched, just a little bit. "Don't look a gift horse in the ass?" she said. "Hey, if the government wants to help ya, let them." She rocked forward and leaned her forearms on the desk. "Maybe your insurance agent went on the lam, and handed over their list of customers to FEMA?"

Maria considered that. "It is possible," she finally said. "Anyway, I will look at the papers and see what it is." She paused. "So many people are here. They are making the office look so nice." She changed the subject. "If the power comes, it will be almost better."

"Not quite." Dar sighed. "We need comms. More than a tin can and string back to a half assed satellite sitting on that damn island."

"You are worried," Maria said, quietly. "Kerrisita is   worried."

Dar regarded her. "I'm more pissed off than worried. Pissed off that we let ourselves get into a mess like this," she said honestly. "I feel like an idiot. I know what these things can do."

For a long moment, Maria just remained silent because there was really nothing to be said to that, and both she and Dar knew that. Finally, she sighed. "Dar, you cannot think of everything. I think no one considered that we would have so much business so quickly."

"Yeah, that's what Kerry said, and I know it's true, but I still feel like an idiot." Dar sighed. "I told her we need to slow down and get our act together." She paused. "And who knows how long it'll take for the power to come back." She paused again, thoughtfully. "Hmm." Her brows contracted a trifle.

"You are thinking of something," Maria said, confidently.

Dar blinked a few times. "Yeah, maybe," she murmured. "Maybe."

Kerry re-entered the room. "Well," she said. "I'm not really sure it was how you or I would have done it, but we still have Brazilian clients."

Both Dar and Maria turned their heads to look at her.

"It involves a posse of out of work Brazilian steakhouse waiters from West Palm Beach, translating for LAN technicians from Smyrna Georgia," Kerry said. "Mark multiplied two and six and divided by a wild chicken and got a working contract."

Dar's brows shot straight up to her hairline. "What?"

"Dios mio," Maria murmured.

"Hey. We always say think out of the box. He did."

****

It was so nice, and so wonderful to be cool and comfortable, surrounded by the conveniences they were used to around them. Kerry picked up a tray with some hot chocolate on it and went back into the living room where Dar lay on the couch, dressed in a pair of cotton shorts and a T-shirt, her newly showered hair still damp around her shoulders.

Spread out across their coffee table near the couch were diagrams, brown and dark blue lines that looked a little dusty and had carefully spaced and written letters in blocks on the bottom right-hand side.

There was a triangular shaped ruler on top of them and a drafting pencil. Dar had several pages of dense notation in her hands that she was studying.

Chino and Mocha were curled up on the loveseat together, very content to be back in their home.

"Dar, was Richard right about us getting into trouble for doing things to this place?" Kerry handed her a cup of the cocoa. "He sounded pretty sure it was going to be a problem."

"Probably." Dar sat up and put the cup down. She set the papers onto the tabletop without mussing them or spilling a drop onto the rest of the pages in a nonchalant display of perfect coordination. "But I don't care. This is the one way we can get this all done, Ker."

"I like it." Kerry sipped her chocolate. "Of course, we're dependent on that telecom to get done what they need to do, but if we have power and comms, and space… hell, why not? Half those guys are living in tents anyway, or underneath desks. We could do it."

"We could do it," Dar agreed. "Bring those RV's in there and get that electrician in to run us feeds. Hell, we don't even need to trench if that's going to be a hassle just run the cables over the ground there. You gave me the idea, we can light the place up with WIFI."

"We need aircon for the servers," Kerry said. "And for us, hon, it's August. We have what, three more months of summer left? Where are we going to put that kind of hardware? I agree on the people. Get them out of that office and over there and we have a wall and gates and plenty of space to work with."

"We can run the cables into the house and into those internal offices. One of them," Dar pointed at a line in the drawings, "just air condition with spot coolers in those two. One for the servers, one for the people."

Kerry studied the drawing. "Better to do the downstairs. That area near the kitchen and the storage rooms back there. We can use this one for the servers." She leaned over and pointed at one of the large walk-in spaces. "We can work on that kitchen table and use the appliances in there if we power that space."

Dar tapped her pencil on the paper. "We could do it," she said. "Drain the spot coolers out the sinks there. Move the office refrigerators." She looked at Kerry. "Run everything temporary, in case we do get our asses nailed for it, and we can pull it all out."

"Spot coolers," Kerry said. "Let me call our national partner. I'm one hundred percent sure they have a bunch of them around here no one's doing jack squat with because they have no power." She wagged a finger at Dar. "Bet they'd send a truck of them over."

"Bet they would."

Kerry thought about it again for a long moment, and then smiled. "This could work, Dar."

"It could."

"Let's do it."

Dar sat back and picked up her cocoa. "Hell, if Mark could wrangle bus boys to support an AWS migration, we can sure as hell make this house a nerd camp."

Kerry lifted her cup in a toast. "To nerd camp!"

****

"Let's take the boat." Dar leaned in the doorway to the kitchen, arms folded.

Kerry looked up from her laptop, one eyebrow quirked. "Given the line to get off the island this morning, it'll probably be faster," She said. "And there's a dozen other people at the office with cars if we need a ride. Sure. Why not?"

Dar nodded. "I'm going to go down and turn the engines over," she said. "I'll run by the cottage on the way and check out the kids. I know they said it was all peaches last night at dinner but…"

"But you want to see for yourself." Kerry chuckled. "I'll catch up on the mail and meet you down at the marina. Did you see on the local channel they already demo'd that whole area near the docks? They have a dome up for the dockmaster's office."

"I saw. That was cool." Dar slid her sunglasses into the front of her collar. "I want to find out where they got that tent, because it would work in nerd camp." She winked at Kerry. "C'mon dogs, let's go."

It was a breezy morning. Dar waited for the dogs to jump into the back of the golf cart and then she backed out of the underground spot and pulled up the ramp and paused, regarding the line of cars backed all the way up past their driveway from the ferry dock. "Holy crap."

Chino, seated in the rear dock with her head out the side of the cart, sniffed the wind. She let out a soft bark.

"Mommy Kerry wasn't kidding, huh?" Dar turned left along the road and rumbled along in the gravel until she got past the cars, then bumped up onto the road and into the right-hand lane heading toward the water. "What a mess."

She hadn't realized there was a line. She had just felt like being on the water, with the bright sunny morning, the breeze and the incrementally smaller amount of humidity in the air. To come out and find it was actually a more efficient commute just brought on a wry smile.

As she parked at the cottage, she saw one of the service staff approach with a small cart bearing a coffee setup and a covered tray. "Morning, Carlos," she called out, as the dogs jumped down and trotted over, sniffing knowingly at the tray.

"Morning, Ms. Dar," Carlos cheerfully greeted her. "I was just bringing over some coffee and some little pastries for the boys and girls here."

"Don't let them hear you call them that." Dar chuckled.

"Oh no they are very nice," Carlos said. "I have heard that you and Ms. Kerry have found a new house. They said it was a big place?"

"True. The old Hunter place in the South Grove," Dar said. "House is as big as that damn mansion up there. No idea what the hell the two of us are gonna do with it really."

Carlos regarded her, his head cocked a little to one side, a faint smile on his face. "Well, Ms. Dar, if you decide it is so big a place you need some help to take care of it, you will let some of us know that, yes?"

Dar was a touch surprised, then realized she really shouldn't be. "We absolutely will."

Carlos smiled more widely, and then winked at her, before he twitched the cover over the tray of pastries and turned the cart once again toward the cottage.

Dar went over and opened the double door for him to roll the supplies inside and gave a brief wave to the greetings from inside. She followed him into the cottage and closed the door.

****

Kerry had just slid her backpack onto her back and put her sunglasses on when a knock came at the door. She pushed the glasses up onto the top of her head and went over, pulled the door open, and took a step back. "Hey, Clemente, c'mon in."

The hospitality manager, sweating as usual, came inside and closed the door behind him. "I am sorry to disturb you, Ms. Kerry, it will only be for a moment," he said. "The booking office asked me to find out for how long you will want the cottage."

"Ah." Kerry considered that. "I'm going to guess about a month," she said. "We have some other arrangements we're working on, but it's kind of tough out there right now."

Clemente nodded. "There is no problem. At the first, there were many people who were also interested in the cottages. But the idea you said, that Ms. Dar said, to contract out the units no one is living in, this was excellent," he said. "Now our problem is with the traffic we have so many people who were so interested in that."

Kerry felt enlightened. "Now I get what the lineup is."

"Si." He nodded. "All the solutions make more problems," he said. "But all the people who were making so much noise, the government and so on, they are happy now. The unit owners getting fees for their units, they are happy. The booking office now has not enough place to keep the money they are making. They are very happy, and you can be sure that I told everyone where this idea came from."

"Well." Kerry hitched her thumb under the strap of her backpack. "It was kind of obvious."

"Si. Now only the ferries are not happy, and we have to find a way to fix that problem," Clemente said. "But at any case, thank you for this, and I will let the booking office know. And if you do not mind, I am also going to say to them they should not charge you for this because you came with such a good idea."

"Hey, we'll take that," Kerry told him, as they both walked toward the door. "I think they owe us a few favors for Dar's fixing the security cameras and setting up Internet for them too."

"Absolutely." He held the door open for her. "And oh yes, Lisette at the desk has told me that the governor is looking to speak with Ms. Dar. He was asking for her last night, but you had not yet come home, and he went on his helicopter this morning."

"Uh uh." Kerry walked out onto the landing and started down the steps as he closed the door behind them. "I'll let her know. We're going to take our boat over to our office, so we probably won't be back until tonight but..." She glanced over her shoulder. "Our cell phones work at the office. Have him give us a call if you bump into him."

Clemente nodded. "I will do that, absolutely," he said. "Would you like a ride to the marina? My cart is just there."

"Sure," Kerry said. "To the cottage, matter of fact. Dar's probably there with ours." She pushed her sunglasses down as she got into the service cart and hoped for another progressive day.

Chapter Nineteen

It felt amazing to be out on the boat. Kerry put her feet up on the aft gunwale and sipped her freshly made cup of herbal tea, keeping Chino and Mocha company as they lay on the deck enjoying the breeze.

Dar was up on the flying bridge threading a course past the causeway and obeyed the speed limit. This gave Kerry a chance to look at the coast on either side of them. She remembered their first trip up the waterway and saw there was some improvement from the wreckage to be seen.

Things that had been half sunken, the overturned boats, and other debris had been towed out of the water. Some just dragged up onto the shore, some completely gone. A few of the boats had been refloated and were bobbing near the trashed piers, tied off onto whatever was available.

Florida Power and Light, who had, truthfully, been working around the clock, reported that morning that while they had a plan for restoring all the power poles that were now probably sunken either in the Everglades or in the Gulf. The plan to fix the two power plants that had taken catastrophic damage would take longer.

One of them was nuclear. Fortunately, the structure of Turkey Point had been thoughtfully considered, Kerry had learned that morning. Possibly by the same people who had built their condos as it had been rated to stand up to roughly fifty percent higher winds than even Bob had managed to produce.

So, they didn't have that problem. But the plant was offline and had no external power to run its management systems and were on a diesel generator to maintain control of the reactors.

Great way to start the morning. Kerry shook her head. "Okay, kids, we're almost there. You ready to see all your friends at the office? Even that cat?"

"Growf," Chino commented, tongue lolling.

"Hey, Ker?" Dar's voice crackled through the intercom. "We're about ten minutes out."

"Yep." Kerry hit the button and responded. "Need anything?"

"Do we have any oatmeal cookies onboard?"

Kerry got up. "Probably not, hon. Maybe peanut butter."

"Even better."

****

There was a lot of activity and yelling voices audible when they walked up the road from the sailing club to the back of the office property.

"Uh oh," Kerry said, as both dog's ears perked up.

"We cursed ourselves," Dar said, "when we said at least it wasn't Monday."

"We did."

They increased their pace and as they reached the side of the building, they saw flashing lights ahead of them in the parking lot. "Oh boy," Dar muttered.

There were at least four police cars in the lot, and as they came around the corner, they saw the staff, en mass, standing in front of the building, fronted by both Carlos and Maria, with Mayte at her side, speaking forcefully to the cops.

"Wait." Kerry grabbed Dar by the back of her cutoff overalls. "Maybe we should let them handle it."

"C'mon." Dar started to move forward and hauled her along. "We own the property and the company, Ker."

"I know, but if we get involved, will Martians land?" Kerry nevertheless released her and caught up alongside. "I mean, the water delivery worked out, didn't it?"

They crossed the front yard and were spotted, and their crew separated to let them through. They looked, without a doubt, relieved to see them.

Dar removed her sunglasses and edged to the front and got between Maria and the police, making the most of her height, and her presence. "What's going on here?" She pinned the closest policeman with her eyes. "You got a problem?"

Kerry sidled up next to Mayte and tugged her sleeve, bending her head close to listen to Mayte's rapid whisper.

"I'm sorry? Who are you, ma'am?" the cop responded, with brusque courtesy. "What's your interest here?"

Dar eyed him. "I co-own the property and the business that's inside it." She indicated with her thumb the building behind them. "So, I'll ask again, what's going on here?"

She glanced at the uniform. State police. Not the city cops, or the county cops, these reported to the governor and the cars in the lot were FHP.

"Ma'am, this area, the whole section of the city, has been ordered closed, and evacuated." The officer said, "This has nothing to do with you. It applies to everyone. You have until four p.m. to leave the premises, or you'll be arrested and taken to jail."

"Why?"

He blinked. "Excuse me?"

"Why?" Dar repeated. "We've been living and working here since the storm. Why now? What happened?"

"Ma'am, it's not your business or even my business as to why. We've been asked to secure this area, and that's what we're going to do. All of these people need to be out of here by four. That's all." He jerked his head at her. "Let's go," he said to the other police officers standing by.

"Hold on," Dar said. "What's the perimeter?"

The man stopped and looked at her. "Ma'am?" He made the word sound like a curse.

"How far do they have to go. What is the perimeter of your evacuation area?" Dar ignored the tone. "How far south does it extend?"

Faced with a reasonable question and no real reason not to answer it, the man looked around. "Jaspert, can you answer that?" he said. "I'm not from this part of the state."

"Obviously," Carlos muttered.

One of the men behind him, a tall, lanky man with a very visible Adam's apple nodded. "Main Highway on the west, to St Gaudan's on the south, on up to Mayfair."

The assembled group looked at Dar, clearly waiting for her to respond.

Clearly expecting some fireworks.

Dar just nodded. "Okay, that works," she said, in a mild tone. "We'll be out of here."

Expecting more pushback, it surprised the cop, and his expression shifted a little "Okay, that's good to hear. Have a great day." He gave them all another nod, and then he, and his officers turned and walked back to their cars, not without a few backward glances.

They got in and drove off, lights still flashing, but in silence.

"Assholes," Carlos said, after a brief silence.

"Payback from them other assholes?" Hank suggested. "So, what're we gonna do, junior? Alamo part two?" he asked Dar. "Sure as hell we're not going to just roll our asses over for those beige pussies."

Dar turned and regarded them, her arms folded. "Actually. We're going to do just what they asked us to do," She said. "Let's get everything loaded into those RV's. Pete. Can you hitch your Jeep up to Scott's trailer?"

Everyone looked at each other in bewilderment.

"Say what?" Hank responded.

"I... can....? "Pete said, his voice full of question.

"But, Dar," Maria said. "Where are we going?"

"Someplace south of St Gaudan's." Dar seated her sunglasses on her nose. "And damn it, I'm going to need another router," she said as almost an aside. "Josh, grab the production router from the server room and all the AP's we have."

Hank had a sudden wave of realization. "Oh!" His eyes opened wide. "Oh yeah! Yeah! Hell yeah." He turned and started back toward the building at a trot. "Hey, Carlos! Get your boys together and put that generator up on my truck."

"What about all that work?" One of the carpenters asked, pointing at the building. "I guess we're done?"

Kerry chuckled and shook her head. "C'mon, let's get going people," she said. "Bring all the tools, too. Where we're going, we're gonna need them just as much as here."

****

It was late afternoon before the caravan started out with Hank and his Humvee in the lead, and the three RV's taking up the rear.

Dar was the last to leave the building, and locked the door behind her while a group of six waited for her on the sidewalk. "Okay." She shoved the key into her pocket and gestured toward the side road. "Let's go."

They headed for the sailing club. Carlos accompanied her and Kerry, along with two of the veterans, Sasha, Josh, and one of their LAN techs.

"Gotta tell ya, boss," Carlos said as they walked along the road toward the water. "That did not go the way I thought it was going to go this morning. I figured it was gonna be a scrap."

Dar chuckled. "Scrapping's fine, but there wasn't really a purpose. We'll end up in a better place this way anyhow, and closer to being functional."

"You think it was those jerks from yesterday?"

"Could be." Kerry had her backpack on her back, full of stuff she'd taken out of her and Dar's office, just in case. They'd locked all the doors, but anyone who really wanted to get in probably could. All the equipment they could carry were stacked into the underneath bins of the RV's, and in trunks of the caravan.

Josh had his own backpack stuffed completely full of gear. "Wild," he said. "But hey, we were just sleeping under desks. Not like it was the Hilton."

"Just roll with it," Dar said. "We're not going to the Hilton now, but at least the view'll be better."

"Place has a wall around it, right? Someone said that," Carlos said. "Hank said it, once he stopped laughing."

"It does," Kerry answered, as they crossed the road between their building and the club. The late afternoon sun was at their back, and the club itself had most of the debris and broken furniture removed and hauled away, leaving it looking bare. "But it's not twenty feet tall or anything. Dar jumped over it."

"Still and all, a wall is a wall." Carlos looked content. "And we got the pooches."

Chino and Mocha trotted along with them; noses busy sniffing the onshore coming air.

The sailing club deck was now easy for them to negotiate. They walked down the concrete dock to where the wood started, and across the pier they'd built that extended out to where the Dixie was sedately tied up.

"Stupid people. But if they are locking everything up, no one to sell to anyway," Sasha said. "Maybe more people stay down there where we're going."

"We haven't been around there long enough to really know, but probably," Kerry said.

They boarded the Dixie and Dar left Kerry to sort everyone out while she climbed up to the flying bridge and settled behind the controls.

Carlos climbed up behind her. "Feels weird to just leave after all we did around that place."

"Yeah." Dar started up the inboard engines, hearing them rumble to life behind and below them. "But I had enough of the jackassery anyway. If it's legit, and they're locking the area down, no point in arguing. If it's blowback from the guard, no point in sticking around for it. Nobody's winning that one."

Carlos sat down in the fiberglass seating area behind her. "Figures you'd show up with a plan though." He chuckled a little. "Never thought of that one, moving ops down to your new place."

"We're loose!" Kerry called up, and Dar engaged the engines and pulled back away from the dock, threading between the two broken columns and the debris she'd moved aside when they'd first gotten there.

She swung the bow around and started south, already looking forward to docking the Dixie into its new home.

She owed the troopers a thank you, for making the shift a mandate, Getting it done all at once removed any second thoughts they might have had. She couldn't repress a smile because she was pretty sure there was some jackassery behind it, and it made her happy it had worked in their favor.

They would make it work. With any luck, they'd started on the trenching and when they got there, she could reveal that part of the plan to offset the loss of their Internet connection, slow as it was. And the loss of the phones and the comfort of all the office's structure and facility.

There was doubt, Dar knew it. Some of the construction workers were reluctant to come along, until Hank talked the place up. That got all their folks a little interested too.

She adjusted the throttles, and they were coursing along, the boat rocking a little in the chop the bow stolidly plowed through, making the most of its V hull and the power of the twin inboards.

It would be interesting, if nothing else, and absent any comfortable couch to rest on, they could sleep right on Dixie. She was glad she'd had them fill up the tanks.

"This is nice," Carlos said, after a period of silence. "Better than that dodge ball road rage freak show on land. Hope those guys all get down here all right."

"Hank and Pete'll get em through." Dar adjusted the course a little bit, watching the depth sounder. "Would you stop a Humvee with a machine gun on the roof?"

Carlos laughed.

"Me either."

****

Kerry passed around some cups as she finished making a pot of coffee in the Dixie's small galley. Their riders were seated comfortably in the living deck and the ride so far had been pretty smooth. "Kinda radical, today, huh?" She brought the coffee pot with its marine gimbal over to the table and put it down.

Then she took a seat in the chair nearest the door and relaxed.

"Yeah." Josh nodded. "Been a freaky week, but I didn't' figure to end today in a big boat moving the office." He stirred some cream into his coffee and sat back in the chair. "Sucks we lost net, though."

"True," Kerry said. "But given that Key Biscayne's between the new place and our old place there's no way a point-to-point would do anything useful." She folded her hands. "We'll think of something."

Sasha was seated cross legged on the couch against the sidewall, her hands curled around the coffee cup. "Too much trouble there," She said. "Lots of people where we're going, Residential. Not so far from the U. They kept those kids there for the storm."

"Dar says those college buildings are built for it." Kerry leaned on her chair arm. "So, they'd probably buy everything you have to sell, Sasha. They've been living on ramen noodles for the last week or so I heard on the local news."

Sasha nodded briskly. "No good back at the other place until the businesses open up again."

"Did you know they were going to shut that down, ma'am?" Josh asked. "You guys showed up and it was like you'd planned for it. We thought we were going to fight about it, but I'm glad we didn't. That thing yesterday was creepy."

Kerry cleared her throat. "Dar and I talked about moving operations last night, matter of fact. We had some things in mind, and we knew that building was becoming a bit of a trouble magnet. I just hope they really are shutting down the area, and we don't come back to a literal dumpster fire."

"That could happen," one of the two veterans said. "This other place sounds safer. Hank said there was plenty of space."

"Oh, there is." Kerry smiled. "That's the one thing that shouldn't be a problem."

Kerry felt the engines throttle down a little. "And I think we're getting close." She leaned over to look out the window of the boat. "Yep. Coming up on the dock. This one, at least, we didn't have to put together from wreckage."

They all turned in their seats to look out, as Dar brought the Dixie around the edge of the trees coming to the water and the stone dock appeared, with its seawall. And overlooking the water, the house.

"Oh. Wow," Josh said, in an astonished tone.

One of the veterans whistled, "Lookit that."

Sasha turned all the way around on the couch and looked outside, as the Dixie slowed and turned for the pier. Then she looked at Kerry, both eyebrows hiked right up to her hairline.

Kerry got up. "We never do things halfway," she said. "Let me go get ready to tie us up." She went to the door and paused, glancing back at them. "Welcome to Hunter's Point."

****

Night found them all in the kitchen. The generator was going outside, and there were long cables run through the open doors to the fans that made it all tolerable.

The three RVs were parked outside the door to the kitchen, where the loading dock was. The RV service company had just left after filling their tanks.

Tents were scattered everywhere, as the group spread out across the grounds. Sasha set up her miniature yurt right by the spring, clasping her hands over and over again in an almost ecstasy of silent delight.

The carpenters took over the garden shed for a workspace. The general construction guys spent an hour outside at the pool deck and now discussed what had to be done to sort it all out.

Along the long counter in the kitchen were the supplies, and in the small courtyard outside in back, in front of the RV's, they'd set up the grills.

"This is actually pretty sweet," Carlos said. "You weren't kidding when you said there'd be plenty of room, boss."

"Heck ya," one of the lifters agreed. "We could set up a dozen gyms around the place, and you'd never even see us." He looked around. "Had no idea this place was even by here, and I used to ride through this area every morning on my bike."

"I love all those trees," Josh said. "And the rocks and everything. It reminds me of some places we used to camp at when I was a Cub Scout."

"Place is built." Carlos reached behind him and thumped the wall. "Looks like it didn't even blink at that storm... but it's up on a little bit of a rise with that deck and everything."

An oddly assorted smorgasbord was spread across the huge kitchen table. A mixture of the sandwiches Sasha had left, along with cookies and doughnuts and boxes of cereal and bags of tortilla chips. No one cared, everyone was content to grab a plate and just munch.

"Tomorrow, we're going to arrange for spot coolers," Kerry said. "Dar and I talked about it last night. We'll set up this area to work in, and that big storage room behind us to the left there we can rig for the servers."

"We can build a platform for them to sit on," one of the carpenters said. "This is some nice woodwork in here. Someone knew what the hell they were doing."

"Someone did," the plasterer agreed. "Six, maybe eight places that need some work, but the rest of it's pretty solid." He looked over at Dar. "You said you had power coming?"

"We do," Dar said.

"You pay someone off for that?" the man meant no offense, his tone held only curiosity. "Cause I heard that guy from FPL talking before. They're screwed."

"Sorta." Dar's pale eyes twinkled a little in the light from the battery lanterns. "Let's say it was a barter. I figure we have to suffer another couple of days and something decent is going to happen. They already started digging over on the property line."

"That the green metal casement I saw on the edge there?" Carlos asked. "At the end of that big trench? What is that?"

Dar nodded, a smile on her lips, but remained silent as Kerry took up the explanation.

"With our usual luck, it turns out one of the major service providers main fiber lines comes in right off the coast there, and of course we happened to be here when they wanted to ask if they could bring it up over our property. And it was a company who had a good idea of who it was they were talking to." Kerry pointed her finger at Dar. "So of course, we traded a right of way for power and Internet."

"Of course," Dar echoed. "Because if that was going to happen, it'd happen here, and to us."

"No shit, really?" Pete sat on the counter, eating a banana. "But they can't get power either, can they?"

Kerry chuckled, and shook her head, she looked over at Dar.

"Actually, they can. It's emergency power. Runs through the conduits from the NAP. Ties into their fiber hub ring," Dar said. "Which is sitting under the sidewalk on the other side of our wall. So, they're running a tap back in the same trench they're bringing the line up over and giving us a feed."

"Of course." Carlos laughed. "And some Internet."

Dar nodded. "Saved them weeks pulling new lines down the coast to their previous landing point."

"So that's why you needed another router," Josh said. "And that big old spool of cable. And those extra APs!"

Another nod. "Yep," Dar said. "We'll run a line in, when they're done, to the storeroom in there, and split service out from there. It's open. We can cover a lot of the grounds." Dar glanced at Kerry. "That was her idea, actually."

Hank was in the corner, a bottle of pop in his hand. "That's some damn funny stuff right there," he said. "Like of all places to have that happen, it comes here? And you happen to buy this place? "

Dar lifted her hands in a silent shrug.

It was, really. Kerry smiled. "Nerd karma. At least once they're done, we'll get our connection back. It's a pain in the ass to not have it after we did." She leaned back against the wall. "Glad we got hold of the RV folks before we lost signal."

"So, we'll have power and high speed like, ten times faster than we'd ever get it at the office," Carlos said. "Damn."

Dar shrugged again, but chuckled. "We talked about that last night. So when we got to the office and the state wanted us to move, I had no issue with it. They did me a favor, got it done faster."

Hank laughed silently.

Kerry got up. "Okay folks, let's get some rest. It's been a day," she said. "Lot more to do tomorrow." She picked up a remaining banana as the rest stood up and filtered out of the room. "Good night!"

Outside the sky was darkening overhead and the clouds had cleared a little, giving them a good view of the stars and with the lack of power in the area, they were more vivid than usual.

Kerry walked outside onto the deck with Dar and looked up. She took a breath of the sea breeze coming off the bay and listened to the soft rush of the tide against the seawall. "You were right about coming here," she said, as she took Dar's hand and they started down the leveled slope toward the pier.

Dar had a flashlight in her other hand, and she lit the path for them. "Maybe. Not like we had a choice," she said. "But it feels a hell of a lot better to be here, then back at the office." They skirted the edge of the deck. "Remind me when we get back onboard to try and contact my folks."

"Let them know where we are?"

Dar nodded, as they walked from level to level, past the empty pool. "Glad we brought our mobile apartment with us, though," she said, as they reached the steps down to the stone pier the Dixie was tied up to. "Wasn't really in the mood to either fight with staff all night or sleep on that wooden floor."

Chino and Mocha climbed down ahead of them, happy and tired from running around their new playground and they walked up the teak gangplank onto the boat and went right over to their large water bowl near the back gunwale and drank from it together.

"I'm glad too." Kerry opened the door to the cabin and went inside. She turned on the inside lights and the air-conditioning that would make the boat a comfortable place to be.

And the queen size bed in the compact bedroom in the bow, with its soft cotton sheets in ocean colors amidst the mellow scent of polished teak, with shaded windows on either side. After the long, hot day, she looked forward to stretching out in it, with the quiet of this dark new dock alongside.

She left Dar at the radio station and went to the refrigerator to remove a bottle of wine and set it on the counter. She then turned and retrieved two stemless, weighted base glasses.

The dogs bumped their way inside and went over to the couch to jump up and curl into contented balls. Chino had a smudge of mud on her head and Mocha turned over onto his back and waved his paws in the air.

"No answer." Dar came over and took a seat in one of the two comfortable bucket chairs in the living area. "I'll try again in the morning. But I let the island marina know where we're docked in case they come in and ask."

Kerry brought the glasses over and handed her one, then sat in the other bucket chair. She held out the glass and touched it to Dar's. "Welcome home, hon."

Dar sighed and lifted her glass in a toasting gesture. "Let's just hope it all works out as good as we hope it will."

"Well, here's to chaos, in any case." Kerry took a sip of the wine and let her head fall back on the cushion of the chair. "It is what it is."

****

The next morning was blessedly quiet. Kerry put things on a platter for a nibbly breakfast and picked it up to carry outside onto the back deck of the Dixie, which was bobbing gently at dock, the rubber bumpers protecting her hull from the stone pier squeaking softly in rhythm.

The pier was also a jetty. It came out from the land and then presented a right angle to the oncoming tide. It extended past the length of the boat with a solid surface to the seabed that protected the docking area from wake. It was large enough to hold two boats the size of theirs, or a handful of smaller ones.

Dar stood on the pier and spoke to two men in work boots, Dickie's shirts and long pants, with a logo patch on the sleeve and tool belts around their waists.

Chino and Mocha had already mounted the steps and now roamed around their new playground. Kerry heard Chino bark, far off, somewhere beyond the house.

She put the platter down on the table on the back deck next to a pot of freshly pressed coffee and seated herself. She picked up half a Pop Tart and took a bite.

It was warm, but not yet hot. The sunrise behind them lit up the edge of the property and gave her a nice bit of shade to have her breakfast in.

Dar gave the two men a genial wave, and they departed, their boots making a soft, crunching sound as they climbed up the steps and moved quickly out of sight. With a satisfied nod, Dar came back onto the boat and took the other seat.

"Everything okay?" Kerry picked up her coffee cup and took a sip.

"They're about to bring the conduit in from the road." Dar put her feet up on the gunwale and regarded the tray, selecting a peanut butter cup. "Did we raid a vending machine?"

Kerry chuckled. "This was left over from when we stocked the office," she said. "I didn't have any perishables stocked onboard, like milk or eggs. We left too fast."

"No complaints." Dar bit the cup in half contentedly. "I hear people getting going up there." She indicated the house. "Our dogs are helping." She took a sip of coffee. "Condensed milk?"

"The very best in hurricane supplies, hon." Kerry relaxed back in her chair. "I feel like we took a step backward in this whole communication thing though. You think it'll be a lot longer before we get that service in? Maybe we should let everyone carry on here and go back to the island."

Dar thoughtfully chewed her tidbit, her pale eyes regarding the seawall, and the neatly set stones in the front of it. "Without a connection it's not much use us being here," she said. "We can get more done back there."

Kerry watched her from her peripheral vision. "But you want to stay here." It wasn't a question, and she saw the corner of Dar's lips twitch into a smile. "Yeah, I do too," she admitted. "I want to explore every inch of this place, because who knows, Dar, we might not have another chance if they get really ratty with us over the legal business."

"Screw them."

"No thanks."

Dar chuckled. "Tell you what, you can go explore and I'll start setting up the infrastructure with Josh. Run those cables and get what I can in place so when they are ready, we can get things moving," she said. "The kids really do have everything under control back there. They're keeping our delivery dates and Angela's in touch with Colleen."

"Did you see Elvis has Celeste doing QA?"

"I did." Dar smiled.

"And..." Kerry suddenly paused and covered her eyes. "Oh my God, Dar I completely forgot to tell you, and we never went back to the island yesterday."

Dar watched her in mild alarm. "And?"

"The governor's looking for you. He wanted to talk to you. Clemente told me as I was going out the door and then... well crap. With everything that went on yesterday it slipped my mind." Kerry lifted her hand and looked up at Dar's profile.

Dar shrugged, blue eyes widening. "And?"

Kerry's brows twitched. "Aren't you curious about what he wants?"

"No. Not really," Dar said in a mild tone. "I'm sure he wants something. I'm sure I don't really want to give it to him. Phones being down is a great excuse not to contact anyone." She picked up another peanut butter cup. "Actually, I'm glad you didn't tell me."

"Well, I didn't so..." Kerry now also shrugged. "Well, maybe they'll work some miracle, and we'll get phone service down here. I'm going to turn on the sat TV inside the boat here and see if I can pick up the local channel, see if there's anything we need to know." She got up and picked up the second half of her Pop Tart. "See you up at the house."

Dar toasted her with the coffee cup, settling back to finish it as she watched a few seabirds circling the edge of the shore, their beady eyes, she was sure, firmly planted on her table with its remaining peanut butter cups. "Don't you sea rats even think about it."

****

"Okay! It's going hot!"

Kerry regarded the large power distribution panel now installed just inside the back door leading out to the deck. There were thick, black cables snaking everywhere, and one of them ran across the stone surface and then off into the ground cover until it reached the big metal box that had been installed.

After a long, almost thoughtful moment, a red light appeared on the device, along with a soft hum. The device seemed to consider the condition, and then a series of other lights lit up on the back side of it. Then a series of lights popped on the front of it, where yet more thick black cables were running off inside the house.

Behind her, she heard cheers.

On the low shelves to her right, she saw lights now on the small switch, and it started its little green and yellow dance. Suddenly she experienced a vivid memory of being in New York, her nose almost smashed against the front of a router, a lime green light blaring into her eyes and almost being able to taste the limey tang of the color on the back of her tongue.

Beautiful and cheery, success defined by its color and tangible light.

There was a wireless antenna on the top of the shelves, just lying there, on top of a square piece of very expensive metal with Dar's laptop on top of it, open, a pale blue cable running from it to the box, her swimming fish screensaver sending a splash of reflection against the pale wood wall.

Dar came back from the inside room, dusting her hands off. She had her hair pulled back in a ponytail and there was dust on the front of her tank top as though she'd leaned against a grimy shelf somewhere. "Is it up?"

"It's thinking about it." Kerry indicated the stack of equipment that hummed and fluttered and made burbling noises as it went about its business of bootstrapping.

Dar lowered herself to the stone floor and settled cross-legged behind her laptop. "Let's see what we got." She cracked her knuckles, in a visible good mood. "This is going along a lot better than I'd anticipated."

"Shuh." Kerry admonished. "Pretend it's a shitshow, please."

Dar smiled, as she unlocked the laptop and regarded the screen it revealed. "Switch is up. Now what's coming from... ah." Her brows wiggled happily. "Port's up."

Kerry came round and sat down next to her and looked over her shoulder as Dar's long fingers sped over the keys in a veritable explosion of cryptic command line call and response. "Is that a ten-gig port?"

"It is," Dar said, with some satisfaction. "If I'd tried to buy that commercially it'd taken me ten years with the age of facility around here."

"We have a ten-gig port on our pool deck?"

"We do. I'm going to steal some of the address space we were going to use for the datacenter Mark was looking for," Dar said. "We'll need a DMZ here... so I'll use that slash 26 for now, and we'll put a slash 23 inside. That should hold us at least for a week."

Her voice trailed off into muttering about masks and gateways as she typed along, her head rocking back and forth a little bit.

Kerry made a snorting sound. "Maybe." She glanced at the shelves, and then jumped a little. "Did you do it already?" she asked, as she dug her phone out of her pocket. "Damn, Dar. That was fast."

"Doesn't take long when you know what you're doing." Dar smiled, in a rare bit of braggadocio. "Tunnel's up. Phones should work now." She observed the wireless point that was now a happy, contented blue color. "They took our routes without any bitching. And our capwap's up. Now let me go figure out where else to light up."

"Just like that." Kerry scrolled through her messages.

"Just like that." Dar leaned over and bit her on the shoulder. "Those jerks from Alabama did us a favor. Maybe I'll call Gerry and get their asses sent up to Palm Beach to guard the governor's country club." She winked at Kerry. "Be right back."

Kerry remained where she was, already imagining she felt the faintest reduction in the humid air from the spot coolers they couldn't possible have running yet. As she went through her texts she paused to respond to two of Colleen's.

Then she turned to her mail, aware of Dar's laptop next to her softly chiming as it picked up mail as well. "What in the hell did we do before we had email?" she asked aloud. "Did we really write in longhand on pieces of dead tree, put them in wrappings of more dead trees, and have someone walk around and hand deliver them?"

"Hey, Kerry!"

Kerry turned around to look behind her, to find Hank coming across the open floor, his boots scuffing a little against the stone surface. One of the contractors trailed behind him with dirt covered gloves and pine needles stuck to the knees of his work pants. "Hey."

"Got some good news," Hank said. "Doug here, he dug round the place and this here's got plumbin."

Kerry paused. "Well, didn't we know that?"

"Useful kinda plumbing," Doug said. "Like, they did the whole deal, ma'am. There ain't no fixtures in place or nothin, but all the lines go out under the ground and y'all are hooked up to city sewer," he said confidently. "All it'll take is some porcelain and caulk and you all are good to go. Don't need to bring in them portos you were talkin bout."

"Oh!" Kerry said, slightly startled. "Really?"

Doug nodded. "Now..." He looked to either side and put a finger along his nose. "I can't say whether that there hookups legal. Know what I'm saying?" he said. "I mean, it's all solid pipes and all, but I didn't see no typical city meet me for it. Just goes in there."

Kerry thought about that. "Well, it's a hell of a lot better than if you'd told me those pipes just went out into that Bay." She pointed over her shoulder. "So now we just need some fixtures."

"Sure, I can find me some," Hank responded. "Ain't no problem... all we need to do after that is get us some water turned on."

"Oh... well so that." Doug pulled off his gloves and stuck them in his back pocket. "There's a tap off that spring out there. It's valved off and I didn't turn the house on cause I wanted to make sure there wasn't no busted pipes first," he said. "I didn't see none, so I'll crank it up a little, and do a quick check."

"The spring," Kerry repeated. "Is it potable?"

Doug nodded. "I tested it. It's pretty good. It's coming up out of the aquifer. But if I were you, I'd put filtering on it, in case cause there's lots of stuff in the groundwater round here. Or in case the salt water comes in." He paused thoughtfully. "Place this size, you want to get commercial water turned on. Not sure it'll give you enough pressure for the whole place and all that. I saw a city meter. It's locked though."

"But the spring's good enough for now?"

Doug nodded again. "Oh yeah. But like I said about the filtering..."

Kerry smiled at him. "Would you like to install filtering for us? I think it's a great idea. Can you do it or do we need to wait?"

He shook his head. "Nope, can do it right away," he said. "Matter of fact, let me go see if I got something I can start with in my truck." He waved cheerfully, and headed toward the entrance door of the house, whistling under his breath.

Kerry hitched up a knee and rested her elbow on it. "That guard captain really did do us a favor," she said, in a wondering tone. "Holy cow that's amazing news. That was the last thing I was really worrying about, getting water supply."

"This place right here? This is righteous," Hank said. "Couldn'ta worked out any better, and whatcha know? Less assholes round." He looked at the machinery. "That all working?" He pointed curiously at it.

"It's all working," Kerry said, with a sudden, grin. "This really is all working." She got up and dusted off her knees. "C'mon. Let's see what else is going on. Maybe Dar found a manatee offering cable tv."

"I can prob'ly find us a television for it to hook up to." Hank hitched his camo pants up. "Lemme to take the Vee out and find us some crappers. Hey Zoe!" he let out a yell as they walked along together. "Ya'll wanna go shoppin?" He glanced at Kerry. "My ass is colorblind. You all don't want me pickin out nothing that goes in a house."

"Are we going to have a choice of colors?" Kerry eyed him. "Or is to better not to ask?"

Hank grinned at her. "Ya'll are learnin fast."

****

The sun was setting in the west, sending long shadows through the trees and spears of red and gold between them. The sounds of work had faded, and now seagulls drifted over the edge of the land, inspecting the goings on with a wary fascination as the deck emptied of strange humans who retreated into and around the house.

Two Labradors came into view, galloping along across the ground heading for the house. There was mud on their coats, and they pattered over the leaves happily, tongues lolling pinkly.

The yellow dog stood up and put her front paws on the tree trunk, and barked commandingly, and as if in response, not a squirrel but a tall, lanky body emerged from the tree, moving down from branch to branch as the dog's tails wagged into a blur.

Dar sat on the bottom limb and regarded her pets, as Mocha whirled in a circle, nearly falling down in his excitement. Then she turned and grabbed onto the branch and swiveled around to lower herself and hang from her arms. She glanced down to make sure the dogs weren't underneath her before she let go and dropped the few feet to the ground. "Cut that out, you mutts!"

She had a backpack on her back, and visible against the tree bark was a long cable. She paused to adjust the cable straight before she turned and walked toward where Pete stood.

Pete enjoyed the moment. Dar was just one of those people who were so unconsciously unselfconscious it was a pleasure to simply watch her stroll along. She moved with that faint swagger and muscularity that was so natural and unstudied.

Dar wasn't cute, and she wasn't what he thought of as pretty, but she was primally beautiful and that was seriously attractive to him in its frank boldness without really having any sexuality involved. "Hey, Dar," he greeted her. "What'cha doin up that tree?"

"Hanging WIFI. Whole area here's lit now," she added in a tone of satisfaction. "It probably reaches out to that shack. Maybe even the gate."

"You could have asked one of your little techie boys to do that, y'know."

"What, and given up the fun of climbing that tree?" Dar's pale eyes widened in mock horror. "Dad's on the way over," she added. "Now that they can call us again, they want to see what the hell's going on over here. They got back a few hours ago."

"There's room down there at the dock," Pete said, "or is he driving over? You tell him the office is blocked off?"

"He's running by there to see if it really is." Dar produced a tiny, somewhat piratical grin. "You know my dad. He's pretty pissed off at the whole thing the way it went down, but I told him it's much better here."

"Truth." Pete glanced past her as Sasha emerged from the house with a large metal bowl of something, and Ben, one of the veterans right behind her with a tray. "Are we going to go rustle up some stores? We could use some resupply."

"I can run the boat out and get some fish." Dar chewed her bitter little orange. "But Sasha seems to have sources."

"Mm."

"Yeah, I don't ask too much either," Dar sighed. "I heard Publix has like five stores they're going to open on generator. I can only imagine the chaos."

Pete's gray eyes widened. "Like Black Friday at Walmart." He paused. "Maybe we should get front in line with that Humvee."

Dar laughed in reflex. "That'll make the news." She swallowed the last of the tiny fruit. "But today was a good day. We're in a lot better place now. With all this space I can house the whole company in there once we get a few more coolers."

"You going to do that? I mean... it's your house," Pete said. "Kinda weird."

"Not our house yet." Dar smiled easily. "Gotta do what's right first, Pete. We've got people counting on us to keep things going."

Andy's image. "Yup, hear that," Pete agreed cheerfully. "Think we got ice in that fridge yet?"

"Let's go see." Dar dusted her hands against her cargo shorts and headed for the door, as the scent of char broiling rose around them from the grills, and the sharp fragrance of jerk seasoning followed.

****

The kitchen was a bizarre mixture of stolid old house and odd techno-logical post-apocalyptic addition, with the spot coolers providing a blessed coolness. Their vent ducts snaked under hastily built wooden ramps and through the windows to release the hot air outside. Their drain hoses snaked out far enough for the slope to take the condensation all the way to the bay.

It was more than large enough to hold everyone, though. Between seats by the work counter on the window side of the room and seats around the huge block table on the other side, everyone was busy with plates full of weirdly mixed grill and Vietnamese charred vegetables and pitchers of cold iced tea.

Just to be able not to sweat, and to be comfortable almost made the menu irrelevant, but Leon's jerk chicken drew praise from everyone and Sasha as usual made magic with the ingredients on hand.

Kerry's contribution had been the iced tea. There were leftover cookies and doughnuts for dessert, but for now they sat back and discussed the day and what had gotten done, and what the plans were for the following morning.

The water was on in the sinks, and Hank had managed to scrounge a total of two toilets the plumber had installed in two of the downstairs bathrooms. They had no hot water, but the sun shower had come over from the office and with the facilities in the RV's, everyone was pretty much okay.

The pop-up tents were moved inside, in the large room just behind the hallway where the spot coolers provided enough drier, more comfortable air to allow everyone a chance to get a good night's sleep.

There was a feeling of peace and safety. John, the ranger who had poked his head inside an hour or so earlier, was seated on one of the stools next to Kerry. He looked around in some amazed alarm at all the people and gear.

"So much stuff's going on," John said. "We weren't sure what all the... I mean, we knew something was happening." He paused. "We weren't sure if it was okay to come over here."

"Of course it is," Kerry said immediately. "You're all welcome here, and tomorrow we should sit down and talk about how we can be partners going forward," she added. "As long as you all want to. It's a big place. We need help."

John smiled shyly at her. "Um... what's with the cables all over?" he asked. "And you all using a generator? I don't hear one going like I thought there was last night."

"It's regular power. The other cables are Internet," Kerry said. "You're welcome to come share."

"How did you do that?"

Dar's phone rang, and she was spared the tale as she opened it and held it up to her ear. "Dar Roberts." She listened for a moment. "I'm sorry about that, we just got phone service back a little while ago." She paused to listen again. "No, I'm not, I'm on the mainland." She listened again in silence for a longer period of time. "I wasn't planning to. We can discuss this tomorrow if you're in the area of Hunter's Point. Anyone local can tell you where it is."

Kerry looked at her with intense curiosity.

"Okay, we can certainly discuss it." Dar's voice had that dry formality that was all business. "Good night." She closed the phone. "Governor," she said, briefly and turned her head to meet Kerry's eyes. "Apparently we're going to have him over for breakfast."

She glanced around at all the surprised, wide eyes looking at her. "He's pissed off at something. Probably that nerd who works for him blamed me for his inability to do crap."

"Dar, you're a private citizen. You don't have to save the planet for him." Kerry rolled her eyes. "Even though we did talk about you actually doing exactly that."

"Meh."

"Well, I'm going to make him pay through the nose for it if that's his problem." Kerry folded her arms. "Not really sure why people being paid by the citizens of this country all think they're anointed by God."

"Meh."

There was an awkward silence, as the entire room looked at both of them with some surprise and alarm. Dar caught the looks and grinned wryly. "We're really not anarchists. Kerry's just gotten a closer look at the inside of politics than most."

Eyes shifted to Kerry, who stuck out her tongue.

Conversation at that point was diverted, because the back door to the kitchen area opened behind them. "Lo there!" A moment later, Andrew Roberts appeared in the doorway, closely followed by Ceci. He paused and looked around. "This here a party?"

"Sure," Dar said. "There's some hot dogs and peanut butter over there on the counter, Dad."

"Nice," Ceci said, as she moved through the crowd and went to the counter, where the dinner buffet was reposing under foil. She retrieved a piece of broccoli from one of the pans and leaned against the counter as Andy investigated the other contents.

"Them folks did close off that area, Dardar," Andy said, as he appropriated a dog and a bun, depositing a glob of peanut butter on top with a grunt of content. "Got it all shut down from that main road there."

"Well, at least that was true," Kerry said.

"Yes, and they were being pretty snitty about it." Ceci munched her broccoli. "We told them we were happy if they were being jerks to everyone, not just us."

"They were jerks," Hank assented. "But like old junior there said, they did us a favor cause we came on down here instead."

Ceci looked around the room, at the lights propped in the corners. "I don't hear a generator."

"Ain't one," Pete said.

"You have power here?"

"We have power here, and the Internet," Dar said. "And some aircon, courtesy of those spot coolers." She pointed. "Enough power to run the servers."

Andy chewed on his peanut butter covered hot dog. "How'd you all do that, Dardar? Everybody's yapping all over how they ain't got none. You run you a cable over to that there island?" He seemed mildly curious but unsurprised.

"Pfft." Hank waved a hand at him. "Easier than that'd be."

Dar got up and edged around the table. "C'mon, I'll show you. It's easier than explaining." She indicated the internal door to the kitchen. "We just got lucky."

"At some point." Ceci grabbed a paper plate and more vegetables, then went around and took Dar's empty seat next to Kerry, "We're all going to admit it's not luck."

Kerry propped her chin on her fist. "Maybe it's karma."

"Maybe it's intergalactic synergy." Ceci picked up a charred pepper. "So," she went on. "Fill me in. We were only gone for two days. Can't take all that long."

Kerry gave her a sideways look.

"Then I can tell you about what we were up to."

****

Dar led the way down the deck past the neatly coiled pressure hoses and sawhorses and the stacks of construction material they'd brought from the office. There was a nice breeze coming off the water and it wasn't uncomfortable to walk in.

"This here's some place," Andy said. "Ah did not realize that when we were here that first time."

Dar angled across the scrub grass toward the large metal box now planted on the edge of the property, freshly dug and covered ground leading away into the darkness toward the road. "Haven't really had a chance to even go over all of it."

"Ah do like it."

"Me too." Dar smiled, as they arrived. "So, this." She indicated the box. "I agreed to let the phone guys install it. They run it off emergency power. So, they gave me a feed, and a connection in return." She half turned and looked offshore. "One of the main interconnects comes in off the coast there. I saw them with a work boat hunting for something, so I asked what was up."

Andy folded his arms and regarded the waist high metal enclosure. "Do tell."

"They had to bring it onshore two miles north, otherwise. So, it was a win win for everyone," Dar said. "There's a hub under the road out there. Saved them a hell of a lot of time, money and labor to hook up here."

"Ah heard there was some all thing that started working at the gov'm,int center. That it?" Andy asked.

"I don't know," Dar said. "I haven't listened to news all day cause we've been busy. They hit us with that evacuation yesterday and we've been going full out getting settled here all day." She looked around at the house, whose lower level now had visible lights on, all the brighter since nothing else in the area had power. "Where did you guys go off to?"

"Had to do me a favor for a buddy up off South Carolina," her father responded. "Turned out all right." He didn't seem to be disposed to explain further, and Dar didn't ask him to. "You all goin to bring them server things ovah here?"

Dar pondered that. "Yeah," she finally said. "I don't know how much longer that sat scam's going to hold up. Better connection here. But I might wait a few days until we can get this place more settled. It's pretty bare right now and they need a place to work."

"Need you some tables and all."

Dar nodded. "Richard's going to have a fit when he sees this place. He thinks that society's going to get an injunction against us using it," she said. "Told him I don't care."

Andrew chuckled softly. "They ain't got time to bother with that there right now, Dardar," he said. "That man's a worry wart, always was."

"Well, he's a lawyer." Dar smiled. "Maybe I should ask him to be here when the governor shows up tomorrow. He's mad at me for something or other."

"Lord."

"Kerry'll deal with him." Dar looked off over the water, where the only visible lights were some emergency beacons on Key Biscayne, and the flicker of what was, perhaps, firepits out on the shore across from them. That and the stolid, low, red and green of the channel markers. "They wanted me to come do something to help them a week ago and I told them to get lost."

Andy cocked his head in question, one brow lifted.

"We had a crap ton of stuff going on," Dar said, lifting both hands in a faint shrug. "So, who knows. Maybe he's going to try and pressure me into it."

"Dumbass."

Dar chuckled. "If hooking this up really did fix something, it'll give us some leverage because I already helped him for free," she said. "I should go check the news sites. See what went on." She considered. "And we can actually research it from the boat. The antenna I put in that tree'll cover the waterfront."

They watched Chino and Mocha run across the pool deck, noses down, tails waving.

"Them dogs do like this place," Andy noted. "Plenty of room."

Dar put her hands in her pockets and drew in a breath of salt-tinged air. "I like it," she said. "We're going to make this into our home. Whatever we have to fix to make it happen." She swung her gaze around to meet Andy's. "Whatever deal we have to make over it."

He smiled at her. "You all going to put you a treehouse up in that tree?"

Dar smiled back. "Maybe. I am going to build a climbing wall."

"Hope you ain't' gonna fall down off it and break your arm again."

"No way."

****

There was a thunderstorm overnight and it woke them, as lightning flashed visibly through the right-hand side bow window, illuminating the inside of the cabin.

Dar lifted her head off the pillow and regarded the window and listened to the wind driven rain spit against the reinforced plexiglass behind the light curtain.

The Dixie floated placidly at dock, the jetty providing protection against any incoming waves and after a moment she put her head back down as Kerry gave her a pat on the stomach. "Rain."

"News said it was going to," Kerry murmured. "Summer in Florida. Isn't that what you always tell me?" She asked. "At least we're here inside and it's not in the middle of the afternoon." She relaxed and closed her eyes. "But damn, for all those people out there with holes in their roofs."

Dar studied the low cabin roof over their heads. It's height just barely enough to clear hers, the doorframe something she had to duck through. But it was fiberglass, and solid, the hull meticulously shaped and sealed. They had plowed through far worse weather with her than tonight's thunderstorm.

But then, this boat, bought new, cost far more than many of the houses that had been wrecked by Bob. Her makers had assumed bad weather, and wind, and the corrosion of sea water and built accordingly.

Like old man Hunter had, building the dock they were tied to, and the stone seawall that protected the pier. Though Key Biscayne was across from them, south of that they were open to the bay, and the bay open to the Atlantic Ocean.

He'd built for it. Dar wondered how he would have felt knowing what he'd built stood up to the worst Bob had brought.

Good, she thought. Satisfied, like she was when some program she'd written tested out. She felt an odd sense of kinship at a distance with the builder of their new home. Though they'd had nothing in common, and he would have likely found her bizarre in the extreme, it would have been interesting to have met.

Thunder rolled again, and more lightning.

"You're not going back to sleep, are you?" Kerry asked, in an amused tone.

"It's almost dawn," Dar said.

"It is, I heard the dogs sit up," Kerry agreed. "So let me go see what I can arrange for all of our breakfasts, because we finished the peanut butter cups and Pop Tarts last night."

"Bummer."

"I'm sure there's a jar of peanut butter in the closet." Kerry pulled back the covers and got out of the comfortable bed in the cabin. She slid on a pair of shorts and pulled a T-shirt over her head as she heard the sound of dog toenails approach down the steps from the living area. "Good morning, doggos."

Thunder boomed and their ears went back, but they followed her into the main cabin and waited next to their bowls while she got out their bag of kibble. She poured them some breakfast then stood back as they munched and regarded the kibble bag thoughtfully.

"It's awful." Dar emerged from the small bathroom and wiped her lips free of toothpaste. "The canned stuff is worse."

"Sure would be easier if we could just have people kibble, huh?" Kerry put the bag back into the closet, it's top carefully rolled and clipped. "Turn on the sat, let's see how long this weather's supposed to last while I concentrate on not asking you how you know that about dog food."

"Maybe it'll delay the governor." Dar flipped on the power for the satellite. "Hell, I can check the marine radar on the console," she said, after a moment. "And it was a bet."

"Did you win or lose? No wait. Don't tell me." Kerry retreated to the bathroom to run a comb through her hair and brush her teeth. "At least we can fill up the water tanks with all that." She came out, to find Dar, arms crossed, watching the Weather Channel. "Florida off the front page yet?"

"Is Florida ever off the front page?" Dar asked rhetorically. "If it's not hurricanes, it's love bugs, or Florida men, or alligators dancing on Miami Beach or a combination of all of the above."

"Mm. That's true," Kerry said. "This state really is weirdo central sometimes."

"Sometimes?"

"What's the deal with the weather then?" Kerry diverted the conversation. "Since we're not likely to get Florida to change any time soon."

"It's actually a tropical low," Dar said. "Slurping after that front that killed Bob."

"That sounds so evil." Kerry went to the kitchen and studied her options. "Can you cope with jerk chicken this early?"

"Yum."

"Okay, jerk chicken street tacos it is, because I have corn tortillas and canned pineapple."

"I'll make Cuban coffee," Dar said. "Since that, and milkshakes are about all I can manage and I'm guessing you didn't refill the ice cream." She winked at Kerry and ducked around her and reached up into the cabinet to remove the small silver coffeepot.

Kerry casually wrapped an arm around her and held her still long enough to lean up and kiss her on the lips. "I'm glad I share the craziness of the world with you, Dar." She looked up into Dar's eyes, pale that reflected the warm, ochre inside light. "I really do love you."

Dar leaned over and kissed her back. "Likewise." She gently bumped heads with her. "We are really the luckiest people on the planet."

"We are." Kerry paused and listened to the thunder outside. "Do we really need to get up?" She wrapped the sleeve of Dar's shirt around her finger and watched her face.

"Do you mean, do we need to actually get out of bed?" Dar's eyes twinkled knowingly.

"Yeah, that's what I mean." Kerry smiled, as Dar's hand cupped her cheek. "It's too early for me to start looking through all that mail and it's raining too hard for us to do anything."

"Anything?"

"C'mon." Kerry dismissed the thought of jerk chicken tacos for the moment and eased past Dar, moving in the direction of the cabin.

****

By the time the sun rose over the horizon, the rain had stopped. Dar walked out onto the back deck and then crossed the gangplank to the dock. She moved out of the Dixie's shadow into a pool of warm pink light as she went to the steps and trotted up them.

There was no railing to them. They were neatly made in a zig zag of the rock wall, but the residual damp made them a bit slippery. Dar pondered having both solar lights and iron tread plates put in to make it a bit safer at night.

She imagined them arriving here in the dark, after a trip, or a dive, or just a ride over to Key Biscayne for some dinner. Having the boat this close to the house made it almost as convenient as a car. She paused and considered again the trade off with having to take the boat somewhere to get it serviced and fueled.

Eh. Crandon Park marina wasn't that far. Dar shrugged and continued upward. She could always arrange for marine diesel deliveries, but given how far the dock was from the edge of the property, probably was faster to just drive it over the cut.

At least for now.

She reached the top of the steps and crossed the pool deck, it's surface now an almost shining deckled white from its cleaning. The pool was now covered with plywood and she stepped over the thick cabling that crossed the space coming from the telco box.

She paused and studied the cables. She traced their route along the edge of the deck and up to the door. They went through one pane of the French doors that had been carefully removed, and then blocked with a square of wood that had a hole cut in the center large enough for the cables to pass, a piece of foam around them for insulation.

It was a nice, thoughtful piece of work and she took the time to appreciate it. She made an internal note to find out who had done it and thank them, as well as whoever routed the cables, the electrical carefully bundled separately from the data, neatly strapped and tucked away.

Not really relevant in terms of its operation, but it showed care and attention to detail. It made her happy to see it. It saved the time it would have taken for her to do it, because she would have. Even now there was a bit of a separation between two cables, and she nudged them together with her foot.

There.

She walked around the side of the house and up onto the long, covered porch toward the back.

It was quiet. She could hear birds in the trees, and the rustle of branches overhead. The wooden boards under her feet creaked and shifted as she crossed them and every few feet a lizard raced from one side to the other, surprised by her presence.

On the east side here, the rising sun speared through the foliage and across the porch, laying down a pattern on the surface of it. Dar paused midway, turned and faced the water. She looked at the view to the southeast, to the ruffled waters of the bay as it met the darker blue of the Atlantic.

She imagined working here with her laptop, listening to the sounds of the water and the investigative creaks of the seabirds. She nodded to herself. "Yeah."

She took a breath, and found it full of the smell of earth, and vegetation, the far off smell of wood smoke, and as she continued walking and got closer to the back of the house, the scent of the barbeque heating up.

Around the back corner she saw the RV's, and if she listened hard, could hear the sounds of people stirring.

Sure enough, one of the grills was open, and as she came to the back entrance, it opened, and Pete emerged carrying a bowl. "Morning," she said and stepped back to hold the door open.

"Morning!" Pete greeted her cheerfully. "It sure was nice to get some shut-eye, without crazies or cops around. Tell ya that." He looked around. "Rained last night, but who cares? We definitely moved up in the world, junior."

"Yeah, thunder woke us up, but we took advantage of that and filled Dixie's freshwater tanks," Dar said. "Kerry's doing some work from the boat. Thought I would come up here and see what we need to get together to move the rest of our guys out here."

"The ones out on the island?" Pete asked. "Why not leave em there? From what those other techie guys said, they're having a ball living the lifestyle of the rich and famous."

"I could. But they'll be more productive here, with the high-speed access we have," Dar said. I just have to figure out how to put in workspace and keep them fed. They probably are enjoying the service out there, though. The staff like them and keep bringing them sodas and chips."

Pete chuckled.

"Ah, it's going to take me a few weeks to get enough furniture around anyway." Dar shrugged. "Everyone get rest in there?" She indicated the house.

"Seems like." Pete set the bowl down on the worktable next to the grill. "Having real power sure does help. I did my share and more of rough living, but boy you don't realize you don't have stuff until you don't have it. You know?"

"I know," Dar said. "One night on our couch in the office was kinda enough for me."

"But you could have stayed out on that island yourselves," Pete said. "I mean, you do live there. You don't have to hang out here. We're pretty savvy and all."

"You are. But we're responsible for all this," Dar said, as the door opened and Sasha came bustling out, carrying a bag full of what appeared to be fresh baguettes. "Besides, I like it," she admitted. "I like being in the middle of all the crap going on. It's interesting. It's problem solving. What the hell would I do back on the island? Probably get my ass in trouble pissing people off or being asked to fix someone else's problems."

"Yeah," Pete said. "Everyone respects that. You do notice, when you're a grunt, when the guys in charge sit in the mess with you and don't have some cook make them something nice delivered to their tent."

Dar nodded. "Yeah."

"Were you ever a grunt, Dar?" Pete asked. "Bet you weren't."

"No." She smiled easily. "I've been running things, legit or not, since I could walk and talk. Ask my mother. Made her crazy. It's why I never really could have gone into the service. Some striped bozo would have told me to do something and first thing out of my mouth would have been— why?—and the second would have been—kiss my ass—"

Pete thought about that briefly. "Andy took orders," he said, after a while.

"I'm not my father."

"He said that last night," Pete said. "And said given how everything turned out, he's absolutely all right with that." He winked at her. "That whole thing with the rig out there and the phone guys... that tickled his ass."

Dar chuckled. "That was sweet. But honestly that was just being in the right place at the right time and seeing those guys," she admitted. "Lucky we had something they really, really wanted. And for them it was worth it. I checked the local news last night. That line brought up the whole state-wide emergency system."

"Win win."

"Absolutely. Everyone won in that carnival of WTF," Dar agreed.

The door to one of the RV's opened and Maria climbed out. She spotted Dar and came over. "Good morning, Jefa," she greeted Dar. "Did you know these things here have a washing machine inside them?" she asked. "It is like having an apartment."

"Well let me get cooking," Pete said. "Want to get everyone fed before the politicos show up. They're not worth Sasha's magic grub." He went over to join Sasha at the prep table, where she was contentedly slicing up the bag full of bread.

Maria observed them for a moment, then turned and regarded Dar.

"Where did she get fresh baguettes?" Dar guessed her thoughts. "Some things, it's better not to ask," she said. "No, I had no idea they had washing machines. That was Kerry's gig. But I'm glad you and Tomas are comfortable. That's what counted."

"And now we have the Internet," Maria said. "Josh so nicely set up a laptop for Tomas and he is very busy now, working to set up insurance claims for all our neighbors. It is good, Dar. I know we have said thank you again and again, but again, thank you."

Dar smiled. "Yeah, this is working out," she said, then paused. "What's going on with your house?" She eyed her longtime assistant, one of her dark eyebrows lifting in interrogation. "Mayte said you all went by there again yesterday."

Maria clasped her hands in front of her and cocked her head to one side. "It seems that by somehow our house is being taken care of by some government program, Dar," she said. "They have shown us the paperwork, there is no mistake. There is our name and our house, on it."

Dar's blue eyes took on a distinct, somewhat piratical, twinkle. "So, they're fixing it?" she asked in a mild, innocent tone. "Cool."

"It is all ruined, the inside, from the water," Maria said. "But they have taken everything out and are doing it again, like they were working at our office. It will take a long time, of course, but it will be okay at the end."

"Good." Dar nodded. "I know that can't replace the things you had in there, Maria."

"No, but they are just things, as Kerrisita said to us," Maria said. "So, Dar, can you imagine how that could have happened, that program?" She looked steadily at her. "We did not ask for it to be like that." She paused, but Dar remained silent and waited. "My neighbors, they want to know how they can have that same program and I do not know what to tell them."

Dar leaned back against the tree they were standing under, the tree that she'd climbed the previous day. "I made that happen," she said, after a long moment. "I know you didn't ask for it. But it's a fee I took for doing someone a favor."

"But, Dar—"

Dar held a hand up. "There were a lot of people in that program. They were there not because of any merit, Maria. They were there because they were friends of some important people, or given money to some politician, or they were rich."

Now Maria nodded. "This is what happens with people all the time, everywhere," she said. "This I understand very well. But..."

"Well, I made it so those people all could get things taken care of. So, for my fee, I added some names," Dar said. "Your house is as important to you as some investment property in Coral Gables, Maria. Sometimes when you get an opportunity to even the scales, you take it. So, I did."

For a moment, Maria was silent. "Will this make trouble for you?"

Dar's eyes twinkled even more. "Not unless you tell someone I did it," she said. "Those guys don't want anyone to really know about that list, Maria. Makes bad press. You can just tell your neighbors that because your employer does some work for the government, it's a benefit."

Maria drew in a breath to answer, then paused, thoughtfully.

"It's true," Dar said. "In fact, it's the absolute truth."

"Yes, that is so," Maria finally said, with a slight laugh. "Tomas said it must be that way. That you had something to do with it. But we can tell everybody this, and they will also understand completely. The government, yes, this is something we understand." She reached out and touched Dar's arm. "We will use our good fortune to help our neighbors."

"Good." Dar slid her sunglasses over her eyes as the sun penetrated the trees and lit up the area. "Now. Where the hell are we going to meet with the governor? Speaking of politicians."

"Ah, this is no problem." Maria reverted to business. "We can use the desk part in our vehicle, yes? They have put up a work area there in any case, and it has some chairs." She patted Dar's arm. "Come look. We will have some Cafecito."

"Lead on." Dar pushed off away from the tree. "I made some this morning but Kerry and I both agreed it was more suited to pour on top of ice cream as a syrup."

"That is too much sucar."

"Spoon stayed straight up so you're probably right."

****

The Dixie wasn't really set up as an office, but Kerry improvised with the small coffee table bolted to the deck and one of the comfortable bucket chairs nearby. She had her laptop on her knees, and a cup of herbal tea in the holder on the chair arm, and on her screen was a video conference.

"So, Col... anyway," Kerry said. "A lots happened in the last few days."

"No kidding!" Colleen said. "Wait, now, Mark'll be here in five minutes. He was just talking to the long-term hotel we're staying at."

"Trouble?" Kerry asked.

"For a change? No." Colleen laughed. "And I ... are... where are you?"

"On the Dixie," Kerry said. "Connected to wireless in a tree on land on our new property. We're hooked up to a high-speed Internet connection courtesy of the telecom company we traded land rights for it."

Colleen propped her head up on her fist. "Y'know, you said something about that in your email," she said. "Great quality. "So, you're parked in the water near there I guess?"

Kerry nodded. "Dar just went up to see what was going on and figure out where to talk to the governor at."

"The governor?"

Kerry nodded again. "We think he wants us to do something," she said. "Don't worry, I'm going to make him pay for the privilege. So, how's it going up there?"

"Not bad." Colleen leaned back in her chair. Behind her were the bland buff walls of the office space they'd rented. "We're holding our own. I found a little company near here that does basic IT outsourcing. We're using them to cover nights for us, so now we're rotating the guys and girls off."

"Good."

"Not that they don't show up here anyway. Not that much to do around here," Colleen said. "I'm afraid to tell them the rest of that lot is bunking up by your new place. They'll run out and hijack the bus back there."

"Still want to come back?"

"They do." Colleen nodded. "And some of them have places and family there they're a bit worried about."

Kerry leaned back and regarded the screen thoughtfully. "That's natural," she said. "If we had a place for them to work out of, we could handle them here now, with this connection. But there's nothing to sit on even. Give us a few more days."

Colleen nodded. "I'll tell them that. It'll make everyone happy," she said. "I thought that place was a historical something, though. They going to go along with you turning it into an IT shop?"

"Probably not," Kerry said, with a smile. "Dar just told our lawyer to deal with it. It's not like we had a lot of choice, and frankly I don't know what they're thinking of doing with ... no, I know what they want it to be, but there's no history to restore here."

"Ah heh?"

"Long story," Kerry said. "But we agreed we wouldn't do anything permanent here, just what we had to do to make things functional. So, if they throw the book at us, we can roll it back."

There was noise behind Colleen, and then Mark walked into camera range and sat down next to her. "Hey, poquito boss!" He had a ballcap on his head and took off a pair of sunglasses. Wow, nice clear pic! Where are you?"

"Sitting in the cabin of the Dixie."

Mark blinked. "Like as in your boat?" he asked, after a moment's silence. "Oh yeah, it must be. I recognize the background." He paused again. "Pops hook you up to a submarine or something? Cause that ain't cellular bandwidth you're on."

So nerd. Kerry smiled back at him. "Ain't cellular," she said. "C'mon, I have Thor the God of the Internets here. How long did you figure it would take?"

Mark laughed out loud. "She take over a military node or something?"

"Sort of. We now have a major pipeline crossing our land that happens to hook into the emergency grid and our fee was power and Internet,"

Kerry said. "Give us a few more days to finish setting up, and you could work from our second floor with a nice view of the bay."

"Once she's done talking to the governor," Colleen said, as he was digesting that. "And hello? Do I get a nice view as well?"

"Let me find some folding tables and lawn chairs first." Kerry chuckled. "It's literally an empty building right now except for a bunch of pop-up tents and cables running everywhere."

"Kerry, that's freaking amazing," Mark finally said. "I mean... it's totally typical and all that stuff, but wow."

"But wow," Kerry agreed. "Dar's pretty intent on moving operations here until we can get the office power and circuits back. And you know, when Dar puts her mind to something, it does usually happen, because the Fates just run screaming from her."

"No that's great," Mark said. "Josh and Leo must have spilled to everyone because they all looked at me when I got here like they expected me to... I don't know what."

"Tell them what's going on," Kerry said. "So go ahead and officially tell them. How's that Brazilian account going?"

Colleen laughed.

"Pretty sweet, actually." Mark sounded surprised himself. "Turns out those outta work waiters from Palm Beach got some IT skills. They're only passing on the stuff they can't handle to the guys here. And it's sweet for them, because they live at the northwestern edge of West Palm, they got a power coop there and they're living in one guy's house."

"Beanbags and laptops?"

"No idea, don't care," Mark admitted frankly. "But they work east in Palm Beach and that's all shut down so they're making their rent doing this. They said if we need more people, they can probably scrounge them."

Kerry pondered that. "Great job, Mark."

"Stupid luck, Kerry," he said. "Like, really stupid luck because one of the maintenance guys here at this building we're in has a sister who's dating one of the guys in that house. All I did was be in the hall talking to Scott about our problem long enough for that guy to hear us."

"So... you think the fact that we just happen to buy the property that happens to be the nearest point of land to a major Internet inroute and happened to be here when some guys were trying to find a way to bring it closer to a node is anything but luck?"

Mark eyed her.

"C'mon, Mark. Listen, I've got some business savvy, and Jesus only knows Dar has a higher IQ than summer temperatures in July here, but we literally did nothing to plan any of this stuff."

"Way higher than summer temps," Mark responded. "But I don't want to take credit for stuff that just happened, and I don't' want you to think I magicked up this awesome plan."

"But you did." Kerry smiled. "Success isn't knowing what to do all the time, Mark. It's taking what life tosses at you and doing the best you can with it. You turned what would have been a contract cancel into a win for the customer, and for us, and all props, you know?"

"I told him that," Colleen said. She'd been listening in silence, her hands folded on the table. "Being in the right place at the right time is just our brand."

They looked at each other in silence for a minute. "I think you just found our company motto, Col," Kerry said. "That's going to look great on a T-shirt."

"Rightyho." Colleen made a note on the pad at her elbow. "I'll get the process started. I may not know what end of a cable to do anything with, but you're right. That's good marketing."

"So anyway, yeah, if this place hadn't been here, and they'd kicked us out, we'd have figured out something else, like hauled everyone over to the island," Kerry said. "Which would have been hilarious. But the service out there for comms sucks."

Mark went with the subject change. "Does, Elvis was saying it. So, about those waiter guys..."

"Did we hire them direct, or are we just paying them per day?"

"Per day."

Kerry nodded. "Give them a choice. Either they can onboard as a support team and we do that like we usually do, or they can incorporate, and we do a B2B contract with them and they handle their own legalities and logistics."

"And taxes," Colleen said. "Same thing we offered Carlos. But make it known they need to complete the contract, hmm? When that restaurant opens back up, no running off and abandoning us until we can wind down."

"Got it." Mark smiled cheerfully.

"Great," Kerry said. "Now let me go find out what trouble Dar's gotten into and figure out where we can get folding tables. I'm hoping a Walmart will open sometime soon."

"Call the Miami Beach Convention Center," Mark suggested. "I bet they got tons of stuff in their back room, and nothing to do with it."

"I'll do that." Colleen took a note. "Send you a note if I can get hold of them."

Kerry sat back and felt a sense of accomplishment. "All right guys let's just keep on rolling. I'll let you know what comes of the meeting with the governor, if anything. It might end up just a pissing match." She paused. "I can't really believe I'm going to say this, but I wish my mother was here so I could throw her at him."

"Maybe she'll show up," Mark said. "Y'never know."

"You never know," Kerry agreed. "Talk to you guys later."

Chapter Twenty

Dar walked along the beautifully finished wooden floors on the third level of the house. Her eyes searched the ceiling intently until she reached the side of the house away from the water and finally found what she was looking for. "Ah."

She was alone. Downstairs she could hear voices and work underway, and now that she was near the land side of the house the sound of a truck backing into the loading area.

But here on the third floor, with its round windows and smaller, anonymous rooms on both sides of the hall it was quiet and untouched.

Nothing really to be done up here, after all. They would use the many closets, rooms, cubbies, sections, and spaces for anything and everything. Maybe even to house the staff for now once they got true air-conditioning and power in the place.

Or nothing, if the legal problems go overwhelming.

Dar shrugged and dismissed the thought and focused on the hatch in the ceiling, conveniently above the start of the stair banister.

She judged the height then put her hands on the banister and vaulted up onto it. She balanced on the narrow beam and reached up to push against the hatch that obligingly gave upward. Then as she shifted to try and move it aside, it surprised her by lowering itself down.

"Ah." She was charmed. There was a wooden ladder attached which helpfully extended itself halfway down to the floor and kept her from trying something stupid to get up into the crawlspace to look around.

She hopped down to the ground then reached up and grabbed the highest rung she could reach and pulled herself up and got her knees on the lowest step, then straightened up and climbed up into the attic.

It smelled of wood and dust, and she was happy to detect no smell of mold or mildew as she looked around. The roof timbers were heavy four by four, and creosote coated, and she walked along one of them over to one of the roof peaks that held the small, round, boat like windows.

Much to her surprise, she found they were more boat like than she'd expected, since they were, in fact, portholes that had been fashioned into the wall of the house, complete with their brass fittings and clamps, as though Hunter had gotten them from a shipyard supply store.

Odd, but she worked the clamps and with a yank, pulled the porthole open and stuck her head through it. She studied the view over the trees and noted the sight lines. "Hmm." She could see past the western edge of Key Biscayne, and past Virginia Key, and had a clear view of the loading cranes for Port Miami.

Satisfied, she pulled her head back in and carefully closed the porthole, fastening the clamps and checking the seal to make sure she hadn't just introduced a leak into the roof. Then she turned and walked along the timbers through the centerline of the attic, the only path she could take that admitted her height.

There was no insulation. They'd have to install that. But the joins she saw were sound and there were no obvious signs of water intrusion, and surprisingly no signs of resident fauna either.

She'd expected at least a water rat, or a racoon. But it was critter less and she finished her circuit of the attic and arrived back at the hatch and climbed back down to the ground.

It was stuffy, and they'd decided it was a better course to leave the windows closed and not add to the onerous task of the spot coolers in removing the humidity that letting in the sea breeze would add. She examined the ladder and found the locking mechanism and unlatched it and watched the ladder retract itself up into the ceiling. The hatch closed with a light, but definite snick.

She admired the workmanship. Like the rest of the house, it spoke of attention to detail uncommon even in the very expensive condo she lived in. "Nice."

The sound of boots on the steps made her turn and look down, to find her father making his way upward to where she stood. "Hey, Dad." She leaned on the banister. "Good morning."

"Morning there, Dardar. We all are parked up next to you on the water there. Ferry's a mess and a half with all that gov'mint whohaa going on," he said. "That dock there's a good one." He came up to stand next to her.

"Hunter knew his stuff," Dar said. "I was just up in the attic, seeing if I could plot out a point- to-point from here to the island. Might have a sightline if I can get enough elevation out there."

Andrew nodded as though he knew exactly what Dar was talking about. "Man knew how to build," He said. "Had him some.. " He made a slight shrugging gesture, his lips twisting a little into an expression Dar could almost feel on her own face. "Didn't have no respect for ladies."

Dar folded her arms across her chest. "What do you mean?"

"Wall, y'know, Dardar." He seemed a mixture of embarrassed and perplexed. "Folks had some thoughts in the past bout who the head of the family was, that kinda thing. Kinda was the way it was."

"Sure." Dar finally nodded. "The whole, women are weak, walk two steps behind the husband kinda thing."

Andrew nodded. "Was how he grew, ah suppose. Same as my old man. He didn't have no use for womenfolk running things or being strong or nothing like that. Felt the good Lord put them on earth to serve menfolk." He paused. "Still people like that, round everywhere."

"Its' true." Dar sighed. "Kerry's father was one of them."

"Yeap."

"Glad you weren't," Dar said, after a moment.

"Your grandmaw done always said ah was cursed with an open mind," he said. "But truly, Dardar, all ah ever done was live by the idea that every'body's equal in the eyes of the Lord. Ah feel like that's done me well in mah life."

Dar nodded slowly. "Wish more people would."

Her father shrugged a little bit. "Anyhow. Ah only talked a few times to that there fella and the last time I done slugged him. Don't matter why."

Dar could well imagine, and she internally, silently agreed it didn't matter, whether it was some insult of him, of her mother, or of her, or just in general. "Maybe that's why that kid was so happy to sell this place to us," she mused. "That makes a little more sense."

"Ah do think so," Andrew agreed solemnly. "So, like your mother says some such, what done go around, done come around and bites you in the behind."

"Huh."

Andy put his hands in the pockets of his cargo shorts. "Don't think on it too much, Dardar. Man's gone, he done a good job building, now it's you all's."

Dar was silent for a minute, and he just stood there, comfortable with the silence and waited. "Well, can't do anything about it." She shrugged. "You're right, he's gone, we're here." She chuckled softly. "It's just so ironic."

"Yeap."

"C'mon, it's hot up here." Dar gestured the back steps and started down them. "I want to see what was on that truck I heard coming in."

"Ah do think I heard some fuss at the gates 'fore I came up here."

"Probably the governor."

"Probly. You all mind if I sit by an listen to his chitchat?"

"Not at all."

****

"We don't have any tables inside yet." Dar opened the door to the RV and stood back, allowing the tall, lean man in short sleeves and slacks to climb up ahead of her.

Behind him were two men in sports jackets, sweat rolling down their faces and down through their collars that had spiral corded earpieces disappearing under them.

"And it's air-conditioned."

Kerry went next, and Dar followed her.

Inside, the workspace was set up neatly for the meeting, and two extra chairs had materialized from the other RV's. Maria stood near the small kitchen, the folding partition behind it closed and fastened. Andy was seated in the driver's bucket seat, big hands folded. Mayte was in the passenger seat, with a small pad and a pen.

On the desk was a computer, a phone and a large monitor screen that now showed the cloud dashboard with lots of impressive graphs and blinking lights and scrolling content on it.

Behind the desk was a built-in credenza, and as though pre-arranged, which of course it was, Kerry settled in the chair behind the desk and Dar leaned back on the credenza behind her. "Please sit down," Kerry said, politely. "Tell us what we can do for you."

"Senor, would you and your people here like a cold drink?" Maria asked. "It is so hot outside."

The governor was a man in his mid-sixties, with a weatherworn face and straight, gray hair. He sat down in the right most chair in the space and hitched up the knees of his slacks. He took out a handkerchief from his pocket and mopped his brow with it. "I'd love some cold water if you have it, thank you, ma'am."

The two security personnel accompanying the governor sat down in two chairs at his back and gratefully accepted the bottles as Maria passed them along.

The governor opened his bottle and took a long swig of the water, not even asking for a glass. He then put the cap back on the bottle. "Thank you," he said. "Let me get to the point, since we're all pretty damn busy people. My tech czar tells me he asked you for help, and you turned him down. I'm here, mostly, to ask why that is."

Kerry nodded, as though she'd expected the question. She removed a small folder from the desk she was sitting at and handed it over to him. "Rather than rambling on, if you would mind taking a minute to read over this recap it should set the groundwork for the explanation."

The two security men both nodded at the same time and settled back in their chairs, one of them hitching an ankle up on his opposing knee and sipped on their water.

"All right." The governor took the folder and removed a single printed sheet and set it on his left knee. He took out a pair of reading glasses and put them on. He then sat there in silence and took his time to read through the text.

Dar crossed her ankles, regarding the scar across one kneecap as she used the time to think about the possibility of getting something tall enough on the island to make a connection to.

She had on a company polo shirt, with the short sleeves rolled up a turn and khaki cargo shorts, a slightly more formal than tank top and denim concession to this governmental intrusion.

Kerry was dressed similarly, and now she sat back in the desk chair, her hands folded on her lap, elbows on the chair arms in a posture of infinite patience.

Outside, through the walls of the RV, was the sound of construction, the buzz of a saw, the rumble of a hammer drill, and voices in varying timbres and languages.

Finally, the governor finished. "Thank you," he said. "That's quite a lot of information."

"It is," Kerry agreed. "The whole point of that was this. We did that," she said. "We performed those services for the government, was tasked with unusual requirements, and succeeded in what we were asked to do, against some pretty significant odds."

He nodded. "You didn't really need to tell me all this, you know. Your competence was never in doubt. Certainly not in my mind. That's why I was so surprised when you turned us down."

"Yep, coming to that," Kerry said. "We did all that no questions asked. But when we went to that same government, and presented a bill for what it cost us, to do that, we were told that we should be grateful that we were allowed to donate our time, our energy, our ability, and success to the country and to go home and shut up."

The governor blinked several times.

"So," Kerry concluded. "My question to you is, please tell me why we should help?"

****

The governor looked at Kerry in silence for a minute or two and turned the paper over in his fingertips. Then he put it back down on the desk and gave it a gentle push back toward her. "Not really sure I have an answer to that but let me ask you this. Do you think it's all right for you to want to profit on that kind of tragedy?"

His voice was mild, but his eyes were not, and one brow lifted in question at her.

"Profit? No." Kerry shook her head. "And if two dozen buddies of various ranking government people hadn't been given lucrative contracts the following month, I might even agree with you that we should have sucked it up and considered it the cost of doing business."

His other eyebrow lifted. "Not sure I heard about that part."

Kerry smiled briefly and without humor at him. "My mother's a senator. I hear things," she said. "At any rate, we have a whole lot of rebuilding to do ourselves, to restore our operations, to help our customers... I get that everything's a mess here, but it's a mess for us too. Is it fair to have us stop what we're doing, and leave our own people in this mess to help out governmental agencies that one would think could handle this sort of thing?"

"We get things going, that helps you too," he countered. "That makes sense, doesn't it?"

Dar shifted a little and wished she had her laptop. She resisted the urge to remove her phone from her pocket and mess with it. She kept her arms folded and let Kerry play out her game. One she knew she had little or no patience for.

Never had. There was an art to negotiation. There had been literally hundreds of people back at ILS who were far, far better than she was at it. And if a contract got to the point where she had to get involved in it no one, including her, had ever enjoyed the process.

It was like having tea with a wolverine, someone once said, and she'd actually taken that as a compliment. So now she was content to let Kerry handle the sparring right up until the point where, if he decided to get nasty with her, she'd lean in.

"It does make sense, but it doesn't really help us," Kerry said. "Because really, we could just pack up in these RV's and head out of town, up to where my support group is holding down the fort in Melbourne."

He considered that. "So why haven't you?"

"We have people here we couldn't leave behind," Dar spoke up for the first time. "We had to make sure they were all okay first."

"That so?" He tilted his head up to look at her. "Well, there are a lot of folks in the same boat, I guess," he said. "I know its popular to blame the government, when things go in the crapper. But when even the crapper is in the crapper, it's hard to know where to start."

"No one expected it to get this bad," Kerry said. "You never do, right? You always assume at the last minute it'll turn, or die, or something like that. We did." She indicated herself and then Dar. "Day before it hit, we were running around trying to get plywood put up."

"You hope you learn from things like this. So next time..." he said.

"Except by next time, that budget went somewhere else," Dar drawled softly.

"Okay." He accepted that. "So then let me ask you, if I sign a contract with you, ahead of time, this time, with Ts and C's, would you give this old man a break and just come help me out?"

Kerry awarded him a smile, a faint twinkle appearing in her eyes as she approved the approach, which showed a fine sense of political acumen and more so, of the ability to read people. "We've helped already," she said. "We saw the emergency center come up this morning."

The change of subject threw him a bit off-guard. "Sorry?" he said. "What does that have to do with you?"

Dar leaned over and pointed out the RV's window that faced the south end of the property. "See that box there? The green one? That's where the connection is coming in that lit up that office." She leaned back against the credenza again.

The governor looked out the window, then he leaned back in his chair. "Well, I'll be damned," he said, after a moment's silence. "That's what that man was talking about." He half turned to look at the two security men behind him. "Johnson, right? That's what he said? Something about a cable?"

"Yessir." The man nodded. "Some crazy story about a boat and a cable—I dunno. But it's workin," he concluded. "Man, those guys were happy, even without no air-conditioning." He wiped his forehead. "I thought it was hot in Tallahassee. This place is brutal. Thank Jesus you have some cooling in here."

"Si," Maria said. "It is terrible for everyone. We are so fortunate that Kerrisita thought to have these trucks for us to be in." She indicated the RV. "And we have everything we need here to do our work."

The man eyed her with thoughtful speculation.

"With a little preparation, it is possible to do this for your locations," Mayte added, from her seat near the front of the RV. "We have learned many things that can help."

He leaned his arm on the back of his chair and regarded her in turn, then after a moment of silence, he looked at Andrew, who had the driver's seat swiveled around and his long legs extended with ankles crossed. "And you, sir?"

"That's my father," Dar said, to prevent the mischief she could see was coming as Andy produced a grin. "He's our director of operations."

"Got it." The governor turned back around and faced them. "All right, Roberts Automation," he said. "Let's talk Ts and Cs."

"You bringing in a lawyer?" Dar asked.

"Nope," he said. "Never bring a lawyer in to do a governor's job, I always say." He half turned again. "Give me that lined pad, willya?" He glanced back at them. "Anyway, I am a lawyer, but Jesus did I get bored with that fast. I think I still remember how to write the lingo though."

"Fair enough." Kerry removed a pad from the drawer herself, and from the pocket of her cargo shorts, removed a calligraphy pen she unscrewed the top of, and put it down on the desk. "Let's do it old school."

Dar and Maria exchanged grins, and then Dar went over to one of the built-in couches near the small service area. She settled behind it and extended her legs out across the carpeted floor.

"Would you like some Cafecito, Dar?" Maria asked. "It is the time."

"Yep," Dar said. "It is the time. Café all around."

****

"Ah think that there fella's all right," Andy said, as they watched the black SUV parade trundle down the lane and out the gates. "Got him some sense."

Kerry stood next to him, her arms folded. "Yeah, he's not bad," she agreed. "A lot less asshole and a lot more let's just get stuff done than I expected from the governor of the national phallic symbol."

Andrew turned around and stared at her.

Kerry's lips twitched. "I heard that on the Internet and it just makes me laugh," she admitted. "Okay, so, we have the rest of today to get all our stuff sorted out before we head down to the emergency headquarters we enabled tomorrow and start fixing things."

Dar came up behind them and draped her arm over Kerry's shoulders, "good job, hon."

"With the contract?" Kerry chuckled. "Yeah, it's not bad. If we're not going to be able to get business the other way at least it keeps money coming in. I liked that he liked the pay for performance clause." She looked at Dar. "Can we actually do what I committed us to?"

"Sure," Dar said, in an unruffled tone. "So, now how much you think we could charge our island over there if I give them access to high-speed Internet?" she asked. "Free up that sat rig for us to go uplink the swamplands and send a point-to-point over there from here."

"I thought you said there wasn't any way to get a signal over the Key?"

"That was before I climbed into the attic. I forgot this is a three and a half story building on a rise." Dar said. "I just need someone to sneak over to our offices and grab that dish."

Andy chuckled. "Ah got that. Be back." He ambled off, attracting the attention of Pete and Hank with a whistle, and then motioning them to follow, which they did.

"Have to make some adjustments over there but it should work," Dar said. "I finally got hold of that VC. Told him we're not going to market this year."

"He pissed?"

"Told me not to bother calling him back," Dar said. "But you know what? If it's meant to happen, some other VC'll come along. Or we'll sell the IP and let someone else do it like we said."

Kerry nodded. "This," she gestured vaguely after the cavalcade. "This is the right thing to do, Dar."

"It is. I'm tickled silly you drove a good deal with them, and that we'll do all right this time because we don't have the unlimited resources to blow like ILS did but..."

"But you'd have done it anyway."

Dar nodded. "Has to happen. We can do this. Our community needs it," she responded, in a brisk tone. "So, let's make the most of today, maybe we can find some grog, throw a party tonight before we go headfirst into the crap farm out there."

"Ride the kids over from the island for it," Kerry said. "They want to see this place anyway. I spoke to Angela about ten minutes ago after I finished with the governor. I took a picture of my chicken scratch and she's turning it into one of our contracts."

"Know what else?"

"What?"

"Lobster season just started."

Kerry turned and looked at Dar. "Are you suggesting we take time out of our last day before chaos and go lobstering?"

"Yup." Dar bounced up and down on the balls of her feet. "Take limit is six per, and we've got at least six divers here. Won't take much time and it'll feed everyone."

"What if people don't like lobster, Dar?"

"More for me."

Kerry started laughing. "Sure. Why not." She lifted her hands and let them fall. "Let me go update Colleen on what happened and see if we have all our gear onboard for it."

"I'm going to get the guys to start to run cable for that dish." Dar started toward the house. "We got this, Ker."

Kerry wrapped her arm around Dar's waist and moved into step with her. "Long as I have you, my love, everything else is what it is."

"Likewise."

****

The party was outside on the pool deck. There weren't enough things for people to sit on yet inside, and no real way to aircon enough of it to hold everyone so they were outside on boxes and crates and benches the carpenters had thrown together.

Luckily, it was a dry night. There was a breeze coming off the bay and tables set up with pieces of plywood that rested on sawhorses. The tables held a true cornucopia of whatever you might find in a radical potluck style. It featured platters of grilled lobsters and a respectable lineup of fish along with two big restaurant style bowls full of Asian seafood curry that was both fragrant and spicy.

And a huge pot of rice.

And a tray of Rice Krispy treats.

There were two large beer kegs with built in chillers.

There were bowls of cut up mangos and a scattering of calamondins and oranges, bananas and grapefruit all gathered from trees on the property.

The amateur musicians had their instruments out and were jamming softly on one side of the deck. Two of the rangers had joined them, and the rest, four guys in khaki shorts and T-shirts, sat with some of the construction guys, talking sports.

Down on the waterside, the Dixie and Andy and Ceci's boat, still unnamed, floated at dock next to each other, each festooned with drying dive gear.

Up near the southern part of the deck Dar and Kerry were in camp chairs next to each other, and roaming from person to person in eternal hope, tails never ceasing to wag for an instant, were Chino and Mocha.

Andy and Ceci were perched nearby, and Hank, Pete, and the other veterans had that contented look that people who'd spent hours in salt water often did.

In a circle nearby, the programmers, along with Celeste and Angela, were seated with Josh and Leon catching up with each other. Everyone was laughing and just enjoying the day.

The sun was low on the western horizon, behind the trees that ringed the property already and it was a warm and purple long twilight of the tropics that they'd lit with the tiki torches brought from the office. The scent of citronella wafted over the deck to mix with the lobster, and the spice, and the beer.

"This was a great idea," Ceci said. "And I think your folks appreciate a break from the bing bongs over on Fantasy Island."

"It's nice," Kerry admitted. "What a gorgeous night." She had a mug of beer in one hand, and she gently swirled it around before she took another sip of it. "And the viz was atrocious but boy were there bugs out there." She regarded her plate, which had four empty lobster tails on it. "I only got two."

"Yeah, it'll take a while for all that to settle down. There was a lot of damage down there. The reef's trashed," Dar said, sadly. "And I can't believe Hank caught an octopus in all that murk."

"You know what is weird?" Ceci had a plate of all kinds of fruits and vegetables she was nibbling at. "It's weird your neighbors haven't come over here to see what the hell is going on." She indicated the ring of trees. "I know there's a wall, and all the plants, and Hunter was a nut job, but we're making a lot of noise here."

"Maybe they all evacuated," Dar said. "It's not like I saw anyone out there walking around, not in this area. Closer to the U, yeah."

"You mean you found neighbors who actually obey the government?" Ceci's voice rose in disbelief. "Are you kidding me?"

Andy laughed. "Could be."

"Someone will, eventually," Kerry said. "Those are pretty high rent houses on both sides there, they might have evacuated, Dar's right. They could afford to, and maybe they're all sitting somewhere in North Carolina in a hot tub watching the news. waiting for things to get back to normal."

"We could have done that," Ceci said. "We could be up in the Adirondacks in sixty-degree weather in some snooty resort. You could have arranged for office space and moved everyone."

"Coulda," Dar said wryly. "Next time, we will. But just like everyone else around here I figured we'd get a skip. We almost always do."

"True. I remember when Hurricane Andy hit," Ceci said. "We hadn't had a storm even close in over twenty years. Year after year of them going every direction but here, or hitting dry air, or a cold current or who knows what, you forget sometimes it happens."

Kerry swirled her mug again. "Oh, I don't know," she said. "If we had, we'd have missed out on this place." Her tone was thoughtful. "Maybe things happen when they're supposed to. You know?"

Dar eyed her. "Remind me you said that if we find out we're being sued. We might be house hunting again the next time Richard calls me."

"You really worried?" Kerry asked her, with a smile.

"No." Dar smiled back. "I think you're right. Things happen when they happen for a reason."

Arthur came over and sat down cross legged at Dar's side. "Hey."

"Hey," Dar responded.

"We were talking," Arthur said, launching into what was obviously a prepared speech. "Me and El, and the gals. We really want to come over here and work here." He glanced around. "Like... the island is cool and everything. It's just too boring. Know what I mean?"

"Uh huh. I do." Dar smiled at him. "I thought you might feel that way after you saw the place." She pondered. "No real spot to work yet though. It's pretty rough."

"What's wrong with right here?" Arthur asked, pointing at the chairs. "Dude, the signal here's kickass. I can just sit here in the shade with a towel under my laptop, so I don't toast my 'nads. You know?"

"Got it," Dar agreed mildly as she heard Kerry stifle a snort of laughter. "Yeah, okay we'll work out a plan to grab the servers and bring them over here. You saw the room they set up for them. We're almost there."

Arthur looked pleased. "Sweet. Thanks, Dar." He got up. "Let me go tell 'em all."

They were all quiet for a minute. Then Ceci chuckled. "Kids."

"Nerd camp." Dar settled back in her chair. She felt pleasantly tired from the diving, and if she licked her lips there was still a trace of salt on them from it.

Tomorrow there would be more chaos, and probably craziness but today she felt content with their decisions and generally... well... they'd just figure it out.

They'd just figure it out.

****

Kerry was sprawled on the back deck of the Dixie as the sun started to rise, a large cup of coffee in one hand and the other resting on the bolted down teak table that held the remains of some lobster benedict and one lonely piece of mango.

She studied the horizon, and the still dark surface of the water. She saw in the distance where the bay met the Atlantic the ruffled white of rollers coming over the shallower reefs and sandbars that came and went with the tides.

A seagull was bobbed near the boat and watched her from the corner of one beady eye, its beak clicking a little bit as he paddled around the stone pilings of the pier.

Kerry knew better, but tossed him a bit of the crust of her English muffin anyway and he zoomed over to capture it. She almost saw the thought bubble *sucker* lift over his sleek white head.

She chuckled. "Yeah, you guys got two live ones here now. Let me tell ya."

Dar stuck her head out of the cabin. "Who are you talking to?"

"Seagull."

Dar emerged and sat down in the other chair. "Did you feed it?"

"Yes."

The slip next to them was empty. Andy and Ceci had cruised on back to the island with their four staff, all of them busy with plans on how to wrap up things and get ready to move over. This time in a more normal fashion involving a liftgate and a truck.

They'd gotten a good night's sleep, with no thunderstorms, and no unexpected events, just quiet gentle rocking until their usual pre-dawn wake up. Kerry spent a moment imagining what it would be like to sit up on the deck of the house and watch the sun come up in just this way.

She could do that now, of course, from the patio of the condo, but there she was always aware of the density of the people and the apartments around them, and the understanding that they were never really alone.

Here, she could see the edges of other properties if she walked to the very edge of the seawall and looked down the coast. But since they were on a point, from the house on the back deck they would see nothing but their own land, and water.

It wasn't quite the same as living on a deserted island, but there was a peace here she really looked forward to and hoped like hell they wouldn't be legally blocked from.

"Now you did it. There's a manatee." Dar said and pointed at a stubby snout emerging from the water not that far away. "He wants his toast."

"He wants greens, and I don't have any." Kerry sighed. "I think they like arugula."

"Seaweed," Dar said. "He's eating sea grapes." She leaned forward and watched the slow-moving mammal, who browsed on the thick purple and green weed washing against the rocks on the tide. "Hey, buddy!"

The manatee peered at her, its nostrils wiggling.

"Dar, don't start that up now." Kerry watched her with wry amusement. "You'll have plenty of time to make friends, after we go and do whatever it is we need to do."

"Me? You were the one who fed the seagull." Dar straightened up and stretched. "Up for another cup of coffee before we head out?"

"Sure."

Dar stood and went into the cabin of the boat, where it was still quietly dim, only slices of sunlight coming in the side windows colored a chromed ochre from the tint on the glass. The two dogs had gone shoreside as the sun started to emerge and she listened for their far-off barking as she poured two cups out of the carafe.

It would be an annoying day. She could already anticipate the arguments, the yelling, the lack of cooperation, the anger, the frustration of the people she'd be dealing with, who certainly wouldn't enjoy some random unknown women coming into their hairball and start to pull on it.

Dar's lips twitched a little, into something close to a smile, finding herself halfway looking forward to it. She took the cups back outside and handed one to Kerry. "I thought you said not to mess with that guy," she said.

"He's cute." Kerry leaned closer. "He has blue eyes." She looked over at Dar. "They sort of look like walruses, don't they?"

Dar sat down with her coffee. "They're most closely related to elephants."

"Really?"

"If you look at his flipper there... "Dar pointed. "See the edge? See his toenails? Look up what an elephants foot looks like, and you'll see."

"Huh."

The manatee decided to cruise along and munch more seaweed, since there didn't seem to be any cabbage or lettuce forthcoming.

"Huh," Kerry repeated and braced one foot against the back wall. "Should we name him?"

"No."

"How about Charley?"

****

They both wore backpacks as they walked up to the deck toward the side porch, the morning sun now fully lighting the stone and the eastern side of the house. Rather than shorts and T-shirts, they were in jeans and company polos, and hiking boots. Both carried one of the nearly useless satellite phones clipped to their belts.

"Are there more birds around?" Kerry asked, as they walked out of the sun and onto the shade of the porch on the western side of the house. "Or am I just paying attention today?"

Dar paused and studied the trees around the edge of the clearing the house was in. "No, you're right," she said, after a moment. "It was... I think they knew about the storm and cleared out."

"Smarter than we are." Kerry hooked her arm through Dar's, and they continued along the planked walk, where a broken board was being replaced by one of the carpenters, despite the early hour. "Morning!"

The man looked up. "Morning, ladies," he greeted them. "Gonna be a hot one."

"They all are," Dar said.

They walked on and passed another man applying a careful layer of paint over a second newly installed board. They reached the side of the house where the RV camp, and the cook pit were. "It's really hard to say what the front and what the back of this thing is, Dar."

"I was just thinking that," Dar said, as they paused. "Those steps up to that entry there could be the front. That's where we went in the first time.

Does it matter?"

"Not really." Kerry regarded the still somewhat quiet area. "Well let's get going. It's almost seven thirty." They started along the path past the RVs to the gravel area beyond that held the rest of the cars they'd brought with them, including Hank's Humvee, and Pete's Jeep. At the back of that Dar's truck they'd brought over late after the traffic to and from the island had settled down. "Where first?" Kerry asked. "Emergency management center?"

"Makes sense."

"Let's get a punch list going I guess," Kerry said. "Then we can see what we need to get them to do for themselves.'"

Dar chuckled under her breath.

"He was right about one thing, Dar. With all the infighting going on a third-party view won't hurt."

"If we can get them all to shut up long enough to listen to us."

"Hah. I've seen you take over a room, Dixiecup. Really won't be a problem."

"Mm. We'll see."

They reached the truck and Dar opened the back door to toss her backpack in, when they both heard barking coming from the direction of the main gate. "Found our dogs," she said and closed the door. "Maybe the neighbors have finally figured out we're here."

"Oh, I hope not. We don't really have time for that this morning." Kerry got in the passenger seat. "Let's go find out."

Dar started up the truck and a moment later they drove across the slightly uneven gravel and stone lined path, the tires of the truck making some slight crackling and popping noises as they crunched on the rocks.

As they came around the bend through the trees, they saw the gates and both Mocha and Chino robustly barking between one of the rangers on one side, and one of the veterans on the other, who were apparently standing guard.

"Y'know, Dar," Kerry said. "We should maybe not be so post-apocalyptic armed camp. You think?"

"Until we fix everything and the power's back on and people can order Domino's pizza, no I don't think actually." Dar slowed as they reached the main gravel roadway. "There could still be zombies, Ker... but in this case, I think it's just our lawyer."

"Ah."

Dar opened her window and stuck her head out and let out a whistle. "Let him in," she called out. "He's a good guy."

The ranger, it was John, she realized, waved his hand and a minute later they pulled the gates open, while Chino and Mocha trotted their way, tails waving in happy pride at their skill in guarding.

Richard pulled his rental car inside and they closed the gates behind him. He pulled up to where they had stopped the truck and rolled his window down. "Good morning!"

He seemed wry, but cheerful, and Dar relaxed a trifle. Whatever news he had could not be completely horrible. "Hey, Richard. We were just on our way out."

"So I see." He opened the door and half stood, holding into the frame. "Got about ten minutes? You probably want to hear what my last twenty-four hours have been like. You headed back to the island?"

"We're headed out to take over the government disaster response," Kerry told him. "Because of course we are."

Richard actually laughed. "Well, if you give me a cup of coffee, I'll make it brief and you can get on your way. I couldn't get a flight back down from Tallahassee, so I just drove."

"C'mon back to the house." Dar waved him back into his car. "You can take a nap in the Dixie after if you want."

They turned and drove back to the house and parked behind the RV's, which now had figures emerging from them, and a group standing around one of the grills, with paper plates.

Inside the kitchen the coffeemaker was lit, and there was a sheet pan full of cinnamon rolls on the counter already well decimated along with a plastic container filled with venison jerky and a block of aged cheddar cheese.

They picked up cups of coffee and then Dar led the way to the newly finished server room, empty of any servers, but with a sturdy wooden work surface along one side of the room and several chairs. There were ethernet cables draped over things, and a power strip on the ground under the table. A large industrial spot cooler pumped away in one corner, tubes extending from it back through a small hatch cut in the door.

There were cable trays up along the ceiling with cables already in them. Clamped to them were work lights, giving the space a blare of slightly green, fluorescent magnificence, industrial and bare, yet with a scent of antiseptic clean and the fresh wood of newly built up floor and rack platform.

Kerry closed the door.

"This was a closet, wasn't it?" Richard said. "Wow."

"IT space is IT space." Kerry sat down. "We need what we need and it's never just a closet."

"Everything's removable," Dar said. "I remember what you said."

"Right." Richard set down a backpack and opened it up. He removed a folder, which he put on the work surface. "I'll make this fast, because if I tell you the whole story, we'll be here all day long. So, there I was in Tallahassee yesterday in the tombs digging out all the records on this place." He pointed at the folder. "Wasn't much. But I was looking for all the proof of land transfer and ownership, anything they had on what this place was. Any old newspaper clippings, visuals, anything that could make the case that the historical designation was invalid."

"Uh huh." Kerry nodded. "Because it's not valid, is it?"

"Because it's not," Richard agreed. "You can see this place, there's nothing here but a building, and some nicely done stonework. Then I looked up the submission, to see if that was legally valid." He paused and took a long sip of coffee." So, there I was in the records office minding your business when I heard a ruckus."

Dar propped her head up on one fist. "A ruckus."

"So, because I am your lawyer and I heard the name *Hunter* mentioned, I went around in the vital statistics area to see what the ruckus was, and what do I find there? I find those folks from the historical society."

"Making the ruckus."

"No, actually," Richard said. "Who was making the ruckus was a big old group of environmentalist activists waving papers yelling to beat the band that those historical folks couldn't touch anything here because they had a prior claim."

"What?" Kerry stared at him.

"Huh?" Dar said, at the same time, her brows knitting in confusion.

Richard seemed pleased with the reaction, and he settled into his chair a little more comfortably and toasted them with his coffee cup. "It was nice to be the witness to the weird for a change, if you catch my drift."

Dar and Kerry exchanged glances, then just looked back at him.

"At that point, I'm thinking to go find me some popcorn and settle in to watch the show," Richard said. "But I was a good boy, and introduced myself as your lawyer and to make what would be a long long story short, ladies, the good news is you can do whatever you want to this house. "Any existing buildings? Whatever your little hearts desire. Improve existing facility? No problem."

Dar eyed him. "What's the catch?"

"You can't mess up any of the plants or trees. It's a protected ecological biome." Richard regarded them, with a wry twist to his lips. "You can't remove any of them, you can't build over them, or move them. You have to protect them."

Kerry started to take a breath to talk, then stopped, and started again. "What the hell?"

"Why would he do both of those?" Dar asked, after a moments silence. "Was Hunter really just nuts?"

Their lawyer produced an exaggerated shrug.

"I've asked for copies of the environmental evaluation and the designation," Richard said. "But I got a look at it and there's no doubt it's legit, and no doubt it was registered almost two years before the old man requested the historical thing." He nodded succinctly. "Those are some pissed off historical people. But they ain't pissed off at you anymore, at least. Now mostly they're mad as a wet hen at Hunter, which, since he's gone and buried, is completely lacking a point."

"Holy crap," Kerry murmured.

Dar chuckled suddenly. "That's awesome," she said. "Thanks, Richard. I really appreciate you coming down to tell us."

Richard grinned. "Gotta tell you. I was laughing all the way down I-

95."

****

Kerry sat on the edge of the wall around what once had been a garden, and now would be again, near the entrance to the kitchen. Dar had walked Richard down to the dock, and she was now waiting here for Dar to come back. She took a moment to just absorb what they'd just been told.

Hot damn.

She looked around and behind her where the property was a mix of wild growth and limestone elevations and felt a sense of pleasure and relief that it would remain just like that. This relatively tiny patch of nature that held such appeal even to her, someone who had been accustomed to pristinely groomed foliage all the years of her life.

And now this house. Kerry swiveled to look at it. She could already imagine it with new shutters, and the stone cleaned and patched, with the troughs around the steps filled with flowers.

The wraparound porch will be full of comfortable chairs, some rockers, some hanging, with little tables and places to work from if they wanted to, or just to sit and play a game of chess at.

She could almost see them doing that in her head, with happy dogs sprawled at their feet or taking a walk through the trees.

This garden here, would be full of herbs. She could taste the mint from it on the back of her tongue and smell the scent of all of it at twilight at the end of a long day of work. She imagined what it would feel like to sit on the seaward deck and just enjoy the breeze from the water.

They would make friends with the manatees, she was confident, and she could spend some time taking pictures of all the birds. The possibilities seemed endless.

She saw motion from the corner of her eye, and she turned to see John the ranger approach, his hands stuck into the pockets of his khaki shorts. "Hey," She greeted him invitingly.

He came over to her and sat down on the wall. "That guy Henry told me you all want us to stay and do stuff for you," he said, straightforwardly. "Like what did you have in mind? We're not computer guys. We don't do any of that, cept maybe we can help run some cable."

"No, we've got plenty of people to do that." Kerry half turned to face him. "We found out something really cool today," she said. "This whole property, the whole area here, it's a protected nature preserve." She met his eyes and held them, waiting.

John smiled, just a little. "Yeah, I know," he said. "I... uh... I went and did that." He glanced around. "I signed the old man's name to all the papers and sent it off, few years back." He looked back at her quickly to see her reaction.

Kerry smiled back at him. "I thought maybe you did," she said, trading his surprise for one of her own. "I thought maybe that was important to you, when you saw I knew about the hammock." She studied him. "And the way you all stayed around here and camped."

He nodded. "You're a smart lady."

"I am," Kerry agreed. "I figured you figured it was a way to make sure it stayed the way it was, if something happened."

He nodded again. "Then when the old man said he was doing the other thing, I was afraid to tell him. Thought he'd get real mad about it, because I signed his name and all that. But he didn't really care about the land and all he just...."

"Just wanted to keep his granddaughter from tearing down what he built." Kerry indicated the house. "That's what he cared about."

"She would have, that girl. That is what he cared about, you're right. Because he made this place, he put his sweat into it. He was proud of every inch of it." John said. "Minnie cared about the land, you know, because she was from it, her people. She didn't care about the house or nothing. She cared about the trees, and she taught us about them."

"Two opposites," Kerry said. "Were they married?"

"Not officially or nothing," John said. "She took care of him, cause that's... she was real traditional. He really liked that." John seemed a touch apologetic. "He liked that she always kind of..." He hesitated. "She did what he told her."

"Served him," Kerry concluded.

"Yeah."

"Wasn't that long ago that was the way it was in a whole lot of the world, and still is, John." Kerry smiled at him. 'My parents wanted me to be a good political wife, just a piece of window dressing to help some guy get elected like my father did."

He studied her for a moment. "Didn't work out I guess." He grinned, a little.

Kerry laughed. "Nah, unfortunately I turned out to be gay."

"And smart."

"And smart, and stubborn, and a rebel. But it's only been a couple generations where women even voting was a thing. You know?" she said. "I'm pretty sure that old man could not in a million years even imagine me and Dar." She paused. "So ... we're going to need help to keep this place safe and take care of the land and the plants and trees. It's a big job. "Hank scientifically knows what to do. He's got a degree in horticulture management. But he needs a good team."

John remained silent for a minute, and they sat there as the sounds of construction and some laughter washed over them. "Of course, we want to help," he finally said. "But... are you saying... is this like—"

"Paid work? Yes." Kerry gently cut him off. "We want to hire you all to work for us. Here, taking care of this place," she said. "So, think about it and maybe let us know tonight? We have to go talk to the folks at the government center. Hank will get with you and show you what kind of pay scale we had in mind."

"Okay," John said. "I think everyone is going to say yes, for sure, but we can talk about it." He paused. "Government people causing a problem?"

"Government people hired us to fix their problems." Kerry caught sight of Dar returning, with her hands in her pockets, grinning to herself. "So, it should be an interesting day." She stood up, and as Dar approached, she gave him a short wave. "Talk too you later?"

He waved back. "Yes, ma'am. For sure we will."

****

They got into the truck and closed the doors, then paused and looked at each other. "Is it a coincidence, Dar, that we decide to help our fellow Floridians here, and the next thing we know, something nice happens?"

Dar regarded her in silence for a minute. "It's karma, Ker," she said. "What you put out in the world, you eventually get back. I'm not sure what that says about us since what we usually get back is—"

"But it always works out all right," Kerry interrupted her gently.

"True." Dar started up the truck's engine. "Doesn't matter, anyway." She put the truck into gear. "So, let's go see what else today has in store for us."

Kerry settled back in the passenger seat and leaned one elbow on the center console. "Mayte and Maria said they'd have the house work areas all sorted out for us by the time we get back."

Dar eyed her, as she paused to let them open the gates again.

"Hank's going to help," Kerry added, with a wry smile. "There's apparently a truck involved."

"Do I want to know?"

"No." Kerry settled her sunglasses onto her nose as they turned and headed up the road. "Let's just hope it's not those convention center folding chairs that pinch you in the ass."

"I can see where this is going. Foraging for beanbags."

The End.

About the Author

Melissa Good is a full time network engineer and part time writer who lives in Pembroke Pines, Florida with a handful of lizards and a dog. When not traveling for work, or participating in the usual chores she ejects several sets of clamoring voices onto a variety of keyboards and tries to entertain others with them to the best of her ability.

You can contact Melissa by email at: merwolf01@gmail.com

Visit her website: http://www.merwolf.com

Books by Melissa Good

Tropical Storm

From bestselling author Melissa Good comes a tale of heartache, longing, family strife, lust for love, and redemption. Tropical Storm took the lesbian reading world by storm when it was first written...now read this exciting revised "author's cut" edition.

Dar Roberts, corporate raider for a multi-national tech company, is cold, practical, and merciless. She does her job with razor-sharp accuracy. Friends are a luxury she cannot allow herself, and love is something she knows she'll never attain.

Kerry Stuart left Michigan for Florida in an attempt to get away from her domineering politician father and the constraints of the overly conservative life her family forced upon her. After college she worked her way into supervision at a small tech company, only to have it taken over by Dar Roberts' organization. Her association with Dar begins in disbelief, hatred, and disappointment, but when Dar unexpectedly hires Kerry as her work assistant, the dynamics of their relationship change. Over time, a bond begins to form.

But can Dar overcome years of habit and conditioning to open herself up to the uncertainty of love? And will Kerry escape from the clutches of her powerful father in order to live a better life?

Hurricane Watch

In this sequel to "Tropical Storm," Dar and Kerry are back and making their relationship permanent. But an ambitious new colleague threatens to divide them — and out them. He wants Dar's head and her job, and he's willing to use Kerry to do it. Can their home life survive the office power play?

Dar and Kerry are redefining themselves and their priorities to build a life and a family together. But with the scheming colleagues and old flames trying to drive them apart and bring them down, the two women must overcome fear, prejudice, and their own pasts to protect the company and each other. Does their relationship have enough trust to survive the storm?

Enter the lives of two captivating characters and their world that Melissa Good's thousands of fans already know and love. Your heart will be touched by the poignant realism of the story. Your senses and emotions will be electrified by the intensity of their problems. You will care about these characters before you get very far into the story.

Don't miss this exciting revised "author's cut" edition.

Eye of the Storm
(second edition)

Eye of the Storm picks up the story of Dar Roberts and Kerry Stuart a few months after the story Hurricane Watch ends. At first it looks like they are settling into their lives together but, as readers of this series have learned, life is never simple around Dar and Kerry. Surrounded by endless corporate intrigue, Dar experiences personal discoveries that force her to deal with issues that she had buried long ago and Kerry finally faces the consequences of her own actions. As always, they help each other through these personal challenges that, in the end, strengthen them as individuals and as a couple.

Red Sky at Morning
(second edition)

A connection others don't understand...
A love that won't be denied...
Danger they can sense but cannot see...

Dar Roberts was always ruthless and single-minded...until she met Kerry Stuart.

Kerry was oppressed by her family's wealth and politics. But Dar saved her from that. Now new dangers confront them from all sides. While traveling to Chicago, Kerry's plane is struck by lightning. Dar, in New York for a stockholders' meeting, senses Kerry is in trouble. They simultaneously experience feelings that are new, sensations that both are reluctant to admit when they are finally back together. Back in Miami, a cover-up of the worst kind, problems with the military, and unexpected betrayals will cause more danger. Can Kerry help as Dar has to examine her life and loyalties and call into question all she's believed in since childhood? Will their relationship deepen through it all? Or will it be destroyed?

This is the revised "author's cut edition." Some scenes were added such as: a shopping excursion downtown where Kerry buys leather; a flashback to Dar's first shopping trip to buy business attire – see how her clothing went from jeans and sweatshirts to power suits; and a mugging.

Don't miss this new edition.

Thicker Than Water

This sequel to Red Sky at Morning is the continuing saga of Dar Roberts and Kerry Stuart. It starts off with Kerry involved in the church group of girls. Kerry is forced to acknowledge her own feelings/experience toward/with her folks as she and Dar assist a teenager from the group who gets jailed because her parents tossed her out onto the streets when they find out she is gay. While trying to help the teenagers adjust to real world situations, Kerry gets the call concerning her father's health. Kerry flies to her family's side as her father dies, putting the family in crisis. Caught up in an international problem, Dar abandons the issue to go to Michigan, determined to support Kerry in the face of grief and hatred. Dar and Kerry face down Kerry's extended family with a little help from their own, and return home, where they decide to leave work and the world behind for a while for some time to themselves.

Terrors of the High Seas

After the stress of a long Navy project and Kerry's father's death, Dar and Kerry decide to take their first long vacation together. A cruise in the eastern Caribbean is just the nice, peaceful time they need – until they get involved in a family feud, an old murder, and come face to face with pirates as their vacation turns into a race to find the key to a decades old puzzle.

Tropical Convergence

There's trouble on the horizon for ILS when a rival challenges them head on, and their best weapons, Dar and Kerry, are distracted by life instead of focusing on the business. Add to that an old flame, and an aggressive entreprenaur throwing down the gauntlet and Dar at least is ready to throw in the towel. Is Kerry ready to follow suit, or will she decide to step out from behind Dar's shadow and step up to the challenges they both face?

This is the first part of the story formerly known as Moving Target.

Storm Surge, (Books 1 & 2)

Its fall. Dar and Kerry are traveling – Dar overseas to clinch a deal with their new ship owner partners in England, and Kerry on a reluctant visit home for her high school reunion. In the midst of corporate deals and personal conflict, their world goes unexpectedly out of control when an early morning spurt of unusual alarms turns out to be the beginning of a shocking nightmare neither expected.

Can they win the race against time to save their company and themselves?

Stormy Waters

As Kerry begins work on the cruise ship project, Dar is attempting to produce a program to stop the hackers she has been chasing through cyberspace. When it appears that one of their cruise ship project rivals is behind the attempts to gain access to their system, things get more stressful than ever. Add in an unrelenting reporter who stalks them for her own agenda, an employee who is being paid to steal data for a competitor, and Army intelligence becoming involved and Dar and Kerry feel more off balance than ever. As the situation heats up, they consider again whether they want to stay with ILS or strike out on their own, but they know they must first finish the ship project.

This is the second part of the online story formerly known as Moving Target.

Moving Target

Dar and Kerry both feel the cruise ship project seems off somehow, but they can't quite grasp what is wrong with the whole scenario. Things continue to go wrong and their competitors still look to be the culprits behind the problems.

Then new information leads them to discover a plot that everyone finds difficult to believe. Out of her comfort zone yet again, Dar refuses to lose and launches a new plan that will be a win-win, only to find another major twist thrown in her path. With everyone believing Dar can somehow win the day, can Dar and Kerry pull off another miracle finish? Do they want to?

Fans of this series should note that due to its length this story will be split into three novels. The determination of where to make that split was a joint decision between the author and the publisher.

See the title Tropical Convergence for further details on the first part and the title Stormy Waters for details on the second part.

Winds of Change (Books 1 & 2)

After 9/11 the world has changed and Dar and Kerry have decided to change along with it. They have an orderly plan to resign and finally take their long delayed travelling vacation. But as always fate intervenes and they find themselves caught in a web of conflicting demands and they have to make choices they never anticipated.

Southern Stars

At last, Dar and Kerry get to go on their long awaited and anticipated vacation in the Grand Canyon. They are looking forward to computer free time, beautiful scenery, and white water rapids. As always, though, life doesn't go smoothly and soon challenges are at hand.

Jess and Dev Series

Partners (Books 1 & 2)

After a massive volcanic eruption puts earth into nuclear winter, the planet is cloaked in clouds and no sun penetrates. Seas cover most of the land areas except high elevations which exist as islands where the remaining humans have learned to make do with much less. People survive on what they can take from the sea and with foodstuffs supplemented from an orbiting set of space stations.

Jess Drake is an agent for Interforce, a small and exclusive special forces organization that still possesses access to technology. Her job is to protect and serve the citizens of the American continent who are in conflict with those left on the European continent. The struggle for resources is brutal, and when a rogue agent nearly destroys everything, Interforce decides to trust no one. They send Jess a biologically-created agent who has been artificially devised and given knowledge using specialized brain programming techniques.

Instead of the mindless automaton one might expect, Biological Alternative NM-Dev-1 proves to be human and attractive. Against all odds, Jess and the new agent are swept into a relationship neither expected. Can they survive in these strange circumstances? And will they even be able to stay alive in this bleak new world?

Of Sea and Stars

Of Sea and Stars continues the saga of Interforce Agent Jess Drake and her Biological Alternative partner, NM-Dev-1, that began in Melissa Good's first two books in her Partners series.

This series chronicles what happens to human kind after a massive volcanic eruption puts earth into nuclear winter. The planet is cloaked in clouds and no sun penetrates. Seas cover most of the land areas except high elevations. These exist as islands where the remaining humans have learned to make do with much less. People survive on what they can take from the sea, and with foodstuffs supplemented from an orbiting set of space stations.

This new world is divided into two factions, and the struggle for resources between them is brutal, pitting one side against the other.

In Of Sea and Stars, Jess and Dev uncover a hidden cavern at Drakes Bay full of growing vegetables and fruit trees. There is evidence that the "other side" has been negotiating with Jess's brother, and with someone on the space station that created, Dev. This sends them on a quest into space to solve the mystery.

Bringing LGBTQAI+ Stories to Life

Visit us at our website: www.flashpointpublications.com